Tall…dark…handsome…and rich!
Who can resist a gorgeous millionaire?

In February 2006, By Request
brings back two collections containing
three favourite romances by our
bestselling Mills & Boon authors:

MILLIONAIRE'S MISTRESS
The Sicilian's Mistress
by Lynne Graham
The Rich Man's Mistress
by Cathy Williams
Marriage at His Convenience
by Jacqueline Baird

BEWITCHED BY THE BOSS
The Boss's Virgin by Charlotte Lamb
The Corporate Wife by Leigh Michaels
The Boss's Secret Mistress
by Alison Fraser

Millionaire's Mistress

THE SICILIAN'S MISTRESS
by
Lynne Graham

THE RICH MAN'S MISTRESS
by
Cathy Williams

MARRIAGE AT HIS CONVENIENCE
by
Jacqueline Baird

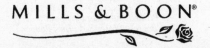

MILLS & BOON®

Harlequin Mills & Boon Limited,
Eton House, 18-24 Paradise Road, Richmond, Surrey, TW9 1SR

MILLIONAIRE'S MISTRESS
© by Harlequin Enterprises II B.V., 2006

The Sicilian's Mistress, The Rich Man's Mistress and Marriage at His Convenience were first published in Great Britain by Harlequin Mills & Boon Limited in separate, single volumes.

The Sicilian's Mistress © Lynne Graham 1999
The Rich Man's Mistress © Cathy Williams 2002
Marriage at His Convenience © Jacqueline Baird 2001

ISBN 0 263 84652 0

05-0206

Printed and bound in Spain
by Litografia Rosés S.A., Barcelona

THE SICILIAN'S MISTRESS

by

Lynne Graham

Lynne Graham was born in Northern Ireland and has been a keen Mills & Boon® reader since her teens. She is very happily married with an understanding husband, who has learned to cook since she started to write! Her five children keep her on her toes. She has a very large dog, which knocks everything over, a very small terrier which barks a lot, and two cats. When time allows, Lynne is a keen gardener.

Don't miss Lynne Graham's fabulous new novel
The Greek's Chosen Wife,
on sale in May 2006
from Mills & Boon Modern Romance™!

CHAPTER ONE

STUDIOUSLY ignoring Faith's troubled expression, Edward smiled. 'I never dreamt that Mother would make us such a generous offer—'

Faith sucked in a deep, steadying breath. 'I know, *but*—'

'It makes perfect sense. Why go to the expense of buying another property when there's ample space for us all at Firfield?'

At that precise moment Edward's flight was called. Immediately he rose to his feet and lifted his briefcase. 'We'll talk it over when I get back.'

Faith stood up. A slim, beautiful blonde of diminutive height, she had sapphire-blue eyes, flawless skin and wore her hair in a restrained French plait. 'I'll see you to the gate.'

Her fiancé shook his well-groomed fair head. 'Not much point. I don't know why you bothered coming to see me off anyway,' he remarked rather drily. 'I'm only going to be away for three days.'

Edward strode off and was soon lost from view in the crowds. Faith left the café at a slower pace, genuinely appalled at the announcement Edward had just made. They were getting married in four months and they had been house-hunting for the past three. Now Faith sensed that as far as Edward was concerned the hunt was over: his mother had offered to share her spacious home with them.

It was a really ghastly idea, Faith acknowledged in guilty dismay. Edward's mother didn't like her, but she carefully concealed her hostility. Mrs Benson was no more fond of Faith's two-year-old son, Connor. But then the fact that Faith was an unmarried mother had first fuelled the older

5

woman's dislike, Faith conceded ruefully as she walked back through the airport.

Her troubled eyes skimmed through the hurrying crowds. Suddenly she stiffened, her gaze narrowing, her head twisting back of its own volition to retrace that visual sweep. She found herself focusing on a strikingly noticeable man standing on the far side of the concourse in conversation with another. As her heartbeat thumped deafeningly in her ears, she faltered into complete stillness.

The compulsion to stare was as overwhelming as it was inexplicable. The man was very tall and very dark. His hard, bronzed features were grave, but not so grave that one glance was not sufficient to make her aware that he was stunningly handsome. Her tummy somersaulted. A fevered pound of tension began to build up pressure behind her temples.

A smooth dark overcoat hung negligently from his wide shoulders. He looked rich, super-sophisticated, that cool aura of razor-edged elegance cloaking immense power. Perspiration dampened her skin. Sudden fear and confusion tore at her as she questioned what she was doing. A wave of dizziness ran over her.

Simultaneously, the stranger turned his arrogant dark head and looked directly at her, only to freeze. The fierce intensity with which those brilliant dark eyes zeroed in on her stilled figure disconcerted her even more. But at that point the nausea churning in her stomach forced a muffled moan from her parted lips. Dragging her attention from him, Faith rushed off in search of the nearest cloakroom.

She wasn't actually sick, as she had feared. But as she crept back out of the cubicle she had locked herself in and approached the line of sinks she was still trembling. Most of all, she was bewildered and shaken by her own peculiar behaviour. What on earth had possessed her to behave like that? What on earth had prompted her to stop dead and gape like some infatuated schoolgirl at a complete stranger?

Infatuated? She questioned the selection of that particular

word and frowned with unease, the way she always did when a thought that didn't seem quite *her* came into her mind. But she wasn't feeling well. Maybe she was feverish, coming down with one of those viruses that could strike with such rapidity.

There had to be some good reason why a total stranger should inspire her with fear...unless he reminded her of somebody she had once known. She tensed. That was highly unlikely, she decided just as quickly, and began to scold herself for her overreaction to a fleeting incident.

But she knew what was the matter with her. She understood all too well the source of her basic insecurity. But *that* was something she had learnt to put behind her and never ever dwell on these days. With conscious care, Faith suppressed the scary stirrings at the back of her mind and blanked them out again.

But what if she *had* once known that man? The worrying apprehension leapt out of Faith's subconscious before she could block it again. Aghast, she stared blindly into space, suddenly plunged into a world of her own, a blank, nebulous world of terrifying uncertainty which she had believed left far behind her. *The lost years...what about them?*

A crowd of noisy teenagers jostled her at the sinks, springing her back into awareness again. She blinked rapidly, once, twice, snatched in a shuddering breath to steady herself. Discomfited by her uncomfortably emotional frame of mind, she averted her head and shook it slightly. You saw some really interesting people at airports, she told herself squarely. Her attention had been momentarily distracted and she wasn't feeling too good. That was all it had been.

But when Faith vacated the cloakroom and turned back into the main concourse, she found her path unexpectedly blocked.

'Milly...?' A dark, accented voice breathed with noticeable stress.

Faith glanced up, and it was a very long way up, and met flashing dark eyes so cold and deep her heart leapt straight

into her throat. It was the same guy she had been staring at
ten minutes earlier! Her feet froze to the floor in shock.

'*Madre di Dio…*' The stranger stared fixedly down at her,
his deep, accented drawl like an icy hand dancing down her
taut spine. 'It *is* you!'

Faith gazed up at him in frank surprise and sudden powerful embarrassment. She took a backward step. 'Sorry, I
think you've got the wrong person.'

'Maybe you wish I had.' The intimidating stranger gazed
down at her from his incredibly imposing height, slumbrous
dark eyes roving so intently over her face that colour flooded
her drawn cheeks. '*Dio*…you still blush. How do you do
that?' he drawled very, very softly.

'Look, I don't know you, and I'm in a hurry,' Faith responded in an evasive, mortified mutter, because she
couldn't help wondering if her own foolish behaviour earlier
had encouraged him to believe that she was willing to be
picked up.

Eyes the colour of rich, dark golden honey steadily widened and her heartbeat started to thump at what felt like the
base of her throat, making it difficult for her to breathe. 'You
don't know me?' he repeated very drily. 'Milly, this is
Gianni D'Angelo you're dealing with, and running scared
with a really stupid story won't dig you out of the big deep
hole you're in!'

'You don't know me. You've made a mistake,' Faith told
him sharply.

'No mistake, Milly. I could pick you out of a thousand
women in the dark,' Gianni D'Angelo murmured even more
drily, his wide, sensual mouth curling with growing derision.
'So, if the nose job was supposed to make you unrecognis-
able, it's failed. And what sad soap opera did you pick this
crazy pretence out of? You're in enough trouble without this
childish nonsense!'

Her dark blue eyes huge in receipt of such an incompre-
hensible address, Faith spluttered, 'A nose job? For goodness' sake—'

'You have a lot of explaining to do, and I intend to conduct this long-overdue conversation somewhere considerably more private than the middle of an airport,' he asserted grittily. 'So let's get out of here before some paparazzo recognises me!'

As Faith attempted to sidestep him he spontaneously matched her move and blocked her path again. She studied him in disbelief. 'P-please get out of my way...' she stammered, fear and confusion now rising like a surging dark tide inside her.

'No.'

'You're mad...if you don't get out of my way, I'll scream!'

He reeled back a full step, a deep frown-line of impressive incredulity hardening his lean, strong features. 'What the hell is going on here?' he demanded with savage abruptness.

Faith broke through the gap he had left by the wall and surged past him at frantic speed.

A hand as strong and sure as an iron vice captured her wrist before she got more than two feet away. '*Accidenti*...where do you think you're going?' he questioned in angry disbelief, curving his infinitely larger hand right round her clenched fingers.

'I'll report you to the police for harassing me!' Faith gasped. 'Let go of me!'

'Don't be ridiculous...' He gazed unfathomably down into her frightened and yet strangely blank eyes and suddenly demanded with raw, driven urgency, *'What's the matter with you?'*

Faith spun a frantic glance around herself. Only her instinctive horror at the idea of creating a seriously embarrassing public scene restrained her from a noisy outburst. *'Please* let go of me!' she urged fiercely.

The ring on her engagement finger scored his palm as she tried to pull free. Without warning he flipped her hand around in the firm hold of his and studied the small diamond solitaire she wore. A muscle jerked tight at the corner of his bloodlessly compressed lips, shimmering flaring eyes flying up again to her taut face.

'*Now* I understand why you're acting like a madwoman!' he grated, with barely suppressed savagery.

And Faith's self-discipline just snapped, right then and there. She flung back her head and tried to call out for assistance, but her vocal cords were knotted so tight with stress only a suffocated little squawk emerged. But surprisingly that was sufficient. Gianni D'Angelo, as he had called himself, dropped her hand as if she had burnt him and surveyed her in almost comical astonishment.

Shaking like a leaf, Faith backed away. 'I'm not this Milly you're looking for…never seen you before in my life, never want to see you again…'

And she rushed away her tummy tied up in sick knots again, her head pounding, a kind of nameless terror controlling her. She raced across the endless car park as if she had wings, and then fell, exhausted, to a slower pace, breathless and winded, heartbeat thundering. Crazy, crazy man, frightening her like that all because she resembled some poor woman who had clearly got out while the going was good. Gianni D'Angelo. She didn't recognise that name. And why should she?

But wasn't it strange that he should have attracted *her* attention first? And only then had he approached her. Almost as if he genuinely had recognised her…

As her apprehensions rose to suffocating proportions release from fear came in the guise of an obvious fact. Of course he *couldn't* have recognised her! She couldn't believe that she had ever been the kind of person to run around using a false name! And she was Faith Jennings, the only child of Robin and Davina Jennings. True, she might have been a difficult teenager, but then that wasn't that uncommon, and her parents had long since forgiven her for the awful anxiety she had once caused them.

Half an hour later, sitting in her little hatchback car in heavy morning rush-hour traffic, Faith took herself to task for the overwrought state she was in. Here she was, supposedly a mature adult of twenty-six, reacting like a frightened teenager desperate to rush home to her parents for support. And yet what had happened? Virtually nothing. A case of mistaken identity with a stubborn foreigner unwilling to accept his error! That was all it had been. A nose job, for heaven's sake!

And yet as she gazed through the windscreen she no longer saw the traffic lights; she saw Gianni D'Angelo, his lean, bronzed features imposed on a mind that for some reason could focus on nothing else. As furiously honking car horns erupted behind her Faith flinched back to the present and belatedly drove on, strain and bemusement stamping her troubled face.

Gianni D'Angelo stared fixedly out of the giant corner window of his London office. An impressive view of the City's lights stretched before him but he couldn't see it.

His sane mind was telling him that even twelve hours on he was still in the grip of shock, and that self-control was everything, but he wanted to violently punch walls with the frustrated anger of disbelief. He had searched for Milly for so long. He had almost given up hope. He certainly hadn't expected her to do something as dumb and childish as try and pretend she didn't know him, and then compound her past offences by attempting to run away again. And why hadn't it occurred to her that he would have her followed before she got ten feet away from him?

Milly, whom he'd always called Angel. And instantly Gianni was beset by a thousand memories that twisted his guts even after three years of rigorous rooting out of such images. He saw Milly jumping out of a birthday cake dressed as an angel, tripping over her celestial robes and dropping her harp. Milly, impossibly beautiful but horrendously clumsy when she was nervous. Milly, who had given him his first and only taste of what he had dimly imagined must be a home life…

And you loved it, you stupid bastard! Gianni's lean hands suddenly clenched into powerful fists. Punishing himself for recalling only pleasant things, Gianni made himself relive the moment he had found his precious pregnant Angel in bed with his kid brother, Stefano. That had put a whole new slant on the joys of home and family life. Until that moment of savage truth he hadn't appreciated just how much he had trusted her. And instead of proposing marriage, as he had planned, he had ended up taking off with another woman. What else could he have done in the circumstances?

He had wanted to kill them both. For the first time he had understood the concept of a crime of passion. The only two people he had ever allowed close had deceived and betrayed him. A boy of nineteen and a girl/woman only a couple of years older. The generation gap had been there, even though he had been too blind to acknowledge it, he reflected with smouldering bitterness. And naturally Stefano had adored her. Everybody had adored Milly.

Milly, who had called him on the slightest pretext every day and never once failed to tell him how much she loved him. So she had spent a lot of time alone. But business had always come first, and he had never promised more than he had delivered. He had been straight. He had even been faithful. And how many single men in his position were wholly faithful to a mistress?

As a knock sounded on the door Gianni wheeled round and fixed his attention with charged expectancy on his London security chief, Dawson Carter. His child, he thought with ferocious satisfaction. Milly *had* to have had his child. And, whatever happened, he would use that child as leverage. Whether she liked it or not, Milly was coming back to him...

'Well?' he prodded with unconcealed impatience.

Dawson surveyed his incredibly rich and ruthless employer and started to sweat blood. Gianni D'Angelo ran one of the most powerful electronic empires in the world. He was thirty-two. He had come up from nothing. He was tough, streetwise, and brilliant in business. He didn't like or expect disappointments. He had even less tolerance for mysteries.

'If this woman *is* Milly Henner—' Dawson began with wary quietness.

Gianni stilled. 'What do you mean *if*?' he countered with raw incredulity.

Dawson grimaced. 'Gianni…if it is her, she's living under another name, and she's been doing it successfully for a very long time.'

'That's insane, and utterly impossible!' Gianni asserted in instant dismissal.

'Three years ago, Faith Jennings was found by the side of a country road in Cornwall. She had been seriously injured and she had no identification. She was the victim of a hit and run. The police think she was robbed after the accident—'

'*Dio!*' Gianni exclaimed in shaken interruption.

'But she *was* pregnant at the time of the accident,' Dawson confirmed. 'And she does have a child.'

Gianni drew in a stark breath, incisive dark eyes flaming to bright gold in anticipation. 'So the child must be two and a half…right? A girl or a boy?' he prompted with fierce impatience.

'A little boy. She calls him Connor. He'll be three in May. He was born before his mother came out of the coma she was in.'

Gianni screened his unusually revealing eyes as he mulled over those bald facts. 'So…' he murmured then, without any expression at all. 'Explain to me how Milly Henner could possibly be living under another woman's name.'

'It was a long time before she was able to speak for herself, but she was apparently wearing a rather unusual bracelet. Her face had been pretty badly knocked about and she needed surgery.' For the first time in his life Dawson saw his employer wince, and was sincerely shaken by the evidence of this previously unsuspected vein of sensitivity. 'So as a first move the police gave a picture of the bracelet to the press. She was swiftly identified as a teenager who had run away from home when she was sixteen. Her parents came forward and identified her—'

'But Milly doesn't *have* parents alive!' Gianni cut in abrasively.

'This woman never recovered her memory after the hit and run, Gianni. She's a total amnesiac—'

'A total amnesiac?' Gianni broke in, with raised brows of dubious enquiry.

'It's rare, but it does happen,' Dawson assured him ruefully. 'I spoke to a nurse at the hospital where she was treated. They still remember her. When she finally recovered consciousness her mind was a blank, and when her parents took her home she still knew nothing but what they had told her about her past. I gather they also discouraged her from seeking further treatment. The medics were infuriated by their interference but powerless to act.'

'Normal people do not take complete strangers home and keep them as their daughters for three years,' Gianni informed him with excessive dryness.

'I should add that the parents hadn't seen or heard from their missing daughter in seven years, but were still unshakeable in their conviction that the young woman with the bracelet was their child—'

'Seven years?' Gianni broke in.

'The police did try to run a check on dental records, but the surgery which the daughter attended before she disappeared had burnt down, and the most her retired dentist could recall was that she had had excellent teeth, just like the lady in the hospital bed. This is a very well-known story in the town where Faith Jennings lives—her miraculous return home in spite of all the odds.'

'There was no return, miraculous or otherwise…that *was* Milly at the airport! Seven years…' Gianni mused with incredulous bite. 'And Milly was in a coma, at the mercy of people no better than kidnappers!'

Dawson cleared his throat. 'The parents are respectable, comfortably off—the father owns a small engineering plant. If there's been a mistake, it can only have been a genuine one, and most probably due to wishful thinking.'

Gianni was unimpressed. 'While Milly was still ill, that's possible, but when she began to recover they must've have started to suspect the truth, so why didn't they *do* anything?' he demanded in a seething undertone. 'What about the fiancé?'

'Edward Benson. A thirty-eight-year-old company accountant.'

Gianni lounged back against the edge of his desk like a panther about to spring. 'An accountant,' he derided between clenched teeth.

'He's her father's second-in-command,' Dawson filled in. 'Local gossip suggests that the engagement is part of a business package.'

'Check me into a hotel down there.' Gianni straightened, all emotion wiped from his lean, strong face, eyes ice-cool shards of threat. 'I think it's time I got to meet my son. And isn't that going to put the cat among the pigeons?'

Dawson tried not to picture the onslaught of Gianni, his powerful personality, his fleet of limos and his working entourage without whom he went nowhere on a small, peaceful English town...and the woman who against all reason and self-preservation had contrived to forget her intimate involvement with one of the world's richest and most influential tycoons. A lot of people had a lot of shock coming their way...

'So you just tell Edward you *refuse* to live with his mother!' Louise Barclay met Faith's aghast look and simply laughed. A redhead with green eyes and loads of freckles, Louise looked as if she was in her twenties but she was actually well into her thirties, and the divorced mother of two rumbustious teenage boys.

'Sometimes you're such a wimp, Faith,' Louise teased.

'I'm not—'

'You are when it comes to your own needs. All your energy goes into keeping other people happy, living the life *they* think you should live! Your parents act like they own you body and soul, and Edward's not much better!' Louise informed her in exasperation.

Faith stiffened. Louise was her best friend and her business partner, but she had little understanding of the burden of guilt that Faith carried where her parents were concerned. 'It's not like that—'

'Oh, yes, it is.' Louise watched Faith carefully package a beautiful bouquet for delivery and leant back against the shop counter. 'I'm always watching you struggle to be all things to all people. Once you wanted to be a gardener. Your parents didn't fancy that, so here you are in a prissy flower shop.'

Faith laughed. 'Alongside you.'

'But this *was* my dream. And if you don't watch out, you're going to end up living with old Ma Benson. She will cunningly contrive, without Edward ever noticing, to make your home life the equivalent of a daily dance on a bed of sharpened nails!' the lively redhead forecast with conviction. 'You think I haven't noticed how stressed-out and quiet you've been since Edward dropped this on you the day before yesterday?'

Faith turned her head away. For once, Louise was barking up the wrong tree. Faith hadn't told anybody about that incident at the airport, but she still couldn't get it out of her mind. Her mother didn't like to be reminded that her daughter was an amnesiac, and got upset whenever Faith referred to that particular part of the past. Her attitude was understandable: after running away, Faith hadn't once got in touch to ease her parents' distress.

How could she ever have been so selfish and uncaring that she had failed to make even a single phone call to reassure them that she was at least still alive? Conscience had given Faith a strong need to do whatever she could to please her parents in an effort to make up for her past mistakes.

She was also painfully aware that both her parents viewed those missing years as a Pandora's box best left sealed. As far as they were concerned, seven years on she had turned up again, pregnant, unmarried and seemingly destitute. Nobody she might have known during that period had listed her as missing. Those bald realities suggested that prior to the accident she had been homeless, unemployed, not in a stable relationship and bereft of any true friends. Frankly, she'd been desperately lucky to have forgiving parents willing to take her home and help her back to normality again, she acknowledged humbly.

Only what was normality? Faith wondered, with the lonely regret of someone who had learnt not to discuss her secret fears and insecurities with anyone. It could never be *normal* to possess not one single memory of what she'd been told she'd lost—the first twenty-three years of her life. But if she wanted people to feel comfortable with her, if she wanted people to forget that strange past and treat her like everybody else, she always had to pretend that that vast gaping hole inside her memory banks was no longer any big deal...

'A fresh start.' In the early days of her convalescence that had been a much-used parental phrase, the implication being that an inability to recall those years might well prove an unexpected blessing. So Faith had concentrated instead on trying to retrieve childhood memories. She had dutifully studied the photo albums of the much-loved and indulged daughter who had grown into a plump teenager with a sullen face, defiant blue eyes and make-up like war paint. Self-conscious about her weight, the teenage Faith hadn't liked photos, so there had only been a handful after the age of twelve.

Faith had walked through the schools she had once attended, met the teachers, wandered round the town where she had grown up and paid several awkward visits to former schoolfriends, always willing her blank brain to remember, recognise, sense even token familiarity…

Repetition *had* created a kind of familiarity, and she had exercised her imagination until sometimes she suspected that she did *almost* remember and that real memory was hovering cruelly just out of reach on the very edge of her mind. She had rebuilt a quiet, conventional life round her family, but Connor was the true centre of her world. She loved her parents for their unquestioning support, loved Edward for his calm acceptance of her, but she adored her son with a fierce maternal joy and protectiveness that occasionally shook even her.

'There's something more up with you than Edward's sudden penny-pinching desire to regress and stay home with Mother,' Louise remarked with sudden insight.

The silence thickened. Faith reached a sudden decision and took a deep breath.

'A man spoke to me at the airport. He was very persistent. He insisted that he knew me by another name…Milly, he called me.' Trying to downplay the incident even now, Faith loosed an uneven laugh, but the pent-up words of strain continued to tumble from her. 'Maybe I have a *doppelgänger* somewhere. It was daft, but it was a little scary…'

'Why scary?'

Faith linked her hands tightly together in an effort to conceal their unsteadiness. 'You see, I noticed this man first…to be honest, I really couldn't take my eyes off him…' Her voice trailed away as embarrassment gripped her.

'So he was trying to make a move on you—but do tell me more,' Louise invited with amusement. 'Just why couldn't you take your eyes off this guy?'

'I don't know. He was very, very good-looking,' Faith conceded, colour flaming into her cheeks. 'And at first I thought that my staring at him had encouraged him to approach me. But when I thought about it afterwards… I don't think it was like that.'

'Why not? You might wear fuddy-duddy clothes and

scrape your hair back like a novice nun, but your kind of beauty would shine through a potato sack,' her friend advised her drily.

'This man was angry with me...I mean...with this woman, Milly,' Faith adjusted hurriedly. 'He accused her of having run away. And he was really astonished when I said I didn't know him and when I threatened him with the police.'

'That's persistent.' Louise looked more serious now.

'He said his name was Gianni D'Angelo...it means nothing to—'

Louise had straightened, an incredulous light in her eyes. 'Say that name again.'

'Gianni D'Angelo.'

'Did this guy ooze money?'

'He was very well dressed.'

'Gianni D'Angelo owns Macro Industries. He's a hugely important electronics mogul. My ex-hubby once worked on a major advertising campaign for one of his companies,' Louise informed her with dancing eyes. 'And if I thought a gorgeous single guy worth billions was wandering round Heathrow trying to pick up stray women, I'd take my sleeping bag and move in until he tripped over me!'

'It can't have been the same man,' Faith decided. 'I must've misheard the name.'

'Or perhaps you once enjoyed a champagne and caviar lifestyle, rubbing shoulders with the rich and the famous!' Louise teased with an appreciative giggle. 'I think you met a complete nutter stringing you a weird line, Faith.'

'Probably,' she agreed, with a noticeable diminution of tension.

With a sense of relief, Faith decided to put the entire silly episode out of her mind. And, just as she had arranged a couple of days earlier, she called in at the estate agent to collect the keys of the house which was her dream house for a second viewing.

True, Edward had not seen the sadly neglected Victorian

villa in quite the same light. But Faith knew she had to tell her fiancé why there was no question of her agreeing to move in with his widowed mother after their marriage. Perhaps then he would be more amenable to a property which needed a fair amount of work, she reasoned hopefully.

Set on the edge of town, in what had once been open countryside, the house rejoiced in a large garden screened from the road by tall hedges. Faith unlocked the front door and walked into the hall. The stale air made her wrinkle her nose, and she left the door wide on the weak morning sunlight. She wandered contentedly through the shabby rooms and finally into the old wooden conservatory which still possessed considerable charm. Edward had said it would have to be demolished.

A faint sound tugged Faith only partially from her cosy reverie. She half turned, without the slightest expectation of seeing anybody. So the shock of seeing Gianni D'Angelo ten feet away in the doorway was colossal. A strangled gasp escaped her convulsing throat, all colour draining from her face to highlight sapphire-blue eyes huge with fear.

'All I want to do is talk to you. I didn't want to walk into the shop. I didn't want to go to your home. At least here we're alone, on neutral territory.' He spread fluid brown hands in a soothing motion that utterly failed in its intent. 'I won't come any closer. I don't want to frighten you. I just want you to listen.'

But, in a state of petrified paralysis, Faith wasn't capable of listening. She started to shake, back away, her entire attention magnetically pinned to him, absorbing every aspect of his appearance in terrifyingly minute detail. His smoothly cropped but luxuriant black hair. His fabulous cheekbones. His classic nose. His perfectly modelled mouth. And the devastating strength of purpose dauntingly etched into every feature.

His charcoal-grey suit just screamed designer style and expense, moulding broad shoulders as straight as axe-

handles, accentuating the lithe flow of his lean, tightly muscled all-male body. 'P-please…' she stammered sickly.

'*Per meraviglia!*' Gianni D'Angelo countered rawly.
'Since when were you a bag of nerves on the constant brink
of hysteria? All right, I'll just give you the proof that we
have had what you might call a prior acquaintance.'

'I don't want to have had a prior acquaintance with you!'
Faith exclaimed with stricken honesty. 'I want you to go
away and leave me alone!'

He withdrew something from the inside pocket of his
beautifully tailored jacket and extended it to her.

Faith stared, but wouldn't move forward to reach for the
item, which appeared to be a photograph.

'This is you just over three years ago,' he breathed in a
gritty undertone. 'And if you had your memory right now,
we'd be having a major fight.'

'A m-major fight…' Faith parroted weakly.

'I crept up on you with the camera. You were furious.
You made me promise to destroy the photo. I said I would.
I lied. I'm afraid it's the only photo of you I have left.'
Stooping with athletic ease, he tossed the glossy snap down
on the pitted tiled floor like a statement.

It skimmed to a halt about two feet from her. Faith stared
down at the snap where it lay. Her eyes opened impossibly
wide. She saw a slim, bare-breasted blonde semi-submerged
in bubbles in a giant bath. She saw a slim, bare-breasted
blonde with her face, her eyes, her mouth…her breasts. She
didn't want that brazen hussy to be her! Shock rolled over
her like a tidal wave.

'Keeping it was kind of a guy thing,' Gianni admitted,
almost roughly.

A strangled moan of denial slowly hissed from Faith's
rigidly compressed lips. Her head swam, the photo spinning
out of focus, her legs turning hollow. And then the great
well of darkness behind her eyelids sucked her down frighteningly fast into a faint.

Gianni caught her before she hit the floor in a crumpled
heap and swore vehemently.

CHAPTER TWO

FAITH drifted back to awareness in a complete daze. Her lashes fluttered and then lifted. A dark male face swam into stark focus, but it was those eyes, those stunning lion-gold eyes fringed by black spiky lashes, that entrapped her attention and held her still. Her breath feathered in her throat.

The oddest little tugging sensation pulled deep down inside her, heralding a slow burst of heat that spread from the pit of her stomach up, and then down to more intimate places. Faith quivered in extreme disconcertion, extraordinarily conscious of the strange sensitivity of her full breasts, the sudden straining tightness of her nipples. She couldn't breathe, she couldn't speak, she couldn't think. Her body had taken on a frightening life of its own, yet she couldn't muster the power to either question or control it.

'Gianni…Gianni,' a breathless voice she barely recognised as her own pleaded achingly inside her mind. Seemingly of its own volition, her hand lifted and began to rise towards that strong, aggressive jawline…

Gianni's eyes shimmered chillingly. He broke the spell by tilting his proud dark head back out of her reach. Then he flashed her a look of raw derision. 'When I want sex, I'll tell you, Milly. In the meantime, keep your hands to yourself.'

That assurance was so shattering it sprang Faith back to full awareness. As he slid back upright from his crouching position by the sagging basketwork chair on which she sat, all that had happened in the minutes before she had fainted flooded back to fill her with frantic, frightening confusion.

She had been viewing the house. He had arrived. He had shown her the photo, that awful photo of herself flaunting

22

her bare breasts like a tart. He *did* know her. He *had* known her. Dear heaven, she conceded in drowning mortification, he had to have known her in the biblical sense. This man had actually slept with her.

Disorientation engulfed her. She heard afresh that pleading voice whispering his name inside her head, and wondered in stunned disbelief if after three long empty years she had *finally* remembered something from the past. Something she didn't want to remember, something that made her squirm with discomfiture. Perhaps it had been her imagination playing a trick on her. Why now and never before? She lifted her head and then suddenly dropped it down again, shutting her eyes tight, unable to meet Gianni D'Angelo's cool, measured gaze. A dulled throb of tension now pulsed behind her temples.

She recalled his derision, the blunt immediacy of what had been a rejection couched in the most humiliating terms. And then she relived what had prompted that crushing response from him. Oh, dear God, she thought with stunned shame, in those first moments of recovering consciousness she had focused on him and experienced the most unbelievably powerful surge of physical hunger. She was shattered by that realisation. It rewrote everything she had believed she knew about that side of her nature.

The sound of brisk footsteps sent her eyes flying open again. She gaped at the sight of the uniformed older man who appeared in the doorway to extend, of all things, a brandy goblet. Gianni took it from him with a nod and a dismissive move of one authoritative hand. He strode back to Faith and slotted the glass into her nerveless fingers. 'Drink it. You're as white as a sheet,' he instructed grimly.

'Wh-where did that man and this drink come from?' she stammered in unwilling wonderment.

Gianni frowned, as if that had been a very stupid question. 'When you passed out, I called my driver on the car phone and told him to bring it in.'

Faith slowly nodded, studying him with slightly glazed

eyes. Did he have a bar in his car? It had to be a big car. He wasn't giving her a bottle to swig out of. Her sense of dislocation from reality increased. The gulf between them felt immeasurable. According to Louise, Gianni D'Angelo was a very wealthy and powerful tycoon, and certainly he looked the part. What sort of relationship could she possibly have had with such a man? Suddenly she really didn't want to know.

'Drink the brandy,' Gianni pressed with controlled impatience.

'I hardly ever touch alcohol…'

'Well, you weren't on any wagon when I knew you,' Gianni informed her without hesitation.

Shaken by that come-back, and the daunting knowledge that was his alone, Faith tipped the glass to her lips. The spirit raced down her dry throat like liquid fire and burned away the chill spreading inside her. She swallowed hard and then breathed in deep. 'It seems you once knew me…I want that photograph back!' she added the instant she recalled its existence, anxious eyes lowering to see if it still lay on the floor. It didn't.

'Forget it; it's mine. But isn't that just like a woman?' Gianni growled with incredulous scorn. 'I only showed you that photo to make you accept that we once had a certain bond, and now you can only concentrate on a complete irrelevance!'

It didn't feel irrelevant to Faith. Right at that moment she saw that revealing photo as shocking evidence of a past she wanted to leave buried, and she certainly didn't want it left in his possession. 'Look, Mr D'Angelo—'

'*Mister* D'Angelo?' he queried, with a slashing smile that chilled her to the marrow. 'Make it Gianni.'

That ice-cold smile was like a threat. It shook her. He was poised several feet away, still as a predator about to spring. She recognised his hostility and recoiled from it in sudden fear. 'You hate me…'

He froze.

The silence thundered.

Suddenly he swung away from her. 'You don't remember me…you don't remember *anything*, do you?'

'No…I don't,' she conceded tautly.

'I thought you would've been full of questions. This isn't any easier for me,' he ground out in a charged undertone, spinning back to her with graceful but restive rapidity. Stormy dark eyes assailed her and she paled even more. 'At the airport, I admit I wanted to strangle you. I didn't know you'd lost your memory. I don't like you looking at me like I'm about to attack you either!'

Intimidated by the powerful personality that he was revealing, Faith did nothing to soothe him when she instinctively cowered back into the chair.

'Milly…'

'That's not my name!' she protested.

He let that go past.

'Look…' He spread the fingers of one lean and eloquent hand. 'You're scared because I'm rocking your cosy little world. It's not me you're afraid of. You're scared of the unknown that I represent.'

Faith gave a slight wary nod that might or might not have signified agreement, but her expressive eyes revealed her surprise that he could make that distinction. She wasn't used to the sensation of someone else trying to get inside her head and work out how she felt.

'I don't want to frighten you, but anything I tell you is likely to cause you distress, so I'll keep it basic.'

'How did you find out where I was living? How did you know I was an amnesiac?' Faith suddenly demanded accusingly.

'Naturally I had you followed from the airport. Then I had some enquiries made,' Gianni supplied with a fluid shrug.

Rising in one sudden motion from the chair, Faith gave him a stricken look of bemusement. 'But why would you do something like that? Why would you go to so much trouble? Why are you here now? Just because we had some relationship years ago?'

'I'm working up to that. I did have this rather naïve hope that you might start remembering things when you saw me again,' Gianni confided with a sardonic laugh, his smooth, dark features broodingly taut. 'But it looks like I'm going to have to do this the hard way. I suggest you sit down again.'

'No.' Faith braced her slim shoulders, a sudden powerful need to regain control of the situation driving her. 'I don't need to put myself through this if I don't want to. I don't need to listen to you—'

Gianni murmured, 'I'm afraid you do…'

'No, I don't. I just want you to go away and leave me alone,' Faith admitted truthfully, suppressing the little inner voice that warned her that that was craven and short-sighted. For here it finally was, the opportunity she had once yearned for: the chance to knock a window, however small, into that terrible wall that closed her out from her own memory. Yet because she didn't know, indeed strongly feared what she might glimpse through that window, she was rejecting the chance.

Gianni D'Angelo surveyed her with disturbing intensity, brilliant eyes semi-screened by his lush lashes to a glimmer of gold. 'That's not possible. You asked me why I was here. So I'll tell you. It's quite simple. When you disappeared out of my life, you were pregnant with my child…'

A roaring sounded in Faith's ears. Her lips parted. She stared back at him in horror as that cosy little world he had referred to with such perceptible scorn lurched and tilted dangerously on its axis.

'Connor is *my* son,' Gianni spelt out levelly.

The very floor under Faith's feet seemed to shift. Her eyes were blank with shock.

As she swayed, Gianni strode forward. Curving a powerful arm to her spine to steady her, he took her out of the conservatory and back through the hall. 'No, don't pass out on me again. Let's get out of this dump. We both need some fresh air.'

The winter sunlight that engulfed her at the front of the house seemed impossibly bright. She blinked and shifted her aching head. 'No, not Connor…it's not possible…not *you*!'

Ignoring those objections, Gianni guided her over to a worn bench and settled her down on it with surprisingly gentle hands. He hunkered down in front of her and reached for her trembling fingers, enclosing them firmly in his. 'There *is* no easy way to tell you these things. I'm working really hard to keep the shocks to the minimum.'

That one shock had temporarily left her bereft of the ability to even respond. And yet he could call that one bombshell keeping the shocks to the "minimum"? Dear God, what worse could he tell her than he had already told her? Her face was pale as parchment. 'My head hurts,' she mumbled, like a child seeking sympathy in an effort to ward off punishment for some offence.

Gianni's hands tightened fiercely on hers. 'I'm sorry, but I had to tell you. Why do you think I'm here? Why do you think I've spent three endless years trying to trace you both?' he demanded emotively.

Faith focused on him numbly. The father of her child. Why hadn't that possibility occurred to her sooner? But she knew why, didn't she? Connor might as well have sprung into being without benefit of any male input whatsoever.

Once she had been frantic to know who had fathered her child, but when she had admitted that need to her parents they had gone all quiet and looked at each other uncomfortably. And when she had questioned their attitude to what seemed to her an absolutely crucial question that had to be answered, she had recognised what they didn't want to put into words.

They were afraid that she had been promiscuous, that she might not even know for sure who had actually got her pregnant. And she had been very upset to realise that her parents could harbour such sordid suspicions about a life she could no longer remember.

'The father of my baby might love me…might be looking for me right now!' she had sobbed in distraught self-defence.

'If he loved you, why were you on your own?'

'If you disappeared, why hasn't he been in touch with the police?'

'And why hasn't he come here looking for you? Surely he would at least have known where your parents lived? Even though you hadn't been in touch with us recently, wouldn't he have arrived here to check us out as a last resort?'

Faced with those unanswerable questions, Faith had finally let go of the idea that she might have conceived her baby in a caring relationship. And from that moment on she had begun suppressing her own curiosity, shrinking from the idea that Connor might be the result of some casual sexual encounter. Yet those suspicions had only fronted worse fears, she conceded now, a hysterical laugh lodging like a giant stone in her throat. These days you read so many horror stories about the level penniless and homeless teenagers could be reduced to just to survive…

'Milly…' Gianni tugged her upright.

'That's n-not my name,' she stated through chattering teeth.

He raised his hands to capture her taut cheekbones and she shivered because he was so very close. 'That's the name I knew you by,' he murmured softly.

'Please let go of me…'

'You're shaking like a jerry-built building in an earthquake,' Gianni countered drily.

She realised that she was. Involuntarily, she braced her hands on his chest. Instantly the heat of him sprang out at her and she swiftly removed her hands again, almost off-balancing in her eagerness to put some distance between them. But the distinctive scent of him still flared in her nostrils. Clean, warm, intrinsically male and somehow earthy in a way Edward was not. Edward always smelt of soap. *Oh, my God, Edward,* a voice screamed inside her pounding head.

Another moan was dredged from her. She covered her distraught face with trembling hands in growing desperation. Connor, whom she loved beyond life itself. Connor's father was here to stake a claim in his son's life. What else could he be here for? Why else had he searched for them?

'Let me tell you something…' Gianni breathed in a charged undertone that reeked of menace but somehow didn't frighten her. 'Three years without me has turned you into a basket case! I'm taking you back to my hotel and getting a doctor to look you over!'

By sheer force of will he got her down the path and out onto the pavement. She wasn't capable of matching the speed of his reactions, but she dimly registered that what he thought he acted on simultaneously, with terrifying decisiveness. She gawped at the sight of the long silver limousine waiting, not to mention the chauffeur surging round the bonnet as if he was running a race to get the passenger door open in time.

'Your hotel…?' she repeated belatedly, her brain functioning only in tiny, cripplingly slow bursts of activity. 'I can't go to your *hotel!*'

Gianni ducked her head down as carefully as an officer of the law tucking a suspect into a police car and settled her onto the rich leather-backed seat. He swung in beside her, forcing her to move deeper into the opulent car, and a split second later the door slammed on them both.

'I'm not going anywhere with you!' Faith protested frantically. 'I've got to get back to the shop—'

'I'm sure your partner will manage without you for a couple of hours.'

'I have to pick up Connor from the nursery…no, I don't…I *forgot*,' she lied jerkily. 'The kids are out on a trip today and they won't be back until—'

Gianni subjected her to a derisive appraisal. 'Wise up,' he

breathed in cool interruption. 'You can't hide Connor or keep him from me. When I want to meet my son, I will, but I'm unlikely to stage that meeting when you're on the edge of hysteria.'

He had seen right through her, and that terrified her. 'I'm not on the edge of hysteria...my car...the house...it wasn't locked up—'

Gianni held up the keys. 'I pulled the door shut behind us. If you give me your car keys, your car will be picked up and driven over to the hotel. You're in no condition to drive.'

Faith surveyed him with huge haunted eyes. She passed over her car keys. He was like a tank, rolling over her to crush her deeper and deeper into the dust. And so cold, so very, very cold, she sensed with a shiver. He had tried to calm her, gripped her hands, made an effort to show that he understood why she was so distressed. But none of that had worked. Why? There was no human warmth in him. His brilliant, beautiful dark eyes now chilled her to ice.

Connor's eyes were lighter in shade, but his skin always had that same golden tint even in winter, she reflected numbly. Maybe he was lying about Connor being his child! Even as her head pounded unmercifully into what felt like the onset of a migraine attack she discarded that faint hope. Gianni D'Angelo wouldn't be wasting his time tracking down a child he didn't know to be his.

Stray, unconnected thoughts kept on hitting her from all directions. She had shared his bed. She shifted on the seat, totally unable to look at him any more. She had bathed in his bath. It had to have been *his* bath. Nothing would convince her that she had ever been in the bracket of owning so luxurious a bath. But he had avoided the usual word 're-lationship' to describe their former intimacy. 'A certain bond'. That was the phrase he had used. Such an odd choice to describe their...their what?

Not an affair, not a relationship? Oh, dear heaven, had she been a one-night stand? Or worse? And she knew what was worse. No, no. She discarded that melodramatic suspicion. If she'd been a hooker, he would hardly be so sure her son was his. Dear heaven, what was she thinking? It was as if her brain had just been unhinged, torn open to let all her most deep-seated anxieties flood out.

In silence, Gianni reached into the built-in bar and withdrew a glass. He poured another brandy and settled it meaningfully into her trembling fingers.

Had she drunk a lot when he knew her? Been a real boozer with a strong head? She raised the glass to her lips, the rim rattling against her teeth. The nightmare just went on and on. What did he want from her? She was too terrified to ask, was in a state of complete panic, incapable of rational dialogue.

She didn't even notice where the limo had been going until he helped her out of the car. It was a big country house hotel about three miles out of town. Faith had dined there on her twenty-sixth birthday. Even her father, who liked to make a show of sophistication, had winced at the cost of that meal.

'I don't want to go in here…just take me home,' she mumbled. 'I'm not feeling very well.'

'You can lie down for a while,' Gianni assured her. 'Get your head together.'

'You're not listening to me—'

'You're not saying anything I want to hear.'

'Did I ever?' she heard herself whisper as he pressed her into the lift and the doors slid shut on them.

His superb bone structure tautened. 'I don't remember,' he said flatly.

Her tummy twisted. Was he making fun of her?

Gianni stared down at her from his imposing height. His mouth curled. 'I guess you could say I don't *want* to remember. It's irrelevant now.'

Her head felt woozy, her legs weak and wobbly. As the lift disgorged them into a smoothly carpeted reception area containing only one door, he settled a bracing hand on her spine. 'I don't want to be here,' she told him afresh.

'I know, but I have a habit of getting what I want.' He made her precede him into an incredibly spacious and luxurious suite. Closing the door, he bent, and without the slightest hesitation scooped her off her feet.

'What are you doing?' she gasped.

'You should've said no to that second drink. But possibly I did you a favour. The alcohol has acted on you like a tranquilliser.' Thrusting open another door, he crossed the room beyond and laid her down on a big bed. 'The doctor will check you out in a few minutes. I brought him down from London with me.'

'I don't need a doctor.'

Gianni studied her without any expression at all and strode back out of the room, leaving the door slightly ajar.

A doctor did come. He was middle-aged and suave. If he gave her his name, she didn't catch it. She was finding it impossible to concentrate, and she was so tired, so unbelievably tired, it took almost incalculable effort to respond to his questions…

Gianni watched Milly sleep. Grudging pity stirred in him. She looked so fragile, and it wasn't an illusion. Right now, Milly was like a delicate porcelain cup with a hair-fine crack. If he wasn't very careful, she would break in half, and he might never get her glued back together again. Connor needed his mother. Connor did not need a mother having a nervous breakdown over the identity crisis that was soon to engulf her.

Porca miseria, Gianni swore inwardly. He wanted to wipe Robin and Davina Jennings from the face of the earth for screwing Milly up. She wasn't the same person any more. She was a shadow imprint. Anxious, nervous as a cat, apologetic, scared. She didn't know him from Adam and yet she had just let him bring her back to his hotel suite. In her current condition she was as foolishly trusting as a very young child.

But there was nothing immature about Gianni's response to her. He wanted to rip her out of that buttoned-up white blouse and gathered floral skirt she wore and free her glorious hair from that ugly plait. And then he wanted to jump her like an animal and keep her in bed for at least twenty-four hours, he acknowledged, with grim acceptance of his own predictability.

He had really hoped she would leave him cold. But she didn't. Sooner or later she would. She was a woman, like other women, and eventually all women bored him. Only she never had in the past, he conceded reluctantly. And if he hadn't caught her with Stefano he would have married her. His dirt-poor Sicilian background of traditional values had surfaced when he'd got her pregnant. He had been ready to buy into the whole dream. The wife, the child, the family hearth. And this tiny, fragile woman, who would only reach his heart now if she stood on literal tiptoes, had exploded the dream and destroyed his relationship with his brother.

He had wanted revenge so badly he could still taste it even now. He had come down to Oxfordshire intending to let revenge simply take its natural course. He emitted a humourless laugh. He hated her, but he craved the oblivion of her sweet body like a drug addict craved a fix. He hated her, but he couldn't bring himself to hurt her. He hated the Jenningses for making him the weapon that had to hurt. He had no choice but to blow Milly's cosy little fake world away. She had to take her own life back, and she couldn't do that without him...

A slight, slanting smile eased the ferocious tension stamped on Gianni's features. She was *his*. He cursed the rampant stirring in his loins. He had been in a state of near constant arousal ever since the airport. Only rigid self-discipline and cold intellect restrained him. For the foreseeable future, she was untouchable. He had waited three years; he could wait a little longer. The fiancé had to be seen off.

How *was* Mr Square and Upwardly Mobile likely to react to the news that Milly wasn't really the boss's daughter?

Milly shifted in her sleep and turned over. The plait lay temptingly exposed on the pillow. Gianni moved forward, and before he even knew what he was doing he was unclasping the stiff black bow, loosening the strands, running his long fingers through her beautiful silky hair. His hands weren't quite steady. Instantly he withdrew them, studied them broodingly, clenched them into defensive fists.

When she had her memory back and he had enjoyed her for a while, he would dump her again. But he would retain a lot of visiting privileges. Purely for his son's benefit, of course. The cascade of half-unravelled wavy golden hair hung over the side of the bed like a lethal lure. It might be quite a while until he dumped her. So what? He asked himself. You couldn't put a price on pleasure.

But how did he tell her the truth about herself in a way that didn't make her hate him? How did you wrap up the fact that at heart she was a gold-digging, cheating tramp who had fooled him right to the bitter end? And if she got her memory back she was going to remember that she had run rings round him right from the minute she'd jumped out of that birthday cake. She was his one weakness, but he could afford to indulge himself just one more time. As long as he never let himself forget for a second what she was *really* like...

'Angel...?'

Somebody was shaking her awake. Faith began to sit up, opening her eyes, only to freeze into immobility.

Gianni D'Angelo stood over her. So very tall, so exotically dark.

'What did you call me?' she mumbled, remembering everything, attempting to block it back out again until she felt better equipped to deal with it.

Faint colour scored his hard cheekbones. 'Milly...I called you Milly.'

'My name's Faith,' she told him flatly, refusing to consider his assurance that he had known her by that other name because such an astonishing claim raised questions about her past she could not yet bring herself to ask. 'Why on earth did you bring me here?'

'You needed time out.'

With a sudden start of dismay, Faith checked her watch. It was almost one. She began to scramble off the bed with alacrity. 'I need to pick up Connor—'

'Call Mrs Jennings. You should eat before you get back behind a steering wheel.'

Mrs Jennings? What an odd way to refer to her mother! Struggling to regain her equilibrium, Faith was even more disconcerted by the untidy cascade of hair now falling round her face. The clasp must have fallen off while she slept. Thrusting the waving mass back behind one small ear, she frowned in Gianni's general direction. 'Eat? I have to pick up Connor—'

He extended a mobile phone to her. 'Ask Mrs Jennings to do it today. We need to talk.'

'No, I—'

'You can't run away from this.'

You can't run away from this. That blunt statement unnerved her. Her lower lip trembled, and then firmed. She twisted her golden head away and snatched in a shuddering breath. Once again Gianni D'Angelo had seen right through her. Her parents and Edward had always been content to accept what they saw on the surface.

And how *was* her fiancé likely to react to the sudden appearance of Connor's natural father? Badly—probably very badly, Faith acknowledged dully. Edward was a very conservative man. And he had once admitted that the very fact he was the only man involved in Connor's life had made it easier for him to accept her son.

The mobile phone was pressed into her tense fingers.

'You think you can just tell me what to do—' she began accusingly.

'Right now, you'd seize on any excuse to walk out of here again!'

Reddening at the accuracy of that stab, Faith turned back reluctantly to look at Gianni D'Angelo.

And, like a slap in the face, she saw all the cool control she craved etched into the arrogant angle of his dark head and the steadiness of his burnished dark gaze. He had complete dominion over himself.

'When you've made your call, we'll have lunch.'

Her teeth ground together. She couldn't hold back her hostility any longer. 'I really don't like you.'

Gianni stilled with one brown hand on the door. 'I know... The Sleeping Beauty woke up to a kiss—'

'She also woke up to a prince!' Faith heard herself interrupt, and then she stiffened, disturbed by the speed of her own retaliation. She never argued with anybody. She was far better known as a peacemaker.

'If I'd kissed you, you might have screamed assault...although possibly that's only what you'd prefer me to believe.' Gianni surveyed her, a sardonic slant to his expressive mouth. 'I think your body remembers me better than your brain does.'

Faith was aghast at that suggestion. 'How *dare* you?'

Gianni gave an exaggerated wince. 'Tell me, how do you square the outraged prudish virgin act with the reality that you're a single mother?'

Beneath his coolly enquiring gaze, Faith's soft mouth opened and closed again. Colour flooded her complexion.

'When something irritates the hell out of me, I usually mention it,' Gianni shared, before he turned on his heel and left her alone.

In his wake, a combustible mix of anger and chagrin engulfed Faith. She punched out her home phone number with a stabbing finger. Her mother answered.

'It's Faith. I'm sorry, but I won't be home for lunch...and I hate to ask you at such short notice but could you pick up Connor from nursery for me?' Faith asked tautly.

'Of course I can, darling,' Davina Jennings responded instantly. 'You sound flustered. Is the shop very busy or is Louise away? Never mind. I'd better get a move on if I'm to collect my grandson *and* still have lunch ready for your father!'

'Thanks, Mum.'

Faith laid down the mobile. As she did so she caught a glimpse of herself in a mirror. *Outraged virgin?* Her cheeks burned afresh. Was that really how she came across?

During her convalescence her mother had warned her that she had a reputation to rebuild, that folk would be quick to pass final judgement on an unmarried mother. Already the target of considerable local curiosity, Faith had been painfully aware of her parents' concern about how she might behave. Her parents were very private people, but they were pillars of both church and community. So Faith had followed her mother's guidance when it came to her wardrobe and had worked hard at cultivating an acceptably low profile.

Distractedly, Faith lifted one of the silver brushes on the dresser to try and tidy her hair as she couldn't find her clasp anywhere. There had been nothing prudish about that blonde in the bath…and, whether she liked it or not, that blonde *had* been her! Yet she still found that so hugely hard to accept. It was like the sudden discovery of an identical twin, who was her exact opposite in personality and behaviour.

After all, in three long years Faith had never had the slightest urge to go to bed with anybody! Quite a few men had asked her out. Unfortunately most had had definite expectations of how the evening should end. Repulsed by those pushy advances, Faith had come to believe that she had a pretty low sex drive, and had occasionally marvelled at Connor's very existence.

Edward had been a family friend long before they had started seeing each other, and she had been grateful that he seemed so ideally suited to her. Her fiancé was neither physically demonstrative nor sexually demanding. He had informed her that he preferred to save intimacy for marriage.

He had even told her that he would respect her more on those terms, particularly when she had made what he called 'a youthful mistake'. When it had dawned on her that the 'mistake' Edward was referring to was Connor, she had been mortified and hurt.

When Faith walked back into the beautifully furnished reception room next door, she saw a waiter standing by a trolley in the elegant dining area. Gianni was poised by the window. He watched her approach with unfathomable eyes. Her tummy flipped and her breathing quickened.

'Let's eat,' he suggested smoothly.

She was surprised to discover how hungry she was, and was grateful for the restraining presence of the waiter. Gianni embarked on an impersonal conversation. He questioned her about local businesses and the recent bankruptcies on the industrial estate. His razor-sharp intellect swiftly outran the depths of her economic knowledge. Where another man might have centred his interest on local history, or the sights to be seen, Gianni functioned on an entirely different level.

Involuntarily, Faith was fascinated. In the midst of her nightmare, Gianni D'Angelo could behave as if nothing remotely abnormal was happening. It was intimidating proof of a very resourceful and clever male in absolute control of a difficult situation.

When the waiter departed after serving them, Faith tensed up again. Gianni surveyed her with slumbrous dark golden eyes and her throat tightened, her heartbeat speeding up.

'Now it's time to talk about Connor,' he told her with immovable cool.

'Connor? How can we?' Faith protested without hesitation. 'As it is, I can hardly get my mind around the idea that you *could* be his father!'

'Not could be, *am*,' Gianni countered with level emphasis. 'You had a test shortly before your disappearance for the child's DNA. I am, without a single shadow of a doubt, Connor's father.'

Faith's knife and fork fell from her loosening hold to rattle jarringly down on her plate. She stared back at him, appalled by that revealing admission. 'You weren't sure that…well, that… You mean you didn't trust me…you suspected there might've been room for doubt?' She struggled valiantly to frame that horribly humiliating question, and her strained voice shook.

Gianni's lean, dark devastating face was now as still as a woodland pool. He cursed his error in referring to the DNA tests to convince her that Connor was his son and murmured evenly, 'I'm a very rich man. The DNA testing was a necessary precaution.'

'A n-necessary precaution…?' Faith stammered.

'A legal safeguard,' Gianni extended with a slight shift of one broad shoulder. 'Once Connor was proven to be my child I could be sure that if anything happened to me his inheritance rights would not be easily contested.'

Faith nodded uncertainly, thoroughly taken aback by the obvious fact that Gianni D'Angelo had already thought to make provision for her son in his will. She also registered that she herself had already moved on in terms of acceptance and expectation. Only three hours ago she had wanted Gianni to vanish, had denied any need to know what ties they might once have had. But now she badly needed to be reassured that they had had a stable relationship which would *not* have entailed DNA testing simply to confirm the paternity of her child.

'You said I was trying to run away from all this,' she reminded him tautly, her clear blue eyes pinned anxiously to his hard bronzed features. 'At first, yes, I was. I was so shocked. But now I have a whole lot of questions I need to ask.'

'About us,' Gianni slotted in softly. 'Unfortunately it would be a bad idea for me to unload too many facts on you right now.'

Faith frowned in complete confusion. 'Why?'

His stunning eyes veiling, Gianni pushed away his plate

and lounged back fluidly in his chair to study her. 'I talked to a psychologist before I came down here.'

'A psychologist?' Disconcerted pink surged up beneath her skin at that admission. The embarrassed distaste with which her parents had regarded all such personnel had left its mark on her.

'It was his view that wherever possible you should only be expected to deal with one thing at a time. That's why we're concentrating on Connor,' Gianni explained, with the slow quiet diction of someone dealing with a child on the brink of a tantrum. 'At this moment, that's enough for you to handle.'

'Let me get this straight,' Faith muttered unevenly. 'You are telling me that you are not prepared to—'

'Muddy the water and confuse you with what is currently extraneous information,' Gianni confirmed, watching her eyes darken and flare with incredulous anger.

Abruptly thrusting back her chair, Faith rose to her feet. 'Who the heck do you think you are to tell me that?'

'Sit down and finish your meal,' Gianni drawled.

Faith trembled. 'I have the right to know what role I played in your life. That is *not* extraneous information!'

'I think it is. I want to talk about my son because I've waited three years to find him and now I would very much like to meet him.' Gianni's measured gaze challenged her.

'You're not meeting Connor until you tell me what I need to know!' Faith's head was starting to pound, not least because a temper she had never known she had was tightening its grip on her, no matter how hard she strove to contain it. 'What was I to you? A one-night stand? *A hooker?*' she slung furiously. 'Or a girlfriend?'

With pronounced cool, Gianni came upright to face her. Even in the overwrought state she was in, his striking grace of movement caught her eye as he stepped out from behind the table. 'No to all of the above. Leave this for another day, *cara*,' he advised very quietly, incisive dark-as-night eyes resting on the revealing clenching and unclenching of her hands. 'When the time's right, I'll tell you everything you want to know.'

'Stop treating me like I'm mentally unfit to deal with my *own* life!' Faith launched back at him in furious condemnation. 'I'll ask you one more time before I walk out of here…what was I to you?'

Gianni expelled his breath in a slow hiss. 'You were my mistress.'

Faith stared back at him, eyes widening and widening, soft mouth rounding but no sound emerging. The angry tension evaporated from her. Sheer shock stilled her, leaving her looking vulnerable and lost. Then she sealed her lips, forced her feet to turn her around and walked to the door. There she hesitated, wheeled back, and hurried across the room again to retrieve her handbag. Not once did she allow her attention to roam back in Gianni's direction.

'Are my car keys in here?' she asked woodenly.

'Yes. This is ridiculous,' Gianni murmured drily.

'How long was I…your mistress?' Faith squeezed out that designation as if her mouth was a clothes-wringer.

'Two years…'

Faith flinched as though he had struck her a second body blow. Then, pushing up her chin and straightening her slight shoulders, she moved back to the door and paused there. 'I hope you paid me well to prostitute myself,' she breathed through painfully compressed lips.

In the thunderous silence that greeted that stinging retaliation Faith turned her head. Gianni gazed back at her, not a muscle moving on his darkly handsome features. But for once she could read him like an open book. His golden eyes blazed his fury. Oddly soothed by that reaction, Faith stalked rigid-backed out of the suite and headed for the lift.

CHAPTER THREE

FAITH's tenuous control crumpled and fell apart the instant she reached the sanctuary of her car.

Snatching in a gasping breath in an effort to calm herself, Faith stared blindly through the windscreen. *His mistress!* It made a horrible kind of sense. He was filthy rich. She wasn't from the same world. So of course she hadn't been his girl-friend, his *equal*, she reflected bitterly. Now she knew why he had been challenged to quantify their relationship. The commercial element had figured. For two years. *Two years*, an agonised inner voice screeched in condemnation. It had taken her an inexcusably long time to wake up and see the error of her ways.

For two years, two of her missing years, she had been a kept woman. In exchange for sex he had probably paid for the roof over her head, her clothing, all her bills. Faith shud-dered, mortified by the self she had clearly been before she'd lost her memory. What kind of woman could she have been? This woman who had called herself Milly? What further humiliating discoveries still awaited her?

Striving hard to get a grip on her wildly seesawing emo-tions, Faith started the car and drove away from the hotel. Gianni had said she had disappeared. OK, she told herself, it might have taken her a long time but at least she had finally decided to leave him. She must have planned to make a fresh start. And a fresh start was exactly what she had made, she reminded herself doggedly.

Then, just as she came off the roundabout on the outskirts of town, her searing headache became suddenly so much worse that her vision began to blur. Immediately she pulled off the road and parked. Perspiration beaded her short upper lip.

And then it happened. As if somebody was staging a sudden slideshow inside her head. A picture slotted into her mind. She saw herself clutching a phone like a lifeline, and then her awareness shifted and she was suddenly inside that self.

'Gianni…I haven't seen you in three weeks,' she was saying, and tears were stinging her eyes, but she was working really hard at keeping her voice light and teasing because like any workaholic Gianni hated it when she nagged.

'Book yourself a seat on Concorde.'

'OK…' she agreed with studied casualness, furiously blinking back the tears.

'I didn't realise it had been three weeks.' Gianni paused, and then continued with innate superiority and instinctive attention to detail. 'No, it hasn't been three weeks, *cara*. Don't you remember I stopped over one night before I went to Rio?'

'Gianni, much as I love you,' she groaned, 'there are times when I just want to reach down this phone line and *hit* you! You were here for less than five hours!'

And then, just as quickly as it had come, the picture vanished and Faith was left sitting behind the steering wheel of her car in complete shock. But every emotion she had experienced during that slide back into the past had stayed with her, and the revelation of those powerful emotions now took her by storm.

Winding down the window with a shaking hand, Faith drank in great gulps of fresh air. It had happened, this time it had really, definitely happened, and she had genuinely remembered something. But that tiny slice of the past she had relived had been incredibly disturbing.

She had loved him. She had *loved* Gianni D'Angelo! She had had a capacity for emotion then that had virtually eaten her alive. Until now Faith had never dreamt that at any stage of her life she could have experienced such strong feelings.

And it was even more devastating to be forced to accept that once she had adored Gianni D'Angelo, lived from one day to the next on that love, needed him as she needed air to breathe, felt she was barely existing when he wasn't around…

Emerging from that shattering new awareness, Faith tried to block it out again. It had already been a hell of a day. Tomorrow she would take it all out again and deal with it. Not now.

She drove through town and parked at the rear of Petals, the flowershop she ran with Louise.

Gianni D'Angelo's mistress. If she had once been *that* crazy about him, she could even begin to see how she might have ended up trapped in such a relationship. Love had made a fool of her. Love, she told herself urgently, was a lot more presentable an excuse than avarice.

But how was she to tell Edward? Edward was such a conventional man. Faith's heart sank. Edward had chosen to assume that some flash young man had seduced her and then abandoned her when she fell pregnant. That was how Edward had dealt with getting engaged to an unwed mother. He had effectively excused her from all real responsibility and decided to view her as an innocent victim.

But being kept by Gianni D'Angelo as a mistress was a very different kettle of fish. And how could she not tell Edward, when Gianni was here in the flesh demanding to meet his son? It was *all* going to come out. Nothing she could do could prevent that. Gianni D'Angelo's mistress. It was sordid. Why had she tried briefly to persuade herself otherwise? Edward and her parents would be extremely shocked. And Gianni wasn't likely to sink back into the woodwork again. Climbing out of her car, Faith paled at that awareness.

The shop was empty of customers. Louise was dusting shelves and humming to herself. Her partner turned round, and as Faith moved into the light she frowned. 'Heck, what's happened to you?'

Faith stiffened defensively like a hedgehog under sudden attack. 'Nothing…nothing's happened to me.'

'What have you done with your hair?' Louise demanded. 'My goodness, I never realised you had that much of it!'

'I had a headache…have a headache,' Faith corrected awkwardly. 'I'm sorry. I should've called you to tell you that I would be out for so long.'

'Nonsense. Go back home this minute. You look awful,' Louise told her bluntly.

Relieved by that advice, Faith went back out to her car and drove slowly home to the rambling old farmhouse her parents had bought and renovated when she was a child. In the cosy front hall, the scent of beeswax polish and the ticking of the old grandfather clock enveloped her like a healing blanket.

Connor ran out of the kitchen, loosed a noisy whoop of welcome and flung himself at her. 'Mummy!' he carolled.

Faith reached down and lifted her son. She hugged him so tightly he gave a yelp of protest. Instantly she loosened her grip and pressed an apologetic kiss to his smooth brow. A great gush of love had just engulfed her, but for the first time there was a piercing arrow of fearful insecurity inside that love.

He was a gorgeous little boy. The combination of her blonde hair with his dark brows, sparkling brown eyes and golden skin tone was unusual. But all of a sudden Connor wasn't exclusively her little boy any more. He was the son of a very rich man, who wanted a share of him. How much of a share?

Her mother emerged from the kitchen. 'Are you taking the rest of the afternoon off?' she asked, and then frowned. 'Oh dear, what's happened to your hair?'

'I lost the clasp.'

Davina Jennings, a small, comfortably rounded woman with short greying fair hair and an air of bustling activity, sighed. 'You should take time off more often. You do look tired, darling.'

'Do I?'' Averting her head, Faith lowered Connor to the floor.

She would talk to her parents tonight after dinner. There was no point putting it off. Gianni might just arrive on the doorstep. Possibly storming out on him hadn't been the wisest move. It might have made her feel better but it would have increased his hostility. And how could she blame *him* for the reality that she had been his mistress? She had been an adult when she had made that choice, not a helpless little girl.

'Since you're home, I think I'll just pop down to the church hall and check that everything's ready for that choral do this evening,' Davina Jennings continued. 'I know Janet Markham said she would see to it, but I'm afraid the younger women on the ladies' committee aren't always as reliable as they like to think.'

Faith knew that her mother would be out for the rest of the afternoon. Davina loved to be busy. She would go down to the church hall, seize with alacrity on the idea that the floor wasn't quite clean enough or the kitchen looked a little dingy and roll up her sleeves.

Faith went upstairs to her bedroom. Connor got down on his knees to run a toy car along the skirting board, making phroom-phroom noises while she got changed. She pulled on a sweater and a comfy denim skirt and took Connor out to the garden.

It was a lovely mild winter day. But the sense of tranquillity that usually enveloped her outdoors refused to come. What would Gianni do next? She was just sitting here on pins waiting to find out, wasn't she? Suddenly ashamed of her own passiveness, Faith walked into the kitchen and reached for the phone. It made sense that she should contact Gianni to arrange to meet up with him. The last thing she wanted was for him to arrive unannounced at her home...

But the receptionist at the hotel didn't seem to know whether they had a Gianni D'Angelo staying or not. Yet she still requested Faith's name and address before she might condescend to pass on such privileged information. Exasperated, because she was afraid she might lose her nerve, Faith decided to leave a message instead.

'Tell him Milly would like to see him. I'll be…I'll be in the park at four,' she dictated tautly, and hurriedly replaced the receiver.

Cloak and dagger stuff, but why give her own name when it wasn't necessary? And this way she would get the worst over with, she told herself bracingly. She would let him see Connor and find out exactly what he wanted. She was dealing with a very rich and powerful male, who was already hostile towards her. At this point, antagonising him without good reason would be foolish.

An hour later, Faith drew into the car park. There was no limo, so Gianni hadn't arrived yet. In fact there were no other cars parked at all. With Connor holding her hand, Faith walked down the sloping path that ran between the steeply banked wildflower meadows towards the playground and the artificial lake. Her heart was now beating so fast she pressed a hand against her breast.

She rounded a corner and saw a man in a dark suit talking into a radio. She tensed, wondering what he was doing, suddenly appreciating that she had come to a very lonely place at an hour when it was likely to be deserted. The man fell silent as she moved past. Connor pulled free of her hold and ran ahead into the playground, his sturdy little legs carrying him towards the slide he loved at a steady rate of knots.

'See me, Mummy!' he shouted breathlessly as he reached the final step, his face ablaze with achievement.

And at that exact moment Gianni appeared, striding down the path she had just emerged from. Something disturbingly akin to excitement flashed through Faith, freezing her in her tracks. The man with the radio spoke to him, but Gianni slashed a silencing hand through the air. Gianni's entire attention was already fixed on the little boy carefully settling himself to the top of the slide, tiny hands holding the toddler grips tight.

The whole atmosphere seemed to charge up. Faith couldn't take her eyes off Gianni. She watched him swallow, slowly shake his gleaming dark head in an almost vulnerable movement, and suddenly ram his hands into the pockets of his exquisitely tailored trousers. He stared at Connor as if he was the Holy Grail, and he did it with a raw intensity of emotional response that shook Faith to her innermost depths.

Did he ever look at *me* like that? she found herself wondering. She wouldn't have credited that Gianni D'Angelo had that much emotion in him. But the stark prominence of his superb bone structure, the shimmering brilliance of his ferociously intent eyes and the hands that he didn't seem to know what to do with any more as he jerked them back out of his pockets again all spoke for him.

Her throat thickened. Suddenly she felt on the outside, looking in. She had picked a guy who loved children but she had run away with his child. Why had she done that? He had known she was pregnant before she left him. Why *had* she left him? Hadn't she realised that he might feel like this about their baby?

Without the slightest warning or expectation, Faith was beginning to feel guilty.

He had known her by another name. Clearly she had lied to him and given him that false name. Why had she done that? Had she been ashamed of the life she was leading with him? Had she been trying to ensure that nobody could ever connect Faith Jennings with Gianni D'Angelo's mistress? Well, her lies must have hampered his every attempt to find them again. He couldn't possibly have known where her parents lived, or indeed anything about them.

'Whee!' Connor screeched as he whooshed down the slide, scrambling off at the foot to race back round to the steps to do it again, totally uninterested in the adults watching him.

'He's blond...' Gianni breathed gruffly from his stance several feet away, still not sparing her an actual glance. 'Somehow I never thought of that.'

Faith's breath feathered in her tightening throat. 'He has dark eyes and dark brows and he takes a tremendous tan,' she squeezed out unevenly. 'And he's pretty tall for his age, which he certainly didn't get from me—'

'He's just tremendous,' Gianni incised almost roughly, his foreign accent far more noticeable than it had been earlier in the day.

One day, in fact considerably less than twelve hours, Faith acknowledged. But today, in the space of those few hours, Gianni D'Angelo had changed her whole life.

Suddenly he turned his proud head, cold, dark flashing eyes seeking out hers in a look as physical as a blow. 'I've missed out on two and a half years of my son's life. You owe me...' he murmured in sibilant condemnation.

Faith went pale and crossed her arms jerkily. 'I didn't know...I didn't remember.'

'You knew when you did your vanishing act,' Gianni reminded her darkly. 'Now go and get Connor and tell him who I am!'

Faith blinked in disconcertion. 'I can't do that—'

'Why not?' Gianni shot back at her.

'I mean, he doesn't know you...it's far too soon,' she argued.

'I won't allow you to introduce me to my own child as some passing stranger,' Gianni spelt out. 'I'm his father. At his age, he's hardly likely to be traumatised by the news!'

Put squarely on the spot, Faith studied him with strained eyes. She hadn't been prepared for that demand. Foolishly, she hadn't thought beyond letting him see Connor, and even that decision, she recognised now with sudden shame, hadn't been made for the right reasons. Playing for time, she had dangled Connor like a carrot, in an effort to soothe Gianni and prevent him from taking any other form of action.

'*Porca miseria!*' Gianni suddenly gritted in a fierce undertone, striding forward, dark eyes flaming threat. 'Does he call your fiancé Daddy?'

Faith backed off a startled step and trembled. 'No, of course not!' she gasped.

Equally as suddenly, Gianni stilled. Dark, feverish colour had sprung up over his spectacular cheekbones as he surveyed her: a slight, shivering figure with replaited hair, drawn features and frightened confused eyes. Now clad in an ugly mud-coloured jacket, flat walking shoes and a shapeless denim skirt, she looked like a waif. The bitter anger sparked by his first emotive sight of a son who didn't know him drained away. One thing hadn't changed, he acknowledged ruefully. Without him around she was still a fashion disaster, choosing comfort and practicality over style.

'It's all right, *cara*,' Gianni murmured quietly. 'Really, it's all right.'

'I don't know what I'm doing here,' Faith whispered truthfully, her vision blurring with sudden tears.

'I don't know about the location, but this meeting was definitely a step in the right direction,' Gianni told her bracingly, checking that Connor was still wholly entranced by the slide before extending a supportive arm around her. 'Take a deep breath and let it out again…'

'I might fall over…' She tried to joke, but her taut voice emerged flat as a pancake. As he eased her into the shelter of his lean body she was alarmingly conscious of his male warmth and his intimate scent. Her tummy flipped, leaving her feeling desperately ill at ease.

'Not when I'm around.'

'I really don't know why I gave you a false name,' Faith heard herself confide. 'It seems such a strange thing to have done, and I've always thought I was an honest person…I really did think that.'

Gianni tensed and suppressed a groan. The plot thickens, he conceded grimly. Of course she was going to assume that her real name was the false one. What else was she to think while she still fondly imagined that the Jenningses were her parents? But by the end of the day he would have dealt with that problem as well, he reminded himself grimly. Handling one problem at a time had become an impossible challenge.

'Take me over to Connor,' he urged.

His lack of comment surprised Faith. But then it had hardly been the right moment for that confession, she decided dully. His sole interest right now was naturally his son.

As she headed for Connor, Gianni let his arm slide from her. It felt oddly like being pushed away. Confusion assailed her. She was uneasily conscious of the change within herself. Since she had had that flashback Gianni no longer felt like a stranger. Now she was hugely aware that she had once loved him. A terrifying, all-or-nothing, no-sacrifice-too-great love, which she had apparently offered freely. But she didn't think he had ever loved her. She had sensed her own insecurity during that phone call, relived her own determined attempt to conceal that insecurity.

When he saw them coming towards him, Connor perched on the end of the slide, restlessly swinging his legs, only curiosity in his eyes as he studied Gianni. He was a friendly, confident child, who had never been shy.

'You're *big*!' he said to Gianni, his blond head falling back to take in the height of a male at least six feet three inches tall, big brown eyes wide as the sky above and openly impressed.

Gianni laughed, and immediately hunkered down to his son's level. 'I think you're going to be big too,' he commented, half to himself.

'This is…' Faith had to stop and start again as Connor gazed up at her with innocently enquiring eyes. 'This is your father, Connor.'

Connor looked blank.

'Your daddy,' Faith rephrased in a taut undertone.

He recognised that word. 'Daddy?' he repeated, small legs falling still, a puzzled look on his face. Then his dark eyes rounded and he studied Gianni with dawning wonderment. 'Peter daddy?'

As Gianni tensed, Faith crouched down beside him. 'Yes, that's right…like Peter has a daddy. This is your daddy,' she explained.

'Who's Peter?' Gianni enquired out of the corner of his mouth.

'His friend at nursery,' Faith whispered back. 'He's been to his house to play.'

'Play ball?' Connor demanded, suddenly bouncing upright in excitement. 'Daddy play ball?'

Gianni released his pent-up breath. 'Not for a long time, but willing to learn,' he muttered not quite steadily. 'Why didn't I think of bringing something like that?'

Connor danced on the spot. Peter's daddy was more of a favourite than even Faith had appreciated. 'Play cars? Phroom-phroom?' he carolled hopefully, withdrawing a tiny toy car from his pocket.

'Phroom…phroom,' Gianni sounded obediently. 'I *love* playing cars!'

Connor grinned and raised his arms to be lifted. 'Phroom…phroom…phroom!' he said exuberantly.

Gianni reached out and eased his son into his arms and then slowly came upright, a slightly stunned light in his usually keen dark eyes. He held Connor awkwardly, at a slight distance from him, visibly afraid of taking too many liberties too soon and spoiling the moment.

Reacting to the amount of attention he was receiving, Connor spread his arms and proceeded to noisily intimate an aeroplane going into freefall.

'Connor, behave!' Faith scolded in dismay, but Gianni saw his mistake and hauled his son closer before he could divebomb out of his arms.

'Daddy!' Connor exclaimed, and wound his arms round Gianni's neck to plant a big kiss on his cheek. 'My Daddy…*mine*!' he stressed, with all the satisfaction of ownership.

Faith's eyes smarted. Even at this age, her son had clearly felt the difference between himself and his friend Peter. She would never have suspected that. She had thought he was too young to appreciate the absence of a father in his life, had once assumed that the presence of her own father would fill that gap. Unfortunately, Robin Jennings worked long hours, and Connor was invariably in bed when his grandfather was at home. And Edward found the high-octane energy of a toddler difficult to handle, had frankly admitted that he would feel more at home with Connor when he was a little older.

Yet Gianni's damp eyes shone. Edward had never looked at her son with such pride and emotion and fascination. And why should he have done? Edward was not Connor's father.

'Down!' Connor demanded.

Gianni lowered him to the thick carpet of bark on the ground. Connor got cheerfully down on all fours, stuck his bottom in the air and cried, 'Woof! Woof!'

'He's doing his dog impression. You're getting his whole repertoire,' Faith explained tightly. 'He's showing off like mad.'

'He's so full of life...so sweet,' Gianni murmured huskily, hunkering down again, careless of the muddy bark welling round his superb Italian leather shoes, to stay close to his son.

Connor got bored with being a dog very quickly. 'Ducks!' he reminded his mother.

Gianni regarded Faith enquiringly.

'On the lake. He likes to see them.'

Connor had already scampered off in the direction of the lake path and Faith hurried after him. The light was fast beginning to fade. Gianni fell into step beside her. The mature trees on the woodland trail cast dark shadows. When a man suddenly stepped into view several feet ahead of them, Faith gave a start of dismay.

Gianni spoke to him in Italian, and only then did she recall the other man who had been standing above the playground.

'What's going on?' she questioned nervously as they moved on. 'Who are those men?'

'I was really surprised when I got your message earlier, particularly when you styled yourself "Milly",' Gianni admitted.

Faith coloured. 'It seemed more discreet to do that.'

'Unfortunately my security staff were convinced the message was a set-up.'

'Security staff?' Those men worked for him?

'The park is swarming with them. They've had the time of their lives staking out this place over the past hour. They love stuff like this,' Gianni conceded with wry amusement.

'Why a set-up?' she queried. 'Why would anybody think that?'

'People don't, as a rule, ask me to meet them in such public places. I did wonder if the press had finally got on to us and whether you might have received a similar message purporting to be from me. The tabloids would pay a fortune for a photo of us all together—'

'Tabloids?' she exclaimed, thoroughly taken aback.

'Wake up, *cara*. The news that I have a child will be a major scoop. And sooner or later it *will* come out,' Gianni informed her. 'I could only protect you from that exposure by staying away from my son, and I'm not prepared to do that. I won't behave as if Connor is some grubby secret in my life.'

Faith was horrified by what he was telling her. His very arrival had already exploded her quiet life out of existence. Now he was calmly admitting that there would be worse to come. Naturally the press would have an interest in the private life of a male as wealthy and powerful as Gianni. But threat of such public exposure made Faith feel ill. If it happened, her parents would be devastated, and once again she would be responsible for hurting them.

Since Connor had got down on the grass verge to play with the gravel on the path, Faith came to a halt and rested back weakly against the trunk of a tall beech tree. 'You don't give a damn, do you?' she muttered shakily. 'No matter how it affects me and my family, you'll still go ahead and demand access to Connor.'

'Guilty as charged,' Gianni said drily. 'I've been excluded from my son's life long enough.'

In the twilight, Faith focused on his lean bronzed features with a heart that was chilled even as its beat involuntarily quickened. His dark, deep-set eyes had an aggressive golden glimmer that challenged. He was tougher than titanium and he wasn't going to quit. 'You're so unfeeling,' she condemned unevenly.

Moving fluidly forward, Gianni braced one lean hand against the trunk and stared down at her, spiky black lashes low over his slumbrous gaze. 'Am I?' he questioned in a lazy undertone as smooth as black silk.

That deep, dark drawl sent tiny little shivers running down her taut spinal cord. Her bemused eyes locked to his and feverish tension snaked through her. For the space of a heartbeat she wanted to move away, and then she wasn't sure what she had wanted or even why she might have wanted it. As rational thought blurred, other more intrusive physical sensations took precedence.

That close, Gianni truly mesmerized her. Her breathing quickened, her mouth running dry. Dark excitement flowered into being inside her. Her muscles tightened on a delicious thrilling edge. The sudden aching fullness of her breasts and the urgent sensitivity of her nipples made her tremble, every pulse racing at fevered speed.

She could hardly breathe as Gianni watched her with the still golden eyes of a hunter. He brought up his other hand and let his thumb slowly graze the full curve of her lower lip. At the first touch of his hand, heat burst into being low in her pelvis, and she was betrayed into a tiny startled gasp. As Connor played at their feet, Gianni let long fingers curve to her flushed cheekbone and slowly he smiled. Faith braced herself against the tree to stay upright. That smile dazzled her, knocked her sideways, and filled her with an elemental hunger so powerful it hurt.

'Poor Edward…' Gianni husked with indolent satisfaction as he withdrew his hand and straightened again with innate grace. 'This is all about to blow up in his face. Let him go before it gets dirty, *cara*.'

Only slowly emerging from what felt vaguely like a partial black-out, Faith stared with darkened eyes up at the tall, dark male towering over her as if he had suddenly become the devil incarnate. Now she recognised the studied insolence of that smile. The frantic heat that had filled her with such mindless yearning seconds earlier now engulfed her in shame. How could she be attracted to him like this? How *could* she be? Maybe it was the disorientating sense of having one foot lodge in the past and the other foot threatening to buckle in the present. All of a sudden it was so difficult to know what she was really feeling.

'Leave Edward out of this!' she told him, with all the fierceness of her own guilty mortification.

'But he's right in the middle,' Gianni responded with supreme cool. 'So why drag out his demise? There's no contest, is there?'

'I don't know wh-what you're talking about,' Faith stammered, although she was dreadfully afraid that she did, and what he was now suggesting terrified her.

Gianni dealt her a long, slow, sardonic look. 'I don't have much compassion to spare in Benson's direction, but I'm fair enough to concede that he didn't know he was poaching on my territory…so let him go now.'

'Your territory?' Faith parroted, scarcely believing her ears.

Gianni ran a mocking fingertip down the exposed line of her extended throat and watched her jerk and instinctively lean closer. 'You're still mine, *cara*. You don't have any resistance to me at all. But then you never did have… I want you back, Milly.'

'You couldn't possibly! You're nothing to do with me any more. Our only connection now is Connor!' Faith asserted in a feverish rush of protest. Hurrying forward, she stooped to grab her son's hand and turn back the way they had come. 'It's getting dark…it's time I went home.'

'Ducks?' Connor cried in plaintive surprise.

'The ducks have gone to bed,' Faith told him with desperate urgency.

And the last sound she heard was Gianni's husky appreciative laughter.

CHAPTER FOUR

AFTER buckling a squirming complaining Connor into his car seat, Faith ruefully acknowledged that she had done it again. She had reached saturation point and fled when she could take no more. Once more Gianni D'Angelo had breached the boundaries of her expectations and forced her into uncharted waters.

His territory. She recalled that assertion with a shiver. *Gianni wanted her back.* And with that shattering statement of intent Gianni D'Angelo had plunged her into shock again. Just as she was struggling to regard and accept him as Connor's father, Gianni had revealed a motivation she had never dreamt might exist.

He had been so casual about it too, but in the cool fatalistic fashion of a male referring to an inevitable event. And he had totally unnerved her when he had urged her to let Edward go. Edward was the man she *loved*, the man she was to marry in a few months' time! Yet with frightening confidence Gianni had talked as though her fiancé was already on the way out of her life.

But mightn't she herself have unwittingly encouraged that attitude? Faith squirmed, steeped in shame over behaviour which had merely increased her emotional turmoil. Gianni was incredibly attractive, but he had one trait more disturbing and more dangerous than all the rest put together, and that was a high-voltage aura of pure sex.

She had never recognised that in a man before. But she had been susceptible, indeed had found it quite impossible to control her own intense awareness of him. But then, around Gianni she was steadily becoming a person she didn't know...

Edward hadn't come into her mind once while her wretched body had come alive like an insidious enemy. And then, as she sat there fighting to understand what was happening to her, Faith suddenly found an escape route from the daunting conviction that in responding in any way to Gianni she had betrayed Edward.

Why was she being so tough on herself? What a fool she was being! That flashback about that long-ago phone call had destabilised her. The instant she'd realised that she had once loved Gianni it had become a huge challenge to deal with him as a stranger. So for a few minutes her barriers had slipped. The line between the past and the present had blurred. And in the enervated state she was in, she had reacted in a way she would never normally have reacted...

Now that she knew the problem it wouldn't ever happen again, she told herself urgently. She had behaved as if she was still the woman making that phone call, hadn't she? She had behaved as if Gianni was her lover. So she wasn't *really* still attracted to Gianni. Involuntarily, she had responded to an eerie sense of familiarity.

Since Faith hadn't heard the limousine pulling into the car park, and certainly hadn't seen it, she almost leapt from her seat in fright when a hand gently rapped on the windscreen to attract her attention. Her head twisted round. She recognised Gianni's burgundy silk tie and it was like an instant shot of adrenalin.

Gianni opened the car door to subject her to a fulminating appraisal.

'What are you doing?' Faith demanded defensively.

'You're sitting in the dark in an unlocked car in a deserted park. You've got a lot on your mind. Let me run you home,' Gianni urged, his dark, deep drawl sending an odd little shiver through her.

'If I've got a lot on my mind, whose fault is it?' she condemned tautly. 'Why can't you give me five minutes of peace?'

'You shouldn't be on your own here.' Delivering that assurance with the supreme confidence of a male making an unarguable statement, Gianni lowered his arrogant dark head to glance into the back of the car. His brilliant dark eyes connected with hers again. 'Connor looks pretty miserable too.'

'Daddy!' Connor squealed in sudden excitement.

Flinching from that cry of recognition, Faith bowed her forehead down against the steering wheel and fought off an urge to bang it hard. But she had seen the reproof in his gaze. He hadn't needed to say anything. 'Go away, Gianni...'

'Only if you go straight home and go to bed. You're exhausted.

Faith tensed even more. She didn't *want* to go home. No longer did she feel up to dealing with her parents, who were likely to be very upset by the news that Connor's father had surfaced. Her past had caught up with her with a vengeance, and nobody was going to escape the fall-out, she acknowledged guiltily.

Lifting her head again, Faith turned the ignition key. 'I'll phone you tomorrow. I'm taking Connor to a fast-food restaurant for tea,' she announced defiantly, and, reaching out, she slammed the door loudly on Gianni.

Connor sobbed when she drove off, which really bothered her. Had he already taken that much of a liking to Gianni? Half a mile down the road, she stopped at a callbox to ring home and yet again excuse herself from a family meal. The phone rang a long time before it was answered by her father.

After she'd explained why she wouldn't be home, her father said in a curiously quiet voice. 'That's fine. Actually, we're dining out ourselves, and we'll probably be late back, so don't wait up for us. By the way, Edward's home.'

'He is?' Faith exclaimed in surprise.

'He caught an earlier flight and called in at the plant just as I was leaving,' Robin Jennings told her.

Faith drove to the restaurant. Connor ate with gusto. Faith nibbled at the odd chip and surveyed her son with her anguished heart in her eyes. Gianni had rights she couldn't deny. Gianni had had a tough deal. At lot of men who fathered children outside marriage sought to evade their responsibilities, but her son had a father who had spent three years trying to track him down. A father who showed every sign of wanting to be very much a part of Connor's life. But a father whose very existence was likely to cause Connor's mother endless hassle and grief.

Edward was home, so she knew where she was heading next. More than anybody else, her fiancé deserved to hear her news first. Edward was always calm, she reminded herself. He certainly wouldn't be happy, but surely he would ultimately take this unexpected development in his stride?

Beginning to feel like a traveller who had no place to lay her head, Faith wearily parked outside the Edwardian villa where Edward still lived with his mother. She thanked heaven that it was one of Mrs Benson's bridge nights. Connor was half asleep, and she carried him up the steps feeling like the worst of mothers for keeping him out beyond his bedtime.

Edward opened the front door and studied her in surprise. 'Faith?'

Faith chewed at her lower lip. 'Dad told me you'd got back early and I needed to see you...so here I am.'

'But why didn't you leave Connor at home?' Edward enquired.

'Mum and Dad are dining out.'

'Are you sure of that? Your father's with your mother? When I walked into Robin's office this afternoon, he was cancelling the business dinner he had arranged for tonight.' Her fiancé continued with pronounced disapproval, 'And, believe me, Bill Smith is too valuable a customer to cancel at such short notice!'

Engaged in settling Connor's limp little body into a corner of the sofa in the chilly lounge, Faith made no response. She was too worked up about what she had to tell Edward.

'Something rather unexpected has happened,' she said stiltedly.

'Everybody does seem to be acting in a very unexpected way today. Your father's evasive manner with me was distinctly odd,' Edward informed her flatly, his pale blue eyes reflecting his annoyance at what he had clearly taken as a snub.

'Look, this is *really* important, Edward,' Faith stressed.

Edward planted himself by the fireplace, a rather irritating air of indulgence in his scrutiny. 'What's up? Wedding stationery not up to scratch?'

'Something I never, ever thought was likely to happen. Connor's father, Gianni D'Angelo, has turned up!' Faith shared in a driven rush.

Edward stiffened. She certainly had his attention now. He began shooting questions at her as if she was in the witness box, charged with some kind of crime.

'Gianni D'Angelo…' Edward repeated incredulously. 'Let me get this straight. You are telling me that the electronics tycoon Gianni D'Angelo is Connor's *father*?'

'Yes, I was pretty shocked too,' Faith admitted heavily.

'Stop talking as if when all this took place it happened to somebody else!' Edward suddenly snapped accusingly. 'Believe me, I'm not too happy with the sound of all this. It's hardly what I expected, is it? Gianni D'Angelo! How on earth did you meet a man like that?'

'I don't remember, Edward—'

'Did you work for him?'

'No…' Faith began pleating a fold in her shirt with tense fingers.

'I'm starting to suspect your loss of memory might be based on a very sound instinct to bury a less than presentable past,' Edward told her in a derisive undertone.

'That's a horrible thing to say. It's not like it's something I can help,' Faith whispered painfully.

'Gianni D'Angelo…so once you moved in distinctly rarefied circles,' Edward remarked snidely, and she winced. 'What sort of relationship did you have with him?'

Stress made Faith's stomach twist. Edward's anger was already greater than she had naively anticipated, and his contempt was an equally unpleasant surprise. I can't tell him the whole truth now. I *can't*, she thought in desperation.

'As your future husband, I have the right to know, and if you don't tell me I have every intention of asking him!'

'He said...he said I was his mistress,' Faith admitted in a deadened voice. She was too exhausted to withstand any more pressure.

The silence went on and on and on. Finally she raised enough courage to look up.

Edward had gone all red in the face. He was also surveying her as if she had turned into an alien before his eyes.

'I'm very ashamed of it,' she told him unevenly.

'So that's who I'm about to marry...Gianni D'Angelo's slut.' Edward labelled her with cold venom. 'Thanks for telling me.'

Pale as milk, Faith got up and bent down to lift her son back into her arms. 'There's not much point continuing this conversation,' she replied tightly. 'You're shocked, and I understand that, but it's my past, *not* my present, Edward.'

'*Shocked* barely covers it...a sleazy association of that nature!' Edward fired back in furious disgust. 'If this gets out locally, I'll be a laughing stock!'

'Gianni's not likely to go around telling people. I only told you because it's not something I felt I could keep to myself.' Only now, she acknowledged, she very much wished she had.

Edward vented a humourless laugh. 'My mother once said I didn't know what I might be taking on with you. Clearly I should have listened!'

'Do you want your ring back?' Faith heard herself ask, without any expression at all.

Edward went rigid, bitter resentment showing in his eyes.

'Of course I don't! My God, can't I let off a little steam without you asking me that?'

'Calling me a slut is more than "a little steam",' Faith countered jaggedly, already wondering if, after their marriage, Edward would throw her past in her teeth every time she annoyed or disappointed him. 'You might as well know the lot. I was Gianni's mistress for two years…and I loved him.'

Edward surveyed her in near disbelief. Whether Faith realised it or not there had been a decided edge of defiance in that final announcement.

'Faith—' he began brusquely.

'I just want to go home, Edward. Could you open the door, please?' she asked woodenly.

Connor restored to his car seat, Faith drove off. Edward was never likely to see her in the same light again. Could she blame him for that? Edward was always very conscious of what others might think. A lot of people had seemed surprised that he should ask a single mother to be his wife. Now Edward was questioning that decision. Were his feelings for her strong enough to withstand such damaging revelations?

Arriving home to find all lights blazing, Faith carried her son straight upstairs and quickly put him to bed. Only when she went downstairs again did it occur to her that the house had the strangest air of being like the *Marie Celeste*. The kitchen even showed every sign of her mother's initial preparations for an evening meal. Faith began to tidy up, amazed that the older woman had gone out leaving potatoes half-unpeeled and the radio still playing.

Where had her parents gone in such a hurry? Her father had cancelled a business dinner and her mother should have been attending the choral evening in the church hall. It wasn't their anniversary or either of their birthdays. Their behaviour didn't make sense, but Faith was already so tired that she fell into bed, determined to suppress every anxiety and every thought.

Once she had caught up on her sleep nothing would look so bad, she assured herself. Edward would have had time to come to terms with her bombshell. He had hurt her, but possibly she had expected too much from him. After all, she too had been upset by what she had learnt about her own past today. Let the dust settle, she urged herself wearily. Tomorrow would be a whole new day.

Accustomed to being rudely awakened by Connor bouncing on her bed, Faith woke the next morning to a curious silence. Glancing drowsily at her alarm clock, she stiffened and then leapt out of bed in dismay. It was just after ten! For goodness' sake, why hadn't her mother roused her?

On her way into the bathroom Faith registered that her son's bed was already neatly made. After washing at speed, she pulled on a brown skirt and a burgundy sweater. This morning it had been her turn to open the shop early for the deliveries. A perplexed frown on her face, she hurried downstairs.

She stilled at the sight of her parents sitting together in silence in the lounge. They looked odd: stiff and strained, and somehow aged.

Robin Jennings rose heavily upright, a stocky well-built man with grey hair. 'We thought we should let you sleep in, so I called Louise first thing and said that you weren't well,' he explained. 'Then I took Connor to the nursery as usual. We need to have a serious talk with you and we felt—well, Mr D'Angelo felt it would be wiser to keep the child away from all this.'

'Mr...? Gianni...?' Faith echoed in growing confusion. 'How...I mean...oh, so you *know* about Gianni?' she suddenly gasped.

'Please sit down,' her father urged.

A hectic flush on her cheeks, Faith was instantly convinced that she knew what was happening. At that moment she absolutely loathed Gianni D'Angelo. Obviously he had gone over her head and contacted her parents. That was probably where they had been last night. *With him.* And her poor parents looked very much as if they had been completely crushed by what they had learnt about her.

'Gianni had no right to interfere!' she exclaimed furiously.

Her father grimaced. 'Faith, Mr D'Angelo—'

A slight movement at the edge of her vision made Faith spin round. She stared, dumbstruck. Gianni now stood in the archway between the lounge and the dining room. She shook her head in urgent negative. Bewildered anger and resentment burned in her questioning gaze. 'What are *you* doing here? How dare you interfere like this? How dare you go behind my back and talk to my parents?'

'That's enough, Faith,' Robin Jennings said stiffly.

'Why did you let him into this house?' Faith demanded fiercely.

Gianni strolled forward with measured steps. 'Keep quiet and sit down,' he told her, his stunning dark features stamped with gravity, his eyes impenetrable. 'I asked to be present. Robin and Davina have a rather disturbing confession to make and they need you to listen to them.'

A confession? A confession about what? Complete confusion made Faith sink slowly down into an armchair. Her accusing stare stayed on Gianni. He dominated the low-ceilinged room, with his height and presence, as alien against the backdrop of the cosy décor as a tiger prowling a busy city street. He didn't belong here, she thought bitterly, and she couldn't credit that her parents could have been influenced by any request of his.

He wore a silver-grey suit, fabulously well cut to his lithe, lean and powerful frame. The fabric had the smooth gleam of wildly expensive cloth, his shirt the sheen of silk. She clashed with dark, deep-set eyes, and suddenly it was an effort to summon up a single connected thought.

'Faith…' her father breathed curtly.

Faith looked back to her parents with some embarrassment. 'What's going on?'

'When we identified you at the hospital three years ago,

we didn't have the smallest doubt that you were our child,' the older man told her flatly. 'You were wearing the bracelet we gave our daughter on her sixteenth birthday. You were blonde, blue-eyed, about an inch taller than you had been when you left. You were a lot thinner, but then why not? Seven years is a long time.'

'Why are you talking about this?' Faith frowned.

Her mother crammed a tissue to her lips and twisted her head away with a stifled gasp. 'I can't bear this—'

'What Robin is trying to tell you is that he and his wife made a very unfortunate mistake.' Gianni advanced, sounding every word with precision.

'We were so overjoyed at getting you back,' Davina Jennings confided jerkily. 'It was over a year before I even admitted to myself that there might be room for doubt about your identity…'

Faith was now as still as a statue, her shaken eyes the only life in her taut face. 'I don't understand what you're trying to say…'

'At the start you were very ill. Then you came round and you had no memories,' Robin Jennings reminded her tensely. 'Our daughter had no distinguishing marks that we could go on. Nothing jarred at that stage. You had grown up. Naturally you had to have matured and changed.'

Gianni shot Faith's perplexed expression a perceptive glance and murmured levelly, 'They're trying to tell you that they are *not* your parents.'

'Not my parents,' Faith repeated like an obedient child. She couldn't believe that, she just couldn't believe it, couldn't even take such a gigantic concept on board long enough to consider it. 'This is crazy…why are you telling me this stuff?'

'We came to love you very much,' her father—who, according to Gianni, was *not* her father—explained almost eagerly. 'In fact as we got to know the person we believed you had become we couldn't have been happier.'

'But eventually we began making discoveries about you

that we couldn't just ignore or explain away,' Davina continued reluctantly. 'You have a lovely singing voice. Our
daughter couldn't even sing in tune. You speak French like
a native...our daughter failed French at GCSE. She was
hopeless at languages.'

Locked suddenly into a world of her own, Faith remembered the evening her father had brought a French client
home for dinner. The instant the man had uttered a French
phrase she had turned without hesitation to address him in
the same language. Dimly she recalled how astonished her
parents had been. But at the time she hadn't thought anything of that. In fact she'd been delighted when the
Frenchman had told her that she had a remarkable idiomatic
grasp of his language. In those days it had seemed to her
that she had no useful talents, and it had felt good to discover she had at least one.

'All the little discrepancies we'd so easily explained away
at the beginning came back to haunt us. Your handwriting
is so different.' Robin Jennings sighed. 'You like cats. Faith
was allergic to cats. It wasn't really very likely that you'd
grown out of that. We began to look rather desperately for
you to remind us in some way of the daughter we remembered, but there was nothing.'

Faith sat there in the kind of shock that felt like a great
weight squeezing the life force from her. 'But the bracelet...I was wearing Granny's bracelet—'

'Our daughter must've sold it. Although she took it with
her when she went, she wasn't that fond of it. Perhaps you
bought the bracelet, or somebody else gave it to you. We
were foolish to rely so much on a piece of jewellery,' Davina
conceded curtly.

'This isn't possible,' Faith said very carefully, but as the
bracelet that she had long regarded as a kind of talisman was
dismissed her voice sank to a mere thread of its usual vol-
ume.

Gianni released his breath in a charged hiss.

'If she doesn't want to believe it, I'm quite content,'

Davina Jennings announced, shooting a glance of bitter dis-like at Gianni. 'In every way that matters she is our daughter and we love her and we don't want to lose her. Neither Robin nor I want anything to change. We told you that last night—'

'And I asked you what you intended to do if the *real* Faith showed up,' Gianni reminded the older woman without hes-itation.

Davina stiffened defensively. 'Not very likely after ten years.'

'This is really happening,' Faith registered finally. 'You're telling me that I'm not really your child, that I was never your child…that this life I'm living actually belongs to an-other woman.'

'Your name is Milly Henner and you're twenty-four years old,' Gianni delivered. 'And while I'm here there is nothing to be afraid of.'

Milly, she thought numbly. My name *is* Milly. She fought to concentrate on thoughts that were whirling like tangled spaghetti inside her blitzed brain. She studied the people whom she had believed were her parents with a deep sense of pain and dislocation. 'How long have you known that I wasn't your daughter?'

The silence thundered. Seemingly neither wished to dis-cuss that point.

Gianni had no such inhibition. 'They've known for about eighteen months. They only admitted their suspicions to each other then—'

'We sat up all night talking,' Robin Jennings cut in heavily. 'We just didn't know what to do. You'd accepted us. We loved you and Connor. We'd introduced you every-where as our daughter—'

'You kept quiet sooner than face the embarrassment of admitting that you could make such an appalling mistake,' Milly, who still so desperately wanted to be Faith, con-demned, at that instant hating everybody in the room. They all knew who they were and where they belonged. But she was an outsider.

'We were happy with the way things were,' Davina argued vehemently. 'Nor do we see why anything should change!'

Milly surveyed her dully.

'I will make every possible effort to trace your real daughter,' Gianni promised the older couple. 'But Milly can't stay here any longer.'

'She can if she wants to,' Robin Jennings asserted curtly.

'She can stay in touch with you. She can even visit. But as who she really is, *not* as who you'd like her to be!' Gianni's attention was on Milly's stark white face and the blank horror growing in her eyes. 'She had another life, and she needs to see that life before she makes any decisions.'

'For heaven's sake, she's engaged…she's getting married!' Davina exclaimed.

'And how do you think Edward is likely to react to this fiasco?' her husband groaned. 'I'll deal with that. I'll see him this morning and explain everything.'

With a sense of numb disbelief, Milly studied them all. Gianni stood apart, his self-discipline absolute. His dark, deep flashing eyes held hers, and she saw the pity he couldn't hide and just wanted to die. She stood up, and walked out of the room.

As Davina leapt up to follow her Gianni planted a staying hand on her arm. 'You can't help Milly with this, Mrs Jennings. Not right now, you can't,' he asserted. 'She feels betrayed by the two people she relied on most. She needs time to come to terms with this.'

'And what exactly are your plans for her, Mr D'Angelo?' the older woman demanded bitterly.

Gianni viewed his companions with concealed hostility. They might love Milly, but they had damaged her. Three years ago they had denied her the further professional help she'd needed. They had done nothing to help her regain her memory. And, unforgivably, when they had realized their mistake they had selfishly refused to put it right. They had ignored the reality that the unknown woman they had erroneously identified as their daughter must have had a life elsewhere.

They also acted as if they owned Milly, and as if she couldn't speak or think for herself. It was an attitude which filled Gianni with violent antipathy. After all, if Milly belonged to anybody, she belonged to him!

She was the mother of his son. He knew her better than anybody alive. He could put her back into the world she had left behind. Leaving Milly anywhere within reach of the Jennings would hamper her recovery. They didn't want to let go even briefly. They wanted her to go on living a fake life while he could not wait to free her from an existence that struck him as suffocating. Milly was very much a free spirit…

The free spirit stared at herself in the bedroom mirror.

Who am I? Who is Milly Henner?

This was not her home. This was not where she had grown up. Those people downstairs were not her parents. Nothing that she had believed was hers was really hers. Not the share of the shop her supposed father had insisted on buying for her, not her car, which had been a birthday present—presented on a day that probably wasn't really her birthday. Only Connor was *really* hers…

As the world she had innocently believed and trusted in caved in around her, Milly experienced an instant of pure terror that threatened to wipe her out entirely.

'Milly…come back to the hotel with me.'

She spun round and focused on Gianni. Naked loathing rippled through her. *He* had done this to her. *He* had ripped her life apart. 'I hate you…' she framed, trembling with the force of her emotions.

'You'll get over that,' Gianni informed her, without an ounce of uncertainty.

'I want Edward,' she admitted shakily, and turned away again.

'You'll get over that too,' Gianni asserted harshly.

'You can't take *him* away from me!'' Milly suddenly slung wildly. 'You can take everything else but not Edward!'

'You can't love him.' Gianni's gaze was black as a stormy night, his tone pure derision. 'You can't. He's nobody; he's nothing!'

Milly's teeth gritted. 'He's the man I love!'

Gianni breathed in deep, his eyes flashing gold with raw menace. 'You couldn't possibly love a calculating little creep like that!'

'Edward is none of your business! Haven't you done enough damage?'

Gianni studied her with shimmering eyes, and then he reached for her without any warning at all. He pulled her into his powerful arms and brought his mouth down on hers. Suddenly she was on fire, her breath rasping in her throat, her slim body burning at every point of contact with his. The heated onslaught of that wide, sensual mouth was a revelation. Nothing had ever felt so necessary. Hunger clawed up through her with such greedy force that her head spun, her senses reeled. Riven with wild excitement, she pressed herself into his hard male frame with a shaken moan of surrender.

'Faith!' Davina intervened, shrill with condemnation.

As Gianni held Milly back from him she trembled in a daze of shock. She focused in startled embarrassment on the older woman lodged in the bedroom doorway.

'I'm not Faith,' she heard herself say unevenly, for she could hardly get air back into her lungs. 'I'm Milly.'

'You're still an engaged woman!' Davina turned to address Gianni. 'She's upset and confused. Why can't you leave her alone?'

Momentarily, Milly was in a world of her own. She could not credit the terrifying intensity of what Gianni had made her feel. She had behaved like a wanton, pushing closer to him and clinging. If she was mortified now, she deserved to be. But then, as the older woman had pointed out, she was upset and in no state to know what she was really feeling…

'I think it's time you told Milly the truth about her engagement,' Gianni murmured silkily.

'I haven't a clue what you're trying to imply,' Davina said thinly.

Gianni gazed down at Milly. His expressive mouth twisted. 'On your wedding day, Edward becomes a fully-fledged partner in the family firm.'

Stunned by that statement, Milly stared back at him. 'That's not true-'

'That news was to have been our wedding present to both you and Edward.' Davina tilted her chin, defying further comment.

Gianni loosed a sardonic laugh. 'Why don't you tell her the truth, Mrs Jennings? Benson got that promise before he even *asked* her to marry him!'

'That's a lie!' Milly's hands curled into tight fists by her sides as she gazed expectantly at the older woman, willing her to shoot Gianni's humiliating aspersions down in flames.

Coins of colour now embellished Davina's cheeks. 'It was a simple business agreement, Mr D'Angelo. Edward is my husband's natural successor.'

'Free partnerships are not the norm in the business world, Mrs Jennings. And you should've warned Benson to keep the news from his mother. She's ensured that half the town knows why her son is prepared to take on another man's child. You made it well worth his while,' Gianni countered very drily.

Tell me it wasn't like that, Milly wanted to beg the older woman strickenly, but she bit back the plea and straightened her shoulders to walk to the door. Only Edward could tell her what it had been like. Only Edward could convince her that he hadn't needed the bribe of a partnership in the firm to persuade him to propose.

'Where on earth are you going?' Davina demanded.

'To see Edward,' Milly looked at Gianni D'Angelo, and, try as she could, she could not suppress the sheer loathing raging through her. 'You are a complete and utter bastard!' she raked at him, heedless of the other woman's shocked gasp. 'And I don't need a memory to tell me why I left you!'

CHAPTER FIVE

REFUSING to be turned from her purpose, Milly snatched her car keys from the hall table and drove over to Jennings Engineering. On the way, she thought back over the months since she had started seeing Edward.

Right from the start he had been attentive and caring. The *dream* boyfriend for an unwed mother? a more cynical voice enquired. Certainly her pseudo-parents had heavily encouraged the relationship, but why not? As a family friend and a trusted employee, Edward had naturally impressed them as being ideal.

But Milly had been more impressed by Edward's apparent indifference to her amnesia. She had relaxed in his company. Other men she had dated had assumed that she was promiscuous just because she already had a child; Edward's respectful attitude had come as a very welcome relief. It was hardly surprising that she had fallen in love with him.

So what if it was a different kind of love from that which she had once felt for Gianni D'Angelo? From what she recalled of those emotions she imagined a lowering form of enslavement, made all the more dangerous and destructive by the strength of her sexual craving for him. There, it was out at last, she acknowledged angrily. An admission of the physical weakness which had probably got her involved with Gianni in the first place.

Yet sex barely figured in her relationship with Edward. But then what she felt for Edward was a more mature and lasting love. So cymbals didn't clash and fireworks didn't go off when Edward kissed her. But where had the cymbals and the fireworks got her before? Down and out and pregnant by a male so frighteningly ruthless she could only admire herself for walking out on him three years earlier.

Milly parked the car outside the small office block beside the engineering plant. She was relieved that Robin Jennings was still at home. She had had enough of other people's interference.

A nightmare mistake had been made, but she was OK, she told herself bracingly; she was coping. Gianni had tried to destroy everything, but as long as she still had Edward she would manage to come to terms with all the rest. She blocked out the little voice that warned that she was hanging by her fingernails onto her last shred of control.

Edward was in his office. Her unannounced entrance made him rise from behind his desk in surprise. Strain from their contentious meeting the night before showed in the stiffness of his greeting.

'I was going to call you this afternoon,' he told her rather defensively.

'I needed to see you to talk. This morning I found out something that I wish you'd thought to share openly with me,' Milly admitted tautly.

'Unlike your life, mine is an open book,' Edward retorted crisply. 'I've kept nothing from you.'

'What about the partnership you get the day you marry me?' Milly enquired, wanting him to tell her that that was a very twisted version of the truth.

Edward stiffened. 'Your parents told me they wanted that news to be a surprise. Naturally I didn't discuss it with you.'

Her knees now unreliable supports, Milly dropped down on the arm of a chair. 'Would you have asked me to marry you without that partnership, Edward?' she asked tightly. 'Please be honest.'

Edward's fair complexion reddened. 'That is a very unfair question.'

'But you're not denying that the partnership was put on the table *before* you decided to propose, are you?'

Edward studied her with unconcealed resentment. 'I don't

see why you should have a problem with that. Your father's generous offer meant that we could have a financially secure future together. Of course it made a difference.'

Nausea pooled in Milly's stomach. 'What about love?'

'I'm very fond of you. But I'd be a liar if I didn't admit that I was also very concerned about the risks of forming a lasting relationship with you.'

'Risks?'

'Do I have to spell it out? That bombshell you dropped on me last night wouldn't have occurred in a *normal* relationship!' he reminded her with derision. 'Like any other man, I want to feel confident that I know everything there is to know about my wife's past. You can't give me that confidence.'

'But the assurance of a financially secure future persuaded you to overlook those drawbacks,' Milly gathered, struggling to keep her voice level. 'Yet you *said* you loved me.'

'For pity's sake, you're talking like a silly teenager-'

'I think maybe I still am just a teenager inside, Edward. If I had had any idea how many reservations you had about me, I'd never have agreed to marry you.' Tugging the solitaire from her finger, Milly stood up to place it on the edge of his desk.

Edward was outraged. 'You *asked* me to be honest!'

But he had been cruelly belittling her from the minute she started speaking, Milly reflected painfully. 'When you hear what your boss has to tell you, I think you'll be relieved to have that ring back. I imagine he'll offer you the partnership anyway. I do wish you well, Edward.'

Striding forward, he snapped bruising fingers round her slender wrist to prevent her departure. 'Who do you think you are to talk to me like this?' he demanded contemptuously.

Milly was shaken. 'Let go of me…you're hurting me—'

'I found your attitude equally offensive last night,' Edward snapped furiously. 'It seems to me that the minute you discovered that Connor's father was a rich man, you got too big for your boots! Now put that ring back on and we'll say no more about this nonsense!'

Taken aback as she was by his aggression, Milly was relieved when a knock sounded on the door and his secretary interrupted them. Edward released her immediately. Milly hurried down the corridor, ignoring his call in his wake. And then, out at Reception, she hesitated and looked at the car keys still clutched in her hand. She left them with the receptionist for Robin Jennings to collect. Suddenly she wanted *nothing* that had belonged to Faith Jennings...

Edward had never loved her. Indeed, right from the start Edward had had serious reservations about a woman with a past she couldn't remember. Without the partnership deal he would never have proposed. And why had she never noticed what a bad-tempered bully Edward could be if he was crossed? The answer was that until last night she had never crossed or challenged Edward. She had been a doormat, ashamed of her unwed mother status, thinking herself very fortunate to be the intended wife of a respectable professional man. And who had given her such low expectations and such a poor self-image? Her fake parents, who had packaged her up with a lucrative partnership to persuade Edward to marry her.

There was a stiff breeze blowing and it was cold. Milly had left her jacket locked in the car, but she still hurried away from the engineering plant. When she found herself on the main road she just kept on walking, insensibly soothed by the noise of the anonymous traffic. All the shocks she had withstood over the past twenty-four hours were hitting her now full force. Edward had seemed like a safe and sturdy post to clutch in the storm, but the post had toppled when she had reached for its support. The oddest thing was that she couldn't yet feel a single shard of grief. But then, she acknowledged dully, she wasn't really feeling anything...

'Where the hell is she?' Gianni raked into the phone.

'We've found her. She's OK. She's sitting on a bench by

the lake in that park.'

'*Madre di Dio!*' Gianni launched, paling at that information. 'I want two of you within six feet of her until I get there!'

After telling his driver to go as fast as the speed limit would allow, Gianni threw back a brandy to steady himself. He was furious with himself. He had known he had to go slowly with Milly. The psychologist had warned him to be careful. But from the first moment he had wildly overplayed his hand.

He should have kept quiet about Benson and the partnership. He had planned to hold that in reserve for a few days. Yet he, who had the reputation for being a brilliant tactician with a superb sense of timing, had ploughed in like a bull in a china shop. The prospect of reaping his own just deserts didn't bother him. But he went into a cold sweat at the threat of Milly reaping them for him...

Milly knew she was being watched at the lake. The instant she recognised the dark-suited men trying not to draw attention to themselves and failing abysmally in their efforts to lurk behind winter-bare trees she almost smiled. Gianni's employees. He must have had her followed. As long as they left her alone, it was almost comforting to think that somebody was looking out for her.

That sound of brisk footsteps made her lift her head. Gianni was bearing down on her, his hard, bronzed features set in grim lines which detracted not one iota from his devastating good looks, she conceded absently. A light grey cashmere overcoat protected him from the chilly breeze ruffling his luxuriant black hair.

'This is a very dreary place.' Both disapproval and impatience rang from every syllable. Gianni slung a deeply unappreciative glance over his surroundings. '*And* it's freezing. Why haven't you got a coat on?'

Even before he peeled off his overcoat and dropped it round her with the pronounced casualness of a male who didn't want to make a production out of doing it, Milly's sense of isolation lessened. Gianni was exasperated and he was letting her see the fact.

'What the hell are you smiling at?' Gianni demanded, thrown by that slight undeniable tilt to her formerly tense mouth.

Almost drowning in the heavy, enveloping folds of his overcoat, and curiously soothed by the warm scent of him that still clung to the silk-lined garment, Milly gazed up at him with rueful blue eyes. 'I don't know.'

'Why did you leave your car behind at the engineering plant? Did it break down?'

'It's not my car. The Jenningses bought it when they still thought I was their daughter. I guess I'm not in a very practical mood,' Milly conceded.

As she lifted her hand to prevent his overcoat lurching off her shoulder, Gianni muttered something raw in his own language and caught her fingers in his. Milly stiffened as he scrutinised the blue-black bruising encircling her wrist.

'You damned well didn't do that to yourself!' Gianni bit out wrathfully.

Milly tugged her hand free and hurriedly curved it out of sight again.

'*Per meraviglia!* The cowardly little bastard,' he growled, well-nigh incredulous, it seemed, that anybody should have dared to lay a rough hand on her. 'I'll make him pay for hurting you!'

'No, you won't,' Milly whispered flatly. 'Those bruises came cheap at the price of what they taught me. Maybe I'm wronging Edward, but I suspect he would have lashed out in temper again once we were married. He really did feel that he was marrying beneath himself. He could never have accepted me as I am.'

Gianni glanced at her other hand, only now noticing the absence of the diamond engagement ring. Milly watched his eloquent dark eyes shimmer with unadulterated satisfaction. On the most basic level, she was beginning to understand

Gianni. He was delighted that her engagement was broken. He wouldn't waste his breath uttering empty conventional regrets.

'I don't have *any* close relatives, do I?' Milly prompted abruptly.

Gianni frowned.

That frown was answer enough for Milly. She averted her head, determined not to betray that a foolish glimmer of hope had just been extinguished.

'How did you work that out for yourself?' It was the tone of a very clever male unaccustomed to being second-guessed.

'If I'd had a genuine suffering close relation waiting somewhere for word of me, you'd have been sure to tell Robin and Davina so that they could feel even worse.'

A laugh of reluctant appreciation was torn from Gianni.

'So, since everybody starts out with parents,' Milly continued doggedly, 'I presume mine are long gone.'

'Your mother when you were eight, your father shortly before we met,' Gianni confirmed unemotionally. 'You were an only child. As far as I'm aware there were no other relatives.'

So, but for Connor, she really was alone.

'Let's go,' Gianni reached down, closed his hand firmly over hers and tugged her upright to walk her back along the path. 'Why did you come here anyway?'

'I've spent a lot of happy times here with Connor...but today I felt lost,' she admitted reluctantly.

'Even the worst situations have at least one positive aspect. You've had an extraordinary experience,' Gianni told her. 'How many people get the chance to live more than one life?'

Disconcerted, Milly blinked. That reality hadn't crossed her mind once.

'Right now you're between lives, but no way are you lost. You've got me,' Gianni delivered with supreme cool.

'You make it all sound so simple.'

'It is. You don't belong here. That's why you feel strange. I know you care about the Jenningses, but they didn't do you any favours. If they hadn't claimed you, I'd have found you ages ago,' Gianni reminded her grimly.

'Did you list me as missing?'

'Of course I did!' Gianni growled, as if he was insulted by the idea that she could think otherwise.

'I *so* wish you'd found me first...' That thought had translated itself into charged admission before she could think better of it. She tensed. All the barriers she had tried to put up against Gianni had somehow tumbled down. It made her feel very vulnerable.

'Luck wasn't on my side. You walked out of the apartment of your own free will. There were no suspicious circumstances, so the police weren't interested. Adults have the right to lose themselves if they want to,' Gianni informed her wryly.

As they reached the park exit the limousine drew up, and Milly climbed in without protest.

Only a couple of hours ago she had hated Gianni D'Angelo like poison. He had been the destroyer. He had been the target of all her furious disbelief and bitter resentment. But now, as he used the car phone and talked in fluid Italian, she studied him with helpless intensity. The strong bone structure, the straight, arrogant nose, the firmly chiselled mouth. The dangerous dark eyes that knew too much, saw too much, and which he could turn on her like a weapon to express more than most people could say in five minutes. Those eyes were spectacular in the frame of that lean, dark face.

His gaze narrowed slumbrously, his arrogant dark head tilting back almost as if he was inviting her appraisal to continue. The elegant, sexily indolent sprawl of his long, lean, powerful body made her breath shorten in her throat, her heart thump against her breastbone. He really was *so* beautiful...

Colour ran up beneath her complexion and she tore her

attention from him, dismay and embarrassment darting through her. How could she be thinking such thoughts now? And she could feel herself wanting to trust him, but how could she trust him when she couldn't even trust herself? If she had learned anything over the past hours, it was that every single thing came at a price.

'Did you say you wanted me back because of Connor?' She got even redder as she spoke, knowing that she was being too blunt.

'No,' Gianni drawled, with all the cool she lacked. 'I wouldn't pretend even for the sake of my son. If you tried to deny me access to him, I would fight you through legal channels, but I believe you already accept that Connor has a right to get to know his father.'

'Yes.' Milly was impressed by that clear-minded reading of the situation. Succinct, realistic, fair.

On the drive through town, the limo pulled up on the main street. Gianni buzzed a window down. One of his security men passed in a large shallow box stamped with the logo of a newly opened pizza parlour. Seconds later, the limo rejoined the traffic.

Gianni settled the box on her lap without ceremony. 'You're crazy about pizza.'

'Am I?' Pizza wasn't something that featured on the menu in the Jenningses' home, and Edward despised all fast food.

'You didn't even have breakfast this morning. You need to eat something before we go and collect Connor.' Gianni poured her a soft drink from the built-in bar. 'Why are you staring at me?'

'No reason...' Possibly it was the combination of the vast, opulent limo, the humble pizza box and Gianni's total lack of snobbery. Or possibly it was the regularity with which he seemed to act to ensure her well-being. And always without comment or fanfare, as if it was the most natural thing in the world that he should take care of her.

Touched by that comforting thought, after the lack of caring Edward had demonstrated when the chips were down,

Milly opened the box. She lifted out a warm, flavoursome wedge and was surprised to feel her tastebuds water. 'Aren't you having any?'

'I'm not hungry.'

But Milly was ravenous, and nothing had ever tasted so good as that pizza. When she could eat no more, she sat unselfconsciously licking her fingers clean until some sixth sense made her lift her head. Gianni's burnished gaze roamed intently from her wet fingertip to her moist pink rounded mouth and flashed a message of very masculine hunger straight into her widening eyes. The atmosphere was electric.

Her breathing fracturing, Milly shifted on the seat. A starburst of heat blossomed between her thighs, making her flush with discomfiture. Shaken by a response that she couldn't control, she shivered. All of a sudden she was painfully conscious of the ripe fullness of her breasts and the swollen tightness of her nipples. The sexual sizzle in the air unnerved her. And Gianni's tension was patent. Feverish colour lay in a hard line over his taut cheekbones. Her pupils dilating, she stared wordlessly back at him, torn by a bewildering mixture of excitement, fear and fascination.

'I know I can't touch you. Don't tease me, ' Gianni breathed in charged reproof.

In sudden embarrassment, Milly closed her eyes to shut him out. 'I'm not like that…like *this*!' she stressed in denial.

'Stretch your imagination. Once you regarded a healthy desire to rip my clothes off as the most natural thing in the world.' His deep-pitched drawl was as abrasive as sand sliding over silk. 'It was the same for both of us. I once withstood a flight of sixteen hours just to spend two hours with you and then fly right back again.'

That deep, dark drawl scent erotic images that made her squirm skimming into her mind's eye. He had flown halfway across the world just to spend two hours with her? She was stunned by that knowledge. And was there a woman alive who wouldn't feel her self-esteem enhanced by such an extravagant gesture?

'Every time we made love felt like the first time. Endless variations on the same glorious theme. The hunger was never satisfied. I don't like anything that comes between me and control,' Gianni confessed huskily. 'But nobody else has ever made me feel the way you can make me feel. So if I'm not ashamed of it, why should you be?'

And Milly listened, *of course* she listened, drinking in every word, taken aback and then impressed by his honesty. It no longer felt quite so indecent to experience a sudden violent longing to be in his arms. Past chemistry had to be operating on her, a powerful physical sense of familiarity. And at least Gianni really genuinely wanted her, she found herself thinking helplessly. Edward hadn't, not really.

And Gianni had nothing to gain and no reason to lie to her. She respected his need to forge a relationship with his son. He already knew she wouldn't try to keep them apart. He was being so kind today. So why had he seemed so very cold and hostile to her yesterday?

Perhaps he had just felt awkward. Perhaps he had been apprehensive of her reaction to the idea of having to share her son. She had been overwrought, confused and angry. Her initial reactions to him would have been far from reassuring, she decided.

'I've booked the suite above mine for you and Connor,' Gianni divulged lazily as the limo pulled up outside Connor's nursery.

Milly glanced up and met his eyes in dismay. 'I—'

'You have to make that break. It's up to you whether you do it now or later. But if you stay with the Jenningses you're likely to find yourself being put under more pressure, and you have enough to cope with right now. They're not ready to accept that things have changed.'

Things have changed. Such a bland description of the shattering new knowledge that had virtually wiped out the past three years of her life. But to move straight out into a hotel? Gianni's hotel? She needed to stand on her own feet, no matter how difficult it was. But Gianni *was* Connor's father. Surely she could trust him that far? She badly needed a quiet corner where she could lick her wounds, pull herself together and decide what to do next.

'Would you leave me alone?'

'If that's what you want.'

She wasn't at all sure it was, but somehow it had seemed safer to give him that impression.

'But I'd like to spend time with Connor,' Gianni completed.

'I'd have gone to my friend, Louise…but she wouldn't have room for us.'

She went to collect Connor. He did an excited dance on the pavement when he saw the big car. One look at Gianni and his whole face lit up. Connor scrambled into the back seat and wedged himself cheerfully as close as he could get to Gianni.

'Phroom-phroom!' he urged with a grin, impatient for the limo to move off again.

Milly's heart clenched when she saw Gianni meet that satisfied grin with one of his own. A startlingly easy, natural smile such as he had never shown her. It wiped every scrap of reserve from his lean bronzed features and was, she sensed, a rare event. Can I trust him…dare I trust him? What have I got to lose?

Gianni watched Milly pace restively round the dimly lit and spacious reception room, her slender body rigid as a bowstring.

So far her control had been too good to be true. A return visit to the Jenningses' home had been yet another distressing experience for her. She had been greeted with recriminations about her treatment of Edward and shocked reproaches at the speed with which she was moving out. And Gianni had been as welcome as the Grim Reaper calling in at a christening.

However, Milly had still sat down with Robin and Davina

Jennings to tell them how truly grateful she was for all they had done for her. In fact, Milly had shone like a star. She had said and done all the right things. She had come across as loyal, compassionate and forgiving. It had been a hell of an impressive show. But Gianni had watched her like a hawk, waiting for a fleeting expression to reveal to his cynical eyes at least that it was all just a clever act.

Yet once Gianni had fully believed that what you saw *was* what you got with Milly. But no decent woman would have betrayed him with his own brother for the sake of a quick sexual fix. He had realised then that Milly had to have a really shallow core which she was outstandingly good at keeping hidden. Bitter anger lanced through Gianni at that knowledge. No way was he about to allow her to suck him in with that I'm-so-nice act again!

So why *was* he still hanging about, holding her hand and being supportive? She didn't deserve that sort of stuff any more. She was playing him like a little lapdog on a lead! Just because she looked all fragile and forlorn, so touchingly brave in the face of adversity! Gianni slung her a brooding appraisal and then stiffened. What a total idiot he was being! A billionaire turning up to reclaim her had to be of considerable comfort! No wonder she wasn't coming apart at the seams! Suddenly he wished he had shown up in a battered old car and pretended to be poor...

His lean, strong face grim, Gianni strode rigid-backed towards the door. 'Call Room Service when you want to eat,' he told Milly.

Milly stopped pacing, shadowed blue eyes flying to him in unconcealed dismay. 'Where are you going?'

'Look, all this stuff is taking a large chunk out of my work schedule,' Gianni informed her flatly. 'Just thought I'd mention it.'

Milly's lower lip trembled. He sounded so fed up with her, but when she thought about what he had had to put up with over the past day or so, suddenly she wasn't the least bit surprised by the way he was behaving. Her wobbly mouth made a determined stab at an apologetic smile. 'I'm really sorry, Gianni.'

Gianni shifted one broad shoulder in an infinitesimal and very Latin shrug. 'What for?'

'Because I've been really selfish,' Milly acknowledged guiltily. 'You've been dragged into the midst of all my problems and this morning I was even calling you names! If it wasn't for you, I'd still be thinking I was Faith Jennings. But not once have I stopped to say thank you—'

'I don't want gratitude.'

Milly looked uncertainly at him. Sensing his eagerness to be gone, she suppressed the awareness that she didn't want to be alone with only her own thoughts to keep her company. She wasn't a baby. She had to manage.

'Could you bring your work up here?' she nonetheless heard herself ask.

'I have half a dozen staff working flat out. I doubt if Connor would sleep through the racket.'

Milly nodded slowly, forced an understanding smile and turned away.

Gianni opened the door.

'How do I get in touch with you if I need to?' she suddenly spun back to demand.

Gianni stilled. 'I'm only one floor below you,' he pointed out drily.

'So what's the number of your suite?' she prompted anxiously.

Gianni studied her for a long, tense moment, brilliant dark eyes veiled. 'I'll send a mobile phone up…OK?'

Her throat thickening, she nodded again.

He compressed his expressive mouth even more. 'You can call me as much as you want…all right?'

Milly kept on nodding like a puppet.

She wouldn't call. He wouldn't want to be interrupted. But didn't he realise that she needed to talk? She stopped herself dead on that censorious thought. Exactly when had she begun pinning so many expectations on Gianni? Maybe right at this moment she badly needed to believe that Gianni really cared about what happened to her, but that didn't give her an excuse to cling to him.

Yet Gianni was the only person who *knew* Milly Henner, her one connection, her sole link to twenty-three years of her life. Everything she had ever told him about herself was locked inside that proud dark head of his. But he wasn't parting with any of it in a hurry, was he? He was sitting on all that information like a miser on a gold mountain!

With Gianni gone, Milly made herself order a meal. Connor was fast asleep in one of the two bedrooms. He had had tea before she'd left her former home. After the fastest bath on record, she had changed him into his pyjamas and tucked him into bed. Already overtired, he had slept within minutes.

Milly took her time eating, but tasted nothing. Then she went for a long shower, donned a pale blue cotton nightdress and carefully dried her hair. When she emerged from the bedroom, the mobile phone Gianni had sent up was buzzing like an angry wasp on the coffee table.

She picked it up. 'Yes?'

'Why the blazes haven't you called me?' Gianni demanded rawly.

'I didn't want to bother you.'

'How am I supposed to work when I'm worrying about why you haven't called?' Gianni gritted.

'I'm sorry. I didn't realise you were worrying.' Milly sank down on the nearest sofa, much of her extreme tension evaporating under that comforting assurance. 'Gianni, can I ask you some questions now about us?'

'You're limited to three.'

'How did we meet?'

'You jumped out of my birthday cake. Next question.'

'I...I did *what*?' Milly gasped, thunderstruck. 'Honestly?'

'Honestly, and only two more questions to go,' Gianni reminded her.

'Why...why did I leave you?' she asked awkwardly.

Silence thundered on the line.

'That one's on the forbidden list,' Gianni responded flatly.

'That's not fair,' Milly protested. 'I mean, obviously I want to know that!'

'I'm not telling you. When you've come up with a replacement question, call me back,' Gianni suggested drily.

The line went dead.

Had Gianni done something dreadful to make her walk out? Had she done something dreadful? Or had they had a foolish argument in which one of them or both of them had said too much? An argument which struck Gianni as so stupid in retrospect that it really galled him to even think of it now?

She waited ten minutes and then she punched out the number that had arrived with the phone.

'It's me,' she announced.

'I know it's you,' Gianni breathed wryly.

'Second question,' she began rather tautly after his last response. 'Was I happy with you?'

'I thought you were deliriously happy, but that's not really a question I can answer for you.'

In the last three years, Milly had known not one minute of what she could have termed *delirious* happiness. The concept of such an extreme couldn't help but impress her to death.

'Gianni…what was I like then?'

'Stubborn, quick-tempered, full of life, unconventional…hell, this isn't a safe subject!'

Milly snatched in a ragged breath, still reeling in astonishment from that disturbing flood of adjectives.

'Are you OK?'

A choked sob was lodged in her throat. 'Fine,' she managed. 'I think I'll go to bed now.'

Milly Henner, it seemed, had been another woman entirely. A definite individual. Lively, strong…*unconventional*? A humourless laugh escaped Milly as she climbed into bed. Gianni's description had knocked her for six.

She had judged their past relationship on the basis of the narrow outlook she had developed over the past three years. His mistress. She had been shocked, ashamed. She had immediately seen herself as a victim. But Gianni hadn't described a woman who was a victim; Gianni had described an equal. Where had that stronger and more confident woman gone? And was she ever going to find her again?

Exhaustion sent Milly to sleep quickly, but dreams full of disturbing and increasingly frightening images kept her tossing and turning. Terror began to rise notch by notch until finally she came awake in a complete panic, shaking like a leaf and sobbing out loud, so confused she didn't even know where she was.

'*Dio mio, cara*…calm down!'

The instant she heard Gianni's voice she froze, and then just crumpled into the shelter of his arms, sick with relief that he was there.

CHAPTER SIX

A SOB catching in her throat, Milly pressed her damp face into Gianni's shoulder. The faint tang of expensive cologne underlying his own distinctive male scent made her nostrils flare. She breathed him in deep, like a drug.

'That must have been some nightmare, *cara*.' Gianni held her back from him.

Her eyes were huge and shadowed in the stark white triangle of her face. 'I was struggling with someone in the dark…it felt so *real*!'

'But it couldn't have been. Nothing like that ever happened to you, at least not when I knew you.' Gianni spread long fingers across her taut cheekbones, dark, deep flashing eyes scanning her still frightened face.

Some of her tension drained away at that comforting assurance, but not all of it. She had never had a dream like that before, could not help suspecting that something she had once experienced had summoned it up.

'Before you woke up, you called my name at the top of your voice,' Gianni imparted softly, mesmeric dark eyes glinting.

'Did I?' Milly didn't want to talk about the dream any more. It had scared her too much. Her brows drew together. 'How did you hear me…I mean, where on earth did you come from?' she belatedly thought to ask.

'About thirty feet away,' Gianni told her. 'I'd moved to work in the room next door. I didn't think you should be alone tonight, so I came up about an hour ago. If you hadn't wakened, you'd never have known I was there.'

In the dim light, Milly studied him properly for the first time. Shorn of his jacket and tie, his white silk shirt open at

92

his strong brown throat and his black hair slightly tousled, he looked infinitely more approachable than he usually did. A faint blue-black shadow had already darkened his aggressive jawline. Even stubble, she thought guiltily, added to his appeal. Hurriedly she turned her head away and made herself rest back against the pillows.

'I'll get back to work.' Gianni began to stand up.

Milly tensed in dismay. 'Do you have to?'

'You want me to stay?'

Milly nodded agreement. 'And talk about something cheerful. You could tell me about my parents, if you like.'

Gianni folded down on the bed, stretched his long, lean frame out with intrinsic grace and sent her a winging glance from beneath heavily lidded eyes. 'You know what's going to happen, don't you?' he murmured, like an indolent tiger.

'Nothing's going to happen.' Milly reddened. 'Think of the bed as a sofa.'

Gianni loosed a low-pitched laugh and tilted his arrogant dark head back against the white pillows. 'Your parents...you told me they were crazy about each other. Your father was called Leo and he was a Londoner. Your mother, Suzanne, was French—'

'*French?*' Milly rolled over in surprise to stare at him.

'You're practically bilingual. Didn't you find that out yet? You spent the first eight years of your life in Paris.'

'You're supposed to start at the beginning. Do you know when my parents got married?'

'They didn't...they weren't into matrimony.'

Milly was stunned. 'You mean, I'm...?'

'Yes.'

She slowly shook her head. Her throat tickled, and then the laughter just bubbled out of her.

Gianni leant down, curved his hands to her shaking shoulders and tugged her up to his level. 'What's so funny?'

Struggling to get a grip on herself again, Milly released a rueful groan. 'It's just so ironic. In the world I've been living in for the past three years illegitimacy is a very serious issue, and now I find out that *I* was born out of wedlock too! Tell me about Leo and Suzanne,' she urged.

'They were pavement artists.'

'Pavement artists,' Milly repeated weakly, and then she smiled. 'I like that.'

'Suzanne was knocked down and killed by a drunk driver in Paris. Your father never really got over it, and that was the end of your settled home life. He took you roving all over Europe with him. You didn't see the inside of too many schools, but you adored your father and you always talked as if you'd had a wonderful childhood.'

Milly gazed up into Gianni's lean bronzed face like a child listening to an enthralling bedtime story. 'I'm glad.'

'But then you always were a sunny optimist.' Gianni skimmed a lazy forefinger lightly through the glossy strands of blonde hair tumbling across his forearm and stared down at her with glittering dark golden eyes.

Her heart skipped a beat and then began to thud heavily. Her stomach clenched. The silence lingered and Gianni's eloquent mouth tipped into an indolent smile that welded her attention to him.

'I'm a real pessimist about most things,' Gianni shared softly. 'But in one field I'm rarely disappointed...'

A curious languor had crept over Milly. Her body felt weighted, yet incredibly alive, every sense feeling somehow keener, sharper. What a wonderful voice he had, she thought absently, as a little tremor ran down her taut spinal cord. Like sinfully rich chocolate. *Sin*... Her abstracted brain began to play with the word. *Sin*fully stunning, *sin*fully sexy...

Hot pink staining her cheekbones, she attempted to concentrate on what he was saying—which was a little difficult, she discovered, when he wasn't actually saying anything!

Slumbrous golden eyes framed with lush ebony lashes rested on her. And, like a tidal wave, Milly felt an enormous rush of yearning well up inside her. She remembered that sensational kiss. The cymbals...the fireworks. Unwittingly, she began to lift her head, push up on one elbow, soft lips tremulously parted, her slim length beginning to curve towards him as if he was a magnet and she was a nail.

'And you have never once disappointed me in that field,' Gianni informed her huskily.

Milly hadn't a clue what he was talking about, and couldn't have strung two rational thoughts together. 'Didn't I?' she managed breathlessly.

'In that one corner of our relationship I had total and absolute control.' Gianni's wide, sensual mouth curved into a wickedly charismatic smile that squeezed her heart in a sneak attack.

The dim light accentuated the smooth dark planes and hollows of his chiselled features. His bronzed skin was vibrant against the pristine whiteness of his shirt. With one long, lean and powerful thigh raised in a very masculine attitude of relaxation, Gianni was so physically arresting he just took her breath away.

In fact, she was so tense her muscles hurt. Yet she couldn't make herself move, couldn't drag her eyes from him, couldn't suppress the increasingly desperate craving holding her so still. Gianni bent his dark head slowly. His breath fanned her cheek. He let his tongue dart between her parted lips and she jerked and moaned and reached up for him, her hands spearing fiercely into his silky black hair.

He did it again, and her whole body leapt, electrified. Just one kiss, just one kiss, she promised herself, like an alcoholic craving what she knew she shouldn't have.

'Oh Gi-anni…' she gasped on the back of an aching sigh.

He pressed his mouth to her cheek, her brow, her lowered eyelids, teasing her with feather-light kisses until she strained up to him even more. 'Any time, any place, any way I want,' Gianni murmured thickly. 'I don't have to say anything, I don't have to do anything. I just start thinking about sex and you are so tuned in to me you just *melt*…'

He kissed her, and it was like being shot to heaven on a rocket. She melted to boiling point in seconds. He made love to her mouth with an intimacy that shook her. He delved and tasted and skimmed until she was burning up, clutching at him, living from one second to the next on the single terrifying thought that he might stop.

Peeling her hands from him, Gianni lowered her back to the bed. He sat up and ripped off his shirt in one impatient movement. Struggling to get air back into her constricted lungs, Milly was totally transfixed. He had a torso like a Greek god. Wide brown shoulders, rippling pectoral muscles roughened by a triangle of black curling hair and a stomach as flat as a washboard.

A tiny pinching sensation attacked low in her pelvis. She felt light-headed, but her body was so tense it screamed at her, every sense recognising Gianni as her lover. The scent of him, the touch of him, the very taste of him. She couldn't believe what was happening to her. She shivered in shock laced with a kind of death-defying excitement.

'Gianni...' she whispered jaggedly, struggling to reinstate some form of control, some sense of reality to her own mounting disorientation. 'I...*we—*'

Gianni came back down to her, dark eyes now bright as flames, his feverish tension as marked as her own. She saw a hunger in him that twisted something painfully inside her, and with a muffled little sound of surrender she reached up instinctively and opened her lips to him again.

With a dark, driven groan of satisfaction, Gianni lifted her up to him with two powerful hands and ravaged the tender interior of her mouth with a raw, demanding passion that overwhelmed her.

'We both need this,' he said thickly. 'You want me; you *always* want me...'

She looked at him, her heart pounding like crazy. She raised a trembling hand and touched his beautiful mouth with tender caressing fingertips, controlled by instincts that filled her with almost unbearably powerful feelings. 'Like I need air to breathe,' she whispered shakily.

Gianni raised her up and divested her of her nightdress

with an easy expertise that somehow shocked her. And suddenly that wholly inborn feeling of security abandoned Milly. She stared in dismay down at the ripe swell of her bare breasts, her face hot with colour. She felt wanton, and then very, very shy as Gianni's gaze burned over her exposed flesh like the kiss of fire.

'*Dio…*' he growled, raising an unsteady hand to cup a pale, pouting breast adorned by a straining pink nipple, lingering to rub a thumb and forefinger over that stiffened peak.

The violence of her own response tore a startled moan from Milly. Her mind closed in on itself again, stripping away that brief awareness of anything beyond the physical. She shut her eyes tight, letting her head fall back. As he toyed with the achingly sensitive bud her own heartbeat thrummed in her eardrums.

'I always adored your breasts. You're exquisite,' Gianni groaned, knotting one possessive hand into her cascading mane of golden hair and letting his mouth swoop down to replace his fingers.

Excitement took hold of her like a bushfire, blazing out of her control. The erotic mastery he unleashed with the tug of his teeth and the wet rasp of his tongue dragged her down so fast into a world of pure sensation that she was lost. She moaned and twisted, suddenly hotter than she could bear. She was wildly aware now of the maddening burn at the very core of her body, the pulse of damp warmth beginning to beat and ache between her thighs.

Gianni wrenched back from her to dispose of the remainder of his clothing. Milly opened passion-glazed eyes. She was trembling, her whole body just one gigantic pleading ache. 'Gianni…*please*…' She didn't even know where the words came from.

'It hurts to want this much, doesn't it?' Gianni leant over her, his long, lean body golden and tight with leashed power in the lamplight. His brilliant eyes savoured her quivering tension, watched her look at him with wonder.

'Yes…' It hurt like a knot tightening and tightening inside

her. Her spellbound gaze roamed down over his powerful frame, lingering in sensual shock on the aggressive masculine thrust of his virility. Her mouth ran dry and it was like something unlocked inside her, loosing a hot flood of honey to pool heavily at the very heart of her.

All conquering male, Gianni pulled her close. Then he stared down into her hectically flushed face, his spectacular bone structure ferociously taut, his bright eyes curiously chilling, his beautiful shaped mouth hardening. 'We always connected best at this level, *cara mia.*'

Something in that dark sardonic drawl spooked her, but before she could try to identify that apprehensive dart of unease Gianni eased her slender thighs apart and began to explore her wildly sensitive flesh. Her body jack-knifed under that surge of almost intolerable pleasure. It was mindless, all-encompassing, and she craved its continuance with every tortured and sobbing breath she drew.

But it was still a surprise when Gianni came over her, sinking rough, impatient hands beneath her squirming hips. And suddenly he was there, where the ache was worst, entering her in one powerful thrust that made her cry out.

Excited beyond belief by him, Milly clashed with the charged darkness of his eyes. 'Gianni…?' she gasped.

'*Madre di Dio*…I have to black out *my* memory to do this!' Gianni gritted savagely, driving into her again, making her tender flesh yield more fully to enclose him.

And even as she struggled to comprehend what was wrong, what he meant, the primitive rhythm of his possession engulfed a body too long starved of such sensation. Her confusion was not equal to the overpowering hunger he had awakened. With every driving invasion Gianni sent excitement hurtling through her at storm-force potency. Hot, aching pleasure took her over. Release came in a shattering ecstatic surge that jolted and freed what felt like every fibre of her being.

Within seconds, Gianni hit that same peak with a shuddering groan. Her arms came round him, tears flooding her eyes. That didn't surprise her. It always happened. Sometimes she loved Gianni so much she wanted to scream it from the rooftops, she thought helplessly. She pressed her lips adoringly to a satin-smooth shoulder damp with sweat and whispered it instead.

With startling abruptness he pulled back from her. With a bitten-off Italian curse, he shoved himself away from her. Then he surveyed her with blazing anger and condemnation. 'Bye-bye, Edward, hello, Gianni—all in the space of one day?' he ground out raggedly, strikingly pale beneath his naturally dark skin. 'What sort of a fool do you take me for?'

And Milly went into deep shock then. The cloaking, blinding veil of physical satiation was torn from her mind and dissipated as though it had never been. Every scrap of colour drained from her stricken face as she stared at Gianni, and she stared at him and registered that both past and present now existed in a seamless joining inside her head.

Gianni snatched in a shuddering breath. 'OK…you didn't mean to say it and I overreacted,' he conceded, a slight tremor interfering with his usually even diction, his Sicilian accent very strong.

Sicilian to the backbone, Milly recalled absently, locked into the terrifying enormity of the memories hitting her now from all sides.

'Stop looking at me like that,' Gianni told her.

He thinks he's going to have to apologise, and he hates apologising, so he's digging himself into a deeper hole because when he's really upset about anything he will go to enormous lengths not to confront that reality. All the strength in Milly's body just seeped away as she completed that instant appraisal. She was immobilised by what had happened inside her own head. She had finally got her memory back. Now the shock was telling.

'Milly…' Gianni sat up, dark, deep flashing eyes narrowing on her anguished face and the distance in her eyes. A distance which suggested that though she might appear to be looking at him, for some reason he wasn't really registering.

Gianni, the love of her life, Milly labelled him, in a growing haze of emotional agony. Walking away, acknowledging defeat, had been like driving a knife into her own heart.

'You *hate* me...' she framed sickly, shaking her head back and forth on the pillow in urgent negative, soundless tears beginning to track down her cheeks. 'You *touched* me, hating me!'

Gianni was stunned.

'And how do I know that?' Milly gulped strickenly. 'I know that because I can remember *everything*—but I don't want to...I don't want to remember!' she lashed at him in passionate pain.

Gianni laid Milly down on the great canopied bed in the master suite of his country house—which he had yet to spend a single night in. Back at the hotel, the doctor had given her a sedative, and had then told Gianni in no uncertain terms exactly what he thought of him.

There had been no hiding the fact that that hotel bed had harboured more than one body. With a humility that would have astounded all who knew him, Gianni had withstood being called a selfish swine. At that instant, hovering while Milly shivered and shook with those horrible silent tears, Gianni would have welcomed far stronger censure if it had in any way lessened his own appalling sense of guilt.

He had traumatised her. *Him.* Nobody else. The Jenningses had loved her, and would have protected her while she tried to come to terms with what was happening to her. But he had deliberately severed every tie she had and then quite ruthlessly seduced her back into sexual intimacy. She hadn't been ready for that. She might never have been ready for that again. He had hit on her like a stud when she was weak and confused and scared. She had trustingly turned to him for comfort and he had let his driving need to re-establish a hold on her triumph. He had never sunk so low in his life…

And it was no consolation to know *why* he had done it. Jealousy, bitter and angry, seething up inside him like hot, destructive lava. The thought of Milly loving Benson, wanting him, sleeping with him. Thinking about her with Stefano had been bad enough, but he had learned to block that out. Iron self-discipline had worked for three years. Only it had come apart at the seams the instant he'd tried to make love to her again, suddenly terrified for the first time in his life that he might not be able to do it and then acting like an animal in rut. Great footnote, Gianni. The one and only thing that was ever perfect, you blew!

'Not sleeping?' Connor asked, his little face full of hope.

'Not sleeping,' Milly confirmed gruffly as she set aside her breakfast tray and dragged her son down into her arms to tickle him, listening to his delighted chortles with a sudden lightening of her heart. She kissed his soft cheek and ran a fingertip lovingly down over his small nose. 'I gather I've been sleeping *too* long.'

Connor scrambled down off the bed at speed. Retrieving something from the floor, he clambered back up to show it to her. It was a child's board book. He pointed to the golden-haired princess sleeping on the front cover and said with tremendous pride, 'My mummy!'

As she noted the title, Milly breathed in very deep. *The Sleeping Beauty.* Gianni was very creative in tight corners, and explaining Mummy's sudden need to sleep the clock round and more had evidently not over-taxed his agile brain. Gianni, she reflected tautly, for so long never more than a heartbeat away from her next thought.

Why, oh, why hadn't he just let her stay lost? Connor. But not *only* Connor. Revenge, she decided with a helpless shiver. Revenge as only a Sicilian could enact it. In a reckless drunken attack of lust, Stefano had destroyed them. On his deathbed Gianni wouldn't forgive her for what he believed she'd done to him. And at his coldest Gianni was at his most dangerous. If *only* she had been armoured with the knowledge that she was dealing with a male who hated and despised her when they'd first met again…

But then how many 'if onlys' already littered her history with Gianni? So she had ended up in bed with him again. So she had had a fantastic time. That was the painful crux of the matter, wasn't it? That she had sobbed with ecstasy and clung to a guy who had invaded her eager body with all the rampaging finesse of a stud on a one-night stand!

Gianni, who had taught her that making love could be an art form, Gianni, who was endlessly creative in the bedroom but never, ever rough. Quite deliberately he had set out to use and humiliate her. But it had been the shatteringly sudden return of her memory which had torn her apart. And Gianni was in for a very big surprise if he fondly imagined she was about to greet him with shamed eyes and streaming tears at their next meeting!

But life went on no matter what, Milly told herself with feverish urgency. Gianni was Connor's father now. Nothing more. Her problem was that she needed to learn a whole new way of thinking. Time hadn't passed for her in quite the same way as it had passed for Gianni. Three years ago she had still been hopelessly in love with him. At the instant her memories came alive again she had been engulfed in a devastatingly intense storm of emotion, the most bitter sense of betrayal, loss and anguished pain. Because the man she loved had turned his back on her and walked away. It was those feelings she had to deal with now, and then she had to put them all away again, back where they *really* belonged—in the past.

From her magnificent bed, she surveyed her imposing new surroundings with grudging curiosity, and then, pushing back the fine linen sheet, she got up. When she'd arrived, she had used the bathroom, which had been left helpfully lit with the door ajar. Now that she registered that there were three other doors to choose between she knew why.

Wandering over to one of the tall windows to glance out, she almost tripped over Connor in surprise. Beautiful gardens gave way to rolling fields and distant woodland. She had dimly assumed that she was in a townhouse, hadn't thought to question the lack of traffic noise. Gianni now owned a country home? Gianni, who had once regarded the countryside as the long, boring bit between cities? But then what did she know about Gianni's life these days?

Tensing, she instantly reminded herself that she didn't *want* to know anything! With Connor tagging in her wake she went for a shower, and was drying her hair when a brisk knock sounded on the bedroom door. A youthful brunette peered in, and then flushed when she saw Milly in her bathrobe. 'I'm sorry, Miss Henner. I didn't realise you were up and about. My name's Barbara Withers—'

Connor interrupted her with an exuberant cry of recognition. 'Barb!'

'I'm Connor's temporary nanny. Mr D'Angelo did stress that a permanent appointment would be subject to your approval,' she advanced anxiously.

'Yes…' Conscious of the younger woman's discomfiture, Milly concealed her own disconcertion.

'I was about to offer to take Connor outside to play. Since Mr D'Angelo left him with you after breakfast, I thought you might be tired now,' Barbara explained.

So Connor hadn't wandered into her bedroom under his own steam. Milly had been concerned that no adult appeared to be in charge of him. But it seemed that Gianni had sneakily fed their son in through the door without making a personal appearance. But then with Connor around perhaps that had been a wise decision, and she didn't want him present when she saw Gianni again.

'I'm sure Connor would enjoy that.' Milly's smile was strained by the thought of what lay ahead of her. And that was facing up to the male who, after that dreadful night three years ago, had refused to meet her again, accept her phone calls or answer her letters. Closure had not been a problem for Gianni. He had judged her, dumped her, and replaced her at spectacular speed.

Suddenly cold inside herself, Milly leafed through the garments she had found unpacked in the adjoining dressing room. She had a curious aversion to wearing the clothes she had worn as Faith Jennings, but she had nothing else available. With regret she recalled the wonderful wardrobe she had loftily chosen to leave behind when she had left Paris three years earlier.

In the end she pulled on a pair of faded jeans she had used for gardening and a long-sleeved black polo shirt. Leaving her tumbling mass of golden hair loose round her shoulders, she set off in search of Gianni.

She emerged onto a huge galleried landing dominated by superb oil paintings. For 'country house' she now substituted 'stately home'. The stamp of Gianni's ownership was everywhere. The most magnificent furniture, the most exquisite artwork. He surrounded himself with beautiful possessions and he had fabulous taste and considerable knowledge, all acquired as an adult.

An extraordinary man, she conceded reluctantly. Always a target for the paparazzi, rarely out of the newspapers, inevitably a focus of fascination for others. Precious few men rose to Gianni's level from a deprived and brutalised childhood. A drunken, abusive father, a prostitute mother who had abandoned him, followed by a stepmother who had fed him alongside the dog and chucked him out on the streets of Palermo to fend for himself at the age of ten. Why was she remembering all that? she asked herself angrily.

But all of a sudden it was as if a dam had broken its banks inside Milly's subconscious: memories gushed out against her volition, demanding her attention, refusing to go away…

The year Milly had turned nineteen her life had changed out of all recognition. Leo, her feckless but very charming father, had died of a sudden heart attack in Spain.

After eleven years of sharing her father's gypsy lifestyle,

Milly had wanted to put down roots and make plans. She had applied for a place on a two-year horticultural course at a London college. With not a single educational qualification to her name it had taken courage to put herself forward, and she had been overjoyed when she'd been accepted as a full-time student.

She had lived on a shoestring in a dingy bedsit, working part-time in a supermarket to supplement her tiny grant. Her first real friend had been the bubbly blonde who'd lived across the landing. Lisa had worked for a strippergram agency and had lived in considerably greater comfort than Milly.

One afternoon, Lisa had come to her door in a real state. 'I have to do a booking in the City tonight and I can't make it,' she groaned. 'Stevie's just called to ask me out to dinner and you *know* what he's like! If I'm not available, he'll ask someone else!'

Lisa had given her heart to a real creep. The saga of her sufferings at Stevie's ruthlessly selfish hands could have filled a book the size of the Bible. Yet when Stevie called Lisa still dropped everything and ran, because he had trained her that way.

'Please do this booking for me,' Lisa pleaded frantically. 'You don't have to take *anything* off. All you've got to do is jump out of this stupid fake cake dressed as an angel and smile!'

Milly grimaced. Lisa raced back to her bedsit and returned with an armful of celestial white robes and a small gilded harp. 'It's a really dated stunt, but these executive-types want something tasteful because they're scared witless of offending the big boss. It's his birthday and his name is D'Angelo...*angel*—get it?'

So that was how Milly had ended up jumping out of Gianni's birthday cake. She had thrown herself upright and found herself looking straight down into dark eyes that flashed to the most amazing shade of gold. Those eyes had spooked her. Tripping in her oversized robes, she had lurched off the trolley, careened into the board table beside it to send half the drinks flying and had finally landed in a tumbled heap at Gianni's feet. The ghastly silence her clumsiness had evoked remained with her even now.

'Happy birthday, Mr D'Angelo,' she had muttered doggedly.

'What do you do for an encore?' Gianni enquired in silken enquiry. 'Level the building?'

Severe embarrassment flipped into sudden fury at that sarcastic sally. 'Don't be such an insensitive prat!' Milly hissed in angry reproach. 'Go on—help me up...don't you have any manners at all?'

A swelling tide of gasps, sharp, indrawn breaths and muted groans rose from the executives still glued to their seats round the board table.

Gianni looked stunned. Then, disorientatingly, he threw back his arrogant dark head and laughed. 'For a little titchy thing, you've got quite a tongue, haven't you?'

'You are one ignorant pig!' Milly told him, even as he extended a lean hand to help her upright. She pushed his hand away and sat carefully untangling the robes from her legs so that she could rise without assistance and take a step back to impose some distance between them.

Gianni then helpfully extended the harp she had dropped on him. 'What do you do next?' he asked, lounging back in his imposing chair with an air of sardonic anticipation.

Milly snatched the harp back. 'If you're hoping I'm about to start stripping, it's not your day! I keep all my clothes on.'

Gianni studied her with even greater amusement. 'Aren't you supposed to at least *sing* many happy returns?'

At that reminder, Milly stiffened resentfully. 'I couldn't hold a tune in a bucket.'

'You...are...priceless.' Gianni savoured her, brilliant eyes fixed like lasers to her expressive face.

Rising from his chair to his full intimidating height, Gianni closed one hand over hers and turned to address their gaping audience. 'Check the Health and Safety rules next time you decide to give me a surprise. This particular angel could have sued the pants off us if she'd been hurt!'

'Let go of my hand,' Milly urged as he carried her across the room with him.

He thrust open the door that led back into the corridor. 'Was this your last booking?'

'My only one—'

'Then I'll take you home.'

'No thanks.' Pulling free of his hold, Milly hurried back to the cloakroom in which she had earlier changed out of her own clothes.

When she emerged, clad in jeans and a sweater, Gianni was still waiting for her.

'You're a bit like a dog with a bone, aren't you?'

'You're very beautiful. Don't act so surprised when I tell you that. It doesn't wash with looks like yours,' Gianni drawled with a cynical smile. 'I'll take you home. You can get dressed up. We'll go out to dinner.'

'No, thanks,' she said tautly, annoyed that temptation was flickering when he was so screamingly unsuitable. Dressed up? Dressed up in *what*? Did he think she had a designer wardrobe to fall back on?

'Why not?'

'How many reasons do you need?'

'This is very entertaining. Feel free to speak your mind.'

'All right. One, you're too slick for me. Two, you look filthy rich. Three, you have to be at least ten years older than me, and I can't imagine that we'd have a single thing in common.'

'Are you always this…sharp-tongued?'

She picked up on the deliberate hesitation, recognised the coolness that had quenched the vibrancy in his extraordinary eyes and felt herself shrivel up inside, but still she said, 'No, you bring out the best in me.'

'Instant loathing?'

She shivered, and then, ashamed of her disturbingly unfamiliar need to continually attack him, she decided to be honest. 'No, I fancied you like mad the minute I laid eyes on you, but it's not something I want to follow up,' she admitted, suddenly finding herself alarmingly short of breath. 'Bye. Have a nice birthday!'

The following afternoon, Gianni was waiting for her to come home from college. Having tripped over him on the landing, Lisa was bending over backwards to entertain him in Milly's absence.

'How on earth did you find out where I lived?'

'Bribed the sleazebag who owns the strippergram agency. He told me your name was Lisa. Then I met Lisa and she explained who you *really* were.' Gianni angled a slanting smile over her—a smile that had megawatt charisma.

'You shouldn't have come here—'

'*Dio mio*…what did you expect? You think I'm about to walk in the opposite direction when you're feeling the same way I feel?'

'Tell me one thing we have in common?' Milly invited.

'Sex.'

'When you think of something else, I'll have dinner with you,' Milly told him, hot-cheeked.

Gianni stuck a swift foot in the door she was trying to close on him. 'Quick tempers.'

'You are *so* persistent!'

'OK.' Strong jawline squaring, he shrugged with eye-catching elegance. 'I'm out of here.'

She let him get as far as the floor below, and then, stabbed by the sudden realisation that she would never see him again, she darted back out to the landing and hung over the banister to call, 'Just dinner…all right?'

'What about breakfast?' Gianni asked without hesitation.

'No chance, but I appreciate you being this honest about your intentions. Honesty is very important to me, even if the truth isn't always welcome. So I should tell you now that I'm not into casual sex and I'm very romantic.'

Gianni sighed softly. 'One of us is set to crash into a solid brick wall.'

'It won't be me,' Milly told him gently. 'I couldn't possibly fall in love with someone like you.'

'*Accidenti*...why would I *want* you to fall in love with me?' Gianni demanded incredulously. 'My sole interest in you is—'

'Shut up before you talk yourself out of a dinner date,' Milly advised.

Emerging from the frighteningly fresh hold of those memories back into the present, Milly blinked and looked around herself. She was still standing on the gallery. Breathing in deep, shaken by the tremendous pull of the past, she walked slowly towards the stairs.

As she descended the sweeping staircase Gianni strode out into the wonderful Georgian hall below. Instantly she felt her tender heart quake like a stupid jelly, as if three years hadn't passed, as if her brain was forever locked in time, incapable of moving on and healing. As she stilled two steps up from the foot of the stairs, so that for once she was at his level, her hands closed into defensive fists by her sides.

CHAPTER SEVEN

'GIANNI…' Milly breathed, and she could hardly get his name past her dry lips.

'You don't look at all well,' Gianni drawled with measured cool, incisive dark eyes resting on her without any perceptible expression. 'You really should have stayed in bed.'

Yes, he could have handled her best as a total invalid, Milly decided. Then she would have been an object of pity, too weak and pathetic to require confrontation. Gianni went to quite incredible lengths to avoid emotional scenes. He could not bear to be vulnerable. He could not tolerate any loss of control. So he attached himself to objects, not to people. Perhaps Connor would teach him to love. She had failed—oh, boy, had she failed…

'I'm fine,' she lied, terrified that he was registering just how much he could still affect her.

Gianni looked back at her. She was so small, so slender, so pale, haunted eyes fixed to him as if he was about to unfurl a set of cloven hooves and a toasting fork. *Fine?* The fear she couldn't hide filled him with seething bitterness.

Suddenly he wished her memory had stayed lost. Memories were bloody painful afflictions! That night in the hotel she had been so sweet. Trusting, open, just as he remembered her. The only person alive who had ever treated him as if he was just an ordinary guy. Nagging him when he was late, complaining when he was preoccupied, yawning through the business news and totally forgetting about him when she was out in her precious garden. In every way she had been different from every other woman he had had, either before or since.

110

Once she would have filled this awful silence, instinctively understanding that he couldn't, that when he was wound up about something he turned cold and aggressive and silent in self-defence. Then he reminded himself that this bit would be over soon. Not for nothing had he spent the past twenty-four hours seeking a rational solution to the mess they were in. And around dawn, he had come up with the answer.

Not perfect, but simple. And the instant he made that proposal Milly would go back to normal—well, maybe not immediately, he conceded grudgingly, but *obviously* she'd be over the moon. He'd also have the tactical advantage of surprise. She'd appreciate that he was making a really huge and stupendously generous effort for Connor's sake. And naturally she'd be grateful. Grateful enough to go back upstairs with him and consolidate their new understanding in the most logical way of all?

Milly knew she was gaping at Gianni like a pheasant looking up the barrel of a shotgun. But the lurch of her heart had appalled her. Feeling that sensitive to dark, deep flashing eyes as chilly as a winter's day was not a good sign. Noticing that he looked shockingly spectacular in a casual designer suit the colour of caramel was an even worse sign. Say something, a voice in her head screeched, for heaven's sake, *say* something. But her mind was a complete blank. She didn't know where to start or how she would ever stop if she did start. Silence seemed a lot safer.

Milly stiffened as Gianni extended a hand to her. It was the very last gesture she had expected from him. Uncurling her fingers, she lifted her arm in slow motion. He got tired waiting. He brought up his other hand, closed both round her waist and lifted her down to the marble-tiled floor.

A slight gasp of disconcertion escaped her. However, the sudden shrinkage in stature she suffered helped. Suddenly her strained eyes were mercifully level with Gianni's chest.

'We've got some talking to do,' Gianni informed her next.

Milly was poleaxed. Only a woman who had been intimately involved with Gianni could have understood that acknowledgement to be ground-breaking and incredible. Whenever she had wanted to talk, seriously talk about personal things, Gianni had had a hundred evasive techniques. 'Later' had been a particular favourite, followed by a sudden rampant desire for her body or a pressing appointment. It had taken her a very long time to appreciate that 'later' meant never.

'A lot…' Milly agreed breathlessly, suddenly experiencing a stark, shameful stab of pained resentment. What had changed Gianni? *Who* had changed him? Who had finally persuaded him that honest communication was the only option when the going got tough? It was what they had once so badly needed, but the offer was coming way too late for her to benefit.

He showed her into a library, where a log fire was burning in the grate. He strode over to the desk, lifted the phone and ordered coffee. Stilling by the hearth, Milly stretched her unsteady hands out to the heat and let her gaze travel around the magnificent room with its warm red décor.

'What do you think of Heywood House?' Gianni asked.

'It's beautiful.' She resisted the urge to admit that it wasn't at all what she had expected. She didn't want to stray onto impersonal topics and deflect him from anything he might want to say to her.

'The gardens are famous. I've ensured that they've been maintained to the highest standards,' Gianni advanced smoothly.

Milly wandered over to the nearest window. She adored gardens, but right now she was so enervated she couldn't even appreciate the wonderful view. 'It looks tremendous.'

'There's a rare plant centre attached to the estate. I rebuilt it,' Gianni continued. 'It doesn't exactly do a roaring trade, but the manager tells me it's a real haunt for the connoisseur.

Bewildered by this flood of extraneous information from a male who barely knew the difference between a rose and a daisy and was content to remain in a state of blissful ignorance, Milly suddenly frowned as her mind homed in on something else entirely, and she exclaimed, 'For goodness' sake, Gianni…I haven't even spoken to Louise! What on earth must she be thinking? She's my partner and my best friend and I didn't even *phone* her!'

The silence spread and spread.

Gianni dealt her a fulminating look. 'I phoned her. She was very concerned. I said you'd be in touch when you were well enough…OK?'

Milly released her breath, relieved by that assurance. But she wondered why he had delivered the news with such an air of impatience. It wasn't as if she had interrupted him when he'd been talking about anything important. The door opened and a maid entered with a tray of coffee. It was a welcome diversion.

She sat down in a leather wing-back armchair and poured the coffee. Without hesitation she added three sugars to Gianni's cup.

'We'll deal with practicalities first, get them out of the way,' Gianni announced with decisive cool. 'And naturally the first thing I want to know is, have you any idea who left you lying badly injured on that road in Cornwall? And how did it happen?'

Milly jerked and froze, her heartbeat thudding loudly in her ears. Such obvious questions. Why hadn't she been prepared for them?

'It must be distressing for you to have to remember that night. But it has to be dealt with.' Gianni watched her with keen, dark expectant eyes.

Milly was shot right back to that night, forced to recall things she would have preferred to leave buried, things that had nothing whatsoever to do with the accident. She lost colour. Her hand began to shake. She set down her coffee again with a clatter. She hoped to heaven Gianni didn't ask her what she had been *doing* in Cornwall in the first place, because if he did ask, she certainly didn't feel like telling him the truth.

'Milly…?' Gianni pressed, more gently. 'Do you remember what happened now?'

'M-mostly…not very clearly.' A taxi had dropped her off at the cottage where Stefano had been staying with his girl-friend. She had forgotten to ask the taxi driver to wait for her: a very foolish oversight. But it had taken a lot of courage to seek out and confront Stefano. And when she had walked back out of that cottage she had felt dead inside and she really hadn't cared about anything. Not the darkness, not the wind, not the rain. She had just started walking away as fast as she could.

'I got lost,' Milly muttered tightly.

'Where was this? Why were you were on foot?'

'I'd gone visiting…and, coming back, I messed up my transport arrangements. So was walking,' she began afresh, staring blindly at the silver sugar bowl, determined not to tell him any actual lies. 'It was a horrible wet night.'

Gianni bent down, closed a hand over her knotted fingers and eased her slowly upright into the circle of his arms. 'It was also a long time ago, *cara*. It can't hurt you now.'

Helplessly, Milly leant into him for support, but she felt like a fraud. 'There really isn't much to remember, Gianni. I *think* I may have heard the car that hit me approaching but that's it. There's nothing else. I don't recall seeing a car or being hit.' She bowed her damp brow against his chest. 'What has always given me the creeps is the knowledge that somebody robbed me while I was lying there hurt. I had an overnight bag with me.'

'The hit-and-run driver and the thief may well have been the same person,' Gianni ground out, and she could feel the massive restraint he was exerting over his anger on her behalf. The knowledge of that anger comforted her. 'I'm afraid the police will be hoping for more details than you've been able to give me.'

'The police?' Milly echoed in surprise.

'Some bastard left you lying by the side of that road like a piece of rubbish!' Gianni reminded her with barely suppressed savagery. 'You'd be dead if a passing motorist hadn't seen you and contacted the emergency services. It's a complete miracle that you didn't have a miscarriage!'

Milly sighed. 'I don't really want to talk to the police about this again.'

Gianni veiled his gaze. 'You'll have to make a new statement, but I can understand that you don't like the idea of it all being raked up again,' he conceded soothingly as he settled her back into the wing-back chair. 'I've still got a few questions I'd like answered, but we'll leave them for now.'

'Yes...' Milly averted her pounding head, stomach still churning. She really didn't want Gianni to know she'd gone to see Stefano. She knew what interpretation he would put on that revelation. And Stefano had clearly known better than to ever mention her visit. That was no surprise to her. Gianni's kid brother had treated her like Typhoid Mary that night. With great difficulty, Milly put away that memory.

'Right,' Gianni breathed in a next-on-the-agenda tone, as if he was chairing a board meeting. 'I imagine you'd like to know where we're heading now.'

Considering that in two entire years with her Gianni had not once even hinted that they might be heading anywhere beyond his next flying visit, Milly was taken aback by that concise assurance. She looked up, sapphire-blue eyes very wide and wary.

Gianni leant back against his desk, looking incredibly sophisticated and elegant in his unstructured caramel suit and black T-shirt. Milly averted her head again and rubbed at a worn seam on her jeans with restive fingers.

'To start with I should tell you why I bought this place two years ago.'

Milly frowned, not understanding why that should be of interest to her.

'Heywood House is convenient both to the airport and the City of London. I hoped that once I found you both, you would move in here—'

'Move in here?' Milly glanced up in frank bewilderment. *'Why?'*

Gianni sighed, as if she was being incredibly slow on the uptake. 'Naturally I want you to live at a location where I can easily maintain regular contact with Connor. Heywood House fits the bill very well.'

'Two years ago, you purchased this property for *me*?' Milly was thinking out loud, and she flushed with embarrassment when reality sank in a split second later.

Gianni had bought a stately home and turned it into a treasure house. Naturally *not* for her benefit but for his child's! Even that far back Gianni had been making plans. Selecting the kind of home he wanted his child to grow up in, filling it with priceless artwork and furniture to create a gilded cocoon of wealth and privilege. Could she ever have dreamt three years ago that he would warm to the concept of being a father to such an extent? With an effort, she forced her attention back to him.

'To all intents and purposes Heywood House *will* be yours, until Connor reaches his twenty-fifth birthday.' Gianni made that distinction with complete cool. 'I intend to sign all the documentation to that effect and this is now your home. I want you to feel secure here.'

Everything to be tied up all nice and tight and legal. Very much Gianni's stamp. Gianni had already worked out how best to control her and, through her, his child. Where they lived, *how* they lived. And, to that end, Heywood House would be put in trust for their son. Milly stared down into her untouched coffee, feeling incredibly hurt and humiliated. He didn't trust her as far as he could throw her now—but then had he ever?

For the first time since she had recovered her memory, Milly recalled the DNA testing Gianni had mentioned. A shudder of very real repulsion ran through her in response. One glimpse of her with Stefano and that had been that. Instantly Gianni had been willing to believe her capable of any evil. Two years of her loving faith had been eradicated in a nano-second. Now, it seemed, he didn't even trust her not to try and make a claim for a share of this house at some time in the future.

'I thought you'd be pleased about the gardens and the plant centre.' Gianni regarded her like a generous benefactor, still awaiting the gratitude he saw as his due and keen to give her a helpful nudge in the right direction. 'Obviously those factors influenced my choice of this particular property.'

Unable to credit that, hating her as he did, he could have been influenced by any desire to please her, Milly swallowed hard. 'Didn't it occur to you that I might want to live somewhere of my *own* choosing?'

'Within certain parameters,' Gianni qualified without hesitation. 'This is my son we're talking about, but let's put that issue aside for now. I have something far more important I want to discuss with you…'

A slightly jagged laugh escaped Milly's tight, dry throat. Her nerves were already stretched tight as piano wires.

'What's so funny?' Gianni asked.

'Once, whenever I said anything like that to you, it really used to spook you,' Milly reminded him helplessly.

His lean, dark features clenched hard, the dark, deep flashing eyes chilling to polar ice. '"Once" is not a barrier we want to cross. I don't want to rake over the past.'

The sudden freeze in the atmosphere raised goosebumps on Milly's over-sensitive skin. She tore her strained and shadowed gaze away. She got the message. Three years ago he had denied her the chance to give her version of what happened the night he had found her with Stefano. And now he was telling her that she would never get that chance. *Never, ever.* Only Gianni, so practised at keeping unpleasant or awkward things in tight little separate compartments, could fondly imagine it possible for her to respect such an embargo.

'For Connor's sake, we *need* to move on,' Gianni added with cool emphasis.

Honest communication? Why on earth had she got her hopes up? They were to move on without ever having paused to consider. Gianni hadn't changed one iota. And Gianni was far too proud to confront an episode that had undoubtedly savaged his ego. So their entire past had now become a conversational no-go area. *For Connor's sake.* That phrase had an almost pious ring of superiority. Naturally it did. Gianni thought Connor's mother was the immoral slut who had lured his kid brother into bed with her.

'I'd like my son to have my name,' Gianni admitted.

Milly raised dulled eyes, wishing he could look ugly to her just once, wishing his flaws would shriek at her loud enough to destroy the dangerous emotions swilling about inside her. But, no, Gianni lounged back against that desk looking drop-dead gorgeous, relaxed and in spectacular control of the situation.

Milly rose to her feet. She parted her lips, and with a defiance she could not withstand breathed raggedly, 'Your brother assaulted me.'

Gianni froze. A kind of incredulous outrage laced with black fury flared in his brilliant eyes.

'Just thought you should know,' Milly completed shakily.

'Keep quiet...' All cool ditched, Gianni studied her with glittering rage and derision, every line of his big, powerful body poised like a predator about to spring. 'I won't listen to your lies. I will not discuss this with you, *capisce*? One more word and I walk out of this room—'

'Go ahead.' Milly stood her ground. Indeed, all of a sudden she felt as if she was wedged in concrete, ready to hold steady through any storm.

'And I head straight for my lawyers and I throw everything I've got at you and fight for custody of Connor!'

Milly's stomach lurched as suddenly as if Gianni had thrown her off a cliff. White as milk, she gazed back at him in horror.

'Now you've got the message,' Gianni murmured grittily, his anger back under lock and key as he recognised her response.

The shock of that unashamed threat savaged Milly. And suddenly she couldn't bear to look at him any longer. She was too damned scared of him. Scared of Gianni for the first time in her life. Before, she had only feared his hold on her emotions. Now she feared a whole lot of other things as well. His innate ruthlessness, his enormous wealth, the dangerous power and influence he had at his fingertips.

She was shaking, and she hated that he should see that. But she didn't need a crystal ball to guess the sort of weapons which might be used against her in any custody battle. A woman capable of spending three years living another woman's life might well fail to impress a judge as a stable mother figure. In fact, her recent past would put her at a distinct disadvantage, Milly reflected bitterly.

'But I wouldn't do that, to you *or* Connor. I think you're a great mother. I have no intention of trying to take him away from you. OK?' Gianni breathed tautly.

Her arms protectively wrapped around herself and her back turned to him, Milly continued to stare blindly out of the window. His words meant nothing to her. She knew she would never forget the way Gianni had just turned on her. His façade of civilised cool and control had dropped to let her see the cold menace that still lay beneath. Why was she so shocked? Hadn't she always known that Gianni was totally incapable of forgiving her for what he believed she had done?

'I suppose I should've expected you to come out with that sort of stuff today,' Gianni continued flatly. 'But you have to accept that I've put all that behind me.'

Her supposed betrayal. Like a gun he concealed behind his back, always primed to shoot.

'To the extent…' Unusually, Gianni hesitated. 'You've really messed this moment up, Milly.'

'What moment?' she muttered in confusion.

'I was about to ask you to marry me. *Accidenti*, I *am* asking you to marry me!' Gianni rephrased, with more than a suggestion of gritted teeth.

Milly went from shock into bigger, deeper shock. She had to consciously will her feet to turn around so that she could look at him again. She *had* to look at him to believe the evidence of her own ears.

A dark line of colour accentuating his stunning cheekbones, Gianni subjected her to a grim, glittering appraisal. 'In spite of everything you've done, I'm willing to give you another chance and make you my wife.'

'Wife...' Milly could hardly get her tongue round that astounding word. 'But you hate me...'

Gianni raised two lean brown hands and spread them at truly impressive speed to indicate his distaste for that subject. 'I don't want to get into emotions here. They're quite irrelevant.'

'Irrelevant...' Milly stared at him with huge wondering eyes.

'All that really matters is that you're the mother of my son. Connor deserves a proper family life and he's not going to get that if I'm just the guy who flies in to visit every week,' Gianni pointed out levelly. 'I want to be a real father. I don't want him turning round and asking me as a teenager why I never thought enough of him to marry his mother and be a genuine part of his life.'

Milly nodded in slow motion.

'Then there's us,' Gianni added in an obvious afterthought. 'Let's be frank, *cara*. You wouldn't kick me out of bed.'

Hot, humiliated colour drenching her former pallor, Milly discovered that she wanted to kick him to kingdom come.

'I don't see any reason why things shouldn't go right back to the way they were,' Gianni told her with complete conviction. 'I still find it a real challenge to keep my hands off you.''

'That's a...a compliment?' Milly prompted unevenly.

Gianni slanted an ebony brow. 'I'm asking you to marry me. I can understand that you're pretty surprised by this development, but you should be really pleased.'

'Why?'

'Why?' Gianni repeated with unconcealed incredulity. 'It's what you always secretly wanted. Do you think I didn't realise that?'

Kicking him to kingdom come wouldn't be enough. It would be too quick, too clean. Milly wanted him stretched on a rack and tortured. How could a male so very clever make a marriage proposal sound so deeply offensive? It *had* to be deliberate. He had decided he had to marry her for Connor's sake, but he was making it brutally clear that his sole use for her would be sexual. Connor deserved a relationship; she didn't.

Gianni surveyed Milly's frozen little face with mounting tension. He could feel his temper rising again, no matter how hard he tried to ram it down. Wasn't she capable of a logical reaction? First she had wrecked everything by actually daring to refer to that disgusting episode with Stefano. Next she had told stupid lies. And now she was reacting to his extraordinarily generous proposal as if he had insulted her beyond belief!

Here he was, striving in the only way he could to make amends for his own errors of judgement over the past few days! He was giving her what she must always have wanted when she least deserved it, but not one ounce of appreciation was he receiving for his impressive ability to rise above *her* unforgivable act of betrayal three years ago! And, finally, he had been *honest* with her, Gianni reflected with smouldering resentment. Right from the instant he had first met her, she had stressed how important it was that he should always be honest with her. So he had been honest. Only somehow honesty wasn't working like any magic charm!

'You said that to all intents and purposes this is my home,' Milly reminded him tightly.

'What's that got to do with anything?' Gianni demanded with stark impatience, brilliant eyes glittering like ice shards.

'If this *is* my home, I can ask you to get out of it,' Milly informed him, her breath catching audibly in her throat. 'So I'm asking...'

Gianni frowned at her. 'Run that by me again.'

Milly thrust up her chin. 'In fact, I'm not asking. I'm *telling* you to get out!'

Wrathful incredulity emanated from Gianni in powerful waves. His eyes flashed shimmering gold. 'How *dare* you talk to me like that?'

Milly's temper rose hot enough to equal his own. She took a step forward. 'You're complaining about how *I'm* talking to *you*? You dragged me back into bed at the hotel just so that you could satisfy yourself that you could still pull me like a Christmas cracker!'

'*Dio*...how can you be so vulgar?' Gianni shot at her thunderously.

'Vulgar? *Me?*' Milly gasped in disbelief. 'Would you listen to yourself? You're the cockroach who had to boast about the fact that I *didn't* have the wit to kick you out of bed! Well, now that I've got my memory back, I know I'd sooner be dead than let you touch me again!'

'Is that a fact?' Before she could even guess his intention, Gianni reached out and simply lifted her up into his powerful arms as if she were a doll.

'Put me down this minute!' Milly shrieked at him furiously.

His mouth slammed down on hers like a silencer. Rage hurtled up inside her, only to be transformed into a blaze of white-hot hunger so intense it literally hurt. It physically hurt to want, to need, to crave to such an extent, for nothing he could do could ever be enough. She always wanted more. The drugging heat of his mouth, the provocative stab of his tongue driving her wild only made her ache unbearably for the fulfilment that he alone could give. Heartbeat pounding, pulses racing, she dug her fingers into his luxuriant hair and kissed him back so frantically she couldn't even stop to breathe.

Gianni dragged his mouth off hers. He was breathing heavily, but his dark golden eyes shimmered with un-ashamed satisfaction. 'Somehow I don't think death before dishonour is likely to figure in this reconciliation, *cara mia*.'

The raging fire within Milly shrank to a tiny mortified flicker and was doused entirely by an all-consuming ache of regret. Her cheeks a hectic pink, she removed her fingers shakily from his hair, tormented by her own weakness.

Gianni lowered her to the carpet again with exaggerated care.

Immediately she spun away in a jerky movement. 'Go, Gianni,' she urged in desperation.

'Call me when you've thought things over,' he murmured silkily, all cool now restored.

Milly listened to the quiet thud of the door closing on his exit and slumped, bitterly ashamed of her own behaviour. He had levelled the score. He had had the last word. Although, as usual, language hadn't played much part in her defeat. But it hadn't always been like that between them, she reminded herself fiercely. Once she *had* been strong enough to hang onto her pride and independence and protect herself from a male determined not to commit himself...

Five years ago, on the very first day they met and admitted to diametrically opposed expectations, Gianni had accurately forecast that *one* of them was set to crash into a solid brick wall.

Gianni had wanted a no-strings-attached affair, but Milly had wanted and needed something much deeper. Within the first week, she had recognised the disturbing intensity of her own emotional response to him. And the discovery that one kiss could set a bushfire burning inside her had been no more welcome.

Milly had tried to back off and protect herself by making loads of rules to ensure that she never emulated poor Lisa with Stevie. No man was going to turn *her* into a puppet on a string! So, if Gianni hadn't called far enough in advance, she'd always been busy. If Gianni had just turned up without calling, she'd always been on the way out of the door to a pressing engagement. If Gianni had been late, she'd gone out and stayed out. And she had never, ever called him.

But then Gianni had gone over to New York for three weeks, and her whole world had turned gloomy grey. She'd begun marking off days on the calendar, hanging over the phone anxiously, and driving herself crazy with the suspicion that he might have other women in his life.

'Have you?' Milly had asked baldly, the first time she'd seen him again.

'Of course I have,' Gianni admitted without hesitation. 'I travel a great deal. Anything else would be impractical.'

Feeling as if she had been slugged by a sack of coal, Milly cleared her throat. 'But if we have an affair, that would change…wouldn't it?' she almost whispered.

Gianni lifted one broad shoulder in an infinitesimal shrug, too slick an operator to be entrapped by a verbal response.

But Milly had got her answer in that silence. And, having naively assumed that even Gianni would concede that intimacy should be accompanied by total fidelity, she was shocked and furious. 'All I can say is, thank heaven I found this out before I slept with you!' she slung as she rose from her seat and stalked out of the restaurant.

'I don't like public scenes. Nor do I admire jealous, possessive women,' Gianni imparted chillingly, outside on the pavement.

'Then what are you doing with me?' Milly demanded. 'I'm jealous and I'm *very* possessive, so get out of my life now and don't come back!'

Gianni stayed away another full month.

Milly lost a stone in weight, but she didn't wait by the phone; she didn't ever expect to see him again. But Gianni was waiting for her to come home one evening when she finished her supermarket shift.

One look and she was sick with simultaneous nerves and sheer, undiluted joy. Gianni took her back to his Park Lane apartment. He dropped the news that she no longer had competition. She asked him how she could be sure of that. Gianni could freely admit that *he* didn't trust anybody, but, faced with her lack of faith in *him*, he was outraged. They almost had another fight.

She was in tears, and then he kissed her—a standard Gianni response when things got too emotional. And the wild passion just blazed up so powerfully inside her she finally surrendered. He was astonished when he realised he was her first lover.

Making love with Gianni was glorious; staying for breakfast feeling totally superfluous while he made calls and read stockmarket reports was something less than glorious.

So Milly drew up a new set of rules. No staying overnight. No asking when she would see him again. Always saying goodbye with a breezy smile. By then, she knew she was in love with him, but she was well aware that he didn't love her. He found her good company. She made him laugh. He couldn't get enough of her in bed. But never once did he do or say anything that gave her any hope that their affair might last.

As part of her college course that year Milly had to spend two months gaining practical experience of working in a large garden or park. She was allotted a place on a big private estate far from London. When she informed Gianni that she would be going away, they had a blistering row.

'How the hell am I supposed to see you up there?' he demanded incredulously.

'You're out of the country at least two weeks out of every four,' she reminded him.

'*Porca miseria*…you can't make a comparison like that!'

'Don't say what you're dying to say,' she warned him tautly. 'It'll make me very angry.'

'I don't know what you're talking about.'

So she said it for him. 'You think your life and your

business empire are one hundred times more important than anything in mine.'

'Obviously they are,' Gianni stated without flinching. 'And, while we're on the subject, I can think of a thousand more suitable career choices than a peculiar desire to go grubbing about in the dirt of somebody else's garden!'

'It's what I want to do. It's what I'll be doing a long, long time after you're gone. So really, in every way, it has to take precedence,' Milly retorted shakily.

'Over *me*?' Gianni breathed chillingly. 'Haven't I offered to find you a decent job?'

'I'm happy with the career choice I'm training for.'

'Fine. Just don't expect me to follow you north to the rural wastes!'

'I never did expect you to. You're far too used to people doing the running for you. You never, ever put yourself out for anybody,' Milly pointed out with quiet dignity. 'So that's that, then. We're at the end of the road.'

'Spare me the clichés at least,' Gianni ground out as she walked straight-backed to the door. 'Tell me, am I being dumped *again*?'

Milly thought about it, and nodded.

'This is a wind-up,' Gianni drawled in icy condemnation. 'This is a power-play.'

'Goodbye,' she said gruffly.

He did come up north. His limo got bogged down in a country lane. He was fit to be tied when he ended up lodged in a very small and far from luxurious hotel. And he was furious when she wouldn't let him come to the estate to pick her up for the weekend. He didn't appreciate being told that she didn't want to shock the head gardener and his wife, who were letting her stay in their guest-room. By the time she had finished explaining that a humble student trainee couldn't have a very rich, flash older boyfriend without her reputation taking a nosedive, and the all too human effect that might have on her receiving a fair assessment of her work, Gianni was not in a very good mood.

'So I'll buy you a big garden of your own,' he announced, in the dark of the night.

'Don't be silly.'

'Then I'll buy the garden for myself. I'll pay you to look after it for me!'

'You're embarrassing me,' she groaned. 'Stop living in fantasy land.'

'When I've got free time, I'd like you to be available *occasionally*.'

'I know how that feels. You're away much more than I am,' she complained sleepily, looking forward to spending two entire nights with him, snuggling up to him with a euphoric smile in the darkness.

'Do you think the head gardener and his wife would be shocked if I delivered you back strangled?' Gianni mused reflectively. 'What am I *doing* here in this lousy dump with you?'

Sex, she reflected. Sex and only sex—and it was an ongoing source of amazement to her that her body could possibly have such a hold on him. It was a perfectly ordinary body. Slender, well-honed, but far from being centrefold material. Yet he kept on coming back to her. She was developing expectations on that basis. That worried her terribly. After all, some day soon he would lose interest and vanish for good.

He came up north three more weekends. She was so happy she couldn't hide it from him. It was getting harder and harder to obey her own rules. It was as if he knew her rules and worked overtime to try and get her to compromise them. That next summer he was away a lot, and she pined, went off her food, couldn't sleep. He gave her a mobile phone and she accepted it, and used it much more than she felt she should.

Then they had their six-month anniversary, and she was stupid enough to mention it. He frowned. 'That long?' he questioned with brooding coolness, and went silent on her for the rest of the evening.

He didn't call her for a week after that. So she called him in a temper and told him he was history and that she was going to find a man who would treat her with the respect she deserved.

'Tell him in advance how demanding you are,' Gianni advised helpfully. 'That you have a very hot temper, a habit of saying things you don't mean and a stubborn streak a mile wide.'

'I'm finished with you—'

'I'll pick you up for dinner at eight, and if you're not there, I'm not waiting. It's time to join the grown-ups and stop playing hard to get.'

Just before she started back at college, she suffered what appeared to be a really bad bout of tonsillitis, and instead of getting better she lost her energy and her appetite. Gianni was in South America. She told him that she thought she had the flu and soldiered on, exhausted, to her classes and her part-time job. By the time Gianni flew back to London she was so weak that walking from the bed to the door was enough to reduce her to a perspiring wreck.

Gianni was furious with her. He got another doctor. Acute glandular fever was diagnosed. She was told she would have to rest for weeks. She wouldn't be fit for her classes or for any other form of work—and by the way, the doctor added, physical intimacy was out for the foreseeable future too. That quickly, her whole world fell apart. At the time she just could not comprehend why Gianni, threatened by weeks of celibacy, should still seem so incredibly supportive.

Forty-eight hours later, she was flown to Paris in Gianni's private jet and installed in a fabulous townhouse with a garden. When she was least able to oppose him Gianni made his move, at supersonic speed.

His every argument had been unanswerable. Who would look after her in London? How could he take care of her from a distance? And she loved Paris, didn't she? If she couldn't study and she couldn't work, she might as well regard her lengthy convalescence as a vacation. And the sad truth was that she was so desperately grateful that Gianni wasn't abandoning her she didn't protest that much.

He was really wonderful when she was ill. She learnt that he liked to be needed, and that in constantly asserting her independence she had been missing out on probably the very best side of him. From that time on, Gianni became the love of her life, the centre of her existence. She stopped trying to contain her own feelings. The last barriers came down. She told him she loved him. He froze, but he didn't back off. The more she told him, the less he froze, and eventually he even began to smile.

And she decided then that maybe if she absolutely showered him in love and trust and affection, if she gave and gave and gave, with complete honesty and generosity, she might break his barriers down too. Her only goal was that he should return her love. So she never did go back to complete her college course.

Gianni became her full-time occupation. He finally got everything the way he wanted. He got to buy her clothes and jewellery, to switch her between the house in Paris and the apartment in New York, according to what best suited his travelling itinerary. She became his mistress full-time without ever acknowledging what she had become. And he was right; she *was* deliriously happy—right up until the day she discovered she was pregnant.

In the heat of passion, Gianni had on several occasions neglected to take precautions. She knew that. *He* knew that. But, like so much else, they had never discussed the fact that he had taken that risk.

Yet the evening she broke the news Gianni went into shock, like a teenager who had honestly believed it couldn't possibly be that easy to get a girl pregnant.

'You can't be…' he said, turning visibly pale beneath his bronzed skin.

'I *am*…no doubt about it. No mistake,' she stressed, getting more and more apprehensive. 'It was that night we—'

'Let's not get bogged down in details,' Gianni interrupted,

striding across the room to help himself to a very large brandy.

'You don't want to talk about this, do you?' she muttered tightly.

'Not right now, no.' Quick glance at gold watch, apologetic look laced with a hint of near desperation.

'You've got some calls to make?'

'No—'

'You have a business meeting at eleven o'clock at night? Well, some celebration this is turning out to be.'

'Celebration?' Gianni awarded her a truly stunned appraisal. 'You're pregnant and we're not married and you want to *celebrate*?'

'Since you're the one who's been playing Russian roulette with my body, maybe you'd like to tell me what end result you expected?'

'I just didn't *think*!' he ground out, like a caged lion, longing to claw at the bars surrounding him, resisting the urge with visible difficulty.

Yet he thought about everything else...incessantly. He thought rings round her. He planned business manoeuvres in his sleep. He was seriously telling her that he hadn't once acknowledged the likely consequences of making love without contraception?

'I'm not having a termination. You might as well know that now,' she whispered sickly.

'*Madre di Dio*...why do you *always* think you know what's on my mind when you don't?' he slashed back at her rawly. 'I don't believe in abortion!'

Only a little of her tension evaporated. 'I'm tired. I'm going to bed.'

'I'm going out.'

'I know.' She closed the door softly, heard the brandy goblet smash and shivered. He was right. So much of the time she did not have one earthly clue what was going on inside him. But that night she believed she did. He might not believe in abortion, but he still didn't want her to have his baby.

The next development shocked her rigid. Gianni walked out of the Paris apartment that night and vanished into thin air for thirty-six hours. He even switched off his mobile phone—an unheard-of development. His security staff went crazy the next morning, questioning her, checking the hospitals, considering kidnapping. They weren't able to accept that Gianni should choose to deliberately take himself off without cancelling his appointments.

Milly convinced herself that he had gone to some other woman.

But Gianni reappeared, looking pale and grim as death, hiding behind an enormous bunch of flowers. And she didn't say a word, behaved as if he had only stepped out an hour earlier. Patently relieved by that low-key reception, Gianni swept her up into his arms and just held her for the first time in his life, so tightly she could barely breathe.

'You just took me by surprise. My own father…if he *was* my father,' he qualified in a roughened undertone. 'He was abusive. I don't know how to be a father, but I don't want to lose you!'

She had never loved Gianni more than she loved him at that moment. It felt like an emotional breakthrough: Gianni trusting her enough to refer to the childhood he never mentioned and actually admitting to self-doubt. Her heart and her hopes soared as high as the sky. Yet, just two short months later, Gianni had almost destroyed her with his lack of his faith…

Coming back to the present to gaze like a wakening sleeper round the library of Heywood House, Milly found that her cheeks were wet with tears. You've got to stop this, she warned herself angrily. There *is* life after Gianni. Three years ago she hadn't felt able to cope with that challenge. But now she was older, wiser…only still as hopelessly in love with him as she had ever been.

CHAPTER EIGHT

'GIANNI...it's me,' Milly announced tautly, her grip so tight on the phone that her knuckles showed white.

'I'm listening,' Gianni responded softly.

'Connor's asking about you all the time.' Milly's troubled eyes were pinned to where her son sat listlessly swinging his feet. 'When I asked you to leave, I overlooked the fact that he's lost a whole life too. The last thing he needs right now is for you to vanish as well—'

'I can be with you in two hours,' Gianni interposed, smooth as silk, but she sensed the buzz of his satisfaction nonetheless. 'Why did you wait four days to contact me?'

Milly tensed. 'I needed some time to myself.'

Before he could ask her what she had decided to do about the marriage question, she finished the call. Then she breathed in very deep to steady herself.

She had lunch with Connor, who could hardly eat for excitement. Leaving him in Barbara's care, she then took herself off outdoors, keen to be elsewhere when Gianni arrived to spend time with their son.

An afternoon spent energetically digging in the walled kitchen garden which had been abandoned to the forces of nature for a good twenty years proved therapeutic. She was going to marry Gianni. *Of course* she was. If he married her, he could hardly use her recent past as a weapon against her in any custody battle. As a wife she would be safer. That way, and only that way, could she ensure that Gianni would find it extremely difficult to try and remove their son from her care.

And if she didn't marry him mightn't he eventually marry someone else? With sudden violence, Milly slashed a bramble out of her path. Once she would not have believed that possible. Once she would have sworn that Gianni would die single. But that conviction had died when Gianni had stunned her by proposing. Even if it was only for his son's benefit, Gianni was finally prepared to offer commitment. If Milly turned him down, sooner or later he would end up marrying some other woman.

And that was a development which Milly *knew* she would not be able to bear. She was possessive. She was very possessive. Currently hating and resenting Gianni to the same degree with which she loved him did not blind Milly to her own vulnerability. To stand by on the sidelines and watch Gianni with another woman would be to tear herself to shreds. After all, she reflected painfully, she already knew what that experience felt like. So there was a lot to be said for choosing to be miserable *with* Gianni now that she had faced the fact that she would be even more miserable without him.

'I really love it when you dress up for me like this, *cara...*'

Milly jerked, froze, and then slowly lifted her golden head. Silhouetted against the fading light of the afternoon, Gianni was poised several feet away, a faint smile on his wide, sensual mouth. His navy cashmere coat hung open to reveal a formal pinstripe suit cut to faithfully follow his powerful frame and his long, long legs. He looked spectacular. Her eyes widened, her mouth ran dry, her heart just lurched.

Milly leant on her spade for support. Her tumbled hair was roughly caught back with a piece of twine. She wore ancient jeans, a warm but shapeless sweater and workmanlike boots. Her lack of elegance didn't trouble her. But she could see it was troubling Gianni, who was reading all sorts of deeper messages into her appearance. Women wore make-up in bed with Gianni. Women spent hours dressing to go out with him. He never had known quite how to handle her unconcern at letting him occasionally see her just as she was, bare of both fashion and artifice.

'You lost track of time. You didn't realise I'd arrived,' Gianni decided instantly.

Milly was not in a conciliatory mood. 'I could hardly have missed the helicopter landing, and that was what…two, three hours ago?'

'Your phone is switched off. Barbara Withers told me where to find you.' Gianni couldn't quite conceal his irritation that he had been reduced to asking such a question. 'You shouldn't be working outdoors in this weather.'

'You're annoyed I wasn't waiting for you at the house,' Milly interpreted without the slightest difficulty. 'But why come all the way down here to get an answer you don't need? The last time you were here you made it clear that you saw my answer as a foregone conclusion.'

His lean, strong face darkened, brilliant eyes veiling to reveal only a watchful glimmer of gold.

'*And,*' Milly continued flatly, aiming a particularly vicious jab of the spade at the undergrowth surrounding her, 'as usual you were right. How *can* I say no?'

'You're going to marry me.' Ignoring the hostile undertones with the practised ease of a male who never looked for trouble with a woman unless it rose up and slapped him smack in the face, Gianni surveyed her with a slow smile curling his expressive mouth. He retained his cool like a cloaking device, but his eyes glittered like the heart of a fire.

'But I have certain conditions,' Milly extended gently.

Caught off guard, Gianni strode closer, stepping off the path to mire his polished Italian leather shoes in mud. '*Conditions?*'

Milly threw back her slight shoulders like a boxer about to enter the ring. 'To start with, I'd like you to have a medical, so that I can be assured that you have a completely clean bill of health.'

His winged brows lifted. 'What are you talking about?'

'Whether you choose to believe it or not, I have *not* been

intimate with anybody but you,' Milly stated, watching his strikingly handsome features freeze, his big, powerful body stiffen. 'However, you can't offer me the same reassurance, and I feel I have the right to ask.'

Gianni drew himself up to his full height, dark eyes blazing derision. '*Porca miseria!* You think that you can make me believe that you didn't sleep with your fiancé?'

'I don't really care what you believe…'

'Then what kind of nonsense is this? I have never been promiscuous…why the hell are you looking at me like that?' he demanded in fierce condemnation.

Milly returned to her digging, thinking with inescapable bitterness and pain of the speed with which he had turned to another woman three years earlier. 'You shouldn't need to be told.'

The tense silence thundered and shouted and snarled. Flailed by pain and anger, Milly hacked at winter-bare brambles. 'I have cause to know that you're not always *careful* with—'

'I have never taken risks like that with anybody but you!' Gianni shot back in a savage undertone.

'Then why with me?' Milly glanced up enquiringly.

His lean brown hands closed into powerful fists. He swung restively away from her. 'That was different…'

'How was it different?'

He didn't answer her. 'A clean bill of health,' he ground out instead, as if he was spitting tacks, apparently choosing to settle for the lesser of two evils. 'OK. I already have that. My most recent medical was less than a month ago.'

But if Gianni thought he was getting off the hook that easily he was mistaken. Milly wasn't finished yet. 'I will also expect total fidelity.'

His eyes shot like flaming golden arrows into hers, his incredulity unfeigned. '*Accidenti*…where do you get the nerve to demand that of *me*?'

'I'm thinking of Connor's need for stability.' Cheeks

burning, because her own needs had risen first and foremost to her mind, Milly focused on the distant wall.

'*Connor?*' Gianni repeated rawly.

'You must set Connor a good example. Our son must be able to respect our marriage. So you can't have a mistress,' Milly informed him, warming to her theme by the second. 'And if I were to discover that you had been unfaithful, I'm afraid I would have to divorce you. I won't have Connor damaged by a destructive relationship.'

All tight-mouthed tolerance now fully breached, Gianni slashed a savage hand through the air. 'You are lecturing me about...*fidelity*?' His Sicilian accent was so thick she had to strain to comprehend that final word.

'I don't think it's a *lecture* to state what I want up front,' Milly responded stubbornly. 'And, after all, you *did* say that you had put the past behind you...'

Sheer rage turned Gianni pale beneath his vibrant bronze skin. In seething silence he studied her, as if he just could not believe that she had dared to remind him of that statement.

'And finally,' Milly added not quite steadily, watching the ice front settle over him like her most dangerous old enemy, 'I'm not prepared to sign a pre-nuptial contract.'

At that provocative announcement Gianni appraised her with eyes that would have chilled a polar bear, aggression emanating from every dangerously still and silent inch of him.

'Not because I have any desire to get my hands on a larger share of your wealth,' Milly explained heavily. 'But because I believe that the absence of a pre-nuptial contract will make it easier for you to respect our marriage. You see, you don't respect me, but I think you *will* respect what a divorce might cost you.'

Gianni stared at her with cold, brooding menace.

Milly shook her head in a sudden helpless gesture of despair. 'Gianni...when I left Paris, I also left everything you ever gave me behind. The clothes, the jewellery, the credit cards. I took nothing. Doesn't that at least prove that I'm not the mercenary type?' Her own voice emerged with a quality of pleading that embarrassed her, and hurriedly she compressed her lips.

Eyes black and reflective as mirrors, Gianni simply swung on his heel and started to walk away.

Milly suppressed a groan.

'Gianni!' she called.

He didn't even pause.

She hurried after him and then forced herself to a halt, watching in frustration as he receded from her with every impossibly long stride. 'Gianni, if you agree to my conditions…I'll try really hard to make everything the way it was!'

Abruptly he stopped dead, but he didn't turn round.

'It's going to be very difficult, but I'll *try* to learn to trust you again,' Milly completed huskily, tears thickening her throat as she thought of what they had once had and had so brutally had taken from them.

Gianni swung back. He sent her a scorching look of rampant disbelief. *You* will try to trust *me* again? Speech wasn't necessary. A split second later, he turned his arrogant dark head away and strode through the crumbling gateway out of sight.

Well, you handled him like a real pro, didn't you? Never had Milly seen a satisfied smile die faster. And her own emotions were all over the place. Until Gianni had appeared, she honestly hadn't appreciated the depth of her own bitterness. But three years ago Gianni had hurt her *so* much. In a blaze of publicity, he had taken off to the Caribbean with a supermodel, infinitely more beautiful than Milly could ever be. And Milly had immediately to her house in Paris, and had sat waiting, torn apart but struggling to understand what he was going through, and still hoping against hope that their unborn child would eventually bring Gianni back within talking distance, even if it only meant he lifted the phone.

With deeply troubled eyes, she watched the helicopter

take off again as she walked back towards the house. She
hadn't meant for that to happen. She hadn't meant to drive
him away again. Connor would be upset. Oh, for heaven's
sake, why didn't she just admit it? *She* was upset!

The following morning Milly's portable phone, switched on
since Gianni's departure, buzzed at seven. She had just got
out of the bath. She leapt for the phone.

'You drive a hard bargain,' Gianni murmured softly. 'But
so do I...'

Sinking down on the carpet, huddled in a towel, Milly
nodded without speaking, tension strangling her ability to
respond.

'You promise me that the past stays buried—'

'I *can't* do that!'

'And you don't ever tell me you love me again.'

Milly gritted her teeth and bowed her head over her knees.

Gianni loosed a cynical laugh. 'I thought you'd be able
to manage that one...'

'I'm damned if I do...and I'm damned if I don't, aren't
I?' Milly countered painfully.

'Only a week ago you were madly in love with another
man—'

'And then I got my memory back and *everything*
changed!' Milly argued vehemently. 'Judging me on that
isn't fair... I—'

She snapped her mouth shut in despair, for she knew now
that she had never loved Edward. She had wanted to love
him and had convinced herself that she did. The illusion had
vanished the instant she got her memory back. But even
before that point she had been responding to Gianni. Dear
heaven, she had gone to bed with him again! Was it any
wonder that he saw that wanton surrender as yet more evidence that her emotions ran only skin-deep?

'Gianni...think what you want,' Milly sighed.

'I always do. I also want to celebrate my way,' he murmured silkily. 'I'll need you tonight at the house in Paris—'

She stiffened in astonishment. 'You still *have* the house?'

Aware that Gianni had only bought that house for her occupation, and equally aware of the ruthless efficiency with which he usually cut loose from the past, she was genuinely amazed that he hadn't long since sold it.

'Around seven,' Gianni continued, as if she hadn't spoken. 'You'll be picked up this afternoon and you'll be back with Connor early tomorrow.'

'But I don't have a passport!' Milly was wildly disconcerted by his proposition. 'I lost it three years ago and I never applied for one as Faith Jennings, so if you're thinking that I—'

'You didn't *lose* your passport, *cara*. You left it behind in the townhouse and I eventually took it back to London with me. Fortunately it's still current, and it'll be waiting for you to collect at the airport. How did you contrive to get back into the UK without it?' Gianni enquired drily.

'I was a ferry passenger. I didn't realise I didn't have my passport until just before I got off. I was ready to panic, but in the end I wasn't actually challenged,' Milly recalled ruefully. 'In the crush I managed to slip through. But I've never been so nervous in my life and it's not something I'd ever try again. I felt like a criminal, waiting for a hand to fall on my shoulder.'

'I wish Immigration had picked you up and thrown you in a cell until I caught up with you,' Gianni confided grimly. 'I wasted a lot of time searching France for you!'

'I don't want to come to Paris tonight,' Milly admitted in a taut undertone.

'It's not negotiable. I'll see you later,' Gianni countered, and finished the call.

Celebrating *his* way? In Paris, where they had been happiest? Stefano had never set foot in the townhouse. The moment Gianni's brother came into her mind Milly tried to push him out again, but her bitterness rose simultaneously and it was impossible to evade her memories...

Gianni had kept Milly and Stefano in separate compartments. If Stefano hadn't chosen to breach those boundaries, Milly believed she would never have met him. Throughout their entire relationship Gianni had maintained his own homes in New York and London, and although he had occasionally mentioned Stefano, he had never once suggested that they should meet.

Stefano was Gianni's half-brother, born of his putative father's relationship with his stepmother. At the age of eleven, Stefano had been taken to Sicily and Gianni had become his legal guardian. Milly had first met Stefano at the New York apartment which Gianni had purchased for her use. By then Stefano had been studying at Harvard. He had just arrived on the doorstep one evening when Gianni was staying.

'I hardly see Gianni any more. Now I now why!' Stefano had laughed.

Initially, Gianni had been uneasy about his kid brother's descent, but, knowing how fond he was of Stefano, Milly had been pleased. It was so hard now to remember that she herself had once liked Stefano.

He had been immature, and pretty spoilt by Gianni's indulgence, but he had been easy company. During the final months of her relationship with Gianni, Stefano had called in whenever she was over in New York. Sometimes Gianni had been there; sometimes he hadn't been. Registering that Gianni had actually been enjoying the fact that he was seeing more of his brother, Milly had made every effort to be welcoming.

'If my brother really cares about you, he should marry you,' Stefano had said once, seriously embarrassing her.

But at the time she'd thought little of that comment— certainly hadn't registered that Stefano's interest in her had become rather too personal. After all, Stefano had had a live-in girlfriend of his own. And Milly had been very wrapped up in Gianni and her own concerns. It had been shortly after first meeting Stefano that she had discovered that she was pregnant.

Even after Gianni had told her that he didn't want to lose her, Milly had gone on feeling insecure. He hadn't ever said up front that he wanted their baby. And although he had been more tender and caring in all sorts of quiet ways she had feared that he was simply making the best of a bad situation. She had also waited for Gianni to tell his brother that she was pregnant. When Gianni had stayed silent, Milly had become more and more uneasy about his attitude.

The night that her world had fallen apart, she had been alone when Stefano dropped in to visit. He had been drinking, and for the first time Milly had felt uncomfortable with him, although even at that late stage she hadn't understood why—until he'd spoken, and shattered the casual camaraderie she had believed they'd had.

'You just don't see me, do you?' Stefano launched at her bitterly, his darkly handsome features flushed as the condemnation simply erupted from him. 'I don't exist for you except as Gianni's brother. I come round here to see you and all we ever talk about is *him*.'

'I don't understand…what—?'

'I'm in love with you!' Stefano shot at her accusingly. 'You haven't even noticed, have you?'

Milly was aghast, exploded out of her self-absorption with a vengeance. 'You've had too much to drink…you don't know what you're saying—'

'Don't talk down to me like I'm some little kid!' Stefano rounded on her furiously. 'You're not much older than I am. But Gianni's *years* older. He's almost a different generation! You've got much more in common with me—'

'Let's just forget you ever said this stuff,' Milly cut in tautly. 'You have to know how I feel about your brother—'

'And how does he *feel* about you?' Stefano slammed back, the words slurring. 'He jets in, takes you to bed and jets off again. All he does is *use* you…can't you see that?'

'I won't discuss our relationship with you,' Milly said shakily, seriously stung by that assessment.

'Don't tell me I leave you stone-cold. I won't believe you.

I've never met a girl who didn't think *I* was something special!' Stefano launched at her like a spoilt little boy, needing to blow his own trumpet. 'I'd treat you like a queen, Angel.'

'I've had enough of this, Stefano. I've only ever thought of you as Gianni's brother and I'm going to forget this ever happened, just like you'll want to forget it tomorrow morning,' Milly forecast witheringly. 'Now I'm going to call a taxi so that you can go home.'

'I'll call my own cab when I'm ready to leave,' Stefano informed her truculently. 'This is Gianni's place, not yours. I've got every right to be here if I want to be!'

While he angrily paced the room, his clumsy gait telling her that he was a lot drunker than she had initially appreciated, a wave of sick dizziness ran over Milly. But the look of utter misery in Stefano's brown eyes still hit her hard, making her feel responsible, even though she was well aware that she had never done or said anything which might have encouraged him. 'Look, it's just a crush, Stefano. That's all it is—'

'It's not a crush! I really, *really* love you!'

Nausea stirred in her stomach. 'But I'm not attracted to you—'

'You could be if you'd let yourself,' Stefano had flung stubbornly. 'I may not be the stud Gianni is, but I'm no teenage virgin!'

Milly's nausea grew suddenly worse. 'Look, let yourself out. I'm not feeling well. I'm going to bed!' she gasped as she raced like a maniac for the privacy of the bathroom that adjoined her bedroom.

She was horribly sick. As she slowly recovered from that bout, she heard what she assumed to be the slam of the front door on Stefano's departure. She meant to go and do up the locks and switch out the lights, but she ended up going for a shower instead. She was exhausted, and very upset. And her distress was exacerbated by the conviction that she would have to keep the whole messy episode a secret from Gianni.

How could she confide in him without causing friction between the two brothers? She didn't want to be the source of the smallest conflict between Gianni and his only living relative. And, although she didn't acknowledge it at the time, she was also afraid to add any further stress to their own relationship.

So, although Milly desperately longed to reach for the phone to talk to Gianni about what had happened, she resisted the temptation and staunchly told herself that it would all blow over. Stefano had got drunk to make that foolish declaration. When he sobered up, he would be angry that he had made a fool of himself. He would stay away from her from now on.

She pulled on a nightdress and climbed into bed. The bedroom door was still ajar. The light in the corridor was still on. Too weary even to get out of bed to turn it off, she stuffed her face in a pillow and went to sleep. It didn't once cross her mind that she might *not* be alone in the apartment...

With an angry shiver, Milly sank back to the present. She still found it so hard to credit that the reckless, selfish arrogance of a teenager unable to tolerate rejection could have devastated her life.

CHAPTER NINE

As THE limo which had picked Milly up at Charles de Gaulle airport wafted her through Paris that evening, her every thought was a memory…

Gianni had bought her the finest chocolates, perfume, and taken her to dine at exclusive restaurants. His knowledge of Paris related only to the exclusive haunts of the rich. Milly had returned the favour by making him queue up for ice-cream from her favourite parlour, browse for books, wander through the flea markets, enjoy the jazz festival and watch French plays in the Shakespeare garden in the Bois de Boulogne.

Employing the keys which had been waiting with her passport for her to collect, Milly let herself into the town-house on the Rue de Varenne. As she discarded her coat, her heart was beating very fast. She scolded herself for her nervous tension. Everything would be different. Since Gianni had retained the house for his own use, he would have made sweeping changes. The vibrant colours, exotic throws and comfortable furniture she had favoured would have been superceded by classic shades, cool elegance and superb antiques.

So it was a real shock for Milly to walk into the spacious reception rooms and see everything exactly as she had left it three years earlier. Her steps quickened as she took a tour and finally hurried upstairs to the bedroom they had once shared. The connecting door stood wide on the fabulous marble bathroom.

Milly focused on the giant bath, her breath catching in her throat as she remembered the night she had bathed in bubbles and Gianni had stolen that photograph. Racing after

144

him, clutching a towel, she had cornered him in the bedroom.

'Give me that camera!' she had yelled furiously.

'Come and get it,' Gianni had invited, stunning dark eyes brimming with vibrant amusement as she had dripped all over the carpet.

'Gianni...I'm warning you!'

As he had stood there, naked but for a pair of silk boxer shorts, his lithe, bronzed body a powerful enticement, a wolfish grin had slashed his mouth and sent her treacherous pulses racing. '*Dio mio*, you're so sexy when you get aggressive.'

Milly had made a wild grab for the camera, but Gianni had cast it aside and caught her up in his arms to crush her mouth with hungry urgency under his.

'I want that film destroyed,' she had told him breathlessly, a long while later, still trembling from the raw potency of his stormy possession.

Gianni had given her a slow-burning smile and had said nothing.

So intense was that recollection that Milly stared at the bed almost as if she expected to see the ghosts of Gianni and herself *still* lying there. She blinked, and turned around in an uncoordinated circle, and then found herself heading for the fitted units in the dressing room. She stared in frank astonishment at the clothing carefully stored in garment bags and then sped into the bathroom to check cupboards.

Finally, with her legs threatening to buckle, she sank down on the corner of the bed. Unbelievable as it was to her, Gianni had left all her belongings intact. Nothing had been changed, nothing had been dumped. It was eerie. But for the garment bags, the past three years might not have happened. The whole house appeared to be locked in an astonishing time warp.

'You wouldn't believe how often I've pictured you here like this...' That deep, dark sexy drawl slashed through her reverie and sent her head flying up, shining waves of hair tumbling back from her oval face to accentuate troubled eyes as blue as lapis lazuli.

Milly looked fantastic, Gianni acknowledged with satisfaction, long past the stage of questioning why this one small woman should excite him to such an extent. It was sex, just sex. He was content with that explanation. It wasn't something he had to think about; the ache of hot, instantaneous arousal was reassuringly familiar. She was wearing something bright and clingy, which for Milly signified a fairly substantial degree of effort on her behalf. She was also trying to smile, but her eyes were strained. She was just nervous; she *had* to be happier than she looked, Gianni told himself impatiently, discarding that initial impression. He just could not see that she had the smallest thing to be unhappy about.

Milly stared at Gianni with colour steadily mounting in her cheeks. He lounged in the doorway, six feet three inches of stunning dark good looks and lean, lithe elegance, his attitude one of deceptive indolence.

Abruptly, she slid upright, smoothing uncertain hands down over the turquoise dress she wore. 'I didn't hear you arrive…'

Shimmering golden eyes roamed over her, lingering on the generous curve of her soft mouth, the defined thrust of her firm breasts and rounded hips in the sleek silky fabric. 'You've been shopping—'

'No. This was an impulse buy last year. I never wore it.'

'Sexy, *cara mia*,' Gianni told her with husky approval, slowly raising lean brown hands to shrug out of his overcoat and let it fall.

Milly's heart started to beat so fast she thought it might burst from her chest. He removed the jacket of the formal suit he wore beneath. Her breath began to rasp in her throat, making her mouth run dry. Without removing his smouldering attention from her for a second, he tugged loose his gold tie and unbuttoned his shirt.

'Gianni…' she began unevenly, her body reacting invol-

untarily to the wild, hot sexual charge in the atmosphere. As
her breasts swelled with languorous heaviness, and her nipples stiffened to push against the confines of her bra, she
shifted uneasily. 'We really should talk.'

'Never got us anywhere before.'

'Because we never actually *did* it!'

'Everything the way it was,' Gianni reminded her with
scorching golden eyes as he took an almost compulsive step
forward. 'You promised.'

Had she promised? Hadn't she just said she'd *try*? But as
Gianni came closer the question became academic as rational thought blurred and infinitely more basic promptings
took over. Suddenly she couldn't wait to get close. She
merged with his outrageously masculine frame on legs that
already felt weak and hollow, eagerly drawing in the familiar
warm, male scent of his skin.

'You want me...' Long fingers curved to her chin, exerting pressure to turn up her face and see the hunger she
couldn't hide.

Breathless, she gazed up into his spectacular eyes, heat
spearing up almost painfully in her stomach to stretch every
nerve-ending taut. 'Always.'

'That's all I need, *cara mia*,' Gianni asserted with complete conviction.

She reached up to him first, encouraging him to drive her
lips apart in a devouringly hungry kiss. Her head spun and
her senses whirled. He tasted like water in the desert, so
sweet, so precious she felt she would die if she didn't drink
deep. Painful memories fell away from her. She met those
dark, deep flashing eyes with an instinctive sense of coming
home.

Unzipping her dress, Gianni peeled it off. She shivered,
pressed her thighs together, seeking to contain the heat he
had already awakened. But in one easy movement she un-
clasped her own bra. Her face burned, but she revelled in
the sudden blaze of gold in Gianni's appreciative appraisal
as her pouting breasts fell free.

'Witch,' he rasped, tumbling her down backwards on the bed with a thrilling lack of cool.

Her spine curved in wondering pleasure as his expert mouth travelled hungrily between her urgently sensitive nipples. As he sucked on a straining pink bud she gasped, her hands clutching at shoulders still frustratingly sheathed in fabric.

'Take your clothes off,' she urged shakily.

Expelling his breath in a driven hiss, Gianni raised himself. He scrutinised her flushed face and moist parted lips with ravenous desire, his lean, strong features taut with the effort self-control demanded. Beginning to sit up, she arched her back, and his mesmerised gaze welded to the projecting peaks of her exquisite breasts.

'*Dio*... I can't spare that much time,' Gianni groaned raggedly.

He curved a not quite steady hand to her temptingly swollen flesh and then drove her flat again with the onslaught of his passionate mouth on hers. His tongue dipped with slow, skilful intimacy between her parted lips, tasting her with an eroticism that released a startled moan of excitement from her throat.

With a roughened laugh of satisfaction, Gianni lifted his head again and surveyed her. 'I might want to jump you like a starving animal, but tonight is going to be different,' he swore, rubbing a thumb gently along the ripe curve of her full lower lip, and she shivered with helpless anticipation.

'Different?'

'*Special,*' Gianni husked thickly against her mouth, and kissed her again. This time she didn't just see cymbals and fireworks, she saw a whole chamber orchestra illuminated by shooting rockets.

'I love the way you kiss,' she confided feverishly as she tried to wrench him out of his shirt. 'But if you don't take your clothes off I'll scream!'

Gianni finally backed off the bed. The slashing grin of

appreciation lightening his strong dark features squeezed her heart as efficiently as a vice.

Her softened eyes roamed over him. Not even the most perfectly tailored trousers could conceal the bold jut of his erection. A twist of almost shocking excitement slivered through her. Dry-mouthed, she watched him strip.

'I like it when you can't take your eyes off me,' Gianni confessed huskily.

Her whole body tingled with the need to touch him. He was awesomely aroused. He strolled fluidly back to the bed and she felt as if her bones were about to melt beneath her skin. He stood her up with gentle hands and went down on his knees to tug her panties down over her hips.

'I have three years of erotic daydreams to live out.' Gianni's deep, dark drawl fractured as he pressed his mouth in a surprisingly tender salute against her stomach. She quivered like a sapling in a storm.

Curving strong hands to her slender hips, he lifted her back on the bed. She was weak with hunger. His first touch was like a match hitting a bale of hay. She was so ready she already ached for him, but Gianni was intent on reacquainting himself with every responsive inch of her wildly sensitised flesh. With silken finesse, he explored the hot, moist centre of her. She writhed out of control. Then he rearranged her, like a gourmet at a feast, and used his wickedly expert mouth and tongue to drive her crazy with an intimacy that drove her from ecstatic moans to choked and frantic pleas for satisfaction.

'*Dio*…I love torturing you with pleasure…I've had nothing else on my mind since the day I saw you at the airport, *cara mia*. I can't work; I can't sleep,' Gianni ground out, startling her.

Rising over her, he settled her beneath him. He entered her with an evocative groan of shuddering satisfaction. She met his shimmering dark eyes, feeling the sheer burning intensity of his pleasure for a split second before he plunged her back into sole awareness of her own.

'You feel like hot satin!' Gianni rasped.

And then, as he moved on her and in her, the hot, electrifying excitement took over and she wrapped herself round him, moaning her pleasure beneath his every thrust. Heart and body exulting as one, she gave herself without inhibition and reached a shattering climax that left her floating in shell-shocked contentment.

Releasing her from his weight, Gianni hauled her back into the circle of his arms. The almost forgotten reassurance of that continuing desire for physical closeness even after satiation filled her with brimming warmth.

He ran a slow fingertip down over one tear-wet cheek. 'Special,' he breathed almost harshly, gazing intently into her drowningly blue eyes, dark colour slowly rising to accentuate his sculpted cheekbones. 'And yet you have driven me crazy more times than any woman I've ever known...'

'Really?' Milly gave him a dreamy, unapologetic smile.

'Really, *cara mia*,' Gianni confirmed, hungrily kissing her again.

Gianni woke up and rolled over. Milly wasn't there. He sat up with a jerk to hit the lights and check his watch. It was midnight. Springing out of bed stark naked, he strode out of the bedroom.

He found Milly downstairs in the dimly lit state-of-the art kitchen. Her slender back turned to him, she was barefoot and wearing an oversized T-shirt that he recognised as having once been his. Humming softly to herself, she was checking something in the stainless steel oven. The almost forgotten aroma of baking apples and pastry assailed Gianni. He turned pale.

Breathing in shallow, quiet spurts to refill his straining lungs, Gianni slowly unclenched his coiled fists. He was in a cold sweat! Swinging soundlessly out of the doorway, he flung himself back against the wall in the dark corridor beyond. Where *did* you think she'd gone? His even white teeth gritted. He was outraged by the recognition of his own fear, alienated by the dark, deep stirrings of childhood memories he always kept locked away.

When he'd been barely more than a toddler, Gianni had learnt the hard way that he couldn't depend on anybody. Not his mother, who had thrown him out of the house for hours on end while she entertained her clients, not his supposed father, who had drunk himself into violent rages and seized on any excuse to lash out with his fists and his belt. Not his stepmother, who had loathed him on sight and humiliated him at every opportunity.

Not even his deeply religious uncle and aunt, who had removed him from the orphanage at the age of thirteen and flown him over to their London home to take the place of their own dead son. For a little while he had believed he was really wanted, until they'd started constantly reminding him of the debt he owed them. They had never formally adopted him, and had washed their hands of him entirely the instant they were forced to accept that he had no vocation to become a priest.

Yet Milly's warmth and affection had drawn Gianni even as he'd marvelled at her naivety in being so foolishly, dangerously open. Didn't she know he was going to hurt her? Didn't she know he had nothing to give back? That deep down inside, where she was all giving and feeling, he was just one big, empty hollow? But fate had had the last and cruellest laugh on him. The day Gianni had found Milly with his brother had been the day he'd finally realised how much he loved her.

Levering himself off the cold wall with sudden force, Gianni went back upstairs and headed straight for the shower, wrenching on the controls with angry hands. Love had been a breeze for Milly. But love had been a killer-chiller for him. So she needn't think that sneaking out of bed in the middle of the night to make some childish offering of his once favourite snack was likely to change the status quo!

*   *   *

Milly carried the tray upstairs. She was so happy. She was just so incredibly happy. Gianni had been so tender, so teasing, so warm. It had honestly been as if the Stefano episode had never happened.

How Gianni could shut it all out, *how* he could be like that with her while still believing what he did, she could not begin to comprehend. But suddenly it didn't seem to matter. If that worked for him right now, that was all right with her. Only once they were safely married Gianni was in for a rather unpleasant surprise, she conceded ruefully. If it took her fifty years, if it took chaining him to a wall in a locked room, she would make him listen to her about Stefano!

Fully awake, Gianni was lounging in bed, intent on his notebook computer. His black hair was still damp from the shower he had evidently taken. His sleek, powerful bronzed body was dark and exotic against the pale bed linen. Milly studied him with wholly possessive eyes. Externally he was absolutely gorgeous, internally he was a little bit complicated, but they finally had a future and she intended to make the most of the opportunity.

'I thought you might be hungry...' She slid the tray down beside him, suddenly feeling self-conscious. Possibly it had been slightly over the top to rush down to the kitchen and turn out a *tarte tatin*.

'I'm not, but don't let me inhibit you,' Gianni murmured, without taking his eyes from the screen.

'It's something you like,' she told him.

Gianni glanced at the laden tray. Then he glanced up at her, brilliant dark eyes cool, questioning, filling her with instant discomfiture. 'I may not employ a chef here, but whatever I want I *can* afford to send out for,' he reminded her with sardonic softness. 'So why the hell did you feel the need to get out of bed at this hour to bake?'

Hot, mortified pink flooded Milly's cheeks. She snatched the tray back off the bed, but she wanted to pitch it at him.

'I don't require cute little domesticated gestures from you now,' Gianni added in measured addition.

The tray rattled in her tensing grasp. But for the two cups of hot coffee, she would definitely have dumped the lot on his lap. Shaken and angered by his volatile change of mood, Milly returned the tray to the kitchen. Why was Gianni behaving like this all of a sudden?

In bed, he had been so different. Dear heaven, why was she always so stupid around Gianni? *In bed*. Within those two simple words dwelt the explanation. The minute Gianni had satisfied that high-voltage sex drive of his, he just went right back to despising her again. Well, she refused to put up with that sort of treatment. She hadn't sunk that low yet. Or *had* she?

Hadn't she let Gianni fly her over for the night like a call-girl? A sure thing? She had definitely been a sure thing. Anguish infiltrated Milly at that acknowledgement. And hadn't she played a full and uninhibited part in her own downfall? Tonight she had been his puppet on a string...his totally abandoned puppet on a string. She squirmed, fingers curling on the stack of plates she had left lying out on the counter.

'Are you coming back to bed?' Gianni enquired with studied casualness from the doorway.

As Milly turned, her eyes lit on him like burning blue stars. She grabbed up a plate and hurled it with all her might. Looking genuinely startled, Gianni ducked. The plate smashed bare inches from him. She sent a second plate flying with similar accuracy. 'If I wanted to hit you, I *could*,' she told him furiously. 'So get out of here before I forget that violence is not an answer!'

Gianni straightened with admirable cool. 'OK...if it's that important, I'll eat it,' he breathed grittily.

Milly studied him with huge blue eyes and slowly shook her golden head. 'Why are you so stupid?' she whispered helplessly.

'Why are you?' Gianni responded, ice-cold.

Milly spun away, denying the cruel message in his diamond-hard eyes. He could make passionate love to her over and over again but he wouldn't allow her to harbour the smallest illusion about the precise nature of their relationship *out* of bed. Sentimental touches of the 'cute' and 'domesticated' variety were out of line. When he had said he wanted everything the way it had once been between them, he had really been lying in his beautiful white teeth. All he really wanted was all the sex he could handle.

'If I hurt your feelings, I'm sorry, but we need to start out straight,' Gianni murmured flatly.

He'd done it deliberately. She knew he had rejected her stupid edible offering deliberately. But she also knew she didn't want to force a major confrontation *before* they got married. Was that proof of her intelligence or proof of her cowardice?

Feeling wretched, she cleaned up the broken plates and then went back upstairs to the bedroom. A small jeweller's box with a very impressive logo awaited her on her pillow. She lifted the tiny box and set it unopened on the cabinet.

Sliding into bed, she was careful not to even glance at Gianni, and she turned her back on him. She had let him see how much he had hurt her and that stung her pride.

'It's a ring,' Gianni advanced, without any expression at all.

Grudging curiosity stirred Milly, because he had never given her a ring before. Reclaiming the box, she flipped it open on a spectacular ruby surrounded by diamonds.

She threaded the ring onto her right hand and said, with all the enthusiasm of a woman confronting a huge pile of dirty washing, 'Fantastic. Thanks.'

'You're wearing it on the wrong finger,' Gianni informed her drily.

Milly frowned. 'Sorry?'

'It's an engagement ring,' Gianni extended in a charged undertone.

Milly flipped right over to look at him, blue eyes rounded with incredulity. 'An *engagement* ring?'

'Why not? We're getting married.' His bold profile rigid, Gianni doused the lights.

End of discussion. In the darkness, Milly fingered her engagement ring with rather more interest than she had been prepared to show a minute earlier. A romantic gesture? She reddened. Hardly. A conventional one? Gianni had yet to mention *when* they would marry. Milly tensed at that belated realisation. Was it possible that this was going to be a *very* long engagement? The sort of engagement that went on year after endless year until it became a positive joke to all onlookers?

'Hi…' Her expressive face pale and stiff, Milly slid behind the table in the dining room. An unfamiliar maid had wakened her.

'I'd have let you sleep, but I know you want to be back for Connor.' With a slow-burning smile that reminded Milly of how very lacking in restraint she had been around dawn, Gianni poured her a cup of coffee. 'You still look pretty tired.'

Milly reddened like an awkward teenager. While she had still been deliciously drowsy and defenceless Gianni had invaded her side of the bed, ruthlessly set on conquest. And even with all her experience of Gianni's incredible expertise she had been quite unprepared either for that level of slow, exquisite seduction or the intensity of his determination to give her the ultimate in pleasure. The intimate ache of her body had powered that smile he now felt able to bestow upon her.

She looked so miserable, Gianni reflected in frustration. He focused on her hand, where it rested on the table only about nine inches from his own. But Gianni was still challenged. Breathing in deep, he reached out suddenly to cover her tense fingers with his hand.

Milly froze in complete disconcertion. Gianni was not given to demonstrative gestures beyond the bedroom door.

She stared at him. His ridiculously lush black lashes semi-veiled his eyes, but his tension was pronounced.

'Last night, nothing went according to plan,' Gianni advanced, with the taut stiffness of a male who never normally allowed himself to explain anything he did. 'We had a reservation at Castel's. We were supposed to dine out. But coming back here, seeing you here again…'

As his hesitation threatened to stretch into a stark silence, Milly instinctively closed her other hand round his as well, literally holding him prisoner. 'Yes?' she encouraged in a breathless whisper.

'It was like we'd never been apart,' Gianni completed flatly.

'I thought that was what you wanted,' Milly muttered unevenly.

Gianni's strong jawline clenched. 'I did…I *do*…but for a while last night I didn't…'

Milly waited with bated breath, but the silence lingered. She was stunned by the extraordinary fact that Gianni had made the effort to explain that his passion had been entirely spontaneous and that he had originally planned a very different evening. Dinner and dancing at the most exclusive nightclub in Paris put the presentation of an engagement ring into a new light.

But his second admission had shaken her most of all. That had been Gianni telling her in as few words as possible that last night their unresolved past had returned to haunt him and caused his change of mood. It was such a gigantic step forward in communication that Milly's eyes glowed as if he had lit a neon light inside her. 'Gianni, I'm so pleased you told me this. I know how difficult—'

'And now that we've got that out of the way, *cara mia*,' Gianni interposed at speed, his lean, dark features lightening with barely concealed relief, 'We should talk about the wedding arrangements. I've applied for a special licence. We can get married this week.'

As a distraction, that change of subject worked. Having

been on the very brink of an emotional speech, Milly was stopped dead in her tracks. *'This week?'*

'Why not?' Gianni elevated a winged ebony brow. 'We have no good reason to wait.'

'I guess not…' Her attention welded to his spectacular dark eyes, Milly's response was rather weak. She had been so totally wrong in her suspicions. Gianni hadn't been using an engagement ring as a delaying tactic. If anything, he was prepared to *rush* her to the altar.

'Connor needs me around,' Gianni pointed out.

Her dreamy smile faded. 'Yes, of course he does.'

Louise Barclay watched Milly twirl in her wedding dress. Reminiscent of a romantic Edwardian tea gown, it was an incredibly elegant confection of silk adorned with exquisite handmade lace which enhanced her slender figure.

'You really, *really* love this guy, don't you?' Louise breathed with a slightly dazed expression on her freckled face.

Milly fell still in apparent dismay at that charge. 'How do you know that?'

Louise assumed a mock air of deep concentration. 'Oh, it might be the way Gianni's name enters just about every sentence. Then again, it might be the totally off-this-planet look you have when you say his name—'

'Louise!' Milly groaned.

'Or it could even be the fact that you've phoned him four times in the last two hours. I've heard of bridal nerves, but the last two times you called he was downstairs under this very same roof,' Louise pointed out gently.

Milly went pink. 'Phone calls are like a jokey thing between us.'

'Hey, I'm not criticising. Obviously he's crazy about you too.'

Eyes clouding, Milly turned away. She hadn't actually seen Gianni for four days. Business had kept him abroad. But, since her return from Paris, Gianni had made regular calls, and on the phone he was Gianni as she remembered him. Tender, teasing and warm. That was why the phone had become her lifeline.

Louise sighed. 'Why didn't Gianni just organise a media man-hunt when you went missing three years ago?'

Milly stiffened. 'Strictly speaking, I wasn't missing. I left Paris because we'd split up. We had some major problems.'

Her friend grinned. 'But nothing the two of you couldn't surmount within a week of finding each other again!'

But Milly knew better. The Stefano episode would never be forgotten. She was certain that her supposed betrayal had come back to haunt Gianni that night in Paris, and it would keep on coming back until she dealt with it. But how *was* she to clear her own name?

What, after all, had changed? It would still be her word against Stefano's. Stefano would never tell the truth; he had too much to lose. But for all that, Milly mused, Stefano would surely be very shocked to learn that she was back in Gianni's life in the infinitely more secure role of his wife.

Her portable phone buzzed. She snatched it up. 'Gianni…?'

'I'm now on my way to the church. We haven't yet met any roadblocks or fallen trees—'

'Don't be snide.'

'Of course, some gorgeous flame from my past could still throw herself across the church steps and prevent me from reaching the altar—'

'That's not funny!' Milly cut in hotly.

'Milly…proceed to the bedroom door. That's the large wooden oblong with the handle. Open the door, walk down the stairs and get into the transport waiting,' Gianni instructed with gentle satire. 'If you keep me hanging around at that church, I'll—'

'You'll what?' Milly whispered in breathless interruption as she moved towards the door.

'You'll find out tonight,' he promised, in a roughened

sexy undertone that made her heartbeat accelerate at the most astonishing rate.

'I'm going to be awfully late, Gianni…'

'I won't wait.'

'You will,' she muttered, smiling, and finished the call.

On her way down the stairs, she was amazed by the number of staff bustling in and out of the ballroom, and she was about to ask what was happening when Robin Jennings strolled out of the drawing room to extend his arm to her with a broad grin.

'Gianni wanted me to surprise you.'

Milly gave the older man a delighted smile and a welcoming hug. 'I'm so glad you're here to share this day with me.'

After that first surprise, the surprises simply got larger. The church car park and the road outside were packed with luxury cars. As Robin helped her out of the limo Gianni's security men surged forward to shield her from a pack of eager photographers and journalists shouting questions.

'What's going on?' Milly voiced her bewilderment in the church porch.

'Gianni did mention that he wanted to show you off to the whole world,' Robin Jennings confided then. 'Only I didn't realise he meant it so literally.'

There wasn't even standing room left in the church.

Gianni watched Milly walk down the aisle with glittering dark eyes of appreciation.

The simple ceremony filled her with emotion and optimism. Some day soon, she swore, she would be able to tell Gianni how much she loved him without him acting as if it was verbal abuse of the most offensive kind.

'Why didn't you tell me you were inviting all these people?' Milly squealed, the minute she got him on his own in the limo. 'We'll be in all the newspapers tomorrow, and you know how you hate that sort of stuff! Everything that's happened to me will come out as well.'

Gianni's dark, deep flashing eyes shimmered with amusement. 'In the words of one of my PR team...''just like a fairytale''. Less than cool, but romantic. You're a living cross between the Sleeping Beauty and Cinderella. I'm still working on being a prince.'

'Did you really say you wanted to show me off to the whole world?'

Slight colour burnished his stunning cheekbones. 'I don't remember.'

Plunged into a reception for five hundred guests back at Heywood House, Milly found her wedding day an increasingly breathless whirl.

Around three that afternoon she slid away to speak privately to Davina Jennings. After the older woman had listened to Connor's excited chatter and cuddled him, she explained that Edward had now become a junior partner in Jennings Engineering.

'He's bearing up very well to having lost you, I have to admit,' Davina confided ruefully. 'With hindsight, I can see that Edward *was* rather more interested in the partnership than he was in you. You made the right decision.'

Davina pressed a very familiar item of jewellery into Milly's hand. 'The bracelet. You left it behind in your room.'

'But I can't keep it. It belonged to your grandmother,' Milly protested.

'You're always going to be part of our family, Milly,' the older woman told her gently. 'But now that you've got your memory back, I'd love to know how you acquired the bracelet in the first place.'

'A couple of days before the accident, I bought it off a market stall.' Milly had turned the silver bracelet over and noticed the word 'Faith' inscribed on the back. It hadn't occurred to her that it might be a name. She had seen it in the light of a message to have faith, keep faith no matter how difficult things might seem. She had clasped it round her wrist like a talisman the same day she'd boarded the train to Cornwall.

'The bracelet belongs with you now. At least you liked it enough to buy it,' Davina remarked wryly. 'Enough of that. Have the police been in touch with you about the accident?'

'Gianni suggested that I get in touch with them, so I made a fresh statement the day before yesterday,' Milly admitted with a rueful twist of her lips. 'I'm afraid that even with my memory back I still didn't have any useful facts to offer them.'

'That can't be helped. By the way, Gianni mentioned the enquiries he's having made on our behalf. If our long-lost daughter *can* be traced, I've no doubt he's the man to do it. Yet that awful day he made us tell you the truth I didn't trust him an inch.' The older woman grimaced. 'I should've recognised that, having found you, he was simply *terrified* of losing you again!'

Milly laughed at that idea. 'Gianni has nerves of steel!'

'Not where you're concerned,' the older woman replied with quiet conviction.

After a light supper was served at seven, Connor fell asleep on Milly's lap. Gianni lifted his slumbering son gently from her. 'It's time he went to bed.'

Barbara Withers was dancing, and very much preoccupied with her partner. Gianni was ready to intervene, but Milly scolded him with reproachful eyes and gave him a little lecture on the need to consider the feelings and the needs of his employees.

'How many employees have you had?' Gianni enquired as he carried Connor upstairs.

'None…but I know what's right,' Milly retorted, not one whit deflated. 'And sometimes you're just a bit too bossy and demanding.'

Gianni met her look of fearless challenge and threw back his head to laugh. '*Dio mio*…how I have missed you in my life!'

At that admission, her breath caught in her throat. ''Sometimes I wonder if I lost my memory because I couldn't handle remembering the pain,' she confided shakily.

The sudden silence that fell seemed to hang on a knife-edge. Aware that she had breached forbidden barriers, Milly scooped Connor out of Gianni's arms and got on with putting him to bed. By the time she had finished their exhausted toddler was no longer fast asleep.

'Play cars?' he mumbled drowsily to Gianni.

Hoping to distract their son until he went off again, Milly picked up a toy car and ran it along the top of his duvet. 'I can give you ten minutes.'

'Boys play cars,' Connor muttered dismissively.

'I wonder where he picks up these sexist ideas,' Gianni remarked, with sudden vibrant amusement.

'It's the Sicilian blood, Gianni. It's in his genes,' Milly teased, highly relieved that the awkward moment had been successfully bridged.

But it wasn't to be the last awkward moment. A pretty brunette teenager hurried up to speak to Gianni when they returned to the ballroom. 'Why's Stefano not here?' she asked baldly.

Gianni's long fingers tensed on Milly's spine. 'He's not well.'

'Gosh, is it serious?'

'I shouldn't think so,' Gianni countered.

'Poor Stefano,' the girl groaned sympathetically. 'He never seems to have much luck these days, and yet he used to be so much fun.'

'Maybe he just grew up,' Gianni suggested flatly.

He whirled Milly fluidly away onto the dance floor. It was some minutes before she could breath normally again, and even longer before she felt the worst of the tension ease in Gianni's big powerful frame. *Had* he invited Stefano to their wedding? Or had she just heard a social excuse to cover the absence of his one and only brother?

'I wanted this to be a wonderful day,' Gianni breathed harshly.

'It *has* been,' Milly argued. 'Don't you ever dare think otherwise! I've met hundreds of people, who have all been incredibly nice to me. I've got to be the centre of attention without anybody thinking I was a show-off! And for the first time in our entire relationship you have switched off your mobile phone!'

His dark, deep flashing eyes roamed over her animated face with an intensity that made her heart sing. Easing her closer, he complained about the frustrating difference in their heights and then, with a growl of very male impatience, he just lifted her high off her startled feet. He kissed her with such desperately hungry need she was trembling when he finally lowered her back to solid earth again.

'I need to be alone with you. I want you all to myself, *cara mia*,' Gianni growled in the circle of her arms.

'Well, you're just going to have to wait.'

'If we'd been able to take a honeymoon, we could have been out of here hours ago!' Gianni ground out in frustration.

'Why weren't we able?'

'Because we couldn't have taken Connor abroad with us. He has no documentation right now—'

Milly frowned. 'What do you mean?'

Gianni sighed. 'Milly, you slipped right back into your true identity because it was already established. Our son, however, was registered at birth as the child of Faith Jennings. That has to be legally sorted out before he can be issued with a new birth certificate.'

'My goodness, I never even thought about that!'

'It's in hand. Don't worry about it. But as soon as Christmas is over I have every intention of finding a hot, deserted beach and bringing in the New Year—'

'With Connor and a bucket and spade?'

'I'm not listening. Fantasy is all I've got right now,' Gianni muttered raggedly, whisking her deftly behind one of the marble pillars that edged the dance floor and hauling her up to his level again to repossess her soft mouth with hot, driven urgency.

Milly caught fire. 'Gianni—'

'You're like too much champagne in my blood.' He bowed his arrogant dark head over hers and snatched in a fracturing breath. 'You push me to the edge. Sometimes I need you so much it *hurts*.'

Already dizzy with desire, Milly experienced a joyous flare of sheer happiness. Had he noticed what he had said? Not want but *need*. Gianni, who prided himself on never needing anybody or anything, whose belief in self-sufficiency was legendary, had admitted that he needed her.

And yet a few hours later, when they were finally in the privacy of their own bedroom, surprisingly Gianni was patience personified. He removed her wedding dress with gentle, almost regretful hands. He told her how gorgeous she had looked all day. He made sweet, tender love to every sensitised, shivering inch of her he uncovered. He took his time—oh, yes, he took his time—until she was twisting and begging, lost in incoherent urgency. And when he at last sealed his lean, bronzed body to hers, and possessed her with aching sensuality, it was the most sensational experience they had ever shared.

Two weeks later, Gianni watched Milly turn on the lights on the big Christmas tree she had sited in the drawing room of Heywood House.

She smiled like a happy child when the lights worked first time. But then she'd had plenty of practice, Gianni conceded. This was the third tree she had dressed within as many days. Several shopping trips to Harrods and other well-known retail outlets had yielded a huge collection of ornaments and other necessities. It was a very big house, she had pointed out, in an apparent attempt to convince him that she was just doing what had to be done. But the truth was that Milly adored the festive season, gloried in every single tradition, no matter how naff, and still left out refreshment for Santa Claus as an adult.

'What do you think?' she prompted expectantly.

'Spectacular.' Gianni looked past the glimmering lights to

Milly, her fantastic hair tumbling round her shoulders, eyes bright as sapphires in her beautiful smiling face. 'Christmas just wasn't the same without you, *cara mia*.'

Milly stilled, veiling her eyes, not wanting to seem too conscious of that easy reference to the past. 'Wasn't it?'

'Like Scrooge, I stopped celebrating it,' Gianni admitted.

'Oh, Gianni!' Milly groaned, troubled by the imagery summoned up by that confession and heading towards him like a homing pigeon.

'And, like grumpy old Ebenezer, I took particular pleasure in doing it.'

Milly linked her arms tightly round his narrow waist. 'We're about to have the most wonderful Christmas ever!'

And it would be, Milly thought with warm confidence. They had spent every hour of the past two weeks together, loving and laughing. She had never been as happy as she was now. She had never known Gianni so relaxed or so content. She loved watching him with Connor, revelling in the rough-housing that little boys enjoy, but she loved him most of all for his acceptance of their son's occasional tantrums.

In fact, from that morning in Paris Gianni had been fantastic in every possible way. He had changed over their three years apart, she now acknowledged. He was more tolerant, more kind, less volatile, less driven. For Milly, it was deeply ironic that Gianni should be capable of showing her more caring tenderness now than he had shown her *before* he'd seen her wrestling on a bed with Stefano! And, unfortunately, that presented Milly with a major problem.

Every hour, on the hour, Gianni was proving that he could successfully put that sordid little scene behind him. As long as the subject was never broached, as long as it was left buried. She still couldn't really understand how he could contrive to achieve that miracle. Could it be because he knew that sexually nothing had really happened that night? Gianni had accepted his brother's lying explanation in its entirety. That *she* had been lonely and *he* had been drunk, that just for a few foolish minutes desire had overwhelmed decent boundaries.

Certainly Gianni had never doubted her guilt. She had been condemned for playing the temptress and punished much more heavily than Stefano. She was still very angry and bitter about that fact. But now she feared the risk she would be taking in challenging Gianni again. She might destroy everything they had recently regained; she might wreck their marriage.

And she still couldn't *prove* that she was innocent. To believe her, Gianni would have to accept that Stefano was an out-and-out liar, capable of behaviour that might well have landed him in court in any other circumstances. That was a very tall order. But, even as Milly confronted that truth, she knew that it wasn't possible for her to remain silent. She would just have to deal with the fall-out when it happened.

That same afternoon, Milly was coiled in Gianni's arms in front of the log fire in the library, telling him between kisses about the new rose garden she was planning, when a knock on the door interrupted them.

With a groan of annoyance, Gianni settled her into an armchair. Milly closed her eyes sleepily.

'Wake up, *cara mia*. We have a visitor.'

Something in Gianni's flat delivery spooked her. Her drowsy eyes opened very wide in dismay when she focused on the young man hovering in the centre of the magnificent rug. It was Stefano.

CHAPTER TEN

STEFANO had so much strain etched on his taut face he looked a lot older then he was. His hair was shorter now. He was a little too thin. His extrovert ebullience appeared to have deserted him. His dark eyes evaded both Milly's gaze and Gianni's.

Milly glanced at Gianni and just winced. The Sicilian side of Gianni's brooding temperament was in the ascendant. He looked grim as hell, but kind of satisfied too, content that his kid brother should be nervous as a cat in his radius. Milly began to revise her assumption that she had been punished more than Stefano. The two brothers had once been pretty close. Stefano, for all his brash talk and swagger, had been heavily dependent on Gianni's approval. And Gianni, she now recognised, had cut him loose from that support system.

Milly stood up. 'Anybody want a drink?' she gushed, to break the awful silence.

'No, thanks…I need to talk,' Stefano announced tautly.

'We'll talk elsewhere,' Gianni drawled, smooth as glass, but he shot Milly a grim, assessing glance, evidently having expected her to be more discomfited by Stefano's presence.

'I don't keep a hair shirt in my wardrobe,' Milly told Gianni defiantly.

'Milly has to be here,' Stefano stated stiffly. 'And you have to promise to hear me out, Gianni. I don't care what you do afterwards, but you've got to give me the chance to explain things.'

'Is there some point to that curious proviso?' Gianni enquired very drily.

Stefano lowered his head. 'You're my brother and I've wronged you,' he breathed tightly. 'I've lied to you, deceived you, and I stood by and did nothing when I could have helped you. I followed the tabloid coverage after you got married. I found out what had happened to Milly…the hit-and-run and everything since…and I guess I just couldn't live with myself any more.'

Milly sank back down into her chair because her knees were wobbling. As far as the two men were concerned she might as well not have been there, and if the knowledge of their marriage had scared Stefano into confession mode, she had no desire to distract him.

Gianni was very still. '*How* have you lied?'

'About that night with Milly in New York,' his brother said gruffly.

'But you had no reason to lie. I saw the worst with my own eyes!' Gianni shot back at him.

'There's no way you'd ever have forgiven me for what I did!' Stefano burst out with sudden rawness. 'You'd have thought I was some sort of pervert. I *had* to lie! It was me or her, surely you can see that?'

Gianni was now the colour of ash beneath his bronzed skin, his hard facial bones fiercely prominent. 'Milly said you assaulted her…'

The silence hung like a giant sheet of glass, ready to crash.

Milly cleared her throat and spoke up. 'Stefano told me he loved me. He was drunk. I was feeling sick and I told him to go home,' she explained. 'I heard the front door slam while I was in the bathroom. I thought he'd left…'

'I opened the door and then I changed my mind,' the younger man mumbled.

'So I got into bed and went to sleep.'

Gianni scrutinised her taut face and then focused with mounting incredulity on his brother.

'I saw her sleeping. I just wanted to kiss her. That's all. I *swear*!' Stefano protested, weak as water now beneath the appalled look of menace and disgust flaring in Gianni's diamond-hard eyes.

'I think maybe you thought that if you kissed me, you'd be able to prove that I could respond to you,' Milly countered with contempt. 'You were angry with me. I'd dented your ego, and just for that you frightened the life out of me!'

'I was drunk as a skunk...I hardly knew what I was doing!'

Gianni's hands coiled into powerful punitive fists, and as he absorbed his kid brother's mute terror a look of very masculine revulsion crossed his lean, strong face. '*Accidenti*...I wonder how many sex offenders say that.'

Milly sprang upright again, her fine features flushed with turbulent emotion, and suddenly she was erupting like a volcano. '*You* needn't sound so blasted pious!' she fired bitterly at Gianni. 'If Stefano *had* been a rapist, you'd have given him open house. You just walked out and *left* me with him!'

Beneath the bite of that derisive attack Gianni froze, to stare back at Milly with stricken eyes.

Stefano's shoulders slumped as he too looked at Milly. 'I didn't mean to terrify you, but when you woke up you went crazy, like you were being attacked—'

'She *was* being attacked,' Gianni slotted in from between clenched teeth, his Sicilian accent thick as molasses as he visibly struggled to control his own rising fury. 'When you touch a woman without her consent, it's an assault.'

'I panicked! When you saw us, I was only trying to hold her still until she calmed down—'

'How the bloody hell do you expect me to believe that?' Gianni roared at the younger man in savage interruption. 'You are one sick bastard! *Per meraviglia*, you came to me that night in tears, sobbing out your penitence, telling me how you couldn't resist her, insinuating that she had led you on. It wasn't *enough* that you had assaulted a pregnant woman; you then chose to destroy our relationship to save your own useless hide!'

Stefano stumbled back against the desk for support. 'I didn't know she was pregnant then, Gianni. I'd never, ever have touched her if I'd known that! *Dio mio*...I pulled a crazy stunt and I frightened her, but I honestly didn't mean to!'

Milly studied the younger man with unconcealed scorn. 'I might be impressed by that defence if you'd thought better of your lies once you'd had time to appreciate what you'd done. But even weeks after that night in New York, you were still determined to keep on lying!'

Gianni's winged brows pleated. 'Are you saying that you saw Stefano *after* that night?' Gianni looked dazed.

'Gianni, once you asked me what I was doing in Cornwall three years ago. I'll tell you now. I went there to confront Stefano,' Milly stated crisply. 'I took a lot of trouble to find him. In the end I had to contact his girlfriend's mother and pretend to be a friend of hers to find out where they were staying.'

Stefano was now staring fixedly at the rug.

'You went to Cornwall to see him? *Why?*' Gianni's open bewilderment told her that shock had deprived him of his usual ability to add two and two.

'Milly wanted me to tell you the truth.' Stefano spoke up again in a sudden rush. 'She tried to shame me into it by telling me that she was pregnant, but I already knew that by then because you'd told me. I was furious she had tracked me down. I didn't want anything to do with her in case you found out. You might've started doubting my story, maybe thinking that we'd been having an affair…'

'*Per amor di Dio…*' Gianni gazed with incredulous dark eyes at his trembling kid brother, and then he simply turned his back.

'When I arrived at the cottage, Stefano had been drowning his sorrows again,' Milly revealed ruefully. 'He'd had a row with his girlfriend and she'd taken their hire car and driven back to London to fly home, leaving him stranded.'

'It was too *late* to tell the truth! I was in too deep by then. There was nothing else to do but face it out!' Stefano protested weakly.

Gianni's dark, haunted eyes were fixed to Milly. 'Tell me

that the night you're referring to was *not* the same night that you were hit by that car!' he urged, almost pleadingly.

'It *was* that night.' Milly shrugged fatalistically. 'I'd gone to the cottage in a taxi and then let it go.'

As Gianni rounded on Stefano, the younger man backed away, looking sick as a dog. 'Until I read about the hit-and-run in the papers last week, I didn't *know* what had happened to Milly that night! How *could* I have known? She just walked out on me. For all I knew she had a car parked further up the road—'

'You didn't give a damn either way,' Milly condemned helplessly. 'In a twisted way, you had started to blame *me* for the mess you were in with Gianni!'

'I called a cab the next morning and flew back to New York,' Stefano continued woodenly, as if she hadn't spoken. 'I had no idea that Milly had been injured after leaving the cottage.'

'But within days you were well aware that I was frantically trying to find her.' Gianni's tone was one of savage disbelief. 'Yet not one word did you breathe! You could have told me you'd seen her in Cornwall but you didn't. I spent months searching France for her. By then she had been wrongly identified as another woman.'

'I knew nothing about any of that,' Stefano reiterated, perspiration beading his strained face. 'And if I'm here now, it's because I couldn't stand all this on my conscience any more.'

'No, you're here now because Milly's my wife,' Gianni delivered with chillingly soft exactitude. 'Because you assumed I might already know all this, and the idea of confessing all and throwing yourself on my mercy seemed like the only option you had left.'

'That's not how it was, Gianni.' Stefano had turned a ghastly colour.

'Your conscience got to you too late. You hurt Milly not once, but twice. You also cost me the first years of my son's life,' Gianni condemned with lethal menace. 'But what I can never, ever forgive is my *own* mistake, Stefano. I put family loyalty first. And here you are, our father all over again. Weak, dishonest, unscrupulous. It's a just reward for my stupidity, isn't it?'

Looking at Gianni, Stefano seemed to crumple entirely. 'I'm not like that. I'm not. I've changed a whole lot since then. I *had* to lie… I was so scared—'

Gianni said something cold in Italian.

Stefano was openly begging now. 'How was I supposed to admit the truth, knowing that you'd kill me? Do you think I didn't realise that *she* came first with you when I saw how you reacted at the apartment? It was her or me…you've *got* to see that!'

Milly did not feel sorry for Stefano, but she was squirming for him. His best quality had always been the depth of his attachment to Gianni. He had always been measuring himself up against Gianni. He had probably developed a crush on her for the same reason. But alcohol, arrogance and sheer stupidity had combined to tear Stefano's privileged little world apart. He *had* been terrified that night in New York after Gianni had walked out on them both, terrified that Gianni, who had been more father than brother to him, would disown him.

'Go home, Stefano,' Milly suggested wearily.

Gianni said nothing. It was as if Stefano had become invisible. His brother slung him one last pleading glance and then hurried out of the room.

A hollow laugh that startled Milly was wrenched from Gianni then. '*Porca miseria!* To think I was jealous of that pathetic little punk!'

'Jealous?' Milly parroted in astonishment. 'Of *Stefano*?'

Gianni half spread expressive brown hands and then clenched them tight into defensive fists, his strong profile rigid as steel. He swallowed hard. 'Yes. Long before that night I saw you together at the apartment, I was *very* jealous,' he bit out raggedly.

Milly was stunned by that revelation. 'I can't believe that... I mean, why on earth—?'

'You had a bond with him. You talked about things I was totally out of touch with...*house* music, clubs. You used the same street dialect, shared the same *in* jokes,' Gianni enumerated with harsh emphasis. 'You were the same generation. I introduced you to dinner dates, antiques and art galleries, and occasionally you were bored out of your skull and I knew it.'

Milly was savaged by that shattering outpouring of feelings she would never have dreamt Gianni could experience. Insecurity, vulnerability concerning the age-gap between them. 'You couldn't expect us to share every taste, every interest...'

'I didn't feel that way until Stefano came into the picture.'

'I thought you were pleased we got on so well.'

'Sure I was pleased.' Gianni's agreement was raw with self-contempt. 'I'd ring you from the other side of the world and in the background my kid brother would be cracking jokes and making you laugh. I was *eaten* with jealousy and there was nothing I could do about it.' He moved restively about the room like a trapped animal, forced to pace round a too small cage. 'But until that night I saw you with him I *knew* it was all in my own mind; I *knew* I was being unreasonable!'

Suddenly Milly was grasping why Gianni had been so quick to believe her capable of betraying him. Jealousy rigidly suppressed—a fertile and dangerous breeding ground for distrust and suspicion. Yet she had never suspected that Gianni was jealous. Once he had even told her that he was grateful she had Stefano for company. His ferocious pride had ensured he went to great lengths to conceal his own weakness.

'I was planning to surprise you that night. I was in a really good mood. But I went haywire when I saw you on our bed with Stefano. That was my every worst fear come true. If I had stayed one second longer I would've torn him apart with my bare hands!' Gianni asserted in a smouldering undertone, ashen pale. 'I couldn't stand to even look at you. So I didn't.'

So I didn't. He always protected himself from what he didn't want to deal with emotionally.

'As usual, you took the easy out,' Milly sighed with immense regret.

The sudden silence seemed to swell.

'It wasn't the easy way out, *cara mia*,' Gianni contradicted from between bloodlessly compressed lips, feverish colour scoring his stunning cheekbones.

Milly hardened herself to the distinct shock spreading in the dark, deep flashing eyes pinned to hers. Now that the truth had come out, she wasn't prepared to allow him to duck that issue. 'Gianni, most men would've confronted us there and then. It's all right saying that you might have ripped Stefano apart. Frankly, I couldn't have cared less what you did to him that night! No, it was what you did *afterwards* that destroyed us.'

Gianni's breathing pattern fractured audibly. 'His *lies* destroyed us.'

'No. Your refusal to see me again did that,' Milly countered painfully, her blue eyes saddened. 'And I'm not interested in what you *thought* I'd done. I'd been with you for two years and I was carrying your child. I had the right to expect a meeting with you. But what did you do? You wouldn't even take a call from me and then you took off to the Caribbean with another woman!'

Gianni latched on to that last condemnation with something very much like relief. '*Accidenti*, you don't need to worry about that!' he assured her. 'We never actually made it between the same sheets. When it came down to it, I wasn't interested.'

'That's not the point,' Milly groaned, refused to be sidetracked into betraying the pleasure she'd received from that information. 'The point is that you let me down by refusing to face up to the situation between us.'

'Let me get this straight, *cara mia*,' Gianni breathed raggedly, as if she had suddenly discharged a shotgun into his back, brilliant eyes burning in stark golden disbelief. 'You're accusing me…Gianni D'Angelo…of running away like a spineless little jerk!'

Milly winced.

'Only you were trying to wrap it up a bit!' Gianni grated, outraged by her silence.

'Why did you take so long to tell Stefano that I was pregnant?'

Disconcerted, Gianni frowned. 'It was private, no business of his.'

'He's your brother.'

'When I hadn't yet decided how I intended to resolve the situation, I wasn't prepared to discuss it with anybody but you,' Gianni framed impressively.

'And not even with me if you could help it,' Milly tacked on helplessly. 'You spent that time trying to decide whether to keep me or dump me, didn't you?'

Gianni glowered at her. '*Dio*…it wasn't like that at all!'

'The speed with which you grabbed the first excuse you had to ditch me isn't in your favour,' Milly informed him.

'At the time, I was thinking of marrying you!'

'*Thinking?*' Milly repeated, unimpressed. 'Only it never got further than that. I trusted you. I relied on you. I loved you for two years and yet it still wasn't enough to convince you that we had something that it might have been worth trying to save.' Feeling her eyes smarting with oversensitive tears, Milly started to twist away.

Gianni reached out for her and pulled her into his arms, refusing to be held at bay by her resistance. 'Don't tear us apart with this,' he said unevenly. 'I made some mistakes. OK, I made a bloody *huge* mistake, but the minute I found out that you'd left Paris, I began looking for you.'

Milly was mutinous, unreachable. 'Because you had your child as an excuse. If it hadn't been for Connor, I'd still be out there, *lost*!'

'You're getting very worked up about this. You don't know what you're saying,' Gianni told her with stubborn conviction. 'OK, I didn't behave the way I should have after that business with Stefano, but once I came to terms with that—'

'Can't you even admit that you were *hurt*, like anybody else would?' Milly demanded emotionally, watching his devastatingly handsome features freeze and aching at the knowledge that he still wouldn't lower his barriers and let her in. 'Or did you stick me in a little compartment and just close the lid? Did you even manage to deal with it at all?'

Gianni's lean hands slid from her with a pronounced jerk. 'I'm going out for a while.'

'No, you are *not*! You walk out of this house now and you'll find barricades up when you try to walk back!' Milly warned him furiously.

'You are really angry with me right now. I have got nothing to say in my own defence,' Gianni spelt out thickly, rigid as a block of wood facing a very hungry bonfire. 'You haven't even given me the chance to apologise for misjudging you!'

'I don't want an apology. I accept that it looked bad for me that night. I accept that you were already jealous and so that much more likely to misinterpret what you saw. I even accept that Stefano is a convincing liar, and that you trusted him more than you could trust me.'

Gianni elevated an ebony brow with the kind of attitude that made her want to strangle him, stunning dark eyes coolly enquiring. 'So what *can't* you accept?'

'An emotional vacuum when we could have so much more!' she responded tautly.

'Enough is never enough for you, is it?'

'I'm not playing our marriage by your rules any more. Once I took all the risks, once I was the one who always went out on a limb…now it's your turn. I think I might enjoy seeing how good you are at expressing anything without sex.'

'Probably pretty hopeless,' Gianni admitted, disconcerting her. 'You want to humiliate me to pay me back for not believing in you three years ago.'

'Gianni…do you really think I'd do that to you?'

Gianni swung on his heel and strode out of the room. Milly emitted a strangled sob, suddenly wondering where all those crazy demands had come from and whether there was a certain unlovely grain of truth in his contention that she was trying to extract revenge.

She rubbed her eyes, knew she was smearing mascara everywhere, and finally she went off in search of Connor to console herself. But Gianni had got there first. He was in the playroom, sitting on the carpet in front of their son.

'Does she ask you how you're feeling all the time?' Gianni was asking broodingly while he set out Connor's toy train set. 'Does she want to know your every thought too?'

Connor gave him a winsome smile. 'Biscuit?' he said hopefully.

'Yes, I suspect that when you share your thoughts with Mamma it works very much to your advantage. Instant wish-fulfilment,' Gianni breathed reflectively. 'Do you think it could work that way for me?'

Milly reeled back against the wall outside the room and struggled to contain her laughter. But they looked so sweet together. Gianni chatting away, Connor giving up on the biscuit idea and getting down to play trains with all the accompanying choo-choo noises.

An hour later, Gianni walked into their bedroom. Fresh out of the shower, wrapped only in a towel, Milly fell still. Gianni sent her a disturbingly wolfish grin, exuding confidence in megawaves. 'Right, what do you want me to start talking about?'

'Us?' she practically whispered.

Gianni breathed in deep.

The silence was thunderous.

Milly couldn't bear it any longer. 'Why did you keep the house in Paris?'

'If you had ever decided to come back, you had to have somewhere to come back to,' Gianni pointed out levelly.

'But in all this time you hadn't changed anything at all!'

Gianni shrugged. 'Yes, I kept it like a shrine.'

Milly was poleaxed.

'When I wanted to feel close to you, I went there and sat for a while. I never stayed over. I used a hotel. Next question,' Gianni encouraged, as if he was competing in a fast and furious game.

'If you weren't able to talk to me like this before, how are you managing it now?' Milly whispered, wide-eyed.

'I've got to trust you. You're my wife.' Gianni breathed rather jerkily, as if that question had gone a little too deep.

Milly sighed. 'I've been so stupid. You wouldn't share things before because you thought I'd succumbed to Stefano.'

'I was protecting myself. I've probably protected myself more with you than any other woman,' Gianni admitted tautly, his strong facial bones now taut beneath his bronzed skin. 'Right from the start, I was vulnerable with you. Every time I walked away, I seemed to double back. I didn't like that. I didn't like the fact that I wasn't in full control.'

'But you were when you kept quiet?'

'It wasn't deliberate.' Gianni grimaced, his wide, sensual mouth tightening. 'You're always analysing emotions. I had learned to tune mine out and I was basically quite content like that. And when I met you you made it easy for me to go on that way. You knew what I wanted or what I didn't want before I had to say it. I didn't have to make an effort until you told me you were pregnant, and then you suddenly went silent and we were in trouble. One voice became no voice, *cara mia*.'

Milly was shaken by a truth she had never faced before.

'I'd always tried to *show* you that I cared, but all of a sudden that didn't seem to be enough. I really felt the change in you. I kept stalling on asking you to marry me,' he confessed ruefully. 'I didn't want you to say yes just because of the baby. I could see you weren't happy. That's why I became so jealous of Stefano. The cracks had appeared before he came along.'

'Yes,' Milly acknowledged, shaken yet again by his ability to put matters in their proper context. She *had* been different those last few months. 'I felt very insecure.'

'So you stopped telling me you loved me.' Gianni released a rather hollow laugh. 'You got me hooked on you saying it all the time and then you stopped. Considering that I never returned the favour, you had remarkable staying power, but I did wonder what was going on with you. I thought possibly you blamed me for getting you pregnant—'

'Oh, no!' Milly was pained by that misconception.

'So I tried not to mention the baby too much. I felt guilty. Of course I did,' Gianni shared heavily. 'I think I took those risks with you because on a subconscious level I was trying to push myself into making a real commitment to you.'

'But you were so upset when I told you I was pregnant.'

'I was scared I wouldn't live up to the challenge of being a parent,' Gianni admitted grimly.

'Gianni, you're a wonderful father,' Milly told him hotly.

'I'm learning.' Gianni shrugged, as if she had embarrassed him, brilliant beautiful dark eyes glimmering. 'You were right downstairs. I did let you down three years ago. I'm not proud of my behaviour. I'm ashamed that I listened to my brother instead of you. But I knew I could cope with him and I wasn't at all sure I could cope with you. And that word "hurt" doesn't cover what I was going through at the time.'

'I know.' Milly closed the distance between them to slide her arms round his lean hard body and feel her own heart beating as fast as a war drum.

'No, for once I don't think you *do* know,' Gianni countered almost roughly, framing her cheekbones with possessive hands. 'When I saw you with Stefano it was like somebody had taken my entire life and just blown it away. You had become so much a part of me that being without you was like being torn violently in two. And the half of me that was left was barely functioning afterwards.'

Milly stared up at him with mesmerised blue eyes.

'It took me a long time to fall in love, and it took even longer for me to realise that I did love you.' Gianni studied her with a raw intensity of unashamed emotion that touched her to the heart. 'And by the time I got the message, you'd vanished.'

'You loved me…' A strangled sob escaped Milly. She was overwhelmed by the poignancy of that confession, three years too late. 'Oh, that's awful!'

Gianni stooped to lift her up into his arms and carry her over to the bed. 'I'm only expecting to talk,' he told her loftily. 'I only want to comfort you.'

He held her close and her towel slipped. He watched the full swell of her pale breasts rise and fall with the rapidity of her breathing and an earthy groan was suddenly wrenched from him.

'I haven't really got that much more to talk about,' Gianni added in roughened continuation. 'You already know just how determined I was to get you back once I found you again.'

'You wanted Connor.'

'Behind every terrified male lurks a big liar,' Gianni shared, splaying long fingers satisfyingly wide over her slim hips and easing her into the hard cradle of his long, powerful thighs. I told you it was Connor I was really after. I told myself it was only sex I was after. I kept on telling myself that I couldn't trust you and then kept on forgetting it. But what I really wanted was everything back the way it was.'

'Your proposal really offended and hurt me…' Milly planted a fleeting kiss to his stubborn jawline.

'So I was trying to be cool. I didn't want to serve myself up on a plate. I certainly didn't want you to know that I was desperate for you to agree because I still loved you. I was trying not to admit that even to myself at that stage.'

'Oh, Gianni...' Milly sighed ecstatically. 'That's *all* I ever wanted, you know.'

'You put me through more hoops than a circus trainer,' Gianni growled feelingly. 'You really were that basic. When I did what you wanted, I was rewarded. When I didn't, I got time out as punishment. The first six months I was with you was like living in an earthquake zone.'

Milly ran a hand with provocative intent along the extended length of one lean, muscular thigh and watched his wonderful eyes narrow to a sexy shimmer of wildly appreciative gold. 'But I always loved you,' she said winsomely in her own favour.

'I adore you,' Gianni groaned with a slight shudder. 'You're gorgeous and smart and sexy and demanding—'

'*Very,*' she asserted.

'I'll never let anything or anybody hurt you again.' The most soul-destroyingly beautiful smile curved Gianni's mouth as he looked down at her.

Her heart tilted on its axis, but she knew she still had something important to say. 'But you still have to look after your brother,' she told him gently.

'Are you out of your mind?' Gianni demanded, staggered by that assertion.

'He was acting like a guy on the edge of a breakdown today, and deep down inside you know he needs you to sort him out. I know the way he was behaving makes you cringe,' Milly continued, with lashings of soothing understanding in her steady gaze, 'but you're all he's got, so he's your responsibility.'

'You couldn't possibly forgive him for what he did!'

'Three years ago, for the space of a minute, he give me a really bad scare...but afterwards he was much more scared than I was. Really scared people are not naturally noble or strong or honest. Think it over.'

'How come you're so compassionate about him but so tough on me?'

'You're like a great big thriving jungle plant and he's

more of a stunted seedling that needs help and encouragement to grow.'

Gianni flung his well-shaped head back on the pillows, dark eyes glinting with appreciation and amusement. 'You really know how to massage a guy's ego, *cara mia*.'

'Yours…oh, yes.'

'Did you realise that I was incredibly hungry the night you dumped that apple thing in Paris?'

'No, but I'm glad to hear it.'

'You can make it again for me.'

'Maybe…' Milly parted her lips with a shiver of delicious expectancy as his sensual mouth drifted downward.

Gianni stilled. 'I don't think we're likely to have a problem in the communication department again,' he proclaimed with satisfaction.

Tempted to tell him that she'd listened to him rehearsing with their son, Milly reared up, pushed his powerful shoulders back to the pillows and moaned in near desperation. 'Please shut up and kiss me!'

Six days later, on Christmas Eve, Milly watched Gianni finish reading a story about Santa Claus and his reindeer to Connor. He was able to answer all Connor's questions. Not a bad performance for a male who had never known a real Christmas as a child, Milly reflected with shimmering eyes.

After tucking their drowsy son in, Gianni straightened with a wry grin. 'We'll never get him to bed this early next year. He'll understand much more than he does now.'

They went downstairs together. Milly thought over the past week. It had been very eventful. All the publicity generated by their marriage and her mistaken identification as Faith Jennings had had stunning results as far as the Jennings family were concerned. Their long-lost daughter had written her parents a tentative letter from her home in the north of Scotland.

Divorced, and with three young children, the real Faith had admitted that the longer time went on the more difficult she had found it to get back in touch. They had since talked on the phone and were planning to meet in the New Year. Robin and Davina were anxious about how that reunion might go, but determined to be accepting of their adult daughter's independence. Milly believed it would be a happy reunion, because Faith had sounded rather lonely in her letter.

Gianni had also gone to see Stefano. They had talked. Gianni had emerged from that discussion feeling rather guilty, never having quite appreciated just how much Stefano relied on his approval, or indeed how devastated Stefano had been when Gianni had stopped treating him like a brother and given him only financial support. It was early days yet, but Milly reckoned that the healing process had started.

Gianni surveyed the drawing room of Heywood House. All the formality and the cool elegance had been banished. In all the rooms Milly used seasonal throws, glittery embellishments, festive padded cushions, unsophisticated home-made log, autumn leaf and berry arrangements and streams of paper chains ruled. Gianni even had to suffer a large fluffy Santa Claus toy on his library desk.

And he just loved it all, he acknowledged with a rueful smile of appreciation. He just loved the rich colour and warmth she brought into her surroundings, her innate ability to transform a house into a real home. He set a small parcel wrapped in beautiful paper down in front of her. 'You get your real presents tomorrow, but this is just a trifle I picked up ages ago,' he admitted, half under his breath.

Milly ripped off the paper and found herself looking at a delicate golden angel inside a crystal snowstorm on an ornate base. 'Oh, Gianni…' she sighed extravagantly. 'This is exquisite! Where did you get it?'

'New York.'

'But you haven't been there since—'

'Last year,' Gianni admitted, bracing himself.

'But you hadn't even found me then!' Milly gasped, instantly leaping up to envelop him in frantic hugs and kisses.

As desire flashed between them to instantaneous heat, Milly jerked back a step. 'Sometimes I love you so much it just hurts, *but* we still have a sooty bootprint to make on the hearth, so that Connor can see which chimney Santa Claus used as an entrance,' she explained apologetically.

'Maybe with the number of chimneys we've got we should put a flag on the roof so that the old guy doesn't get confused,' Gianni suggested deadpan as he curved her smoothly back into the possessive circle of his arms, knowing that bootprints could be faked after midnight as well as before it.

'Magic, doesn't need flags, Gianni!'

Against the backdrop of the flickering firelight and the glittering tree, Gianni scanned her wide, loving smile with softened dark eyes and pulled her close. 'You're the magic in my life, *cara mia*. I love you.'

THE RICH MAN'S MISTRESS

by

Cathy Williams

Cathy Williams is a Trinidadian and was brought up on the twin islands of Trinidad and Tobago. She was awarded a scholarship to study in Britain, and came to Exeter University in 1975 to continue her studies into the great loves of her life: languages and literature. It was there that Cathy met her husband, Richard. Since they married Cathy has lived in England, originally in the Thames Valley but now in the Midlands. Cathy and Richard have three daughters.

CHAPTER ONE

MIRANDA paused and looked behind her, then she slowly turned a full circle. This was a big mistake because the slow beat of panic which had been curling inside her stomach for the past hour mushroomed into full-blown fear as she was forced to contemplate her complete isolation. She had no idea where she was. She had no idea where she was going. All sense of direction had been lost as she had skied rapidly away from the avalanche straight into a blizzard that was now making forward progress laborious and uncertain. And, to make matters worse, dusk was beginning to permeate the great white amphitheatre which had always seemed so gloriously free and now appeared terrifyingly hostile.

She whimpered and found that she was having to make an effort to remind herself that she was an expert skier, had been doing it for twenty-two of her twenty-five years. She could more than handle the challenge of the black runs. With the snow whipping like pellets against the parts of her face which were exposed, and restricting any clear view that might help her to get her bearings, she would have to move slowly and keep her fingers crossed that she was going in the right direction.

Anger gave way to self-pity and she skied slowly towards a small cluster of fir trees which offered the only visual relief from the naked, virgin-white landscape, barely visible now as the light continued to fade.

She was lost, alone, terrified and quite possibly on course for a date with the Grim Reaper, and all because

5

Freddie, her so-called boyfriend, couldn't keep his immature, wandering hands to himself. Not content with having had her there with him, he'd simply had to explore the voluptuous charm of the Italian eighteen-year-old girl who had been assigned to their chalet. And worse, had got caught doing it.

How dared he?

Miranda leaned against the trunk of a tree and closed her eyes. She had to take a few deep breaths to contain her rage or else she would scream at the top of her lungs and, with her luck, probably set off another avalanche. Her woollen hat was soaked from the snow. She should never have worn it. She should have stuck on her faithful, waterproof headgear instead of a flimsy hat simply because it matched the rest of her skiing outfit. Now she could feel the dampness permeating through to her head. As far as everything else was concerned, she was well-protected with all the requisite layers of clothing, including thick, waterproof gloves. But how long would she be able to remain stationary before the cold began sinking its teeth through the layers in search of flesh? She squinted into the dying light and dimly made out a thickish cluster of trees, a dense little patch that would be more protection for her should an overnight stay outdoors become necessary.

Miranda groaned. Why kid herself that she was miraculously going to find her way back to the chalet where Freddie and their fifteen-strong group were right now probably cracking open their first bottle and contemplating what to have for supper? Would they even have missed her? Or, if they had, would they have assumed that she was miserably lost and perilously close to despair in the middle of nowhereland? They were all first-class skiers and they would probably be unaware of the minor avalanche that had thrown her so badly off course. Doubtless Freddie would have made a story about their argument, reducing his despicable behaviour to the level of some boyish jollity that had been misconstrued by a jealous girlfriend and her absence would be put down to a minor blip. Quite possibly they would assume that she had needed to cool off and had taken herself off to one of the hotels in a huff. Her platinum credit card would have gained her entry into any of the hotels further down the slope if she felt she needed time out and they all knew that she travelled with it in her inside jacket pocket.

'Just in case a fabulous shop happens to beckon unexpectedly!' she had always joked.

Fat lot of good a credit card was going to do for her now.

She wearily adjusted her skies and headed towards the vanishing clump of trees, moving at a snail's pace down the steep slope, making sure that desperation didn't propel her to do anything stupid. With luck, the trees would block out the blizzard or at least keep it at bay and, if she huddled into a ball in the centre of them, she might just be able to last out the night. With even greater luck she might find shelter in one of the animal sheds that were dotted around here and there but she wouldn't let any optimism blind her to the stark reality that she might just find more trees.

The vast white terrain was now almost completely swamped in darkness. If she hadn't been so focused on making it to the trees while she could still see them, she might not have stumbled and fallen over the projecting stump, rolling powerlessly down the slope. One of her skies dislodged automatically, the other clung to her foot; and when she finally came to a slow halt and tried to stand, the pain shot through her ankle like an explosion.

The lost ski, which would be essential for her to get out of this mess, was nowhere to be seen. The fast-falling snow had buried it like a matchstick and there was no time to instigate a hunt.

Miranda felt panic turn her bones to water and she gritted her teeth, forcing herself down the last few metres towards the trees, dragging her useless foot and using her ski poles like crutches.

She had been right. The blizzard, at least, was kept at bay by the denseness of the trees. She forced herself forward and was about to pause for a rest when she saw a flicker of light. When she angled her body for a better view, the light disappeared; but then, back in the original position, it reappeared. Something bright through the trees.

She could feel her eyes getting heavy and made herself stand back up, lifting her damaged leg as though she was just about to begin a game of hopscotch. The pain was excruciating, but far less so when there was no weight applied.

If she ever made it back home in one piece, then she would turn her life around. No more flitting from one fun spot to another in search of thrills. No more frantic social life—paid for by her wealthy daddy—in the company of other young, rich, restless friends from similarly wealthy backgrounds. And no more Freddie. That went without saying. In fact no more men. And definitely no more rich, spoiled brats.

The light was getting more constant now.

Miranda was virtually crying from the anticipation of finding it. The trees had become shapeless black towers and she had to weave her way painfully around them until, without warning, they cleared and the source of the light became apparent.

Not an animal shed but a cabin. Fairly small, with the typically pointed roof and, more importantly, inhabited. The curtains were drawn against the darkness but the light inside promised occupation. Help. She gave a deep-throated sob and dragged her way to the door, collapsing in exhaustion after one loud bang.

Which meant that her first view of her rescuer, her saviour, was of his feet. Or rather of his brown, weathered loafers. When he spoke his voice seemed to come from a long way off. A nice voice, she thought distractedly, deep. She lacked the energy to raise her head to inspect the face that went with the voice. She closed her eyes on a sigh and felt him lift her up and carry her into the blissful warmth of the cabin, kicking shut the door behind him.

It felt unbelievably good to be out of the cold. So good, in fact, that she wondered whether she was dreaming and whether, in a minute, she would open her eyes only to find that she was huddled under a tree fending off the same blizzard and any hopes of rescue, cabins, flickering lights and warmth were the delusions of a wandering mind.

Which was why she kept her eyes closed as she was deposited gently on a sofa that felt broad and comfortable enough to be a bed.

'Who,' the voice said from above her, 'the hell are you and what are you doing here?'

Less of a question and more of a demand for an immediate explanation. Miranda opened her eyes and found herself staring upwards at the harsh angles of an aggressively dominant face and at narrowed cobalt-blue eyes that were staring back at her with a mixture of suspicion and hostility.

He was wearing a baggy and very faded dark blue and white striped tee shirt and a pair of loose grey jogging pants that, like the shirt, seemed to have seen better days many moons before.

She forgot the pain in the ankle in the face of this overwhelming show of rudeness.

Never before in her life had any man ever reacted to her like this before! True, she probably wasn't looking her best right at this very moment, but still. She felt her mouth droop into a petulant scowl which only made her unwelcome saviour narrow his fierce eyes even more.

'Are you going to answer me?' he demanded harshly.

Miranda sat forward and then winced as the pain shot straight from her ankle to the remainder of her body. 'My foot!'

The man's eyes travelled from her face to her foot and for a second she thought that he might ignore her expression of pain, but he didn't. He removed his hands from his pockets and bent over to slowly ease her foot out of her ski boot; then he muttered something that sounded very much like an expletive as he saw her swelling ankle.

'What happened?' His long fingers were pressing against various parts of her burning, painful skin. They were cool and skilful and, combined with the relief of not being skewered by those dangerously blue eyes, she sank back against the arm of the sofa and stared upwards at the lofty ceiling.

'I was skiing and I fell,' Miranda said in a small voice and he muttered another impatient oath under his breath. 'I'm sorry,' she felt compelled to add defensively.

'Keep still. I'll be back in a moment.'

She watched his departing back and only felt herself relax when he was no longer in sight.

Trust her to stumble helplessly into a man, the first ever, who intimidated her. He was too tall, too powerfully built, too raw and far too grim. She wondered whether he had disappeared to find something to help her or whether he had simply gone in search of a map so that he could point her in the direction of the nearest other place of occupation and thereby save himself the inconvenience of having her around.

'I don't think it's broken,' he said, emerging with a box in his hand. 'Badly sprained but not broken. How long have you been travelling on it?'

'About half an hour.' Miranda frowned. 'I think. Look, you don't have to do this,' she said as he opened the box and began unravelling a strip of bandage. 'I'm capable of seeing to my own ankle.'

'You mean like you're capable of skiing without injuring yourself? You bloody beginners should stick to the nursery slopes instead of thinking you can ski off-piste because it's more exciting.' He ripped the bandage with his teeth and began stretching it around her ankle, working very slowly and expertly.

'I am not a beginner,' she said coldly. 'I happen to be an extremely good skier.'

The man briefly looked at her with cool disbelief before returning to his task, and Miranda clamped her teeth together firmly. He might have the manners of a warthog but she would not sink to his level. For a start, whether she liked it or not, she was now dependent on him, at least until she could make a phone call and get someone to come and fetch her. She was also too well-mannered to breeze past the normal rules of common courtesy the way he obviously had no qualms about doing.

'How do you know it's not broken?' she asked and he glanced at her again.

'Because I just do,' he said curtly.

'You're a doctor, then, I take it?'

'No, I'm not.'

'Then, who and what are you?'

He didn't answer. Instead he finished with her ankle while she continued to simmer with growing irritation at his attitude. And when he had finished he stood up and strolled towards the chair closest to the fire.

'Are you going to answer me?' She pulled off the woollen hat and her long blonde hair spilled over the arm of the sofa like a sheet of cream silk.

'Let's get one thing straight. You're in *my* house and *I'll* ask the questions. Got it?'

Miranda stared at him open-mouthed.

'When I'm finished asking the questions and I'm satisfied with the answers, you can go and have a bath and get into some of *my* clothes.'

His arrogance hit her like a sledgehammer and left her speechless.

'First of all, tell me just how you happened to be skiing here. Have you any idea how dangerous the vertical slopes to this place are?'

'I—I got caught in an avalanche…'

'Where?'

'Where…what?'

'Where was this avalanche?'

'Near our Val d'Isère resort, as it happens. I…had a bit of an argument with my boyfriend…and…I went skiing to take my mind off things which was when the avalanche happened. Not a very big one but big enough to throw me off course…'

'Bloody irresponsible woman,' he muttered scathingly.

Miranda ignored the interruption. If she had been in possession of her limbs, she would have stormed out of his damned cabin even if the alternative had meant a night on a slope. Unfortunately the option was not available and she bit back her anger.

'Before I could get my bearings, I found myself stuck in a blizzard and, after a while, I didn't have a clue where I was. I—I saw a clump of trees and decided that I'd be better off there if the worse happened and I had to spend the night outside. I was so desperate to get there that I didn't see where I was going and I fell over a protruding stump of tree and sprained my ankle. I then saw the light from your cabin and hobbled over.'

'So no one knows where you are.'

Miranda didn't like the sound of that. She propped herself up on her elbows and looked at him nervously. It occurred to her suddenly that he could be *anyone*. It was a little technicality that had been overlooked in her relief at being rescued from the driving snow and the prospect of hypothermia.

And he was not someone she could fight off should she need to. She was tall, standing a good five feet ten in stockinged feet, but she would put him at least three or four inches taller than her and there was a muscled strength to him that would add power to his height.

She had a sinking feeling when she met his blue eyes that he could read every wayward thought flitting through her brain.

'So...' Miranda cleared her throat '...have I answered all your questions *satisfactorily*?'

'Oh, I haven't asked the most important one yet...' He smiled slowly and linked his fingers on his lap, stretching out his long legs in front of him.

'And what's that?'

'Your name...'

Miranda gritted her teeth in frustration. He had obviously seen the apprehension on her face and had decided to have a little fun at her expense, allowing just sufficient

hint of a threat behind his silences to send her nerves
skittering.

'Miranda. Miranda Nash.'

'Nash…' He tilted his dark head to one side and
Miranda nodded vigorously.

'That's right. You may have heard of my father. Lord
Geoffery Nash.' Her voice implied that whilst it might
very well be true that no one knew her whereabouts, then
it was also true that, should anything happen to her, there
would be serious consequences to be paid.

'*Lord Geoffrey Nash* no less…'

'You've heard of him, then?'

'Is that what I said…?' He gave a low, amused laugh
which for some reason annoyed her.

'Is there a phone here I could use?'

'The land lines are all dead.' He shrugged his broad
shoulders and continued to look at her, though this time
with speculation. 'Thanks to this blizzard. And I don't
expect them to be up and running for some time yet. The
weather forecasts weren't too good for the next couple of
weeks ahead.'

'*Next couple of weeks ahead?*' Where, she wondered,
appalled, did that leave her?

'Fortunately, I have a cellphone.' He raised his eyebrows expressively and Miranda scowled at him.

'May I borrow it? Please?' she added when he made
no effort to move. 'I want to call my dad to let him know
that I'm safe and to tell him to get in touch with Freddie
and the rest of my friends who might be worried…'

'Why, of course.' He gave a mock bow which further
set her teeth on edge, and produced a fist-sized cellular
phone which he handed to her with a flourish.

Miranda rapidly tapped in her father's direct office
number and after a few seconds was connected to him,

smiling as she listened to his frantic overreaction to her situation, which she played down as much as she possibly could. She and her father were members of the mutual adoration society. He doted on her and she adored him. Which was why she guiltily omitted to mention the cause of her predicament, namely an argument with Freddie, whom her father contemptuously referred to as a foolish fop with more money than brains.

'And who is this man you're staying with at the moment?' he rasped down the end of the telephone and Miranda put her hand over the receiver to ask for a name.

'Hand me the phone.' He walked over to her and extended his hand and after a few seconds of internal debate, she let him have it, resenting the way he spoke in a low voice with his back to her, even having the nerve to head out of the sitting room so that all chance of eavesdropping was squashed.

What could he have to talk to her father about? For so long? She impatiently waited for him to return and, when he did, she snatched the phone off him to say goodbye to her father, then she rested the mobile on the table next to her.

'What were you talking to Dad about?' she asked suspiciously. 'And what's your name? Why couldn't you just tell me?'

'Fond of asking questions, aren't you?' He threw another log on the fire and turned to look at her. 'I thought it wise to reassure your father that you weren't going to come to any harm here. My name, by the way, is Luke Decroix.'

'And how did you manage to reassure him?' Miranda asked tartly. 'Did you tell him what a nice, charming, inoffensive gentleman you are?'

'Oh, I think he gathered that from my voice. I also told

him that you would call him every day just to fill him in on how you were. The fact is, I'm stuck with you at least until this blizzard has eased off a bit...'

'*You're* stuck with *me*?'

'That's right.' He gave her a long, measured look. 'I mean, you arrive in a heap on my doorstep and, face it, there's not much you're going to be able to do for yourself for a few days, is there? Not with that ankle of yours?'

'I don't intend to let you take care of me, so you needn't worry.'

'Oh, is that right...? Well, you won't be able to shovel snow and chop logs, will you?'

'You know I can't.'

'What about cleaning...?'

Miranda looked around her—for the first time since she had arrived at the cabin. Downstairs comprised the sitting room, which was quite big with low bookshelves fronting the open fireplace and several battered chairs in addition to the sofa. Through one open door she could glimpse a kitchen and there were a couple of other rooms at the back as well. Wooden stairs led up to a galleried landing which overlooked the downstairs, and off the landing were several rooms, probably bedrooms.

'You've never so much as lifted a duster, have you?' he asked quietly and she flushed. 'What about cooking? Can you cook?'

'I suppose so.'

'You *suppose* so?'

'I—I've never needed to cook. Ethel looks after Dad and me...' Even to her own ears, her résumé sounded woefully inadequate, and she tossed her hair back and glared at him. 'I guess I could try my hand at doing something in the kitchen. It can't be that difficult...'

'What *do* you do?' Luke asked with mortifying curiosity.

'I—I'm a trained interior designer, if you want to know.' Except, she did precious little of that, she thought with a stab of guilt. Her father had funded her course and had even provided her with her first clients, but her enthusiasm had gradually waned; she realised that she had not done anything to further her career for years now. Socialising had left little time for the more serious business of working and, without the need to earn a living, she had found it easy to be diverted.

'That must keep you busy. Does it?'

'Have I asked you what *you* do?' Miranda retorted hotly feeling defensive at the realisation that, if he knew the truth about her idle lifestyle, he wouldn't be very impressed.

'So it *doesn't* keep you busy, I take it,' he replied calmly.

'I never said that!'

'Oh, but your lack of answer tells me that you don't spend your days earning a crust as an interior designer. Which leads me to conclude that you really do nothing with your life except...what...party? Have fun holidays wherever the in crowd happens to be? I know your type.'

'It's important to enjoy life,' Miranda said for the sake of argument, even though she knew that she was on losing ground.

'You'd better go and get changed.' He stood next to her and then grasped her arm with his fingers, help that she reluctantly accepted. 'You can borrow some of my clothes, even though they're probably not quite up to your standard, and then I'll cook us something to eat.'

'Thank you,' she muttered, out of good manners—though she was looking forward to putting on dry clothes.

Whenever she tried to stand, even slightly, on her hurt foot, she could feel her whole body flinch in discomfort. The bandage had made it feel better, or at least had given her the illusion of thinking that it did, but who cared whether she could hop, skip and jump in the morning? She would still be stuck here in ferocious bad weather with this unbearable man who moved from hostility to contempt with the ease of a magician. Through the little panes of the window she could see the snow whipping around outside and she could hear it as well. The low howl of wind and the soft spitting of the snowdrops. It was a nightmare.

'Don't be too proud to ask for help,' he threw in casually, as she clung to the banister and tried to heave herself up, and Miranda looked at him sourly. Blue eyes, a deeper more piercing shade than her own aquamarine-blue and infinitely more opaque, met hers. His eyebrows were dark, the same raven darkness of his hair. But, close to him like this, she noticed his eyelashes, which were thick and long and unexpectedly attractive.

'If you wouldn't mind...' she said, looking away, and he obligingly swept her off her feet and carried her upstairs as though she weighed less than a feather. A huge wave of exhaustion swept over her and she had to fight to keep her eyes open.

It felt so comfortable being carried like this. She could feel the strength of his body against her, like steel. The hands supporting her were large and powerful, like the rest of him; and, unlike most of the men she socialised with, he smelt not of expensive aftershave but of something more masculine and tangy. Very rough and ready, she thought. He would be if he lived here and spent his life chopping logs and skiing.

'There's just the one bathroom,' he said, pushing open

the door with his foot and then settling her on the chair
by the bath. 'So make sure you leave it just as you found
it. I don't intend to have to clean up after you.'

Without bothering to give her a second glance, he began running the bath, testing the water with his hand,
squatting by the side of the bath so that his shirt lifted
slightly to reveal a slither of hard brown skin.

'I'd better get you undressed.' He turned towards her
and she was propelled out of her lazy observation of him.

'No, thank you!'

'You mean you can do it all yourself? With that ankle
of yours?'

'I'm very grateful to have been rescued by you,'
Miranda said stiffly, 'but if you lay a finger on me, I swear
I'll scream this place down.'

'Oh, will you?' He leaned over her, caging her in with
his hands and making sure that there was no place for her
to look but at his face. His features were blunt and over-
poweringly masculine and she cringed back into the chair
like a startled victim of a bird of prey. 'And who do you
think will hear you? But...' as quickly as he had leaned
over her, he stood back, straightening to his massive
height, and looked at her with an insolent lack of respect
'...far be it from me to invade your maidenly privacy.
Just make sure you clean up after yourself. I don't want
to find any of this...' without warning he lifted some
strands of her hair between his fingers so that the long
fine white-blonde hair trailed over his wrists '...clogging
up my plug hole.'

It took one full hour for her to complete her bath. Struggling out of her layers of ski gear was a feat along the
lines of running five marathons in a row. And then, when
she finally decided that her body would shrivel from over-
exposure to bath water, she got out and was confronted

with the further indignity of yelling for him from the top of the stairs with a towel wrapped around her and her hair hanging limply wet down her back.

'I wonder if I might borrow those clothes you mentioned?' she told him when he finally surfaced at the bottom of the stairs with a saucepan in his hand.

'I'm sorry?'

'I asked whether I might borrow those clothes you mentioned?' Miranda repeated tersely. The towel barely covered her body. He must have known how awkward she felt standing here like this but either he didn't give a damn or else he frankly enjoyed her discomfort. Or both.

'I heard that bit. I'm waiting for you to finish your request.'

'*Please.*'

'That's much better.' He deposited the pan on the small wooden table at the bottom of the stairs and then headed up towards her. 'You can use the spare bedroom,' he said, pushing open a door to reveal a small, cosy room with its own open fireplace. There was just enough space for the single bed, a dressing table with a mirror and a chest of drawers. Miranda propped herself up against the door frame and looked around it. She was used to sleeping in a double bed. Even when she stayed in hotels, she always insisted on a double bed, however much extra the room might cost. She liked having a lot of space when she went to sleep. Single beds reminded her of hospitals and hospitals reminded her of her mother who had died in one when she had been barely knee-high to a grasshopper.

'Not good enough for m'lady?' For a big man, he moved with disconcerting stealth, she thought, swinging around to face him and finding a bundle of clothes shoved into her hands.

'It's fine. Thank you.'

'Good. Because the only king-sized bed is in my room and my excessive hospitality does have its limits. Now, shall I help m'lady inside?' Without giving her time to answer, he placed his hand squarely around her waist, leaving her no option but to clutch the loosening towel with one hand and place the other around his neck.

'Now...' He stood back and looked down at her with his arms folded '...you can get changed, and I'll be up in fifteen minutes with something for you to eat. M'lady.' He gave a mock salute.

'Could you please stop calling me that?'

'M'lady?' His dangerous blue eyes widened with an expression of ridiculously inept innocence. 'But why?'

'Because it's not my name.'

He didn't bother to answer that. Instead he moved across to the dead fireplace. 'Cold in here, isn't it? But then, I wasn't expecting company or else I would have lit this fire and had the room warm and ready. You'd better get dressed. You're trembling. I'll put your clothes to dry in front of the fire downstairs.'

'Thank you.'

'And I'll bring some logs up later and get this fire going.'

'I would appreciate that.' Miranda could feel goose pimples on her arms from the abrupt change in temperature after the warm bathroom. 'You needn't worry, Mr Decroix...'

'Luke, please. Why stand on formality when we'll be living together?' He inclined his head to look at her over his shoulder, and she realised, with a little start, that it wasn't simply his face that was attractive, but the whole package. In a primitive, masculine sort of way. He had the kind of unchiselled, powerful good looks that drew stares, and she immediately looked away just in case he thought that she was staring.

'My father will more than compensate you for any trouble.'

This time, he turned slowly to look at her and an expression of contemptuous amusement gathered itself in the corners of his mouth and glittered in the blue, brooding eyes. 'How reassuring. And you think that I might need the compensation, do you?'

Miranda edged her way inelegantly to the bed and slipped under the covers with her towel still in place and the bundle of clothes still in one hand; then she drew the duvet all the way up to her chin. If he insisted on ignoring her chattering teeth and continuing the conversation, then she might as well be warm.

'It's only fair after putting you to all this trouble. But most people wouldn't say no to a bit of financial help,' she finally said, awkwardly.

His blue eyes narrowed coldly on her face. 'Oh, dear. Would you have reached that conclusion by any chance because of my ragged clothing?'

'I hadn't noticed the state of your clothing,' Miranda plunged on. 'I have no idea about your financial circumstances...I don't know what you do for a living. But, well...' His shuttered look was hardly encouraging but now that she'd started, she felt compelled to reach some sort of conclusion to her speculations. '...there can't be that many well-paid jobs that you could do from this remote location...can there...?' Her voice trailed off into silence while Luke continued to observe her with embarrassing intensity.

He shook his head with a low laugh, 'I don't live here all the time, *Miranda*.' He paused for a moment, looking as if he was pondering something very deeply. 'In fact,

I'm just looking after this place actually—for the time being.'

'Oh, I see!' That would explain a lot. His English accent, for a start. He was probably one of these nomadic types who made their way round the world doing manual chores for people. Earning a crust.

He didn't say anything. After a few minutes his expression lightened and he shrugged. 'I'll bring you up something to eat. Your foot will feel much better in the morning.'

He didn't call her m'lady again, although he more than made up for the thoughtful omission by bowing grandly at the door before he left; but Miranda no longer had the energy to feel annoyed. She was too sleepy. She would just close her eyes for a few minutes before she changed and he returned with her food.

CHAPTER TWO

THE room was warm. That was the first thing Miranda noticed when she next surfaced. A warm room and she was changed. Her eyes flickered open and for a few seconds she experienced the disorientation that sometimes attacks when the surroundings are new and unfamiliar. Then her memory returned with a crash and the image of Luke's dark, striking and unpleasantly cynical face filled her head.

It was as though the thought had been enough to summon him, because just at that moment her bedroom door was pushed open and she saw the object of her wandering mind filling out the doorway, with a tray in his hands. Sleep had not managed to diminish his suffocating masculinity. In fact, she literally drew her breath in as he dwarfed the small room, primitively forceful despite the tea towel slung over his shoulder.

'So you're up at last.' He moved across to the curtains and yanked them open, exposing a watery grey light and the sight of fast-falling snow. 'Breakfast.' He deposited the tray on the bed and Miranda struggled up into a sitting position.

'How long was I asleep?' She stretched and the sleeves of the oversized grey tee shirt rode down to expose her slender, pale forearms.

'Over ten hours.'

'Over ten hours!'

'I dutifully came with your supper only to find you sound asleep and snoring…'

'I do not snore!'

'How do you know that?' he asked snidely, pulling up a chair so that he could sit and watch her. 'It's not the sort of thing a lover might bring to your attention. Anyway, I lit the fire to get the icicles off the ceiling and left you.' He linked his fingers together and looked as she bit into the toast and then hungrily began demolishing what was on the plate: A fried egg, bacon, baked beans, just the sort of breakfast she had always avoided.

'After I'd changed you, of course.'

Miranda paused with the last bit of toast *en route* to her mouth and started at him. '*You* change me?'

'Shocking, isn't it?' He clasped his hands behind his head and stretched out his legs, crossing them at the ankles. 'Do you think that Daddy might refuse me my much needed financial compensation if he knew?'

'You're not funny!' She had somehow assumed that she had changed herself, even though she had no recollection of doing any such thing, but she could tell from the gleam in his eyes that the man wasn't lying. He had unwrapped the towel from her and had pulled on a tee shirt, and somewhere along the line those big hands of his had touched her shoulders, her stomach, her breasts. 'You had no right!'

'I do beg Your Highness's pardon, but going to sleep with a wet towel around you in a damp room would just have compounded the sprained ankle with a healthy dose of pneumonia.'

'You still had no right! You should have awakened me!'

'I'll try and remember the next time, if you try and remember to stick to the nursery slopes so that there won't *be* a next time. You haven't eaten all your egg up.'

'I've lost my appetite.' She closed her knife and fork and reclined back on the pillow.

'In which case, you'd better try and find it. You're building your strength up and step one is eating all that breakfast, meticulously prepared by my own fair hands.' He leaned forward. 'Maybe you'd like me to feed the rest to you…'

Miranda gave a little yelp of denial and hurriedly ate what was left on her plate, then she wiped her mouth with the paper napkin and folded her arms.

'Now,' he said implacably, standing up to remove the tray and then whipping the duvet off her so that she yelped even louder, this time in enraged discomfort, 'the next thing I advise you to do is test that foot of yours.'

'And would you like to hear what *I* advise *you* to do?'

'Not really. Here, hold my hand and stand up.'

'Or else what…?'

'You don't want to find out,' he said silkily. 'Now, stand up and try that foot of yours.'

When she remained on the bed, he leaned over her and said in a low, razor-sharp voice, 'Shall I just remind you that you're an unwanted and unwelcome intrusion into my house…'

'*Your* house?'

'While I'm looking after it, it's my house. And if you think you're going to play the grand princess and laze around for the next few days, or weeks if this weather doesn't sort itself out, then you're in for a shock. I'm not a man who puts up with the wiles and tantrums of a spoiled little rich girl!'

'How *dare you* speak to me like that?' Her imperious voice, which reflected more than anything else her be-musement at finding herself in the situation she was in and dealing with the man in front of her, failed to strike a chord. Or rather it did. Luke burst out laughing.

'Oh, dear,' he said, sobering up but not sufficiently to stop the occasional cynical chuckle from slipping through. 'Oh, dear, dear, dear. And you wonder why I call you *m'lady*? Now, up!'

Miranda reluctantly swung her legs over the side of the bed, noting with relief that the tee shirt modestly reached down to just above her knees, and grasped his proffered hand.

'Try and put a little weight on it.'

'I can't.'

'Just try, and stop acting like a baby.'

Which did it. She tentatively touched the ground with her foot and discovered as she applied a bit more pressure that the immediate searing pain she had felt the previous day had become more of a persistent, dull discomfort.

'I'll remove the bandage before you get dressed and soak your foot in some cold water and then I'll truss you up again.'

'There's no need. I can do that myself.'

'Should I allow you to do that, I would live for ever in fear of Daddy's avenging wrath.'

Miranda stopped her halting walk and stared up at him. 'I hate that. Why are you so…horrible and *scathing* about me? You don't even know who I am or what sort of person I am! Yet you feel it's all right to make nasty, derogatory comments about me and my father. Daddy always said that the worst snobs are the inverted snobs. He always said that they're the worst because they never give you a chance to prove yourself one way or another. They just assume that because someone has money, then they can't be worthwhile.' She found herself breathing shallowly as she stared up into his blue eyes.

'Is that what you think I am?' he finally asked curiously. 'An inverted snob?'

'Why else would you be so awful? Just because you don't have any money doesn't make it my fault!'

'No, I guess you're right,' he said in an odd voice, 'it doesn't, does it?'

Instead of feeling pleased at this unexpected victory, Miranda felt suddenly nervous. Nervous because she had become quickly accustomed to his hostility and the lack of it was confusing.

'My foot feels a lot better,' she said, to change the subject, supporting herself on his arm as they headed slowly towards the bathroom, where a further unwanted reminder of his ministrations confronted her in the shape of the blue bath towel she had used the night before, neatly hanging over the towel rail.

She sat on the closed toilet seat and watched as he filled a plastic basin with cold water.

'It's freezing,' she gasped as he soaked her foot.

He said, without looking up, 'It'll reduce most of the rest of the swelling. Don't worry. You'll get used to the temperature. There.' He held up her foot and examined it like a butcher sizing up a joint of meat. 'Not very pretty, but it'll do.' Then he carefully rebandaged it, taking his time. 'Now, there's a change of clothes behind you on the ledge and you might want to do something with that hair of yours. Tie it up, perhaps. Not very practical having that mane swinging around, I shouldn't think.'

'Actually,' Miranda informed him coolly, 'a woman's *mane* is her crowning glory.'

'Oh, is that so? And I always thought of her crowning glory was her mind. How much I'm learning from you.' He shot her a brief, patronising grin and then left.

Miranda gingerly stood up and for the first time took a

long look at her reflection in the mirror. Her waist-length blonde hair had been damp when she had fallen asleep, but even so it had dried and now fell in its usual silky curtain around her face. Her wide blue eyes absorbed the stunning prettiness of her features then, as she stripped off the oversized tee shirt, idly scanned the exquisite, slender proportions of her body. These looks, she thought dispassionately, had turned heads and had opened countless doors to the world of beautiful people in which she moved. If she had been dowdy and unattractive, would she have been as popular? Would men have beaten a path to her door, however much money her father had? Probably not. For the first time, she realised that her looks carried a downside. The had attracted men like Freddie, but looks were disposable. None of the men in her brittle world ever seemed to take time out to search for what lay beneath the sparkling veneer.

She very quickly washed her face and changed into yet another tee shirt and a pair of jogging bottoms that had to be tied with the tan leather belt thoughtfully left along with the bundle of clothes. Then she made her way down the stairs, refusing to yell for assistance.

Luke was in the kitchen clearing up and, for a few minutes, Miranda hovered uncertainly by the door, wondering what to do next.

'Make yourself at home,' he said drily. 'I don't bite.'

She edged to the pine kitchen table and sat down.

'How long does this caretaker job last?' she asked, for the sake of asking something, and he turned to look at her with a momentary expression of bewilderment. Then his face cleared.

'Oh, *this* caretaker job?' he said carelessly. 'Oh, not very long.'

'And then you...'

'Move on.'

'Move on to what?' He made a good caretaker, she thought. The kitchen was tidy, with a stack of logs neatly chopped and piled in the corner.

'Other things,' he said vaguely. 'Now, normally I tend to spend the days outside, but this blizzard has put paid to that, so we might as well work out some kind of routine here so that you don't get in my way.'

Miranda immediately began to bristle. 'I won't *get in your way*. I'm more than happy to spend my time reading.'

'Good.' He paused to sit down, spinning the chair back so that he sat on it with his hands loosely hanging over the back. 'Because I have some business to attend to on my laptop and I don't want to feel that you're lurking around waiting to be entertained.'

'I don't expect to be entertained.'

'Don't you?'

'I'm quite happy in my own company.' Miranda paused to digest this and realised that she was very seldom in her own company. Even at night, when she flopped into bed, sometimes in the early hours of the morning, she was always too tried to really spend any time on her own. 'What work do you have to do?' she asked curiously. 'On a computer? I wouldn't have thought...'

'That I was clever enough to use a computer? Or maybe you thought that I'd never even heard of one?' He grinned wickedly at her blushing discomfort. 'News of technological breakthroughs do sometimes drift even to we yokels, you know. In fact, I'll take a small bet with you that *you're* the one who doesn't have a clue how to operate a computer.'

Miranda's face went a shade deeper in colour.

'Mmm,' Luke said pensively. 'Not much point having

a computer on the ski slopes, is there? Or at the races? Or in Mustique for a few weeks over summer?'

'I—I—'

'You—you—what?'

'I learned everything about computers when I was doing my design course,' she said, holding her chin up to counteract the level of defensiveness in her voice.

'Oh, yes, that interior design course of yours.' He was virtually smirking, and Miranda glowered impotently at him. 'Well, wait right here.' He stood up and she watched suspiciously while he disappeared out of the kitchen, only to return minutes later with a sleek black laptop in his hand.

'There, now.' He flicked it open, pressed a few buttons and the screen unfolded into life. 'Why don't you amuse yourself with this for a little while just while I fetch some more logs from the outside shed and do a bit of chopping.' He moved swiftly around the table so that he was bending over her, one hand resting on the table top, the other pressing various icons until an architectural drawing of a house appeared on the screen.

'What's this?'

'This, my dear interior designer, is a house.'

'Whose house?'

'Oh, just a little dwelling my boss has in mind to renovate. He knows I like playing on the computer now and again, so he lent me this file to have a look at.'

Miranda looked at him narrowly. 'Now, why would your boss do something like that?'

Luke's answer was so swift that she almost wondered whether it had been prepared. 'We go back a ways. If you move this little gadget here, called a mouse, hey presto, you can zoom all over the place.'

Miranda gritted her teeth and allowed him to have his

fun. He would be laughing on the other side of his arrogant, handsome face when she presented him with her ideas, even if the whole lot was erased never to be seen again. The last job she had done of any magnitude had been years previously, but she could feel a stirring of interest in her veins as she glanced at the outlines of a house in front of her.

'You mean you babysit his cabin every year?'

'Oh, yes. It's a long-standing arrangement.' He hadn't straightened, so when he spoke his breath brushed against her cheek and into her ear. 'He must have thought that I might get lonesome, stuck out here as I am, hence this little file for me to play with. Little did he know that I would have unexpected company.' He stood up and flexed his muscles. 'You can mess around however you like. Design whatever you want. It can all be deleted. Why don't you go into the sitting room and relax in front of that roaring fire and show me what you can do with this little toy.'

'I guess you do get lonely here for weeks, maybe months, on end,' Miranda said, half to herself, as she settled onto the big sofa, with the computer on her lap. 'How on earth do you fill your time?'

'Loneliness is a state of mind,' he said over his shoulder, as he slung on his waterproof jacket and then pulled on some very thick wool socks and a pair of snow boots that were by the door. 'And it can only be filled when you're at peace with yourself.'

'Well, if you want to spout philosophy, then I'll just get on with a bit of this interior design, shall I?' She felt herself smile and when she looked up at him it was to find the smile returned. It gave her the oddest feeling.

'When I get back from my healthy outdoor fun, you can phone your father. Although…' he opened the door and swirls of snow blew in '...I did call him half an hour ago. On your behalf.'

Miranda looked up, stunned by this piece of effrontery but, before she could demand an explanation, he had left the cabin, slamming the front door behind him.

Her poor dad probably assumed that the man was a genial, middle-aged caretaker with a family tucked away further down the slopes. He would have a fit if he knew what Luke Decroix was like, she fretted. Ten fits, in fact. He would round up the forces and gear up for a rescue mission, not that that would be possible, given the state of the weather. The windows in the cabin were small, but not so small that she couldn't get a glimpse of the leaden skies, barely visible through the continuing blizzard. Lord alone knew where she was. The skiing resort, her friends, the faithless Freddie and all the bijou little cafés seemed like a dream.

She began experimenting on the computer and the wheels of her rusty memory slowly cranked into life as she played around with ideas. Every so often, she looked up and was treated occasionally to the sight of Luke outside, tramping through the snow with a shovel over his shoulder, making sure that the doorway was kept as clear of snow as possible. He was certainly dedicated to his job, if nothing else.

When he finally came back in, he was carrying a basket of neatly chopped logs slung over his shoulder which he dumped on the ground. He didn't say anything, just looked at her. Then he divested himself of his wet waterproofs and his boots and socks. His black hair was slick from the snow and he went to squat in front of the fire, rubbing his hands together and raking them through his hair.

'So you haven't got bored yet with fooling around on

the computer?' he asked, with his back to her. He pulled his thick jumper over his head and stood up, pulling down the shirt underneath. Another tee shirt, this time with some faded design on the front of what was once a bulldog next to a glass of beer. 'What have you done?' He sat down next to her, depressing the sofa so much that she had a job not to slide straight into him, thigh against thigh.

'Not much. Is the snow just as heavy outside?'

'What do you think of the house? Like it?'

Miranda angled the screen away from him, suddenly shy at exposing her efforts to him. 'You promised I could use your mobile to call Dad. Which reminds me…' yes, a good healthy dose of irritation to bring her back on course '…whoever said you could call my father? And how did you get his number? And what did you have to say to him, anyway?'

'Questions, questions, questions. Didn't your mother ever tell you that when a man returns from some hard labour, the last thing he needs is a whinging woman?'

'My mother died when I was eight.'

'Oh, yes. I'm sorry.' He leaned back on the sofa, hooking one foot around the leg of the table in front and pulling it towards him so that he could rest both his feet on the surface. He had replaced his boots with the same worn, tasselled loafers that had greeted her when she had arrived the previous day. He rubbed his eyes, then folded his arms behind his head and looked at her.

His blue eyes were hypnotic. When she looked into them, she had the strangest sensation of giddiness and a feeling that, if she wasn't careful, she could easily fall into their fathomless depths and drown.

'You haven't answered my questions,' she reminded him tartly.

'Oh, so I haven't. Well, if you really want to know, I

have a little method of obtaining the number of the last call on my phone, which I did last night after you had called him in his office. And I thought I might as well touch base, let him know that nothing untoward had happened to his baby during the night. Here, call him yourself now if you like.' He felt in his pocket and retrieved the palm-sized phone which he handed to her. Except, he didn't quite hand it over, more dangled it in front of her so that she had to reach for it.

Depressingly, her father seemed to have been reassured by Luke's phone call.

'Might do you a spot of good being stuck in the middle of nowhere for a few days,' he joked, impervious to her horror at any such suggestion. Miranda clamped the phone tighter against her right ear and inclined her body slightly away from Luke's undisguised interest in what she was saying and what was being said to her.

'How can you say that, Dad?' she muttered, but the question was bypassed in her father's sudden need to get going to a meeting. His driver, apparently, was waiting. He had to dash but he would be in touch, probably later in the evening when he was back home.

'I hope he's not too worried about you,' Luke said piously, reaching out for the mobile and resting it on the table next to his feet. 'I *did* try and set his mind at rest. Told him how well you were being looked after. I even said that I had lent you my laptop so that you could amuse yourself on it for a couple of hours.'

'I'm sure my father doesn't want lengthy explanations from *you* on how I'm doing,' Miranda informed him haughtily.

'So, what have you managed to do? Anything at all?'

'You never bothered to tell me what your boss meant

by *renovating*. Does he intend to knock walls down? What specifications is he after?'

'My, my. I take it you're wearing your technical interior designer hat now?'

'If you want to sit there and smirk, then why don't we just forget this?' Miranda said. 'You can have your little toy back to do whatever it is you need to do and I can't imagine what, and I'll just content myself with one of those detective novels on the bookshelf.'

Luke pulled the computer towards him so that it was partially resting on his lap and looked at what she had done. 'So, you *are* capable of using a computer. Accept my humble apologies for implying otherwise...' When she looked at him, his face was patently lacking in remorse. He was flicking through the rooms she had designed, seemingly interested. 'There's no need for a dining room that big,' he murmured.

'How do you know? Don't tell me: you're so close to this boss of yours that you have insider knowledge into how often he plans to entertain and for how many people. Are you sure this boss is a man and not a woman?'

'Oh,' Luke murmured softly, scrolling through her work and using various icons to magnify certain aspects, 'I'm most emphatically certain on that point.'

'Well, what *does* this man want to do with the house?'

'I gather he intends to move out of London and use it as a base for his work. So, and I'm presuming here, I expect he would want a fairly large working area.'

'What does this man do?'

'Something to do with finance, I believe.'

'You mean he hasn't bothered to bore you with the details?' It was Miranda's turn to smirk and she did so with relish. 'Perhaps he thought that you weren't up to understanding the technicalities of his job.'

'What's this?'

'It's an archway. I've bashed through those two rooms and linked them with an archway. On either side you can incorporate stained-glass windows as features to break the monotony of the brick wall.'

'Very creative. He'll like that touch, I'm sure. And what's this?'

'I haven't finished with that bit yet.'

'That's not what I asked.'

'Well, that bit, if you can picture it...'

'Which might be difficult due to the dullness of my brain...' he murmured, without looking at her, apparently absorbed by her little efforts at the task he had set her with his tongue in his cheek.

'Is a wrought-iron gate—and he should be able to get an original one—separating the bathroom from the bed-room, so there's a feeling of tremendous space.' She could feel two patches of excited colour on her cheeks and re-membered that her efforts would be deleted before her enforced stay was over.

'Very imaginative.' He closed the screen, shut the lid of the computer and stood up, leaving a void of coldness next to her. He lazily tipped a couple of logs into the fire, so that it sparked up again, hissing, then he glanced over to the bookshelf and selected a book, tossing it lightly to her.

'What's this for?'

'Reading fodder.'

'And what about my design work?'

'What about it?' he asked, perching on the edge of the low bookshelf and inspecting her face coolly.

'Don't you want me to continue?'

'Sure, if you want. Just thought you might want a

break, though, after all the hard work.' He gave her a slow, challenging smile.

'Meaning...what?'

Luke shrugged his massive shoulders casually. 'Meaning that you might need to take a little time out, get accustomed to doing something other than thinking about what your next temporary pleasure might be.'

Miranda looked at him with a sudden flare of anger. He didn't give up, did he? Now that he had grown used to the thought that she might be around for a few days, interrupting his lifestyle, whatever that might be, he had decided to enjoy himself at her expense. The worst of it was that it hurt. His opinions of her shouldn't matter but for some reason they did. Probably, she thought bitterly, because she was forced to sit them out. She couldn't run away because there was nowhere to run to.

'That's not fair,' she muttered.

'Isn't it? I told your father that this wasn't a five-star hotel and that I would make sure that you were all right and delivered back to him safe and sound, but that in the process you would be expected to work for the favour. He seemed delighted. He obviously knows you better than you know yourself.'

'You told my father, *what*? You have *no right* to discuss me with my father!' she found that she was spluttering in outrage. *'Just who do you think you are?'*

Instead of reacting to her tone, he simply raised his eyebrows, and the silence after she had vented her fury stretched between them like a piece of elastic. He went to one of the deep chairs, picked up the computer and opened it, scrupulously ignoring her presence as he quietly examined something on the screen and began typing on the keypad.

'*Will you listen to me when I'm trying to talk to you?*'

He didn't appear to have even heard her protest. He simply continued what he was doing and, in a burst of anger, Miranda stood up. It only took a few seconds for her to hobble to the power point and yank out the plug to his computer which died into blackness.

This time he *did* notice her.

His blue eyes became slits and she felt a thrill of sudden, nervous terror skitter through her veins like alcohol. Then he was on his feet, grasping her by her arms so tightly that she cried out.

'Don't you *ever, ever* do anything like that again! Do you understand me?' He shook her slightly and her long hair, which she had made no effort to tie back, swung around her face. She felt like a rag doll at the mercy of a raging bull. 'I will *not tolerate* you stamping your feet like a toddler deprived of a treat whenever you fancy no one's paying you any attention!'

'I'm sorry,' Miranda choked out, dismayed at what she had done and embarrassed to be likened to a toddler. 'You're hurting me!'

He released her but didn't step back. He just continued watching her as she rubbed her arms and she knew that he was making an effort to keep his temper in check. When she glanced up, she could see the vein throbbing in his neck.

'I'm really sorry,' she repeated, to break the deathly silence and deflect the alarming power of his blue eyes.

'Sit down.' The stillness of his voice was as threatening as his roar had been a few minutes ago and Miranda shakily sat back down, leaning forward tensely to accept the brunt of his reprimands. She deserved it. Yanking that plug out of its socket had been the action of a thwarted child and there was no point in trying to use any ham line about acting in retaliation because he hadn't done anything to her. He had ignored her and his patent indifference had stung and had provoked her into a show of puerile stupidity.

'This won't do, Miranda, will it?' He too was leaning forward, his elbows resting on his thighs, his expression hard. 'You're not a child and you must stop behaving like one. Like it or not, you're here with me and you're going to act like an adult. That little display of temper will be the last, do you read me loud and clear?'

Miranda nodded miserably. 'I...' Oh, God. She could feel her eyes beginning to brim over and she hated herself for the weakness. She couldn't remember a time when she had cried in front of anyone, except for her father. She had certainly never shed a tear over any of her boyfriends nor had she ever felt provoked enough by any of them to cry either in their presence or out of it. Not even when she had caught Freddie *in flagrante delicto*. Her pride had been wounded, yes, but her reaction had been one of fury rather than sorrow. Maybe she was going stir crazy because of the isolation.

He waited for her to continue while she stared down at her slender fingers and tried not to gulp too loudly.

'I...enjoyed doing that design work on the computer,' was all she could think of saying. Her mind had become cloudy and she licked her lips and tried to regain control of her thoughts. She sneaked a glance at him and saw that he was still looking at her at least, his head tilted to one side as though making sure that nothing went unheard. 'It's easy for you,' she said defiantly, but her defiance was stillborn.

'Why is it easy for me?'

'Because…you seem happy with your life, moving from place to place.'

For no reason, he looked momentarily uncomfortable with what she had said, but the shadow of unease was soon gone. 'I get the feeling that your father is worried about you.'

Miranda shrugged, too tired to care whether he mentioned her father or not. What did it matter anyway? She wasn't going to be here for ever. She could unburden herself on this passing stranger if she wanted, safe in the knowledge that nothing would come back to haunt her. Briefly, they were sharing the same space, but not for long.

'What does…' he imitated her shrug '…*that* mean?'

'All fathers worry about their daughters,' Miranda said uncomfortably. 'Especially when there's no one else to share the worry with.'

'And what exactly do you give him to worry about?'

'I don't suppose he's too impressed with my lifestyle,' Miranda admitted. Just saying it aloud made her mouth taste sour. It was an admission she had never made to anyone in her life before. 'He thinks that I should settle down…'

'You mean get married?'

'Oh, good heavens, no! I'm only twenty-five!' She laughed at the idea. 'Besides, I can't think of any suitable candidates for the role. If I had ever considered settling down with any of the boys I went out with, my father would have had a heart attack on the spot!'

'Perhaps you should have been looking for a man instead of a boy,' Luke drawled.

Miranda averted her eyes from the blatantly masculine figure sprawling in the chair. 'By *settle down* I mean get a job.'

'Why haven't you? You're talented enough…'

'I'm what…?'

'Talented.' He gave her a slow, amused smile. 'Like me complimenting you, do you?'

Miranda went scarlet. 'I don't care either way,' she informed him nonchalantly. That slow, measured smile made her feel as though she had been physically touched. It gave her goose bumps.

'Good,' he murmured, his eyes still fastened on hers, 'because the last thing I want are any complications.'

CHAPTER THREE

NOR did she.

In fact, she thought, all she wanted to do was clear out of this wretched cabin and get back to London.

At any rate, it was what she firmly told herself. And she was only forced to confront the truth when, after three days of ferocious blizzard, Luke returned from his daily log-chopping exercise and announced that the sky was beginning to look a little healthier.

'What does that mean?' Miranda looked up from the computer and frowned.

'It means, Your Highness, that our friendly blizzard might be going away.' He sauntered over to the fire and removed his jumper. This time, he removed his tee shirt as well, which was soaked. He had his back to her, and Miranda watched, mesmerised, at the movement of muscle beneath skin as he bent slightly to warm his hands.

'Don't call me that,' she said automatically, while her mind struggled to function.

'Sorry.' He half turned to her and grinned with wicked amusement.

'You were telling me about the blizzard,' she said hurriedly, relieved when he turned back to the fire.

'Oh, yes. I think it's clearing.' He was wearing, for the first time, a pair of faded jeans and he began to fumble with the button.

'What,' she squeaked, 'are you doing?'

'Getting out of these clothes. Bloody tripped with the logs in my arms and fell flat on my face in the snow.'

'Good thing you didn't sprain that ankle of yours,' she said, except the thread of tension in her voice didn't quite turn her remark into the light-hearted quip she had hoped. How could she sound light-hearted when she was finding it difficult to breathe? It wasn't physically possible.

'I won't embarrass you, will I?' he asked, pausing to turn completely around and look at her.

His hand was hovering by the top button of his trousers, which had been undone so that the waistband of his jeans curled open, resting lightly on his lean lips and providing a tantalising glimpse of the flat, hard planes of his stomach down, slightly past, his navel.

'I'd prefer to strip down here and leave these clothes to dry by the fire instead of dripping my way upstairs, but if it makes you feel uncomfortable…'

'Not at all!' Miranda trilled in a high-pitched voice. She made sure to look directly at his face although her racing pulse was all too aware of the rest of him; tanned, muscled and disturbingly intrusive. 'I'm the uninvited guest, after all! You go ahead and do exactly as you please.' She busied herself with the laptop computer, glaring at the framework of the room she was working on with her face pressed as close to the screen as it could get without the image becoming blurred in the process.

She could hear the rustle of clothes as he shifted out of his jeans and arranged them on the wooden contraption by the side of the fire, which was permanently on view and almost permanently draped with some item of outdoor clothing.

Couldn't he move any faster? she wondered edgily.

She sneaked a quick look at his feet and quickly resumed her glaring inspection of the screen without focusing on it.

'Your ankle seems almost healed,' he said conversationally.

Miranda replied to the screen. 'Yup.'

'Which room are you concentrating on?' he asked drily.

She said, clearing her throat, 'The kitchen, I think.'

'You think?'

'It's the kitchen!' she snapped, furiously concentrating just in case he decided that a closer inspection of what she was doing was warranted. But he didn't. He just laughed softly and headed upstairs. She found her wits again, breathing a long, shuddering sigh of relief when she knew that he was no longer around.

What did he mean that the blizzard was going? Miranda gently set aside the computer, which she was now utterly familiar and used whenever it was available, and walked slowly across to the window and peered out.

The snow was still falling, but he was right. Sky was visible, blue sky at that.

'Unfortunately…' came the familiar voice from behind her, and she swung around to look at him. His jeans had been replaced with a more presentable pair of trousers than he had worn over the previous few days although the tee shirt was still of the weathered barely-visible-motto variety '…the break in the weather doesn't mean that you'll be able to leave immediately. Sorry.' He lifted his shoulders ruefully. 'The only way out of here is still by ski and until your ankle can fully support the weight, you're going to have to stay put.'

'What about helicopter?'

'What about it?'

'My father could send a helicopter for me. In fact, he almost certainly will want to…'

She wasn't ready to leave. Not yet. The realisation hit

her like a ton of bricks and left her confused and ready
for an argument.

Luke gave one of those nonchalant shrugs of his that
indicated closure on the subject, and she followed him
into the kitchen. Walking was still uncomfortable, but she
no longer had to support herself everywhere she went. She
could just about manage to lumber along ungracefully but
fairly efficiently.

'Well?' she pressed on behind him as he put the kettle
on to boil. 'What do you think?'

'If you want to mention it to him when you call then
by all means do so.'

'I thought you would have been glad to see the back
of me,' Miranda continued nastily. 'After all, you've told
me often enough that I'm unwelcome.'

Luke turned around and perched on the edge of the
counter, tapping the spoon in his hand softly against his
chin. 'A helicopter's fine but I don't suppose it's occurred
to you that the snow is still falling fairly heavily and vision might be obscured? Or maybe it occurred to you, but
your craving to be back in the swing of the fast lane in
London conveniently overrode any guilt that you might
be endangering other people's lives in the process? Ah,
no. I see that possibility hadn't occurred to you at all.
Now, why am I not surprised when you're so used to
getting what you want?'

'Not with you!' The words were out before she could
call them back.

'No, my darling, not with me.' He said the word *darling* with the brush of soft caress in his voice although
his eyes were dangerously cool and brooding. 'Now
lunch. I think it's time you started investigating what can
be done in a kitchen.'

Which made it sound as though she had spent the past

few days in a collapsed, pathetic and useless heap on the
sofa playing with the toy, as he liked to describe it. She
had obeyed his orders and made sure that the bathroom
was always clean and free from the long blonde hair,
which he apparently saw as a hindrance; her bedroom was
spotless, despite the fact that making up her bed was only
now getting easier.

'I thought you enjoyed cooking,' she said sweetly. 'You
said you liked to cook because the last thing you needed
in your busy, nomadic life was a woman around thinking
that she could win you through her food.' It was surprising
that they had managed to have any conversations at all,
she thought, considering he was fairly beastly to her most
of the time, but she now realised that they had spent most
of their evenings chatting, in the absence of anything else
to do. He had even started teaching her how to play chess,
although, typically, he had refused to play below his high
standard in order to accommodate the fact that she was a
beginner.

'Did I say that?'

'You did,' she said smugly, 'after a bottle of wine.'

'You'll have to get rid of that hair of yours if you're
gong to be of any use to me,' he said abruptly. 'Long hair
and cooking don't make a happy combination.'

'I'll tell it to go away, shall I?' She shook it away from
her face.

'No, I will. Sit down.'

Miranda obligingly sat and watched as he rustled in a
drawer and then moved behind her. When she was about
to turn her head to follow him, she felt his hands on either
side of her face and her body froze in total compliance.

He began to brush her hair. In the small kitchen, with
the snow swirling madly outside and only the noise of the
clock on the wall to compete for sound, the gesture

seemed suggestively erotic. The feel of his hands as the brush stroked her hair away from her face started a drum roll of steady excitement pulsing through her veins and she forced herself to relax, closing her eyes and dipping her head backwards so that he had to gather all her hair in one hand while he brushed with the other.

'Like this, do you, m'lady?' he asked softly, amused as he carried on brushing; Miranda murmured something by way of assent. Her whole body had relaxed now, with her arms falling on either side of the chair like a rag doll's and her legs stretched out in front of her.

'And do you have a little woman who comes in every day to do this?' His deep voice was rich with a hypnotic, teasing familiarity. Miranda didn't open her eyes, although her mouth curved into a smile.

'A little man, actually. Or rather, a great, big, strong hunk. Twice a day he brushes my hair one hundred times.'

'A great, big, strong hunk. Mmm. That's the type you go for, is it?'

Maybe it was because they weren't facing each other and she didn't have to do battle with those penetrating cobalt eyes, but Miranda could feel herself falling in with this light, strangely invigorating, banter. She squirmed like a cat finding a better position and loosely linked her fingers together on her stomach. The jogging pants he had lent her were too long and she had rolled them several times at the waistband. She idly played with the overlap of stretchy material, rolling her thumbs on them, smiling contentedly.

'The hunkier the better.' She giggled. 'Sadly, I have yet to meet anyone fitting that description.'

'You mean Freddie wasn't a great, big, strong hunk?' His voice was lazy and only mildly curious. Just conversationally passing the time of day, it seemed to imply.

'He was tall, at any rate.' Well-built enough, Miranda thought languidly, but soft and well-manicured; baby soft.

'Care to tell me what happened between you two?'

'Oh, the usual. I caught him with his hands on another woman. A curvy, dark-haired Italian who couldn't have been more than eighteen and should have been cleaning our chalet instead of unbuttoning her blouse to my ex-boyfriend.' She gave a snort of derisory laughter. 'I hit the roof, skied off and the rest is history.'

'Were you jealous?'

'I was angry, but, no, I wasn't jealous. I'm not a jealous type of person.'

He began to massage her scalp and Miranda gave a little moan of sheer pleasure. Free of any tangles, her long hair spilled over his rhythmically moving fingers like a waterfall.

'I take it from your tone of voice that you've recovered from your heartbreak?'

There were alarm bells ringing somewhere. In her head, she thought. Because something was telling her that this easy but intensely personal conversation was dangerous somehow.

'My heart was never broken,' she informed him drowsily. 'I was going to break up with Freddie anyway. He was dull, dull, dull. You wouldn't believe the bottles of after-shave he got through! He even had facials once a month.'

'And has m'lady's heart *ever* been broken?' His voice insinuated itself into her head and was as pleasurable as the fingers pressing gently against her scalp.

'Nope. Has yours?'

'When I was thirteen I was forced to face the unpalatable fact that my high school French teacher didn't fancy me.'

'And that's the closest you've come to having your heart broken?' Miranda teased.

'Shocking, isn't it? By the ripe old age of thirty-four, I should have had my heart broken at least three or four times.'

'Maybe your wandering lifestyle doesn't allow women long enough to be around to get to you.'

'Oh, I don't think that's it at all,' he said with a low laugh and she had a sudden, jolting image of Luke with other women and she felt the sour bile of some primitive emotion rip through her. All these women, she thought, who were undaunted by his lifestyle, who were probably prepared to follow him to the ends of the earth because, as she had seen for herself, when he wanted to be charming, he could entice the birds from the trees. Just like he was doing now, lulling her into this little game of confidences, so that she could admit that her love life was a mess and always had been. She pulled herself forward and held her hair in pony-tail.

'Have you got something I could tie this back with, then?'

'Will a rubber band do?'

'Rubber bands are no good for my hair,' Miranda told him irritably, 'but I suppose it'll have to do.' She reached behind her with a free hand and then flicked her hair secure with the rubber band and brought her legs and the rest of herself back to solid ground. She would have to remind herself that solid ground was precisely where she belonged. Reality was waiting for her just around the corner and it wouldn't do to fall victim to any fantasies. Nor to be lulled into imagining that this bizarre relationship, into which she had found herself catapulted, was somehow reality. It wasn't.

'You were going to teach me how to cook? Not that I don't already know.'

'I thought you said that your faithful housekeeper did all those mundane tasks.' He strolled around the table so that he was facing her once more.

'I never said that cooking was a *mundane task*,' Miranda responded tartly. At least they were back to their normal, bouncing-sarcasm-off-each-other routine but, she realised with dismay, that she no longer found his jibes offensive. Somewhere along the line, the tenor of his voice when he referred to her as m'lady or Your Highness had altered. It was no longer laced with the aggressive hostility that had been so apparent when she had first arrived. When, she wondered, had that happened?

And she had stopped being defensive. Her irritation at some of the things he said was a display more of habit than intent.

'Oh, I just assumed...'

'Because,' she rounded on him, 'you spend all your time *assuming* too much!'

'Why the sudden display of vitriol, Miranda? Didn't you enjoy talking to me when I was combing your hair? Or did you think that I was getting a little too close to the real Miranda?'

The man saw far too much! She glowered at him impotently and he smiled with feline, satisfied speculation at her flushed face.

'You're not as shallow as you pretend, are you? You babble along with the best of them but, underneath, something inside is stirring, isn't it? Looking for more? Tut, tut. Dangerous situation.'

'I suppose with all this time on your hands you've got nothing better to do than drone on the minute you find yourself in company!' Miranda shot back, and he grinned, untouched by her wayward dart. 'I detect a severe case of company starvation! Perhaps the owner of this house should give you a dog so that you can bore him to death with your opinions!'

Luke burst out laughing. 'Methinks,' he said when he had sobered up, 'the lady doth protest too much.'

'Methinks,' Miranda replied, 'we'll have no lunch if the so-called chef doesn't stop nosing into my life!'

He was still grinning fifteen minutes later after he had forced his scowling protégé to recite a summary of her culinary abilities.

'Rusty, in other words,' he summarised, when her stuttering résumé had reached a dead end. 'Well, we'd better set that straight if you're going to repay my generous hospitality by looking after me for a change now that your ankle's on the mend.'

'I didn't realise that that was part of the deal.'

'Oh, didn't you? Maybe I didn't make myself clear enough in that case. Look in that cupboard over there and fish out some onions. There's garlic in the fridge. We'll start with something simple, shall we? First of all, fill a saucepan with water and let's put it on to boil. That'll require some ingenuity as you'll have to light the stove and place the saucepan squarely over the fire.'

Miranda was tempted to place the saucepan squarely over his head.

'Now,' he carried on in the overpatient voice of someone addressing a slow learner of dubious intelligence, 'put a pinch of salt in the water. Just a pinch.'

'I know what a pinch of salt is.'

'There, very good. Now onions. Peel and chop roughly.' He slid two onions across to her and Miranda painstakingly removed the brown skin. Really, this was something she hadn't done for quite some time. Not, in fact, since she had experimented in her food and technology class as a kid.

Instead of busying himself by being useful, he adopted a watchful pose by the kitchen counter, perched on the edge, arms folded.

'I'm surprised you're not an expert cook after going to finishing school,' he commented, as she clumsily peeled one layer of onion skin only to be confronted with another layer in need of stripping. 'Didn't they teach you girls all about haute cuisine along with deportment and the importance of knowing how to set a table and identifying which glass to use for which particular alcoholic drink? Useful pointers like that?'

'I didn't *go* to finishing school,' Miranda said coolly. 'Haven't you got anything to do other than stand there and look at me?'

'Nope.'

'I must be more fascinating than I thought, in that case.' She turned to look at him and saw in her mind's eye the image of him with his fingers resting lightly on that top button of his jeans, his torso lean and muscled, and she swallowed convulsively.

'Why didn't you go to finishing school? I thought that was essential on a CV for girls like you.'

'Girls like me?' Miranda paused in her chopping of the onions and turned to look at him squarely in the face, her hand on the knife.

He shrugged. 'Pretty young things with more money than sense.'

Her hand gripped the handle of the knife so hard that it hurt. He made her sound like a Barbie doll and, in all honesty, she could see where his opinions stemmed from, but it stung. She returned to the onions and furiously chopped them.

'My father disapproves of finishing schools,' she muttered grudgingly.

'Wise man.'

'I'll make sure to pass the compliment on. Now, what next?'

'Mushrooms. Canned, I'm afraid. I stock this place to last a certain length of time but, for obvious reasons, fresh food can be a bit dicey if the weather's like this and I can't ski to the nearest shop. Bacon.' He slid a packet across to her and she opened it, her mind still rankling after his high-handed summary of her character. 'Now you need to put the rice to boil. Have you ever boiled rice?'

'Have you ever been pleasant?'

He laughed and pushed himself away from the counter so that he could tip a generous portion of rice into the boiling water, along with a stock cube and some seasoning.

'And since when are you so qualified to launch into speeches about my background?' This time it was her turn to watch him as he took over the cooking, working expertly at frying various ingredients together, letting the lot simmer in a can of tomatoes flavoured with a touch of Tabasco sauce. 'What's your background? The university of life, I imagine?'

He nodded. 'Via Cambridge.'

'*You* went to *Cambridge University*? Ha!'

'Why do you find that so difficult to believe?' He dumped all the dirty dishes into the sink and tossed a sponge so that Miranda could make herself useful by wiping the counters. 'I'm hurt.'

You're hurt? she thought. And I'm the Queen of England!

'What did you study there?'

'Law and economics.'

Miranda burst out laughing. 'You expect me to believe that you went to one of the top universities in England to study law and economics and then ended up dong this to fill in your time?'

'Actually, I expect you'll believe exactly what you want to believe.' He began washing the dishes with the expertise of someone used to doing their own domestic chores; and, after he'd pointedly handed her a dry tea towel, she reluctantly positioned herself alongside him so that she could dry the dishes.

'Why didn't you become a lawyer?' she demanded, not to be deterred by his non-answer of an answer. She couldn't believe that he had any university degree in any such subjects, although there were things that didn't quite add up about him. Nevertheless, she had met so many men in her time who did relatively little with their lives despite their exalted backgrounds that accepting his care-taker story at face value had not been particularly difficult.

'Or an economist? Or whatever it is that people do after they've studied economics?'

'Perhaps the simple life beckoned...' Luke said sanctimoniously. 'Fresh outdoor air in winter, a chance for a poor yokel like me to see the world.'

Miranda looked at him dubiously, wondering why she suspected that he was play-acting when there was no reason for him to do so.

'And in the summer?' she persisted. 'Where do you go?'

'Where do *you* go?' he asked, turning the question on its head and moving away to dry his hands.

'Oh, sometimes to the country,' Miranda said vaguely.

'To enjoy the simple pleasures of rambling and exploring the great British countryside?'

She flushed and tossed her head in a manner that could either have been interpreted as agreement or adamant denial. Fortunately, before he could drag any further revelations out of her, there was the bubbling sound of boiling water spilling over and he forgot his line of enquiry in his salvaging of their lunch. Then the culinary programme resumed, with yet more detailed instructions, which she obeyed with somewhat more alacrity this time considering the other option was to admit to yet more details of her daily life. Her aimless daily life as she was fast beginning to think.

Stuck in this vacuum, she had been forced to confront her life; and what she had seen, even without Luke's heavy handed, patronising observations, had brought a sour taste to her mouth. She couldn't believe that the years had rolled by in a blurry mist of fast-paced, pointless activity, self-indulgence and the company of people whose friendship would probably crumble if ever put to the test.

'At the risk of disturbing your thoughts,' he whispered silkily into her ear and Miranda jumped, 'you still have one or two finishing touches for this meal. Garlic bread in the freezer. Stick it in the oven. I'll open a bottle of wine.'

'At lunch-time?'

'Wildly decadent, I agree, but very complimentary to our little home-cooked risotto.'

Despite the company she had moved in, Miranda had never fallen victim to drink. She enjoyed the occasional glass of wine but anything beyond that made her sleepy and gave her headaches. For the past few evenings, she had sipped at a glass with her dinner, usually tipping the rest down the sink.

'Drink and enjoy,' he cajoled, handing her the glass. 'Who knows? Tomorrow the snow may be back to normal and Daddy can send his helicopter out to rescue you. Then you'll be free to leave this primitive little cabin behind and return to your gilded cage.'

'And not a minute too soon!' she snapped, raising the glass to her lips and swallowing the lot in three hefty gulps. She instantly needed to sit down. And she did, sticking both her feet onto another of the kitchen chairs which she pulled closer to her. 'Anyway,' she continued thoughtfully, 'this cabin isn't primitive. It's small, but it's comfortable. And the furnishings might be old but they're of good quality.'

'You noticed, did you?'

'Of course I did! Have you forgotten that I hold a degree from the university of shopping?' She gave a little snigger at her own expense and accepted another glass of wine from him. 'I can spot quality from a mile off. Handy trait, wouldn't you say?'

'Only in a thief.'

Miranda laughed. 'Now, there's an option I'd never considered. Cat burglar.'

'The hair would give you away. Too blonde. You could never get away with blending into the night.' He drained his glass as he began setting the table for them and she rose to her feet to help him. 'You would have to cut it short and dye it brown.' He ladled two heaping portions of risotto onto plates and handed one to her, then he sat down opposite her.

'That would appeal to you, wouldn't it?' Miranda said, eating voraciously. Her constant weight-watching mechanism of picking at her food had vanished ever since she had stumbled to the cabin.

'What makes you say that?'

'Oh, just the way you disapprove of all this inconvenient hair of mine.' She helped herself to some more wine.

'Now, now. How can you say that when I spent fifteen minutes brushing it?'

There was amused irony in his voice but, when their eyes tangled across the table, she noticed that his expression was unreadable and a little shiver of giddy awareness shot through her. He was all man. Not just in his physical build, but in the way he moved and the manner in which he conducted himself. Rough, raw, sex appeal and, as she finished her second glass of wine, she wondered what it would be like to make love to him, to lie naked in a bed with him and let him turn all his masculine, vital magnetism onto her. What would it be like to be the sole target of those penetrating blue eyes, clouded with passion?

Face it, she thought dizzily as her body responded to the thought, there would be no consequences. He didn't move in her circles, didn't know any of her friends, and she would never see him again once she had left his cabin behind.

The prospect of the snow letting up within the next twenty-four hours, making it possible for her to leave, either by helicopter or on skies to the nearest town, because her ankle was more or less fully recovered, lent her passing speculations an exciting edge of urgency.

'My hairdresser brushes my hair,' Miranda said, her eyes glittering from the heady combination of unaccustomed wine consumption and the tantalising, erotic turn of her thoughts. 'Doesn't mean he likes it or even finds me attractive for that matter.'

A deathly silence greeted this remark as Luke paused to look at her with his food *en route* to his mouth. Even without looking at him, feigning absorption in her food, she was aware of the shift in atmosphere. Suddenly there was a crackling electricity between them. Every pore in her body was aware of it and she wondered whether he was aware of it as well.

'This food's fantastic. How did you learn to cook? Were you taught? A vital culinary course between the law and economics degree?'

'Necessity is the mother of invention, as they say,' Luke murmured. 'Wouldn't you agree?'

'Absolutely.' She sneaked a quick glance at him from under her lashes to find him looking at her. With a quick flick of her wrist she released her hair from its constraining elastic band and shook her head, like a young filly shaking its mane. Then she sat back and sighed.

'I can't eat another mouthful.' Actually, she wasn't lying. She had eaten several mouthfuls too many. 'I have no idea what's happened to my appetite. I've eaten like a horse since I've been here and I don't even have the excuse of good, healthy outdoor exercise to work it all off.' She drained her glass and felt a wild adrenaline rush as she poured herself another. 'I shall return to England horribly fat and be forced to spend six months continuously at the gym just to get back to my former shape.' She twisted in her chair to inspect her supposedly rapidly expanding waistline and was aware that Luke had closed his knife and fork and was inspecting her inspecting herself with a closed expression, his hands nonchalantly behind his head.

'I've an idea!' She could feel the brightness in her cheeks and realised that she had never in her life before felt so *alive*. The world was a wonderful place, laden with possibility. 'Don't you want to hear what it is?' she asked, when he didn't say anything.

'I don't thing you should have any more wine.'

'That's a very boring response to my question,' Miranda told him loftily.

'Perhaps I'm a very boring person.'

They both knew that that was utterly untrue. Arrogant, forbidding, massively self-controlled but also witty, sharp, intelligent. Never boring.

'I think we should go outside,' she said. 'I've been cooped up in this cabin for days now and I need to get a bit of fresh air. Plus the exercise. I need to get a bit of exercise. I haven't been as sedentary as this for years, sitting in one spot, doing nothing. Can't we get all wrapped up and have some fun in the snow? Please?' She would have done her best doe-eyed look but felt that that might put him off rather than spur him on; and spurring him on now seemed to be the one thing in the world she desperately wanted to do.

'It might do you a bit of good,' he murmured, making his mind up and getting to his feet. 'If you think you can actually stand up properly.'

'Oh, my ankle's fine!' Miranda said gaily and he raised his eyebrows in amusement.

'I wasn't actually thinking about your ankle.'

'What were you thinking about?'

'The alcohol level in your blood,' he said drily, holding up the empty bottle of wine, most of which, she realised, she had single-handedly consumed.

The ski clothes she had arrived wearing were folded in

a pile on a chair next to the fire and, without bothering to remove anything, she wrapped the scarf around her neck, stuck on her padded jacket, socks, ski pants, boots and, as an afterthought, her woollen hat, which had not been too clever for blizzard weather on the road to nowhere, but would do for snow outside the cabin.

Then she stood back and looked as he donned his usual waterproof garb.

Tomorrow she would be gone. Or by the latest, the day after. But today…today felt like none other, and she had no intention of letting it go.

CHAPTER FOUR

AFTER the warmth of the cabin, magnified a thousand times by the heat induced by the wine, outside was a shock to the system. Miranda felt her face tingle as the cold slammed against it; then she gradually became acclimatised and tentatively edged her way further outside, like an invalid trying to walk unaided for the first time.

The snow was still falling, but already she could detect its lessening force. She had told her father on the telephone that morning that she would be back home within days but, even when she had said it, home had still seemed a distant place. It didn't seem quite so distant now that she was outside and could see the dramatic clearing of the weather.

Luke had gone ahead of her, towards the small shed, and she followed in his direction, clumping through the drift in her ski boots and only feeling the very faintest of twinges in her ankle as a reminder of her accident.

'How does it feel?' he asked, with his back to her, as he surveyed the pile of uneven logs stacked in the corner.

'Oh, fine. Look.' He turned to look at her and Miranda walked a few paces towards him. 'Would you notice that I'd ever had a sprain?' She had closed the distance between them so that only a few feet separated them.

'No,' he said flatly. 'As good as new.' He returned to his inspection of the log pile and then rummaged around until he had removed a hefty piece of wood, which he placed on a low cutting table against the side of the wall. 'What are you going to do when you get back?' He picked up the axe and with one clean, powerful swoop divided the log neatly into two, then he repeated the process until there was a small bundle of logs which he flung into a basket on the ground.

'Who knows?' Miranda said. For the first time, she wished that he would look at her instead of those damned logs which he seemed intent on chopping. 'Do you think I ought to try and go back to my interior design?'

If the mountain wouldn't come to Mohammed...

She edged sideways, carefully positioning herself more or less in direct line of his eyes.

It was invigorating being outside for the first time in what felt like decades, but even more invigorating was the craving she had brought out into the open. She had aired it, acknowledged it and now it needed to be satiated. Just the thought of that seemed to make her pulses race even faster.

'Why not?' He shrugged, still not looking at her, as though indifferent to whatever future lay ahead of her. 'It might provide more of a challenge than flitting around the globe looking for distractions.'

'It might.' She paused and appeared to give the matter a great deal of thought. 'But then again, thrill-seeking can be quite a challenge in itself.'

Luke glanced across to her but, because the shed was darker than outside, it was impossible to decipher what he was thinking. Not that it was ever easy to see what was going on in that head of his.

'Don't you agree?' she said, pressing him.

'Depends what you want out of life, I suppose,' he said noncommittally. 'But looking for thrill after thrill, as far as I am concerned, is like a drug, and sooner or later the effect wears off, and what then? You still have to confront all those issues you've spent a lifetime avoiding.'

'It's dark in here, isn't it?' Miranda said, diverting what was turning out to be a gloomy subject. She didn't much want to consider any what then? kind of questions. Her head was filling up pretty fast with them already. 'Shall we go outside? Have some fun?'

'What kind of fun did you have in mind, Miranda?' This time he did look at her, and in the cold semi-darkness of the shed, his eyes glittered like a tiger's.

'We could…build a snowman,' she suggested. 'Then, when I'm gone, you can look at it and remember me.' She wondered what she would remember *him* by and realised that she didn't want to *remember* him. She wanted to continue waking up to him, hearing his voice, responding to every nuance of his voice and every glance in her direction.

'Forget it. I'm obviously in your way out here,' she said tightly, and walked out of the shed, back into the glaring light outside.

She hadn't expected him to follow her and was only aware that he had, when he said from behind her, 'All right. Let's build your memory, shall we? A snowman.' He caught up with her so that they were now walking side by side. 'Seems a little inappropriate, wouldn't you agree? Too squat and circular.'

'There's no need to humour me,' Miranda said sulkily. 'I know you find me a bore and shallow.'

'Whoever said that?' He turned to tilt her face up to his, his gloved finger under her chin. 'Did *I* say that?'

'You didn't have to.'

'*Now* who's making the sweeping assumptions?'

She looked at him hesitantly.

'The snow awaits, m'lady.' He gave a large, theatrical bow, still looking at her, and she allowed herself a small smile. 'Of course, we'll have to tone down the curves a bit...'

'How can we build a skinny snowman?'

'Skinny?' He laughed softly and she felt that little tingle of gut-wrenching awareness slither around inside her. 'From what I recall, not all of you is skinny.' He knelt and began to shape some snow into the beginnings of their snow woman and Miranda joined him. Every so often his gloved hand would brush against hers and she didn't pull hers back but pretended not to notice the casual contact.

'I don't think you should feel insulted if there's not much of a striking resemblance when we're finished,' he said, as they completed the base and moved onto stage two.

'I'll try my best,' Miranda promised. Even building a stupid snowman, there was an air of concentration about him that sent a little shiver up her spine. Would he be like that in bed? Concentrating on *her*? 'And will you think of me when you look at it?' she asked lightly and he flicked her a glance. This time, feeling very bold, she held his gaze until he was the first to look away.

'Why do you think I'll need a snowman to remind me of you? In actual fact, I have an excellent memory.'

'Which goes hand in hand with your sense of modesty?'

He gave a low, sexy laugh. 'Which both trail behind my burning inclination to curiosity. Which makes me wonder what game you're playing at the moment.'

'Me?' Miranda opened her eyes wide, genuinely surprised at what he had said. 'Playing games?'

'And don't flash those innocent baby blues at me.' He caught her gloved hand in his and brought his face very close to hers. 'For a lady who lives in the fast lane, you're as transparent as a girl of sixteen.'

'And what exactly do you see on my transparent face?' she asked, cheeks burning.

'What any man would see when a woman follows him around with her eyes.' Out here, in the unforgiving winter sunlight, his eyes looked even more scorchingly blue and she could see the fine lines that added character to his face. 'You've been giving me hot little looks ever since we had lunch. Did you think I hadn't noticed?'

'I have not!' But her declaration of protest was tinged with guilt and he picked up on it with a triumphant little laugh.

'Liar.'

For a few fraught seconds they stared at one another and she could feel her heart thudding like an engine in her chest. His mouth was only inches away from his. She very nearly swooned like some maiden in a Victorian novel at the thought of kissing him, of those sensual lips of his touching hers, exploring her trembling mouth.

'And what I want to know is *why*.' He stood up and she remained a while hunched on the snow with a dazed expression on her face. Then she stood up as well.

'I don't know what you're talking about,' Miranda said faintly. Oh, did she know what he was talking about! She wanted him. She wanted him to want her. She just hadn't realised that she had been quite so obvious about it. Despite her highly social life and the fact that she had always had no end of young men queuing up to take her out, actually *wanting* a man and wanting him to notice her, to want her too, was completely an alien sensation. Handling it was like playing a new game, the rules of which were unknown.

'Shall we carry on this interesting little discussion inside?'

'But what about our snowman? It's not finished yet,' she babbled.

'Oh, I think our little snowman can wait a while, don't you? Like I said, curiosity has always been one of my foibles and right now I can't wait to see where this is leading.'

He walked towards the cabin, raking his gloved fingers through his hair to free the snow, not pausing to look back and see whether she was following or not. Because, she thought helplessly, he knew that she would be. He pushed open the cabin door and then stood back to remain holding it open, allowing her to sidle past him and, in an embarrassed flurry, remove her gloves and hat while scrupulously avoiding eye contact.

She unzipped her jacket with her back to him and struggled out of her waterproof ski pants, feeling like a stripper on a stage, even though the outer layer of clothing only revealed the old clothes she had been wearing underneath. She could hear him behind her, doing the same; and she could *feel* him, could feel his hot, curious eyes on her back, sending little chills of goose bumps skittering along her arms.

'So,' he said, when she had finally found the courage to turn around, 'are you going to continue denying everything or are you going to tell me what's going on?'

'I think I'd like another glass of wine.'

'Dutch courage?' He laughed. 'Sit down right there and wait for me.' He returned minutes later with a glass for them both and sat down on the sofa next to her, depressing it with his weight. 'Now look at me and talk to me. Tell me what's on your mind. I can be a very sympathetic listener.' He was looking at her lazily and Miranda gulped a mouthful of wine, hoping to recapture the heady recklessness she had felt two hours before.

'Are you going to miss me, my darling?' he drawled. 'Do you want me to give you a couple of nights to remember so that when you cuddle down in your cold, cold bed in England you can think of me? You can touch yourself and close your eyes and have a few scorching memories to remember me by?'

'That's crude!' Miranda gasped, but his words had sent a thrill of dampness down through her body.

'But I'm a crude man, aren't I? Is that what turns you on? The fact that I'm nothing like those pretty boys you've been accustomed to dating?'

He might as well be touching her for the electric response his silky words were generating inside her. And he knew it. He could see it written in bold letters all over her flushed face, she was sure.

'Is that the little game you're playing?' He leaned forward and took a strand of hair between his fingers, curling it around them with a little smile on his dark face. 'Haven't I paid you enough attention while you've been here and, now that you're more or less ready to go, you want me to notice you?'

'I...' Miranda's mouth felt as though it was stuffed with cotton wool.

'I don't think your father would approve,' he murmured softly, releasing her hair.

'My father's not here!'

'Ah.' His mouth curved into a knowing smile. 'He's not, is he?' He drained the remainder of his wine and sat back. 'So tell me what happens next. You know the rules of this game. I don't.'

Miranda took a deep, flustered breath.

'Now, don't be shy,' he instructed. He linked his fingers together and cocked his head to one side in expectation.

'This is ridiculous,' she spluttered, lifting her chin.

'Desire, lust…is never ridiculous,' he told her gravely. 'Would you like me to take charge, Miranda?'

As if he would be doing her a favour! She tried to stimulate some self-righteous anger at that but instead found that the thought of him taking charge was even more of a turn on. He stood up abruptly and went across to the windows, drawing the curtains until the room was plunged into darkness, relieved only by two small table lamps which he switched on before sitting back down, this time on the chair.

'Take your clothes off.'

'W-what?'

'Take your clothes off,' he repeated. 'And don't be timid. After all, I've seen your naked body once already; although it has to be said that a sleeping naked figure is quite substantially different from a wide awake and highly charged one.'

'You want to *watch me get undressed*?' she asked, shocked, and he grinned at her bemusement.

'You make it sound like an unnatural desire. Don't tell me you make love by stripping under the covers so that no man can appreciate your body.'

'Well, no…' But pretty close, her frantic expression was telling him. She had certainly never performed a striptease for anyone in her life before, had never even considered it!

'I always say there's a first time for everything.'

Miranda slowly got to her feet and stood in front of him, feeling exposed and, yes, he was right, highly charged. As she reached to the bottom of the tee shirt to pull it over her head, all sense of vulnerability flew out of her head and she gave a little smile as he sat forward slightly, his nostrils flaring as though to capture her scent from where he was sitting on the chair.

She slowly drew the tee shirt upwards, pausing when she knew that a slither of skin would be visible. She had to remind herself that she had been the one to make the advance, which surely must mean that she was in control. She pulled the soft jersey higher, feeling it slide deliciously across the bare skin of her stomach, her ribcage, then over her bra, which, along with her briefs were the only two items of clothing she was wearing from her original garb.

Miranda loved her underwear. She never thought that a woman should give up when it came to what she wore beneath her clothes. Her bra, accordingly, was black, lacy and plunging. She heard him give a grunt of intense satisfaction as she pulled herself free of the tee shirt and tossed it lightly on the ground next to her.

It didn't matter that he had shown her no interest sexually since her arrival. He was interested now. Very interested. And his reaction to her spurred her on. She felt wild with excitement and incredibly daring.

In fact, she had never felt so excited in front of a man before. His drooping blue eyes as they roved over her body was a powerful aphrodisiac.

She slipped her fingers under the waistband of the oversized jogging bottoms, curling them down until her lacy briefs peeped below her belly button.

A little music, she thought, would have been perfect, although the stillness in the cabin was as erotic as any slow number she could think of.

She eased the jogging bottoms slowly down and stepped out of them, kicking them to one side where they joined the tee shirt. When she reached behind her back to unclasp the fastening to her bra, he stopped her.

'Come closer.'

Miranda walked towards him while his eyes followed her every movement.

'Now.' He sat back and watched as she unfastened the bra and her milky-white breasts spilled out of their restraints, settling against her ribcage.

'You have beautiful breasts,' he murmured. 'Nice, big nipples. Let me see you touch them…'

She felt a dizzy rush of blood to her head and was dimly aware of his sharp intake of breath as she rubbed her nipples with her fingers so that the tips jutted provocatively towards him, as if issuing an invitation to plunder.

He crooked his finger for her to step yet closer. Then, when they were within touching distance of each other, he traced a line along her stomach from the curve of her breasts down towards the waistband of her briefs. His touch was feathery and light and sinful in all that it didn't do.

'I thought you warned me against complications when I first landed on your doorstep.' Miranda laughed huskily.

'So I did,' he agreed. Then his finger trailed a path lower to feel the swollen folds of her womanhood pressing against the fabric of her underwear and she groaned. She wasn't sure whether her feet were going to continue to support her and it had nothing to do with the remnants of a sprain! Her hands were desperate to drag down the thin covering which was the only barrier left between herself and this bulky man tenderly touching her, his finger moving rhythmically against her throbbing crease.

'Feel good?' he asked roughly and Miranda moaned in response.

'And how does this feel?' He replaced his finger with his mouth and nuzzled against the damp briefs, pulling her against his face with his hands from behind the rounded cheeks of her bottom. The rough lace rubbed against her and through it she could feel the prodding of his tongue. Then he brought his thumbs around her thighs and slipped them under the elasticated edges of the briefs, ruffling them into the silky hair that enclosed her pulsating womanhood.

Hooking his fingers under the waistband he gently drew her underwear down until she was standing in front of him fully naked, her shallow, rapid breathing making her full breasts rise and fall. She wanted his mouth back there, licking her, rousing her, but he sat back and studied her with a little smile of satisfaction playing around the corners of his mouth.

'Bend over me,' he commanded roughly, 'I haven't even begun tasting you yet, my darling.'

Miranda leaned over him, balancing with her hands on the back of the chair, on either side of his head, so that her breasts dangled tantalisingly in front of his mouth, and he adjusted his body accordingly to catch one dangling nipple in his mouth, suckling on it while his hand toyed with the other hanging breast, rubbing the deep pink nipple with the rough pad of his thumb.

Miranda wanted to scream in ecstasy. He wanted to take his time. He wasn't going to rush anything and she had to force herself to move to his rhythm, even though she was aching to climax.

He let her breasts hang as he licked the deep cleavage with his tongue, then moved to concentrate on her other nipple, sucking and nibbling on it.

The tight bud in the centre of its pink halo was hard and erect and he teased it mercilessly with his mouth and tongue. When she could stand it no longer, Miranda climbed onto his lap, squatting on him so that she could feel, beneath his trousers, his own big erection, pushing against his zip.

'Aren't you going to get out of your clothes?' she questioned urgently.

'In my own good time. You did say you wanted me to take charge, didn't you?'

Miranda nodded.

'I thought so. Lean back. Let me continue with your beautiful breasts.'

Instead of leaning back, she cupped both her breasts in her hands, pushing them up so that the nipples appeared even bigger and more swollen than they were. The pink circles drooped over her fingers and their eyes met as he slowly rubbed the tips with his fingers. They looked at each other, enjoying watching each other's reactions. Making love had never been this explosive. She felt as though someone had struck a match to her, and responses she had never known existed had been ignited.

She wondered whether he was feeling the same thing too, but she wouldn't ask.

He leaned forward and licked her nipple, and Miranda placed her hand behind his head, so that she was pushing him against her with one hand, while the other hand continued to offer him the bounty of her breast, feeding it to him like ripe fruit.

As he sucked her sensitised nipple, she felt his hand cup her between her thighs and she began to move sinuously against his fingers, making soft grunting noises of pleasure as her own tight, female erection brushed against his hands.

She reached behind her and clumsily tried to undo the button of his trousers, desperate to feel him, flesh against flesh, desire pressing against desire.

'Do you want me as much as I want you?' she whispered huskily.

'Can't you feel it?'

'Not enough.'

'Then we'd better set that straight, hadn't we?' He lifted her off him and she watched in open fascination as he removed his shirt and then stood up, gloriously masculine, to shed himself of the rest of his clothing.

He was magnificent. In the subdued light of the room, his torso gleamed with the hard perfection of a fighter's, and when he pulled down his boxer shorts, his manhood rose, proudly claiming his own hunger for her.

He stood in front of her and held her head between his hands, guiding her to it. She felt his big body shudder and he flung his head back with a deep groan of satisfaction, as her mouth circled his powerful erection.

She could bring him to the brink as quickly as he had brought her, she realised with a spurt of pleasure. She licked and sucked until he could stand it no longer and eased himself reluctantly away from the source of pleasure.

'It's a bit cramped here for what I want to do to you,' he murmured and Miranda laughed in thrilled anticipation.

'Shall we go upstairs?' she asked softly.

'I don't promise I can make it that far without taking you on the way,' Luke growled and she laughed again with full-bodied enjoyment at his blatant need. It matched hers.

There was a battered pine chest in the corner of the room, and she watched, sliding her body over the chair in abandonment, as he lifted the lid and extracted a downy quilt which he spread in front of the fire.

'Come and lie down,' he told her. Miranda walked towards him, loving the way his eyes devoured her every movement. He was as single-minded and focused in this as he appeared to be in everything else, and she felt intensely desirable. She lay down and he towered over her, then he straddled her, his knees on either side of her slender hips.

'Lie spread-eagled for me, darling,' he murmured, and she practically purred with heady compliance as she stretched her arms above her head and opened her legs.

'Now, let me pleasure you.' He bent to kiss her lips, her closed eyes, the slim column of her neck. He licked her breasts, his tongue flicking erotically over her prominent nipples, which were dark with arousal. Then he worked his way slowly downwards until his dark head lay between her opened legs and this time there was no lacy barrier to contain the sensation of his tongue against her slippery heat. With his hands on her thighs, making sure that her legs were spread wide for his enjoyment, he licked and sucked and rolled his tongue over her female arousal, flicking against the bud until she writhed and arched with convulsions.

Only when he knew that she could stand it no longer, did he insert himself into her, thrusting powerfully, bringing them both to a shuddering climax and then continuing until wave after wave of pleasure finally melted into blissful fulfilment.

Miranda, exhausted, dozed against him, her body curling into his and fitting into his contours like a hand in a glove. She had no idea how long she would have continued dozing in her contented, dreamy state, if the shrill ring of his mobile phone hadn't jerked her back to reality.

Luke groaned and fumbled around on the sofa with one hand for the phone, finally sitting up and answering it while Miranda twisted around and stroked his stomach with her fingers.

'Yes,' she heard him say down the phone. 'Absolutely fine. Yes. In fact, she's just here. She went outside for the first time today and…' he shot her a wicked, amused smile '…she seems thoroughly exhausted at the exertion.'

He handed her the phone and her father's voice boomed down the end of the line.

'I hope you haven't been overdoing things,' her father admonished, and she tried not to burst out laughing as she caught Luke's gaze and held it. 'You've got to take it easy with that ankle of yours. I know you told me it's all healed up but you don't want to do anything stupid and jeopardise progress.'

'I wouldn't dream of doing anything stupid, Dad.' She watched as Luke settled back down next to her, lying on his side so that he could play with her breast. Miranda smacked his hand lightly and made pointing motions to the phone, which he ignored.

'Pretty much cleared,' she said, in answer to her father's question about the snow. 'Yes. Yes. I'll let you know later…yes. All right. Bye for now. I love you, too.'

Luke removed the phone from her hands and replaced it on the sofa, then he looked at her with a teasing expression.

'So…you wouldn't dream of doing anything stupid…' He laughed and stroked her hair away from her face, propping himself up on his elbow so that he could stare down at her face which was still flushed in the aftermath of their lovemaking.

'Now, I wonder what your father's definition of stupid would be if he knew what his call had just interrupted…'

'Do you think I've been stupid?' she asked anxiously, frowning.

'You mean, do I think *we've* been stupid…? Quite possibly.' He kissed her very gently on her lips but Miranda was too intent on sifting through her emotions to return the kiss. She wriggled onto her elbow so that they were looking at each other on the same level.

'Why do you say that?'

'Sex tends to have repercussions,' he said, sliding his hand along her side to where her waist dipped. 'You're not a child. You know that. Maybe this poor caretaker might start having unhealthy ambitions to have a woman share his cabin with him during those long winter days, now that you've shown me how delightful female company can be...' His hand moved to trace a path along her belly and up to the crease beneath her breasts, showing her precisely what aspect of female company he considered so delightful.

She noticed that he had not specified that he wanted to have *her* as his female company, but who could blame him? She had offered herself to him, no strings attached and, like any red-blooded male, he had accepted the offer. So why should she feel this dull panic because what had been so earth-shattering for her had been commonplace for him?

She took a few steadying breaths to combat the uncomfortable feeling that her life ahead was dawning like a huge, gaping black hole and sternly told herself that everything would be different once she returned to England and left him behind. That was the way it went with holiday romances, and what they had couldn't even be called a romance.

'Dad wants to know when he can expect me back home,' Miranda said. He had been *her* one night stand and she was determined that he wouldn't forget that. Nor that he would imagine that she wanted anything beyond that. She would be the fluffy, self-centre airhead he thought she was and, when she left, she would make it absolutely clear that sex with him had not torn her world apart.

'And what will you tell him?'

'Oh…that he can expect me in a couple of days, when I know for sure that the snow isn't going to turn into another blizzard and that I can ski down to safety.'

'To safety…? Interesting word. Don't you feel safe here with me?' He nuzzled her ear and she squirmed.

'Where's the nearest town?' she asked breathlessly, and he paused.

'About a kilometre away, as the crow flies. In skiing time, no distance at all. When the weather permits, I get my provisions there if I need any, then catch the closest cable car back up and ski the distance to the cabin.'

'You ski with carrier bags in your hands? Must be a bit awkward.'

'I don't usually buy carrier bags full of provisions,' he countered, grinning. 'I buy just enough to shove in my backpack, not that I couldn't manage with ten carrier bags. I'm a very proficient skier as it happens. Unlike some not a million miles away from me…'

'Hang on…' Miranda became very still and cocked her head to one side. 'What's that noise?'

'What noise?'

'Sounds like…your modesty clanking out of control again.' She smirked and he repaid the insolence by kissing her so thoroughly that she only surfaced for air two minutes later.

'And do *you* think this is an act of stupidity?' His breath warmed her ear as she felt the flare of helpless attraction surge through her body once again.

'Well, I barely know you…' she murmured, clasping her hands behind her head, proffering the full vision of her breasts for him to peruse. Which he did with a grunt of satisfaction. 'And you might not believe me, but I don't go in for one-night stands…' He nibbled at her nipple, as she had known he would, and Miranda moaned in response. She could spend the rest of her life watching his dark head explore her body. She lightly ran her fingers through his black hair and followed the line of his jaw as he toyed with her nipple, teasing it with his tongue.

'For someone who doesn't go in for one-night stands…' he looked at her sideways, pausing in his exploration of her breast, '…you certainly seem to have got the hang of them pretty quickly…'

'That's because of you,' Miranda said quickly, regretting her outburst when he heaved himself up so that his face was close to hers.

'Shall I take that as a compliment?'

She shrugged. Now was the time to play it cool, she thought. A casual fling. Women did that sort of thing all of the time, and what had her past three boyfriends been but casual flings? They had lasted months rather than two days, but marriage had never been on the cards.

'I'm not sure,' she said huskily, her eyes drowsy as they met his. 'I might need a bit more to make up my mind one way or another…'

'Minx.' He laughed delightedly.

'If you can,' she murmured. 'I personally think it's a myth that men have the stamina to keep going all night…'

'Then you've never met the right man. You can feel my stamina if you like, my darling.' He blew into her ear and then delicately explored it with his tongue until she squirmed and giggled and forgot. Forgot about that dark hole waiting for her the minute she stepped foot back into the reality that had always been her life.

CHAPTER FIVE

'MIRANDA!'

Miranda's head shot up.

'What on earth is the matter with you?'

'Nothing!' She gazed down at the large breakfast which she had optimistically dished out for herself. Bacon, eggs, toast, marmalade. The toast lay limp and half eaten. The bacon and eggs were pristine and untouched and slowly congealing into an unappetising mass on the plate.

Her father was still peering at her over the rims of his slim reading glasses with his newspaper lowered.

'Why aren't you eating?' he demanded. He abandoned the newspaper altogether and afforded her the full brunt of his undivided attention. He was a tall, slender man with perfectly silver hair and blue eyes the same shade as his daughter's. Right now, he was dressed in his golfing garb. Every Saturday morning for as long as she could remember, her father vanished to the golf course where he played a round of eighteen holes with the same three friends who had been around since his roaring university days a million years ago.

'Spit it out,' he said. 'You've been moping around this house for the past week. Are you sickening for something, my girl?'

'What an antiquated phrase, Dad. *Sickening for something.* No, I'm not sickening for anything. I'm just not hungry.'

He ignored her mumbled explanation. 'And what are

you doing lurking around on a weekend? Shouldn't you be out and about with those friends of yours?'

'Actually, I'm not in the mood for those friends of mine.'

'Don't blame you. Freeloaders the lot of them. I just hope this mood of yours has nothing to do with that Freddie character, because you're well rid of him.'

Miranda gave a snort of disgust at the mere mention of any such thing. Freddie had tried contacting her twice since she had been back and she had told him, twice, that he could get lost. The second time she had added that if he contacted her again she would hang up and she would carry on hanging up until he got the message. For good measure, she had given him a pithy description of what she thought of him, which included the words waste of space, charmless, shallow and in dire need of some growing-up tablets. She didn't imagine that she would be hearing from him again.

'Well, you can't spend your time hanging around. Shall I,' he asked with an unsuccessful attempt to inject delicacy in his voice, 'remind you of a certain design course you took a few years ago?' He removed his specs, snapped them into their case and stuck the case in the top pocket of his shirt, then he stood up and began putting on his golfing jumper: a pale yellow affair with a navy and white diamond pattern and a discreet golfing motto embroidered on one side. 'Perhaps,' he continued, 'you're sickening for a spot of hard work for a change.'

'Why do I detect a certain smugness in your voice when you say that, Dad?' Miranda asked and he chuckled at her. 'I wouldn't know where to begin,' she added.

'I could put the word about at the golf club. Some of those wives seem to spend all their time remodelling their houses. No sooner have they done the whole place top to bottom, than they decide that it's time for a change. And, after they've done that five times, they're ready to move. Can't understand it myself.'

'I can put my own word about.' The task of doing any such thing seemed bigger and more insuperable than a hike up Mount Everest with only a backpack and a pair of walking shoes. Just the thought of it sent her scuttling into a state of panic. Where would she start? An advert in the newspaper? Or at the back of one of those home magazines? Or would she be reduced to standing at the corner of Sloane Square handing out leaflets in the freezing rain? Maybe wearing one of those sandwich boards with the heading, I Haven't Done This For Years, But Please Give Me A Chance.

She would think about it, she decided, next week. Right now, there were more pressing things to think about.

As soon as the house was empty, Miranda wandered aimlessly into the snug, sprawled down on the sofa, closed her eyes and reawakened the memories that were constantly gnawing away at the back of her mind and which coalesced into the haunting vision of Luke Decroix. She gave her mind free rein to travel down roads that she knew would end up hurting her. In fact, she took almost a sadistic delight in wallowing undisturbed in her self-pity.

Her last day at the cabin had dawned with a sense of glorious excitement. They had spent the night making love or at least it had felt that way. In fact, it had been as if time had stood still for them, giving them an eternity in which to explore each other's bodies, and explore them they had. She had touched every part of him, delighting in the feel of his muscled chest, the straining power of his broad shoulders, the girth of his aroused manhood that pulsed between her hands and against her mouth.

And he had caressed every inch of her body, from her

face to her feet, making her spread herself out for him so that he could rifle every part of her.

She had awakened on her final morning with the sun streaming in through the window and the feeling that she had been having the most wonderful dream: a dream about her dark, exciting lover that had left her warm and drowsily aroused.

When she'd turned around and had sleepily opened her eyes, she'd found herself staring into his alert and wide awake ones.

'You look remarkably satisfied,' he murmured with a sultry, knowing look. 'You weren't thinking about me by any chance, were you?' He pulled down the duvet cover so that her pink nipple peeked out at him. 'Oh, yes, I see that you were...'

'What time is it?' She snuggled comfortably into the feathery mattress of his king-sized bed and stretched, arching her arms above her head so that the quilt was pushed further down. When she relaxed, she made no move to re-cover her body and her breasts pointed wickedly at him. She had never felt this strange, powerful excitement at having a man look at her before. He knew how to make her feel weak with craving before he even laid one finger on her.

'Does it matter? I think we should forget about watches today and just make our own timetable up as we go along.'

'Does that mean stay in bed all day?'

'Not *all* day, no...' He blew on her nipple and the rush of cool air further hardened the tight peak and made her sigh with pleasure. 'But mornings are special, don't you agree? Why rush this one when we can laze here for a bit and...' he blew on her nipple again and she dreamily responded with a soft moan that brought a devilish smile to his mouth '…chat…'

'What do you want to chat about?'

'Anything that takes your fancy, my darling…' At which he smoothed his hand along her thighs, still warm and luxuriantly pliable from sleep, thereby ensuring that chat became the very last thing she wanted to do. Or was even capable of doing for that matter.

'Don't mind me,' he said softly, 'I'm listening to every word you're saying.' He gave her a smattering of tiny pecks around her mouth, then proceeded to kiss her thoroughly and devastatingly before turning his attention to her breasts. He pushed her so that she was lying on her back, and began suckling on her breasts, enveloping her warm nipples in his mouth.

'What…are we going…?' Miranda gave a long groan of satisfaction as more than one part of her body was stimulated by his fingers and his mouth simultaneously. She dropped her knees to either side so that he could rub his big hand against her, taking her to dizzy heights of sensation before slowing his tempo to allow her to subside, only to recommence his assault on her senses.

'You were saying?' he queried earnestly, glancing up from her breast briefly.

'To do today?' she managed to struggle out before his mouth travelled possessively down the flat planes of her stomach to the slippery heat that told of her burning arousal.

'Why, it's your turn to fulfil your side of the deal,' he said, 'and look after my needs for the day. And I mean,' he growled, '*all* my needs.'

The day was bright and clear, one of those days where one felt that one might just be able to see to the other side of the world and everything seemed to be in Technicolor.

It was nearer lunch-time by the time they finally descended the short flight of stairs and, still flushed from their languid lovemaking, Miranda bustled around the kitchen, enjoying herself as he watched from a kitchen chair and talked to her about some of the more remote places he had been, making her own travel anecdotes seem puny in comparison.

Her eyes widened at tales of sights in the Far East, the wilds of Canada, even China.

'Are you sure you're not making this up as you go along?' she teased. 'I can't believe you would eat sheep's eyes and insects.'

'When in Rome you do as the Romans do.' He shrugged and smiled at her expression of incredulity. 'It's a wise man who knows how to respect the beliefs and culture of others. Which is why, incidentally, you're doing the cooking. You're doing as the Romans do when in Rome.'

Miranda served a lunch of whatever could be successfully stir-fried and was amazed to find that it tasted fairly good.

She had never felt the slightest enthusiasm for anything culinary, and the lack had always been one of her father's bugbears. Her mother had loved to cook, had devoured cookery books, delighting in experimenting, and Miranda had accredited her father's ideas on women in the kitchen as old-fashioned notions which, she had never failed to tell him, were out of place in the twenty-first century. The truth, though, she uneasily recognised now, was that cooking, like her interior design, like a thousand other things over the years, had just been one more thing that she had abandoned because she lacked the perseverance to see it through.

When, over lunch, she haltingly tried to explain this to

Luke, she found that his reaction was one of sympathy rather than the so-what-was-new attitude she might have expected when she had first stumbled into his life.

'If you can see what you're dissatisfied with in your life,' he said, calling her over to him and then sitting her on his lap like a ten-year-old child in need of comfort, 'then why don't you do something about it when you get back to England?' He stroked her hair and she laid her head on his shoulder, feeling safe, the way she had when she'd been a kid and her father had patiently sat her on *his* lap and had soothed away her childish worries.

'I can't.'

'Why not?'

'Because…'

'Because you're afraid?' he persisted gently. 'Afraid of failing? I know, I know…' He carried on stroking her hair, soothing her, and she realised that he understood everything, things she had never vocalised to anyone before, not even to her father. 'It's easier to succeed at being a beautiful young thing without a care in the world than to allow the world to judge you on your merits.'

His voice, as he continued to dissect her innermost thoughts, was like a wave washing around her, absorbing her, and she had to control the temptation not to burst out crying.

She only had the remainder of this day left! She sat up and sighed but, before she could move away, he pulled her back against him, this time to kiss her with a tenderness that made her weak.

Kissing him was what she needed. She didn't need to think and analyse and end up feeling maudlin! She took his tender kiss and returned it fiercely, her tongue clashing with his. With a lithe manoeuvre, she straddled him, rolling her hips provocatively and pushing him back into his chair with her mouth still possessing his. Right now, all she wanted was to lose herself in his lovemaking because, when she left this cabin, he would be gone for ever and all she would have left would be her memories and an uncomfortable awareness that she would have to start sorting her life out.

'No!' she whispered, when he tried to lift her out towards the sitting room.

'You certainly are taking me to my word about satisfying my needs,' he groaned into her ear and she felt the savage pull of satisfaction at her power over him. Right now. Right at this instant. Tomorrow could wait…

Miranda gave a soft moan of despair as she stared upwards at the ceiling in her father's house.

Playing back the scene of their lovemaking in her head was like watching a film in slow motion. If it had ended there, then she would still be staring at the ceiling in her father's house, she thought, but at least she would have had her dignity intact.

Instead, his little words about not being afraid of failing had somehow wormed their way into her head and had taken root. That, combined with the crippling prospect of never seeing him again, had made her utter something she should have held to herself. Cradling his head against her as they had collapsed, spent after their raw lovemaking, she had asked him if he'd wanted her to stay.

'Just for a few days,' she said hastily and, when his response was not immediate, she sat up and gazed down into his eyes.

'It wouldn't be a good idea,' he told her finally. 'You can't grab a bit of time to hide away here so that you won't have to face whatever you feel you have to face when you return to England.'

His rejection of her offer hit her like a sledgehammer,

but she remained in control of her feelings, willing herself not to shrivel up under those cobalt eyes.

He didn't want her. He had been content to sleep with her because she had offered herself to him, but the bottom line was that he just didn't want her. She wasn't his type and prolonging her stay, far from being a pleasurable prospect for him, was the offer of just a little too much of a good thing.

Who knew, maybe he had even got a kick out of sleeping with a woman who was so far removed from the type of earthy woman he was probably accustomed to. Like sleeping with the boss's daughter: an illicit thrill but not one to be stretched out and with limited novelty value.

'You understand what I'm saying, don't you, Miranda?' he asked and she nodded obligingly, not allowing herself to speak for fear of doing something ridiculous.

'I wasn't talking about commitment and marriage.' She finally found her voice and used it, embarking on a damage-limitation exercise even though her heart, her dignity, her pride were all breaking into a thousand pieces.

'I know that,' he told her impatiently, following her to the bathroom so that he could pursue the conversation to her back.

'I just thought it might have been fun.' She washed, aware of his eyes burning a hole through her but unable to find any excuse to request privacy after they had jettisoned any such notion along the way. To suddenly ask to be alone would be tantamount to telling him how devastated she was by what he was saying.

'But you're right.' She even found the strength from somewhere to give a brittle laugh, though she couldn't meet his eyes. They saw altogether too much. 'It's best to call it a day. Bit of fun but familiarity breeds contempt, or so they say.'

She changed into her original ski gear and had then to undergo the gauntlet of having him ski down with her to the nearest village, which as he had told her, was only a hop and a skip away. Then he waited. Waited so that they could have a cup of coffee until the cable car was ready to take her down to the final stop where a taxi would speed her to the airport and away from him for ever.

And there had been more questions. More shows of sympathy that made her want to scream. And finally she was gone, gone without a backward glance. Just a casual wave to imply that it had all been a bit of a laugh and have a good life.

Miranda wearily sat up and stretched. Her father would be back from his golfing expedition in a couple of hours and it wouldn't do to have him find her skulking around the house like a lost soul. He might not have much experience of honing into women's emotions but he was astute and it wouldn't take him much longer to figure out the reason for her inexplicable lack of energy.

At least, she consoled herself, she hadn't made the mistake of blurting out the confession that would have turned her mortification into downright agony. When she had looked at Luke, lost in his eyes, she had managed not to tell him that she had fallen in love with him.

She waited until her father returned, having changed into a long-sleeved woollen dress and tied her hair back, and greeted him with a bright smile.

'Good game?' she asked, trailing behind him into the kitchen where he began removing his shoes and socks. 'Lost many balls?'

'Since when have you been interested in your old man's golfing exploits?' He gave her a shrewd look from under bushy silver brows. 'Bloody awful game, now that you asked. Putting everywhere but the hole. Damned Gordon had a good laugh at my expense when we got to the nine-teenth hole.'

'I've decided,' she said, taking a deep breath, 'to go out to work.'

Her father paused to look at her. 'Good girl.' He padded out to the utility room where he left his shoes and, when he returned to the kitchen, he said casually, 'What brought about his sudden change of direction?'

Miranda shrugged. 'I'm fed up with doing nothing.' She looked at him and grinned. 'I'm an adult now. Perhaps I just think that the time has come to realise that adults don't spend their lives having good times. They work hard and feel miserable.'

Her father laughed and patted her head as he walked past her to the kettle. 'That's the spirit. So where are you going to begin?'

'Back at design college. I'll go along and hear what they have to say about idlers who want to relaunch their career after years of wasting time.'

'I might be able to help,' he said conversationally.

'The golfing fraternity?'

'Or some such thing. Who knows? You might find that you land on your feet quicker than you think. I mean,' he continued hastily, 'you've always had a lot of talent. Anyone just has to take a look at your portfolio to see that for themselves.'

Unfortunately, she was told the following Monday when she trotted along to the careers office at the design college, a lack of portfolio was something of a hindrance. Especially, she was advised by the impeccably groomed brunette, in a field that was so highly competitive. The time lapse also posed a problem. Were her ideas as fresh as they once had been? Fashions in interior design had moved on. Did she have any contacts at all in the field?

Another problem apparently. A refresher course, she was informed, might be worth thinking about, and Miranda left an hour and a half later with an armful of further course details.

Rather than return to the house and face a long day contemplating her lack of experience, Miranda spent the day out, reluctantly contacting one of her friends for lunch who gave her the full story about the remainder of their skiing trip and Freddie's high junks. Accounts of her own exploits she kept to a minimum. In a small circle, gossip had an unfortunate tendency to spread like wildfire and usually underwent alterations along the way so that the end story bore little resemblance to the truth. Like Chinese whispers.

By the time six-thirty rolled round, she let herself into the house feeling thoroughly beaten by the prospect of her jobless, pointless existence.

'Miranda, darling,' Her father popped out of the sitting room with a drink in one hand as she was divesting herself of her coat and wondering what to do with the lists of courses which had failed to inspire the flurry of interest anticipated by the careers advisor. It was all right for her, Miranda had thought sourly at the time, to sit there and give long lectures about the gaping holes in other peoples' curriculum vitaes, when she herself was ensconced in a nice, cosy career of her own. Perhaps she should scrap all thoughts of returning to interior design and instead try for a recruitment agency so that she could spend all her time telling people without the necessary qualifications that they didn't have the necessary qualifications.

'You're home early, Dad.' She slung her coat over the banister, a habit her father deplored, and ran her fingers through her hair. 'Don't tell me you've decided to take early retirement.'

'Successful day?'

Miranda looked at him gloomily. 'Apparently I need a bulging portfolio, a load of contacts and neither would help anyway because I've been out of the field for so long that all my ideas are outdated and in dire need of a spring-clean.' She waved the course details at him. 'I could always do a refresher course, I'm told, but even then it's such a competitive field that I probably wouldn't get anywhere anyway.'

'Well,' he gave her a long, satisfied look, 'I might just have the answer for you, my girl.'

'What's that, Dad? A position in one of your companies? Or maybe you could let me redecorate your office. It would be a start and I offer hefty discounts to family members.' She grinned. 'I've always thought that hose browns and beiges in your office are a bit on the fuddy-duddy side.'

'Join me in the sitting room for a drink.' He winked at her and spun round on his heels with his daughter tramping behind him. 'And it doesn't,' he threw over his shoulder, 'involve getting rid of my nice browns and beiges.'

'Oh, yes? What does it involve?'

Instead of answering, her father stood back and made a sweeping gesture from the door of the sitting room, allowing her to enter ahead of him.

Miranda, about to continue her speculations about alternative job prospects, stopped in mid-track, with her mouth half open and the ghost of a smile rapidly dying on her lips.

What the hell was *he* doing here? What was Luke Decroix doing in her father's house, sitting in one of her father's chairs, with a drink casually in one hand, the other resting on the arm of his chair?

Miranda blinked rapidly as the air was squeezed out of

her lungs by this sudden apparition who was now raising his drink to his lips and wore the easy self-assurance of someone who feels utterly at home.

In her father's house!

'I believe you two know one another,' her father said from behind her and her wildly spiralling thoughts converged with crashing awareness that this was no illusion.

Luke Decroix, for reasons unknown to her, had left his caretaking job and had dogged her back to England.

'What can I get you to drink, darling?' her father bustled past her, looking suspiciously pleased with himself and oblivious to her rising panic.

'Water!' Miranda gasped, then she took control of herself and cleared her throat. 'On second thoughts, a glass of white wine, Dad. Thanks.'

'So, we meet again.' Luke, who had followed her stumbling progress from doorway to sofa, smiled and raised his glass in mimicry of an old friend. Miranda felt like choking.

'Look at you,' her father said affectionately, thrusting the wineglass into her hand, 'aren't you thrilled?'

'Speechless,' she managed to choke out, before swallowing a generous mouthful of the cold liquid in a misguided attempt to clear her head.

'You do look a bit white, if anything,' Luke said drily. He placed his drink carefully on the polished side table and then loosely linked his fingers together on his lap so that he could give her his undivided attention.

'She's had a bit of a day, from the sounds of it,' her father was saying. 'No wonder the poor girl's white like a sheet. Got a bee in her bonnet about going out to work.'

'Dad, I have not got a *bee in my bonnet*. I'm just giving it some thought.' Out of the corner of her eye, she could see Luke looking at her with a shuttered expression.

Probably trying hard not to smirk, she thought a little wildly.

'That little stay in your cabin must have brought her to her senses.'

His cabin? She opened her mouth to put her father straight on that little point but, before she could utter a word, Luke had smoothly entered the conversation and was suborning her father with a long, philosophical spiel on isolation sometimes being the best cure, giving time to really think about what one wanted to do with oneself, affording the invaluable opportunity to get perspectives right. And her poor father was lapping it all up.

'So what brings you here?' She finally interrupted the monologue on the virtues of isolation.

'Boring you, am I?' Luke asked with a smooth, cutting edge in his voice.

'Not at all. I just wondered what you were doing over here when you should be in France. I mean, what's your er…'

'So not much luck on the job-hunting front? It's a competitive field.'

'I already know that,' Miranda snapped, while her father pointedly cleared his throat to remind his daughter about the rules of courtesy. 'I spent two hours being told it by a supercilious careers advisor. I don't need *you* to launch another sermon on the impossibility of finding work in an overcrowded field. And you still haven't answered my question.'

What would her father be thinking about him? she wondered. He had shown, oddly, very little curiosity about details of her rescuer and her own sketchy descriptions had led him down the road of a thoroughly nice man, by which she had tacitly implied that he was genial and middle-aged.

What would he be thinking at the strikingly good-looking man sitting on his chair, with a faint air of aggression about him? Or maybe Luke had spent however long he had been in the house, inveigling his way into her father's good books so that unanswerable questions about his prized daughter being in the company for a period of days with a man who would turn heads with the best of them, were stillborn. God knew, he seemed to be bringing out the charm in plentiful supply.

'I'm here to help you, actually.' Luke smiled blandly as she tried to work out what precisely he meant by that. He tapped a briefcase which she noticed for the first time was upright on the ground next to his chair.

'Perhaps I should let you two young people discuss this on your own.' He stood to rise and Miranda practically yelled at him to stay put.

'There's nothing that can't be said in front of my father!' she declared on a shout. The thought of being left alone in the room with Luke brought her out in a cold sweat. He had used her, she decided, conveniently forgetting any thoughts that she had led him on. On the back of this, she felt a satisfying rush of antagonism.

Had he come back to *help her* by asking her whether her offer of a bit more uncomplicated sex was still on the agenda? What a nerve! To brazenly come to her house, cosy up to her father and then try and pretend to him that he was actually on a mission to *help*? Miranda felt a bubble of manic laughter at the back of her throat and swallowed it down.

'Luke's come to see you on business,' her father said. 'Now, I might run a number of companies but when it comes to discussing interior design, well, I'm lost.' He beamed at Luke. 'As this little snippet of a thing will be the first to tell you!'

'Is that right, you little snippet of a thing?' He glanced up from his briefcase, from which he had successfully extracted a sheaf of papers. Miranda, who had been watching his activities in open-mouthed silence, snapped her teeth together.

'Why have you got a briefcase?'

'Now, you *will* be polite, won't you, Miranda?' her father said in a warning voice, and she gave him a pitying glance, willing him to read her mind, that whatever nefarious tale Luke Decroix had spun, it was all a lie.

'Oh, I know how to handle your daughter,' Luke said drily, and she caught the double meaning behind his words and felt a rush of colour sting her cheeks.

'Now, young man, how about a spot of dinner when you're through here?'

Miranda gaped but, before she could squawk out her thoughts on any such idea, Luke was nodding his acceptance and making some crack about bringing a bottle of wine if he had known that he would be staying for dinner.

'Sure you haven't got anything else planned?' Her father turned at the door to look at them. He belonged to an era whose idea of casual dress meant no tie or jacket and he looked well-dressed enough to go out in his grey slacks, smart shoes and blue shirt the top button of which he had daringly left undone. Miranda felt a wave of pure love engulf her and her silent rage that this imposter could try and dupe her beloved father made her head feel as if it was going to explode.

'Nothing that can't be put on hold,' Luke was saying, his voice warmly appreciative of the offer.

'Do you mind telling me what's going on here?' Miranda demanded as soon as her father had left the sitting room, tactfully closing the door behind him. 'How *dare* you talk your way into my father's house on some phoney pretext! *How dare you?*' Her hands gripped the edge of the sofa, biting into the cushion.

'You don't seem too pleased to see me,' Luke countered lazily. 'Why not?' His eyes flicked over her flushed face then took in her prim powder-blue suit and blue pumps, the garb she had foolishly imagined would have suited her first day back on the job-seeking front. 'After all we shared... Still, I understand. It's always a bit disconcerting when two separate strands of reality collide.'

'How did you know where to find me?'

'I telephoned your father.'

'And wangled your way into his house by telling him what...?'

'By telling him that I have a little job for you to do.'

Miranda gave a cackle of disbelieving laughter. 'Well, he'll soon realise that whatever little job you might have is all in your head when I let him know who and what you really are!' Actually, seeing Luke there, feet away from her, inspired hysteria. It also revived the bitter taste of his rejection. She bit back the temptation to shriek with demented laughter and lunge for his neck with something very sharp in her hand.

He, she noted, looked perfectly at ease in his surroundings and unfazed by the fact that she was about to uncover his duplicity.

'Why do you think I've come here, then, Miranda?'

'Maybe you think you can somehow get money from my father,' she said callously. 'I don't know, you tell me.'

'What are these?' He handed her the papers he had been holding but, instead of taking them, Miranda just peered at the top one.

'Those are my designs for your boss's house.' She looked at him sharply. 'Why have you got them? I thought you'd deleted them from the computer. What's going on here?' The hostility in her voice was laced with genuine confusion. 'Does your boss know what you're up to?'

'Ah.' Luke dropped the papers on the ground and sat back to look at her. 'It's time you and I had a little chat.'

CHAPTER SIX

MIRANDA drank some of her wine, a taste for which she seemed to have developed ever since her stay in the cabin, and eased her feet out of her pumps. It was imperative that she take the upper hand and not let Luke Decroix try and manoeuvre her in her own home territory. But, when she stretched out to place her wineglass on the table in front of her, she found that her hand was trembling and she hurriedly folded her arms across her chest and looked at him coldly.

'Why,' she asked in a controlled voice, 'are you here *really*? What are you doing with my designs? And what have you told my father?'

'Which question do you want me to answer first?'

'I don't care. Just so long as you answer all of them and then get out of my father's house and out of my life.'

Instead of answering, though, Luke sat back in his chair and contemplated her over the rim of his glass. He took a leisurely sip of his drink, carefully placed his glass on the table next to him and then linked his fingers together on his lap, rubbing the pads of his thumbs together.

In the ensuing silence, Miranda had a good chance to look at him and to notice that his clothes bore no resemblance to the old gear he had worn in the cabin. In fact, he looked smart. Expensively smart. The trousers were hand-tailored, the crisp blue and white shirt bore the hallmarks of quality as did the deep tan brogues. But then, she considered feverishly, he would have dressed up to visit her father if his aim was to try and con money out

99

of him or at least show him a respectable side if he was harbouring some dark hidden agenda.

'I didn't tell your father about us,' he said abruptly.

'There *is* no *us*!'

'Okay, I'll rephrase that. I didn't tell your father that the apple of his eye had made a play for the caretaker and embarked on a passionate, two-day fling, no strings attached. I didn't think that particular version of the truth would be appropriate.'

Miranda glanced nervously over her shoulder just in case her father was hovering. 'I did not...'

'Oh, yes, you did. But don't worry. That's still our little secret.'

Still? Did that mean that he intended to spill the beans if she didn't go along with whatever he had in mind? Her cheeks were flushed with hectic colour. 'If you've come here to blackmail me...' she whispered urgently, leaning forward and impatiently pushing her hair away from her face.

'What would you do about it?' He looked at her coldly.

'It would be your word against mine!'

'Well, I'll just set your seedy little mind at rest by telling you that I don't play those kinds of games. In case you're interested, I have a lot of respect for your father...'

'Having never seen him in your life before!' Miranda burst out shrilly. She snatched the drink from the table and shakily drank some more of her wine in an attempt to steady her nerves.

'That's not quite true.'

It took several seconds for that simple sentence to find its way to her brain and several more for it to gather momentum. Miranda stared at the man sitting opposite her. She was dreaming all of this. In a minute, she would wake up and discover that, in fact, she was still crushed in between two overweight businessmen on the Underground and had in fact nodded off and had begun having a wild, inexplicable dream. She blinked.

'What do you mean? What are you talking about?'

'It means...' He shook his head and then began restlessly prowling through the room, pausing to examine various *objets d'art*, although Miranda got the impression that he wasn't so much looking at them as giving himself time to think.

Finally he returned to his chair but, instead of sitting down, he perched on the fat, cushioned arm of the chair, his long legs extended in front of him. 'I know your father, Miranda. I've met him a number of times before.'

'You're lying.'

'I know you find what I'm saying hard to believe but...'

'You're lying. Why are you lying to me? What are you trying to prove?'

'I'm not trying to prove anything!' he said impatiently. 'Just listen to what I'm going to tell you without interrupting. You can save your thoughts for later.' He raked his fingers through his hair and glanced at her. Under normal circumstances, Miranda would have enjoyed seeing this big, powerful, self-assured man floundering but her mind was too involved along its own tricky path to appreciate his rare failure to be in command.

'When you showed up at my cabin...'

'*Your* cabin?'

Luke shot her another impatient look. 'That's right. *My* cabin.'

'But you said...'

'I suppose it was too much asking you to sit out my explanation in silence. Yes, yes, I know what I said.' He resumed his prowling until she could feel her nerves being shredded by his ceaseless movement.

'I wish you'd just sit down and tell me what you have to tell me!' she snapped, and he gave a little shrug of his shoulders, obediently sitting down, though unfortunately on the sofa alongside her. She sat panic-stricken, frozen on the sofa.

'I didn't actually tell you that I was a caretaker,' he said slowly, 'I just agreed with what you assumed.'

'Why would you do that? None of this makes any sense.' Miranda shook her head in utter bewilderment, hoping to catch a glimmer of revelation and failing. She felt like someone trying to find the way out of a labyrinth with every turn leading to a dead end.

'Why would I do that...?' he murmured, looking at her. 'The fact is I own the cabin. I know I told you it wasn't mine, but it is. It's my bolt-hole. Every year for three weeks I disappear there to wind down from the stresses of my daily life. I take time out. I see no one because I invite no one there to see me. So you can well imagine my annoyance when you interrupted my solitude with your sprained ankle and your expensive, well-bred, pathetic helplessness.'

Miranda was still trying to imagine this man being the owner of the cabin, never mind picture what he'd felt when she'd stumbled into him. Her brain had not quite made it to that particular point of the narration as yet.

'So what do you do?' she asked in a dazed voice.

'I work in London, as it happens.'

'You work in London.' She might have been saying, so you live on Planet Mars.

'I thought that it was just typical of a girl like you to assume that a man like me, holed up in a basic little cabin far from the glamour of the ski slopes, couldn't possibly be anything more than a poor, lowly caretaker and, I admit, I found the assumption amusing. Amusing and convenient. I had no desire to find myself at the receiving end of some impressionable little girl fresh out of a relationship and on the lookout for another rich man to ensnare.'

Miranda felt her cheeks sting and she rested her head in the palms of her hands. 'You lied to me.'

'Look at me.' He gently circled one of her wrists with his fingers and she flinched as though she had been burnt. Flinched and pulled away, shifting further up the sofa. But she did look at him.

'I admit, it suited me. Then you told me your name and I realised that I knew your father. Didn't it ever occur to you that your father was singularly unworried by you being trapped in the middle of nowhere with a stranger?'

'I thought…I thought that even if he was worried, he would be more relieved by the fact that I was safe.'

'Of course he was relieved that you were safe. He was also infinitely more relieved that you had had the luck to be saved by someone he knew personally.'

'I would have met you…'

'No, Miranda.' He shook his head gently. 'Your life and your father's business life barely touched. I'd bet my life that you wouldn't recognise ninety per cent of the people he mixes with through business.'

It was true. When she'd been younger, he had tried to encourage her to play the occasional hostess at some of his corporate events but, after the first one, she had declared herself bored with the concept of having to make polite conversation with people who'd meant nothing to her, and he had never pressed her again.

'And one of those people was me. To cut a long story short, years ago, he helped raise the finance to get my father's business on the road and, from that point on, he remained friends with my father. Despite the fact that your father was born into wealth, he was still imbued with the values of hard work and making his way in the world through his own efforts. He could appreciate similar aspirations in my father. Much later, I wanted some advice on a takeover I was planning and I consulted your father.'

The storyline was getting so complicated that her brain was finding it hard to keep up.

'So Dad and you had a cosy little chat about me and then what…? Decided that I ought to remain ignorant of your true identity? How could he? How could *you*?' She felt tears of mortification sting the backs of her eyes.

'It wasn't quite like that,' Luke said mildly. 'I spoke to your father on the telephone…'

'I remember. You went into the kitchen to do that…'

'I told him that you were with me and made some joke about the fact that you thought I was the hired help; and, after we had laughed a bit about it, he suggested that it might be an idea to go along with the assumption because a bit of hard work might do you the world of good. I agreed.'

'A bit of hard work!'

'Try not to fly off the handle, Miranda,' Luke said sharply. 'Just take a minute to look at yourself from the outside. You've lived a life of privilege, doted on by your father. I doubt you've ever come across anyone who hasn't automatically fallen in line with what you want. Believe me, your father didn't have to twist my arm to go along with his idea. I was one hundred per cent behind it. I thought it would do you the world of good not to have your own way for once. I also had no intention of pandering to a rich young girl's every whim.'

'And letting me play around on your computer was what? Another kindly piece of education to guide me in the right direction? One more addition to your little experiment?' Her voice was laced with bitterness.

'Actually,' Luke said drily, 'I thought it would give you something to do. I remember your father telling me that you were talented and I was curious to see what you could do.'

'And of course,' Miranda said slowly, 'I was working on *your* house, wasn't I?'

'My house.' He agreed.

'And making love?' she blurted out. 'What was that? More home tutoring in how to make wilful Miranda into a more responsible adult?' She clenched her fists and fought down a feeling of nausea.

'That was...' His face flushed darkly. 'That was... unexpected.'

'And should I be flattered by that?' she threw at him. 'That it wasn't part of your grand, master plan?'

'There was no master plan.'

Miranda gave a snort of incredulous laughter that verged on sobbing.

'Stop being so damned selfish,' he grated. 'Your father thought it might be a much needed experience. To understand what it was like to cook for yourself, amuse yourself, do all the millions of things that you have never had any need to do for yourself.

'Now, you may like to take the moral high ground and think that you were somehow betrayed, but let's take a good, close look at it. You've come back to England and you haven't been able to feel too happy about resuming your normal existence, have you?'

His voice was brutal. If she could have fled to another part of the house, then she would have, but she suspected that any thoughts of escape would be well and truly cut off by the man skewering her with his eyes. And she knew from experience that she wouldn't stand a chance against him when it came to flight.

'Well, have you?' he repeated harshly, barely giving her time to repair her battered defences.

'I...' She raised her blue eyes to his.

'You're looking for a job because you can't face the thought of getting back on that mad, pointless merry-go-round, can you? You're fed up with the ride, aren't you Miranda? Fed up with the same old people doing the same old things in the same old places. You've had time to think...'

'For which I should be thanking you, I suppose!'

'And you want out. Which is why you've been tramping the streets of London looking for work...'

'I have not,' Miranda informed him, clutching to the few shreds of self-composure that hadn't yet been demolished under his remorseless litany of accusations, 'been ''tramping the streets of London looking for work''. I've tramped to the careers advisory office at the design college.'

He shrugged dismissively as though her insistence on precision was beside the point.

This was the man she had fallen in love with! She was finding it hard to understand why, even though she knew with frightening honesty that, despite everything he had said and done, she still found herself compulsively attuned to his presence, like a drought victim with water in sight.

'Where you've been told that there's a stiff price to be paid for your years of cheerful abandon.'

'You didn't need much imagination to get to that conclusion,' Miranda said sullenly, 'considering my father announced it the minute he was in the room.'

'Are you all right?' The sudden shift in tone caught her unawares and her eyes flickered hesitantly over his face, then she stared down at her powder-blue lap, her mouth down-turned.

If he thought she was going to admit that what he had said to her or, rather, had rammed down her throat, had made sense, then he had another think coming. She felt like someone who had been unwittingly used as a guinea pig in an experiment and, even though the experiment had worked, still felt like a guinea pig.

No wonder he hadn't wanted her to stay on. The experiment had been over. It had been time for the guinea pig to head home. She felt a wave of self-pity batter the hastily erected walls of her self-control and she inhaled deeply, steadying her ragged nerves.

'Never been better,' she offered icily. 'I've just discovered that I've been the butt of a quality learning experience hatched up by you and my dad, been made love to by someone who loathed me on sight and probably still loathed me when he was making love to me but couldn't resist the free offer, and you ask me if I'm all right. Why shouldn't I be all right?'

Luke looked at her steadily through narrowed, dangerously perceptive eyes. 'Whoever mentioned anything about loathing you?' he asked in a voice that matched the expression in his eyes. 'And if your intention is to insult my intelligence by suggesting that I made love to a woman I loathed, then you've succeeded. I have never laid a finger on a woman I didn't like and I hope to God I never do.' Which was something, she thought resentfully. He *liked* her, meaningless word that it was.

But, before she could analyse what he had said, he was continuing with the same merciless intensity, 'and while you're thrashing about in the throes of self-pity and wounded pride, why don't you spare a thought for me?'

'For *you*?' She gaped incredulously at him and was

tempted to shriek with laughter. 'Why should I feel sorry for *you*?'

'Whatever motives you may credit me with for making love to you,' he told her with a thread of steel in his voice, 'your own motives are firmly rooted in some pretty murky water as well.'

Miranda's disbelieving jaw dropped a few inches further.

'There you were, perhaps not heartbroken after your little fling with the philandering Freddie, but certainly with your pride a bit on the bruised side. Consciously or subconsciously, what better way to restore some of your dented ego than a fling with a robust yokel?'

'Stop referring to yourself as a yokel,' was all she could find to refute this piece of incisive but utterly off-target logic. Trust a man to apply the forces of reason to a situation and unreasonably reach the wrong conclusion. But then, how could he begin to guess the panic that had stifled her thinking processes when she had tried to visualise leaving him behind without a backward glance?

She certainly had no intention of setting the record straight! Least of all on a stomach full of unwelcome revelations!

She decided that a change of subject was called for. Let him remain unenlightened. She pointed to the sheaf of papers, *her* designs, which had been relegated to the floor for a while. 'And so you've come to give me some work, have you? Has my father put you up to that by any chance?'

'No, he hasn't.' He retrieved the papers and resumed his unwanted proximity to her on the sofa.

'I don't need you feeling sorry for me,' Miranda informed him, before he could launch into a patronising speech about lending a helping hand. 'I didn't have much luck with the careers advisor but I'm still confident that I can get things going. I might start by working for someone else and then see where to go from there.'

'You will be working for somebody else. You'll be working for me.'

'I don't need your help!'

'Of course, there are one or two things you'll need to improve on.'

The roaring in Miranda's ears and the gut-wrenching sensation of wanting to drop through the floor melted in the face of this fresh piece of criticism. *Improve on?'*

'There's no need to act as though it's a dirty word.' He rustled the papers on his lap and pulled out one of them. It was her detailed design for the kitchen and she noticed that bits of her work had been changed. 'You'll never get work if you rise up in arms the minute your employer tries to put some ideas forward.'

'You are not my employer!'

'I didn't care for this central island thing. It's going to take up too much space and I don't have enough to fill the cupboards anyway. It's not necessary.'

Miranda snatched the paper away from him and jabbed her finger at one side of the drawing. 'There are only cupboards on one side!' She smirked, unable to resist the opportunity to point out an error, an error *he* had made. 'On the other side, there's empty space for bar stools so you can sit and eat at the kitchen counter if you don't want the formality of sitting at a table. There's also scope for a television to be angled against the wall *there* so you can sit and eat and watch your favourite movie; that would be one involving undercover behaviour and blackmail!'

Before she could turn away and let him stew in his mistake, he had extracted another piece of paper and was drawing her attention to a range of bookshelves she had designed for his den, bombarding her with useless questions about heights and widths and informing her that she hadn't given him enough space for a work area, which was the point of the den in the first place.

'What's the point having an extensive work area if you have an office in London?' Miranda snapped, her eyes furiously scouring the paper and mentally rearranging her design to incorporate a bigger desk with concealed panelling to house filing cabinets.

'That's not the sort of objection that should be raised to a change in design. For future reference. Anyway, I intend to do a lot more work from the house and only commute to London when necessary. I'll keep my apartment on there and use it as an occasional base. And you didn't make allowances for the pool.'

This was getting ridiculous. Miranda felt herself torn between proud and haughty retreat in the face of a job offer she had no intention of taking up, and heated defence of her designs, her first for years. Her blue eyes mirrored the internal struggle and finally she felt compelled to inform him that he had never mentioned wanting a pool.

'I've decided that I want one now.'

'Well, get in touch with some pool people and have one. There's enough land to fit ten pools if you're desperate for a spot of exercise.'

'I want an indoor one.'

'It won't fit.'

'Somewhere downstairs. More of a Jacuzzi than a pool,' he mused thoughtfully. 'Murals on the walls, a couple of columns Roman-style, and a bubbling Jacuzzi so that I can relax in the evenings with a glass of champagne.'

The image was alluring enough to have her mentally

plotting the spot. She brought herself sharply back to reality and thought about the fact that she was discussing Jacuzzis with a man who she had assumed to be a relatively penniless caretaker with nothing more on his mind than his next pit stop. The penniless caretaker she had fallen in love with. The penniless caretaker who had turned out to be an Oscar-winning actor with a degree in lying.

'There's no point going through all this with me. I don't want your job.'

'Fine.'

She watched reluctantly as he stacked the papers and shoved them back into the briefcase, feeling a certain pique that he had surrendered so easily.

'Just so long as you don't object to someone else using your designs, because I thought on the whole they were remarkably good. Very imaginative. Just what I was looking for.'

Miranda stared furiously at him. 'You can't just take my work and hand it over to someone else!' she spluttered and he gave her an implacable smile, lifting his shoulders to imply that he had no problem with that and, besides, what else could he do?

'Why not?'

'Because...because it belongs to me!'

'How do you work that out?'

'And you can stop giving me that innocent, butter-wouldn't-melt-in-my-mouth look! You know exactly why you can't appropriate my work!'

'As far as I know, you never mentioned anything about charging for these designs when you started them...'

'Because I didn't think they were going to be used!'

'Your father will be disappointed. But still, it can't be helped. You've got to find your own feet and if that means turning down my job, for which you would have been more than amply paid and which would have represented something pretty major to add to your portfolio, then so be it. People would have sat up and taken you seriously after a job like this, especially when they knew who the client was. I may not have made much of a mark in the glamorous world of trendy night spots and swinging clubs but my name in financial circles holds quite a bit of credence. You would have found yourself with a number of doors flung open. But there you go. You've got to take the course of action you see fit. Shall we go and join your father now and break the news to him?' He stood up and stuck his hands in his pockets, turning to look at her.

'That's right! If I'm going to get back into this design thing, then it's got to be *my* way, without help from anyone.'

'Because accepting help is something you wouldn't do in a thousand years, isn't it?' he suggested mildly, and Miranda's darkly defined eyebrows met in a frown. 'Because you've never had to expect help from any quarter. You've always been the centre of attention and you've never wanted anything badly enough to need to ask for help.'

'Because accepting help from *you* isn't something I would do in a million years.'

'Then I shall feel no compunctions about handing your work over to someone else and letting them take eventual credit for your designs. Remember *you* would have been helping *me*.'

'But I don't want to help *you*.'

Blue met blue. Although he was clearly waiting for her to stand up so that they could leave the room and join their father for supper, Miranda found that she couldn't move.

'Pride comes before a fall, Miranda,' he murmured, so softly that she had to strain to hear him. The weight of defeat settled on her shoulders like a boulder. Defeat and, she admitted grudgingly, the thrill of a challenge, the thrill of being in contact with this man again, however much he had humiliated her.

'The only reason I would accept this job is because you're using the threat of handing my work to someone else.'

He sat back down, leaning back into the arm of the sofa so that he could cross his legs, his ankle resting on his thigh and affording her the unwelcome sight of fine wool stretching against his big muscular thighs.

'And it doesn't mean that I accept how you behaved. You made a fool of me.'

'That's ridiculous.'

Miranda was not going to be drawn into an inconclusive discussion about rights and wrongs. He and her father had connived to keep her in the dark about who he really was and to teach her a lesson. However much he sat there and tried to rationalise what they had both done, it made no difference: she felt as though she had been subjected to an exercise in humiliation.

But the cards were stacked in his favour and he knew it. She *had* changed; maybe she would have changed anyway, irrespective of their interfering. She wanted to work and he held the trump card.

'But I won't mention it again. It happened and there's nothing I can do about it.' Her voice implied that she would do plenty if she could. 'I'll work for you but the arrangement is purely business.' She reached out her hand for her designs and he gave her a hooded, lazy look from under his dark lashes.

'Not so fast. What makes you think I'm going to hand over your designs before a contract is signed?'

Miranda shot him an outraged look. 'It's called trust.'

'There's no such thing in my world,' he answered lightly while he continued to scrutinise her flustered face with a closed expression. 'In my world, it's a case of survival of the fittest and you would be surprised how many reach survival status by letting other people down.'

'Yourself included, I presume?'

'You're determined to believe the worst of me, aren't you?'

'Wouldn't *you* be if you were in my shoes?' Her restless fingers played with the tassel of one of the deep burgundy cushions on the sofa, threading the silken strands of cloth together then combing them through with her short rounded nails. 'You could have told me the truth…'

'When?' he demanded heavily. 'Perhaps I wanted to, but just couldn't find the right time to do it.'

And perhaps, Miranda thought, piecing together her own jigsaw puzzle of his motivations in her head, it had just been easier to take what had been on offer in the full knowledge that he would never have to see her again and hence would never have to deal with a confrontation he found distasteful. But then he had looked at her designs and had liked them and the confrontation had become an unavoidable reality.

'What else did you lie to me about?' she asked in a small voice. 'Are you married? Do you have a girlfriend? Are those other things you found convenient and amusing to keep to yourself?'

'You know the answers to those questions, so why ask them?'

'I don't know the answers to anything when it comes

to you,' Miranda threw back at him and, gratifyingly, he was the first to look away.

'No wife. No girlfriend. No children lurking in the background.'

'I'm surprised you haven't got hordes of women stampeding you with their attentions.' Why had she said that? She didn't want to go down this personal road of recrimination. She wanted everything to be kept on a purely business level, or else how would she be able to function? But her heart was obviously in disagreement with her head and her bitterness was too close to the surface to allow reason the space to make its own rules and follow them. 'After all, you said it yourself. You're rich, single and eligible. Wasn't that why you were so eager to encourage my assumption that you were a simple caretaker with nothing on his mind but chopping logs and looking after his boss's property?'

'I haven't noticed any hordes of women outside my front door recently.' He didn't appear inclined to enlarge on this simple statement, but she remained stubbornly silent, willing him to continue even though she knew she would recoil from what she heard. It was too easy to picture this man with a woman.

'I finished with my last girlfriend six months ago.' He laughed drily in the face of her incredulous disbelief. 'She wanted marriage, kids, the whole nine yards, and I couldn't promise her that.'

'So you did the kind thing, did you?' Her voice was edged with sarcasm but he didn't rise to the challenge of justifying himself. He wasn't sorry for what he had done, she thought resentfully, he was sorry for *her* and would keep his temper under lock and key, giving her the room to vent her frustrated anger for however long she wanted. She asked tightly, 'What was she like?'

'Tall. Dark-haired.' He shrugged. 'Extremely self-possessed.'

Unlike me, Miranda thought with savage jealousy. 'What did she do?'

'For a living?'

She nodded, determined to go down this road even though it was like walking on broken glass.

'A barrister.'

'Ah. Right. No wonder you thought I was a pathetic, helpless encumbrance.'

'That's not all I thought,' he qualified softly, but Miranda was too consumed by the self-inflicted pain of her own curiosity to hear the indistinct murmur.

'A bruised girl on the lookout for a rich partner to take over from the last one.' She raised fiery eyes to his. 'And what makes you think I won't try to work my feminine wiles on you now that I know what you're worth?'

'What makes you think I...? No.' He shook his head and stood up. 'Your father will be wondering what's happened to us,' he said curtly, moving towards the door and then pausing to wait for her. 'I'll get a contract prepared for signatures by Wednesday, then we can go and see the house. You can get a feel for the place.'

'*We?*' Her mind leap-frogged to the one snag she had not taken into consideration: the fact that she would be in his presence.

'It *is* my house,' he said wryly, as she walked towards him falteringly. 'And I intend to get very involved in every step of the work. If you think that poses a problem, then I suggest you tell me now.'

'A problem? Why should it pose a problem?' She tilted her head to look at him evenly. 'Like I said, Luke, from here on in what we have is solely a business arrangement.'

CHAPTER SEVEN

THREE weeks later, she could barely remember what had led her to assume that their business arrangement would involve him appearing on her horizon on an occasional basis only.

What she had not expected was to have him around, all day, most days, hovering over her shoulder like a guilty conscience while she liaised with the various builders, instructing them what to do. Whenever she bent her head to inspect some aspect of her designs so that she could discuss them with Tom, the architect, his dark head seemed to be next to hers, examining the same piece of paper, asking questions, discussing, pointing out small improvements or alterations on the original design work. He appeared to have nothing of greater importance on which to focus and it was slowly driving her crazy.

He was the constant thorn in her side, never giving her enough space to distance herself from him. And, consequently, their business arrangement, which she had optimistically assumed would kill off all feeling she had for him, was gradually turning into a battleground of unspoken emotion.

She was now so acutely sensitive to his presence that she could feel him even before he made his appearance in whatever room she happened to be in. And because he never gave her any forewarning as to when he was likely to materialise, she spent her days in nervous expectation of his unannounced arrivals. The fact that he was extremely pleased with her progress was little consolation.

'Haven't you got anywhere else to stand?' she asked irritably one afternoon, as she stood running her eyes over one of the bedrooms, trying to ascertain how it would look completed and what colour furnishings she should advise him to try.

'Sure.' He strolled over to the bay window and then perched on the window sill so that he was now in the middle of her visual scan. As usual, his work jacket had been replaced by a weathered Barbour in a similar deep green shade as her own; and his charcoal-grey tailored trousers were incongruously tucked into a pair of func-tional though extremely muddy boots.

Whilst alterations to the basic house were not that ex-tensive, the place was still unfit for clothing of a formal nature. The carpets had all been ripped out in preparation for wooden flooring, which he intended to use downstairs, and the bare floors and lack of curtains lent the entire house an air of work in progress.

'You're still in my way.'

'What are you trying to visualise?'

'I'm trying to visualise you going away and letting me get on with my work.'

'I didn't think I was interrupting you…' His eyebrows shot up in innocent amazement and Miranda clicked her tongue impatiently. He was nothing if not deeply respect-ful of her initial demand that their relationship be kept strictly business. Not once had he mentioned the cabin, or the fraught and life-changing few days they had spent together there. It might not have had existed as far as he was concerned. She had quickly realised that, whilst they may have been fraught and life-changing for her, they were a distant and forgotten memory for him.

'Well, you are,' she snapped, her eyes finally coming

to rest on his formidable body positioned where she could not relegate his presence to the background.

'You're tired,' he suggested mildly and Miranda gave him a dry look.

'I'm tired of you traipsing around behind me.' She sighed, sitting on the ground and resting back against the wall with her eyes closed. She yawned, realising that he was right. She was weary and hungry. 'I mean, Luke, haven't you got an empire to run? I thought you could only spare three weeks out of the year to recover from your stressed existence?' With her eyes shut, she was unaware of him coming towards her until she heard the rustle of his clothes as he sat down beside her.

She felt herself shiver involuntarily and wondered whether he was aware of her reaction to his proximity. She had spent the past few weeks slavishly making sure that she maintained a mask of iron self-control, never letting it slip to reveal the effect his intrusive, disturbing presence had on her. But, while that supported the fiction that he was nothing now but an employer, it also worked against her, allowing their conversations to roam unchecked, allowing his flashes of wit to penetrate her defences and take root in her already treacherous heart.

'My vice president is covering for me,' he murmured, his breath tingling in her ear as he turned to look at her averted profile, nakedly exposed, as it always was now, with her hair ruthlessly scraped away from her face and tightly weaved into a plait that hung down her back like a rope of pale silk. 'And I do keep in close touch with the office. Have laptop, will travel.' They remained in silence for a few moments until Miranda became aware of a more profound silence. The silence of no men working and her eyes flew open.

'Where are the builders?' she asked, edging very

slightly away from him and regretting that she hadn't kept her eyes shut because her vision was now too full of him for her liking. 'Shouldn't they be working?'

'Gone. I let them off early as it's Friday.'

'Gone? But it's only...' She looked at her watch and gasped. 'After six. I have to go!' She stood up, tugging down the Barbour and feverishly sticking her hands in her pockets to make sure that her wallet and car keys were in place. 'I have to get back to London,' she babbled, 'I'm going to be late. I should have left at five.'

'Where are you going?' His tone was expressionless as she flew down the stairs and he followed in her wake, his long legs making it easy for him to keep pace with her.

'Where are my books?' She spotted them on the matting by the window at the bottom of the stairs and snatched them up, struggling under the weight as she fished into her pocket for the car keys and zapped open the car.

'I asked you where you're going.'

'Out,' she said, veering away from the flat insistence in his voice.

'Well, you'll have to cancel.' He trapped her as she leaned against the side of her car, the palms of his hands flat on either side of her.

'What do you mean I'll have to cancel? I made this arrangement a week ago and I have no intention of cancelling! I haven't been out of the house for weeks!'

'Sorry,' he said calmly, without a trace of apology in his voice and he bared his teeth in something approaching a rueful smile but which instead seemed forbiddingly implacable.

'You have no claim over my leisure time.'

'Nor do I intend to,' he ground out, darkly looming as the cold breeze whipped his hair into a black tousle. 'But

I'm going to be out of the country until next Thursday and Tom wants certain decisions made before I go about placement of the conservatory. I need to discuss it with you.'

'Can't it wait?' Miranda asked, as visions of the theatre with her friends began receding into the distance. Having virtually cut off all ties with a number of her friends, bar a handful of her closer ones, she had made a deliberate effort to try and arrange a get together, if only to prove to herself that she was still capable of having a good time without Luke Decroix around. She also vaguely wanted to prove to her father that her social life had not nose-dived, that she had not suddenly turned into a demented workaholic which he seemed to be smugly encouraging.

'Can't yours?'

'How long will you be?' she asked and he flashed her a smile of triumph, pushing himself back from the bonnet of her midnight blue hatchback.

'Oh, an hour at the most,' he said, stepping back to allow her to climb into her car. 'Why don't you meet me at say...' he flicked back the cuff of his Barbour to look at his watch '...eight? In the Scarpetta brasserie in Hampstead. We can discuss these plans over something to eat.'

Something to eat. A brasserie. It would be the first time they would be together without the reassuring chaperone of builders, the house and, usually, Tom. Miranda felt her heart lurch in protest at the prospect of an intimate dinner for two. She licked her lips nervously and tried to think of some reasonable excuse why that idea could be vetoed. Under the expectant, glittering stare of his blue eyes, inspiration failed her and she heard herself stutter out an agreement.

One-and-a-half hours later, Miranda glanced to check

her reflection in the mirror in the hall. Working on the house had negated the need for make-up and, when she had opened the drawer to her considerable array of face paints and had begun applying foundation, blusher and the usual assortment of make-up she had always worn, her fingers had worked the colours uncertainly across her face, hesitant through lack of use. It didn't show. The face that looked back at her was radiant. A little *too* radiant, she thought dismally, considering she was supposed to be heading off for a meeting she did not want in a restaurant.

The outfit, which she had considered prim and suitable for the occasion, now seemed provocatively demure; but it was far too late to change; and she sighed at the ribbed deep-rose turtle-neck which she had matched with a casual pair of black jeans and her mid-thigh black coat which flared as she walked.

'Very fetching,' her father said from behind her. 'And what play will you be seeing tonight, my dear?'

'The play's been cancelled,' Miranda said, turning around and bending to retrieve her black and cream checked bag from the ground. 'In fact, plans have changed and there's no theatre tonight.'

'Why not?' Her father gave her an anxious look and she grinned at him.

'Too boring!' she declared wickedly. 'We decided that we'd just catch a plane to Paris and live it up for the weekend.'

The mild anxiety turned into full-blown dismay. She could read his thoughts as easily as a large-print book. He had been as happy as sandman ever since she had begun working and her social life had spiralled down to zero. He must now be wondering whether her zeal for her new-found career was beginning to flag in the face of all those tempting and pointless activities that she had embraced with such enthusiasm in the past.

'You didn't!' The two words of horror spoke volumes. He was positively bristling with disappointment, she thought, beginning to laugh.

'No, I didn't,' she said, putting him out of his misery. 'Actually, my boss has decided that he needs to see me to discuss this house of his and he's forced me to cancel my evening.'

'*Forced* you? I didn't think such a thing was possible.'

'To know him is to understand,' Miranda replied gloomily. 'The man assumes that he can ride roughshod over anything and anyone if it happens to suit him. Anyway, Dad, the taxi's going to be here any minute. You can reach me on my mobile if you need me.'

'Darling, I wouldn't dream of interrupting your evening with Luke.'

She opened her mouth to tell him that her 'evening with Luke' had nothing to do with enjoyment and could be interrupted at any point for any reason whatsoever, however trivial, but was interrupted by the arrival of the taxi, and she left her father smiling happily in the hall. Much to her chagrin. He had been unrepentant about his part in the cabin fiasco, meekly weathering the storm of her accusations until she had run out of steam, and she hoped that he was not now interpreting her relationship with Luke as anything other than a business deal. If he was, she thought, then he was in for a brutal shock when the job was finished and they went their separate ways.

The brasserie was reassuringly full by the time she made it there. There was no subdued lighting, or atmospheric background music; and Luke, who was waiting for her at the table, had brought his briefcase with him and was inspecting the plans of the house.

With his attention focused somewhere else, Miranda took the opportunity to look at him. He was wearing a cream cashmere jumper and a pair of deep green trousers and, as he perused the papers in front of him, his sensual mouth was compressed with concentration. His clothes, she had noticed, never seemed to conceal his well-honed bulk. If anything, he was one of those men who roused the imagination by sending some sort of subliminal message that underneath all that cotton and cashmere and silk, was a body fashioned for making love. She was still staring blatantly at him when he looked up and caught her wandering gaze, and she felt a tinge of guilty colour invade her cheeks.

'Manage to cancel your plans?' he asked, putting away the papers as she sat opposite him at the small round table.

'If I remember, you didn't give me much choice.'

'Oh, no,' he agreed, as if the thought had just suddenly occurred to him, 'I didn't, did I?' He beckoned to the waiter and ordered a bottle of wine; then he sat back in the chair and looked at her as if, now that the pleasantries, such as they were, were out of the way, he was free to study her; while she, in turn, attempted not to miss a beat.

'You're wearing make-up,' he observed, 'and your hair's out. Do you know, I've become so accustomed to seeing you with your face bare and your hair pulled back, that it's like seeing someone else.'

'I always wear make-up when I go out,' Miranda countered in a muffled voice.

'Mmm. Shame you had to cancel your dinner date.' He watched her in silence as the wine waiter poured a measure of wine for him to taste, filling both glasses when it had been passed acceptable. 'Were you going anywhere exciting?' He took a sip of wine and continued to look at her over the rim of the glass, his disturbing cobalt eyes strangely unreadable.

Miranda briefly toyed with the idea of a lie, but any such thought was stillborn. Luke would never believe her if she said that she was going to Paris for the weekend. In some weird, unspoken way, he seemed to know her. He certainly knew that she was no longer interested in the superficial life she used to lead. He had managed to prise that much out of her during one of his many infernal wanderings through the house, glued to her side, asking just the right number of pertinent questions to allow a few less pertinent ones to slip in. It was to her credit, she thought snidely, that she had managed to glean a fair amount about him as well in the process.

'It would have been exciting for me,' she answered truthfully, 'I'd planned on going to the theatre, actually, to see *Les Misérables*. I know it's been on for centuries, but would you believe I've never got around to seeing it?' She played with the stem of her wineglass before raising it to her lips and taking a few sips.

'I would, actually,' he confessed with a little laugh. 'Theatre times tend to clash with club hours.'

Miranda looked at him in sheepish agreement. 'Well. No matter. I've rearranged it for next Saturday. Anyway, you wanted to discuss the conservatory. I didn't think there was any problem with it.'

'Just making sure that it's absolutely spot on,' Luke murmured, rubbing his thumb across the cool, wet side of the glass before finishing the contents in one swallow. 'After all, this house is not going to be like my apartment.'

'No?' Miranda felt the tell-tale signs of curiosity. 'What's your apartment like? My designer nose is twitching,' she elaborated hastily, just in case he thought that she was angling for an invitation.

'My apartment…is…very uncompromising, very masculine. Maybe masculine isn't quite the right word. Maybe I should say that there are no feminine touches. Everything is functional.'

'I thought you liked that,' Miranda said lightly, pausing to give her order to the waiter. 'You told me,' she reminded him, 'that you didn't like lots of intrusive women around. I assume that meant bringing bunches of flowers in cut-glass vases and little ornaments as presents.'

'I did say that, didn't I?' He seemed to be playing with the memory, turning it over in his head, trying it on for size. 'But now…' he watched as her glass was refilled, '…now, I'm beginning to think that my apartment days are drawing to an end. A man can only survive happily for so long with minimal furniture, minimal kitchen equipment and an exercise machine in the guest room.'

'So you're hankering for the perfect family home,' Miranda said with a tight smile.

'That's a bit strong, but maybe it's time to think about putting down roots and seeing what happens.'

'And is there anyone you have in mind to fill the vacancy?' She could feel a constricting tightness in her stomach, as if a fist was slowly squeezing her intestines. Of course, it was natural for any man to want a family. Perhaps the house had initiated those thought patterns. Perhaps he had bought the house in response to them. What came first, the chicken or the egg? It seemed bitterly ironic to be renovating the house for the man she loved so that he could lay it at the feet of the woman he would eventually want to share his life with.

'Can I pass on that question?' He laughed as if in response to a joke. It was lost on her, and Miranda grimaced in response. She hoped he would interpret the sour baring of teeth as a chummy, unthreatening smile.

'And you intend to have children?' she asked politely, fighting off an inclination to violent nausea. 'The house is certainly ideal for bringing up a family. Lots of space and a large garden.'

'It certainly is ideal, isn't it? I couldn't contemplate raising a family in London. I grew up in the rolling countryside of Warwichshire and I can't imagine what it would be like to have pavements as your playground and parks on a weekend, weather providing.'

Which, over the superb meal, led to a conversation about the relative values of the countryside versus the city. It was an invigorating argument if she could see her way to thinking that it was all theoretical; but she got the distinct impression that there was now a woman in his life and the thought nagged away at the back of her mind until three glasses of very good wine managed to dull it into relatively obedient silence.

It was only when they were finishing their coffee that the reason for their meeting in the first place occurred to her. They had spent not a minute discussing the plans for the conservatory, an oversight he smoothly brushed over by suggesting that they adjourn to his apartment to view the plans at leisure.

'You didn't bring a car, did you?'

Miranda shook her head and started to say, 'but—'

'Good. My driver can take you home when we're through.'

'It's a bit late…'

'My fault,' he said humbly, holding his hands up in surrender. 'But I really do need to discuss this with you before I leave the country, so that you can make sure that Tom knows what he's doing. If you think your father's going to worry if you're not home, then why don't you call him. I promise you, though, I'll make sure you're back before the witching hour.'

He gave her a smile of such persuasive charm that Miranda's protests shrank into low, inaudible grumbles; and she watched in silence as he called his driver on his mobile to collect them outside the restaurant.

While she feverishly contemplated this fresh, night-marish development looming ahead of her, a trial for her already frazzled self-composure, Luke conducted a smooth and effortless conversation. He told her about his views on the stupidity of driving while under the influence of alcohol, hence the necessity for him to have a personal driver if he thought he might be over the limit; he told her about his job, making her laugh weakly as he por-trayed himself as a slave to the office, barely having time to exercise and therefore needing to install an exercise machine in his guest room.

In response, Miranda huddled into her coat despite the warmth in the back of the chauffeur-driven Jaguar and stuttered out an occasional observation when the only other alternative would be a telling silence.

They couldn't have been in the car for longer than twenty-five minutes, although it felt like hours. She heard Luke tell his driver that he would be ready in about an hour. She slid out of the car in a flurry of panic-driven nervousness, following him into the expansive marble-tiled reception area and up three floors to his apartment.

It turned out to be a suite of the kind usually viewed in magazines. True, he hadn't been lying when he had said that it was furnished in the most spartan of styles, but there was an abundance of muted taste in the décor. The absence of bright colours lent a starkness to the black leather furniture in the sunken sitting area, as did the util-itarian nature of the lighting, which appeared to be comprised solely of spotlights and burnished-silver standing lights. Only a Persian rug in the centre, a wash of deep warm hues, gave colour to the room.

But she was not allowed to linger very long in fascinated inspection, drinking up all the outer details that filled the mental image she had of the man himself in her head. He led her into the kitchen, which was almost as large as the sitting room and expensively equipped with chrome appliances, including an impressive cappuccino machine on one of the counters.

'I'm an addict of fresh coffee,' he said wryly, following her gaze to the black and silver machine, 'and I'm particularly fond of cappuccino. Something about all that frothy milk always seems wickedly decadent.'

The words 'wickedly decadent' brought a flush to Miranda's cheeks. She could cast her mind back to one or two wickedly decadent things herself and none of them included the consumption of fresh coffee!

He expertly began operating the complicated-looking machine and, after a few minutes, she was handed a cup of steaming coffee with the requisite one-inch layer of froth on top.

Then he laid out Tom's plans on the kitchen table. The kitchen table was black, solid black wood, with clean, uncluttered lines and was ringed with six metal chairs with hessian seat pads. Miranda looked at it sceptically, then she turned her gaze to Luke who had pulled one of the chairs out and had sat down, his large hand cradling the mug of steaming coffee.

'None of this makes any sense,' she said slowly, moving to join him at the table. Any after-effects of the wine had winged their way out of her head the minute they had left the restaurant and her mind was as clear as a bell. Clear, if still tensely wary.

'What doesn't make any sense?' He had divested himself of the cream jumper and had rolled the sleeves of his plain cream shirt to the elbows. Everything about him was so intensely real; but here, in this apartment, she felt as though she had uncovered yet another layer of this complex man. How many layers could one person have? She wondered. Shouldn't *she* be the complex and mysterious one? No wonder his initial opinion of her had been of a shallow airhead. Probably still thought along those lines. Not nearly as deep, complicated and enigmatic as the lawyer types he associated with.

'This is nothing like the cabin, is it?' Miranda said bluntly. 'All this chrome and black everywhere. The furniture in the cabin was so rustic and, well, lived in. *What sort of man are you?*' she added accusingly. He raised his dark eyebrows in amusement.

'You make me sound like a split-personality misfit,' he said, his mouth curving into a smile. 'Do all your clothes look the same? Are all your shoes the same colour? I'm a man who likes a bit of variety. Don't we all?'

'You know what I mean.'

'I know what you mean,' he concurred obediently. 'I guess, the cabin's much more my style. Old and battered. But three years ago I had someone come in to do this apartment out for me when I bought it and she must have figured that I was the kind of guy who liked being in a high-tech environment.' He shrugged. 'It suits me. I just sleep here. If I need to entertain, I tend to go out to do it.'

'Why didn't you complain when she did it? You're under my skin like a tick,' she said, unable to resist the snide sarcasm, 'so how is that you let someone get away with kitting out an apartment you didn't like? I'm surprised you didn't dog her footsteps every inch of the way.'

'We were lovers when I agreed to let her furnish this,' Luke said bluntly. 'We even had vague plans of moving in together but, by the time it was finished, so were we, and I just never got around to doing anything about changing it.'

'Is that why you're so cynical about the opposite sex?' Miranda asked quietly. 'Because someone you loved let you down in the past?'

Luke lowered his eyes. 'Perhaps. I don't like to think I'm vulnerable—what man does? But perhaps I am. Perhaps there's a part of me that still clings to the wreckage of that disastrous relationship, hence my inability to get rid of all this stuff.' He shrugged his broad shoulders fractionally. 'Perhaps, subconsciously, I feel that if I part with all of this, then I shall finally have to say goodbye to the one woman who broke my heart. Who knows, maybe this whole house business is just an empty hope that I can recreate the thing I've lost.'

Miranda felt tears spring to her eyes. She hoped that they were tears of sympathy for this man sitting before her, head lowered, humbly admitting his own frailty. Unfortunately, she suspected that they might well be tears of self-pity and misery. Every word he had said, had sent a dagger straight to her heart and every syllable had twisted the dagger until she felt as though she was bleeding inside.

'I'm sorry,' she whispered. She placed her hand on his wrist, feeling the fine dark hairs against her palm. His warm hand stirred under hers and he clasped her fingers tightly. His other free hand went to his down-bend head, cradling his forehead, forming a shield against her concerned gaze.

'I hope you won't think less of me,' he murmured, not

looking at her, 'because I've succumbed to this show of emotion.'

'I know it's not easy for you to express your feelings,' Miranda said softly. 'But don't be ashamed.'

'Will you comfort me in my hour of need?'

'Will I *what*?'

He peeped through two fingers and she saw that his shoulders were heaving. Heaving but not with the uncontrollable sobbing of a man who could no longer contain a flood of emotion: his shoulders were heaving with laughter. Silent laughter until the silence could no longer be repressed and he collapsed, still clutching her hand.

Miranda yanked her hand out of his grasp and sat back. 'You…*you*…'

'I'm sorry. I couldn't resist.' He could barely form a coherent sentence amidst his splutterings of mirth.

'That's it!' she yelled. 'You fraud! I'm going!'

'Oh, where's your sense of humour?' he asked, sobering up, but only just. 'The last time I got philosophical with you at the cabin, you didn't hesitate to switch me off. I was just responding to your psychobabble.' He grinned unrepentantly at her and Miranda felt her lips begin to twitch in reciprocal humour. She sat back down and assumed a lofty air of indifference to his infantile clowning.

'Very ice-cold maiden,' he told her, still grinning.

'You mean it was all a lie?'

'Not the bit about us being lovers,' Luke admitted. 'I really did go out with Lizzie; and she really did kit this disaster of a flat out for me as a surprise when I was in New York for a fortnight on business; and we really had planned to move in together; but it all fell apart at the seams. We weren't suited for anything more durable than meals out.

'As it happens, we're still friends. She's gone back to America to live, got married six months after we broke up and has a daughter with another kiddie on the way.'

'I never redecorated this place because I could never be bothered. Always too busy, and eventually I guess I just got used to it—the way you do. Your face,' he added for good measure, 'was a picture.'

There was a strange singing in Miranda's ears. She felt light-headed. He had led her up the garden path, something he seemed very good at doing, but this time she was not annoyed, just stupidly ecstatic that the story that he had concocted and which had sent her spirits plummeting had been untrue.

'If you're quite finished with your little joke, perhaps,' she said in a tetchy voice, 'we might get down to business?'

'Business,' he agreed, looking at her and not moving a muscle. Eventually, he shook himself and gathered the various papers together and, for the next half an hour, they inspected the designs of the house, while Miranda busily took notes about measurements and placement of ceiling lights.

When they had finally finished, he handed the papers to her in a plastic file and sat back with his arms folded behind his head.

'You're enjoying this, aren't you?'

Miranda looked back at him, stuck for words. 'You dragged me away from my plans for the evening. How can you ask me whether I'm enjoying this? I mean…yes, it's been a nice enough evening as evenings go… The food at the restaurant was very good… And I suppose as company goes…' she could feel her heart thumping behind her ribcage and her skin felt hot and tight. It was because of the way he was looking at her, as though every pore, every ounce of his concentration was focused on her '…well, yes, you can be an amusing enough companion when you try…' Why kid herself? Just being in his company, for whatever reason, was enough to make her feel as if she was walking on cloud nine. Without him around, her life was flat.

'Actually, I meant that you seemed to be enjoying your work.'

It took a few seconds for her to realise that she had misconstrued his innocuous observation, and then she went bright red as she frantically tried to recall if she had said anything incriminating.

'Yes, of course!' She breathed in deeply and made a great show of checking the time on her watch. 'Yes, it's fun. I mean, I feel as if I'm doing something useful, which is nice.'

'Nice.'

'That's right!' she snapped. 'Now, what time did you say your driver was coming to fetch me?' She stood up and gathered her hair in one hand, scooping it over her shoulder and, after a few lazy minutes of studying her edginess, he stood up, just as there was a ring on the doorbell. The driver! She could have hugged him!

'You know,' he said softly, as she began walking towards the door, 'there's no need to be nervous around me. Haven't I respected your wish that we keep things purely on a business level?'

Miranda could feel his words stroking the back of her neck, lazily feathering her spine and making the hair on her arms stand on end.

'Yes, and just as well, because I wouldn't have taken this job on if you hadn't,' she said, stoking up some healthy aggression and eyeing the lift door with relief. She pinged the button and waited in silence, with her back to him, as the lift finally arrived and the doors slid open.

'Thank you for the meal.' She eventually turned to look at him, with her bag and the papers clutched defensively against her chest.

'Oh, I'll see you down.' Before she could protest, he had stepped into the lift. He swamped the confined area. If she moved two inches she would bump into him, feel his hard bulk against hers. She kept resolutely to one side, determined not to babble herself into embarrassed silence.

'In case you were wondering,' he said conversationally, as the lift finally bumped and the doors opened, 'it's taken a lot of will-power.'

He held the doors so that she could step out.

'Don't you want to know what I'm talking about?'

'No!'

'Coward. Of course you do.' He strolled past the reception desk, nodding briefly at the uniformed porter. 'Well,' he said at the outer glass doors, 'I'll tell you anyway.' He put one finger under her chin and turned her face to his. 'I remember us making love, Miranda, and it's taken a lot to keep my hands off you.'

Miranda sucked in her breath and half closed her eyes. He would kiss her and she wanted him to with a desperation that terrified her. Never mind logic and reason and the absence of love.

'But business is business,' he said to her parted lips, and he kissed her chastely on the forehead. 'Good night.'

CHAPTER EIGHT

SO WHAT did that mean? That he wanted her? Wanting had a time limit that love didn't have, she dismissed categorically for the hundredth time. Wanting was fine when that was what both partners in the game agreed to, but when the scales were top heavy, wanting became a liability. That was just the sort of equation that led a woman to feel desperate, and Miranda had never felt desperate in her life before.

She frowned and stared at the samples of tiles in her hand. It should have been peaceful this past week, working in the safe knowledge that Luke was far away in another country, but she missed his intrusive presence. She missed the way her heart lurched whenever her radar picked up the sound of his car pulling up on the drive outside the house, and that keen feeling of light-headed anticipation as she heard his footsteps getting closer. She missed those wayward conversations that always seemed to sneak like a thief into their normal business discussions, and the little asides of wit that made her smile even when she made a great show of looking up to the ceiling in feigned exasperation. She missed the casual brush of his hand against hers and his proximity as he leaned to inspect some detail with her, his breath whispering against her hair.

She felt like a woman who had finally met her match and, having met her match, no longer knew how to control the situation. Worse, the situation was controlling her. In the uneven balance of their relationship, she was the loser;

and the more she fought to maintain her charade of composure, the more she felt herself sinking into a quagmire that was slowly but surely sucking her into its bottomless depths.

He should have been back in the country on Thursday, but he had called to explain that business was keeping him abroad longer than he had anticipated, so that he wouldn't be around until the beginning of the following week.

'But you have to choose what tiles you want for the kitchen,' she had told him accusingly.

'You choose them for me.'

'Me? I can't do that.'

'Why not? I trust your taste.'

Miranda didn't want to choose the tiles on his behalf. She wanted, she realised dismally, to have him stand next to her, discussing what he wanted and firing her soul with the nearness of the forbidden. But here she was, choosing them. The Aga was to be a deep bottle-green and, rather than clutter the background with an array of patterned tiles, she decided on plain hand made green and cream ones to give a clean look. It would go with the terracotta flooring and with the cream units which would be installed when everything else had been completed.

Tomorrow couldn't come quick enough as far as she was concerned. Her planned theatre visit in mixed company would be a welcome distraction from her thoughts which were driving her crazy. A few men might be just what she needed to get her errant mind back on the straight and narrow path.

She would dress to impress, something she had not done now for so long that she could barely remember the time when her choice of clothing was an all-consuming pastime. She would laugh gaily and shimmer with allure.

She would be witty and provocative and flirt madly with the three men Clair and Jesse had arranged as their dates even if the men in question looked like close relatives of the Hunchback of Notre Dame.

She would, she decided grimly, *have fun*. She used to have fun all the time, and she would get back into the habit of it if it killed her.

Consequently, Saturday found her shopping for something new and thrilling to wear, having been kindly patted off on her trip by her father who had murmured something about all work and no play and what it did to Jack.

'I never thought I'd be telling you this, darling, but it's time you got out and had a good time.' He had raised his eyebrows in mild interrogation. 'One or two chaps going along with you and the girls, I take it?'

'Three chaps, three girls. Who knows, Dad, I might find the man of my dreams.' Ha, ha. The current holder of that particular title was thousands of miles away in America, probably having a very good time without her around.

'On the other hand,' her father had replied with unsolicited pragmatism, 'you might find yourself in the company of another Freddie.'

Which, Miranda thought hours later as she dressed for the theatre, was a very likely prospect. At least, though, they all had jobs. Proper jobs and not token occupations carved out of family businesses which paid lip-service to the concept of hard work.

She had bought a calf length clinging black number with a flatteringly wide scooped neck. Her blonde hair looked almost white against the dark backdrop and her height was further accentuated by three-inch heels. She kept her jewellery to a minimum, slipping on only a thick silver bracelet which was minutely carved with dancing figures and a tiny thread-like choker with a deep aquamarine stone that neatly fitted against the hollow of her neck.

She felt like a million pounds and she told herself fiercely that she would act the part, and act it she did, scintillating for her escort as they all enjoyed a drink before the curtain call. Claire had kindly heeded her request that she never laid eyes on another Freddie clone again, and James was physically the opposite. Tall, dark-haired with wire-rimmed spectacles and a consuming interest in computers. He positively glowed with satisfaction as his date lavished her avid interest in every word he said, her blonde hair radiating like a waterfall of shiny cream silk down the length of her back.

The noisy rumble of voices all around her fuelled her need to sparkle; and in a strange, disembodied way she heard herself chattering animatedly to her date, asking him question upon question about the one subject in the world in which she had minimal interest.

This, she thought, as she settled into her seat and welcomed the dark shroud of the theatre, was what it was all about. Never mind moping and longing for a man who didn't love her! Never mind analysing every word he said and dissecting them for hidden meaning! Never mind her skin tingling at every accidental brush and her imagination being fired by the mere thought of him!

'So tell me a bit about yourself,' James said, as soon as the intermission bell had sounded and they had trooped out to the bar to retrieve the drinks they had ordered before curtain call.

'What is there to tell?' Miranda sipped her white wine and fluttered her eyelashes coyly, feeling a fraud for implying that she was little more than a girl without a care in the world.

'Miranda's a born again work horse,' Clair interjected

laughing, which meant that she had to launch into some spiel about her design work.

'And who are you working for at the moment?' James asked, when eventually she had run out of steam and was contemplating hurrying down another glass of wine before the second half. She would not let herself flag at this early point in her fun evening!

'Oh, no one interesting. Luke Decroix. You won't have heard of him.'

'Everybody's heard of him,' James said depressingly. 'He's a pretty big cheese in the city.'

'Oh, really,' Miranda said indifferently. 'He doesn't seem that much of a big cheese to me when he's dithering over what should go where and why. In fact...' she couldn't resist stabbing home her point '...when he's with me he's an incredibly small processed-cheese-spread triangle.'

'Oh, is that right?'

They all turned and Miranda blinked at Luke, who had edged towards their small circle and was looking at her with an amused smile on his darkly handsome face. *What was he doing here? On her wild fun night of forgetfulness?*

'A processed-cheese-spread you were saying?' which made her shut her astounded, half-open mouth.

'What are you doing here? I thought you were in America!'

'Aren't you going to introduce me to your friends? Where have your manners gone?'

'You didn't tell me you were going to be coming to see this play.'

'I didn't realise that I had to let you know my intimate movements from dawn till dusk, actually.'

Her five-strong party was watching this little sketch

with such obvious curiosity that Miranda could positively feel the questions burning in her girlfriends' minds as they tried to tally together the man standing in front of them with the image she had portrayed of an unexciting employer with too much money and the onset of a paunch.

She skirted over the introductions and was about to turn away, pointedly towards James, when Luke signalled to someone behind her.

'This is Eleanor,' he said, broadening the circle to accommodate a tall, dark-haired woman with a handsome, angular face. Not technically beautiful, but with an attraction that came from the suggestion of a powerful intelligence. Her long hair had been pulled back to the nape of her neck and her clothes spoke of practicality rather than frivolity. A complete contrast, Miranda thought with such overwhelming jealousy that she leaned against James to steady herself, to her own slinky black number which outlined every curve of her long slender body and made no concessions to female modesty. Her fun-at-all-costs dress now seemed silly by way of comparison to Eleanor's severely tailored trouser suit.

'Look...' he finished his drink and glanced around his audience '...Eleanor and I were planning on going on to a jazz club after this with the rest of our party. Why don't you lot troop along with us?' His lazy blue eyes, that had somehow managed to eliminate the rest of the group so that they could focus totally on her, sent her already skittering nerves into free fall.

'Actually,' Miranda announced, 'we were all going to head out for something quick to eat after this.'

'But we'd love to change our plans,' Claire interceded quickly. 'Miranda could do with a night out.'

'Good idea,' James murmured to Miranda, slipping his hand around her waist in a proprietorial fashion; which,

she guiltily acknowledged, she could hardly object to.
'Give us some more time to get to know one another.'

She was on the verge of quelling any such hasty objective when she glanced sideways to see Luke looking at her, the expression in his cobalt eyes screened by his thick, dark lashes, and she gave a high, tinkling laugh. 'Why not?' she said gaily. 'Might be fun. The last time I went to a jazz club was four years ago with my father. He'd be very impressed if he thought I might be rediscovering his taste in music.'

Luke gave them the name and address of the club and then, as the bell sounded for them to return to the play, he nodded and shoved his hand in his pocket, his other hand moving to usher Eleanor back to their seats.

'Later, then,' he said, just as Miranda linked her arm through James's and tugged him away, gracefully exiting the bar area and wondering whether Luke's eyes were following her. She might not be the world's most ferocious intellectual, she thought darkly, and she might not possess his date's particular brand of appeal, but she had a good body and she derived a childish kick from flaunting it all the way back to their seats.

There was no sign of Luke in the exodus from the theatre forty-five minutes later; and by the time the taxis had been hailed and they had all been deposited outside the jazz club Miranda's edgy enthusiasm was beginning to feel a little worn.

In fairness, she had told James that, lovely though he was, she was not attracted to him.

'And I'm really sorry if I gave you the wrong impression,' she said, holding him back from their crowd so that she could explain herself.

'You're a bit out of my league, anyway,' he responded with a resigned sigh. 'Still, it was good while it lasted.'

He gave her a shrewd, assessing look from behind his glasses. 'In fact, I would say that you're more in Luke Decroix's league. You're the equivalent to a bottle of champagne and I'm more a house wine kind of guy.'

'*His* league? Ha. Bottle of champagne? Only for to-night, I can assure you.'

And the bottle of champagne was beginning to feel re-markably flat, as they walked into the jazz club and her eyes adjusted to the dark interior.

She had had the duration of the taxi ride in which to contemplate Luke, his relationship—whatever that might be—with the woman he had brought to the play, and the temporary appeal of herself. She was, she decided, like a Christmas toy; all fun in bright new packaging; and while it was being unwrapped, it continued to thrill and excite, as maybe it could for a few days or a couple of weeks; but after that it would no longer be a shiny, sparkling, brand new Christmas toy and it would eventually and in-evitably get stuffed to the back of the cupboard to join all the other used toys that no longer thrilled and excited.

Whereas Eleanor, she thought with miserable dejection, was that long-lasting board game that might not look so glamorous when the wrapping came off, but it would never see the back of that damned cupboard.

So big deal if she was no longer prancing around the world in search of enjoyment. So what if she had decided to work and put her frivolous past behind her, to concen-trate on developing the talent she knew she possessed but had always sidelined? It hardly turned her into a board game like Eleanor, did it?

The rush of daring that had made her accept Luke's proposal that they all meet at the club had well and truly fizzled into a need to get back home and go to sleep by the time she spotted his group in the corner of the room.

As she might have expected, he dominated the small party of five. For a start, they were all seated, while he was standing, his restless eyes flicking towards the door then back to his table. Miranda sought out Eleanor and spotted her sandwiched between two men, speaking and gesticulating and obviously expressing a strong opinion on something, judging from her body language. Probably, Miranda thought with a touch of malice, the state of the world, or some such large, consuming issue.

She trailed behind with James, following her friends as they weaved their way amongst the tables, all of which were occupied. On a raised podium, the jazz group were grinding out an evocative slow piece that spoke of sadness, and it struck an unwelcome chord in her.

There was a bustle of shouted introductions, following which several members of both groups went to the dance floor. Amidst the general shuffle of chairs being brought to add to the table, Miranda found herself sitting next to Eleanor with Luke towering behind them. From the brief snatches of overheard conversations, he was quizzing James about what he did, asking questions about where he lived and firing such informed remarks about the world of computers that poor James was forced to adopt a stance of self-defence lest he was steamrollered into silence.

As the sound of their voices washed above her, Miranda tried desperately to cling to the veneer of sparkle that was growing more tarnished with each passing minute. Eleanor, she managed to glean, worked as a tax lawyer but the sound of the music effectively killed any detailed questions. Eventually, Miranda rose to her feet and turned to James with outstretched hand, ignoring Luke who was a good three inches taller than his defenceless victim and who vibrated with restless energy in a way that Miranda thought might well be deliberate.

'Dance, James?' she shouted, barely making herself heard above the wailing sound of the saxophone.

'Okay, but I'm not very good, I warn you! Look out for your feet! You might find that they're not that recognisable after a few dances with me!'

'Aren't you going to ask your date for a dance, Luke?' Miranda's voice was freezingly polite. 'You surely can't leave her sitting on her own while you lurk behind her. The poor thing might get intimidated.'

'Oh, I intend to dance,' he said, bending towards her so that she could hear him. 'When I'm good and ready.'

Miranda swept James onto the dance floor, her body quickly catching the rhythm of the music and swaying in time to the beat, while James looked desperately uncomfortable as he tried to keep up. She deliberately faced away from the table so that she couldn't let herself be tempted into seeing what was happening between Luke and Eleanor. With her back to them, she could pretend that they weren't there at all and that the evening, which she had started out on with such high hopes of having a swinging time and recapturing some of the carefree gaiety of her former days, had not dissolved into stomach-turning tension.

She was in the midst of encouraging a reluctant James to throw caution to the winds and attempt some more complicated manoeuvres when a hand descended on her shoulder and Luke cut in with no attempt at apology, merely applying sufficient pressure on her arm to make her spin around with seeming alacrity, leaving James to head back to the table and embark on a conversation with Eleanor.

'I told you I would dance when I was good and ready,' he murmured into her ear. His arms were wrapped around her, a lover's embrace.

'And what about your girlfriend?' Miranda asked. 'Don't you think it's rude to ignore her so that you can lurch around on a dance floor with your employee?' He wasn't lurching about. Anything but. His movements were as graceful and attuned to the music as hers were and their bodies fitted together with the familiarity of two people who have shared the intimacy of lovemaking. Aware of this and aware of the beady eyes of her girlfriends, Miranda tried to pull back; but as soon as she did, he tightened his grip so that any more attempts to put some space between their bodies might have resulted in an all out scuffle.

'It certainly is the height of rudeness to ignore a girl-friend,' he agreed into her ear, 'but I doubt Eleanor would mind.'

'Oh, I see. You have that kind of relationship, have you? A new-age, liberal, open-ended partnership which means that you can do exactly as you please and she's denied the privilege of objecting?'

'Oh, you're on Eleanor's side now, are you? That surprises me. I think you're jealous...

'You don't know me at all!' Miranda said urgently. 'And why would I be jealous of someone just because she holds down an important job in the city somewhere and dresses in clothes that would look good on a man?'

'Eleanor doesn't look like a man,' Luke said mildly, and she chewed her lip, regretting her jealous outburst. 'In fact, many people think she's a remarkably good-looking woman. It's to her credit that she hasn't allowed the rigours of her job and working in a male-dominated field to smother her femininity.'

'If you're that enamoured with your date,' Miranda shot back tartly, 'then would you mind telling me what you're doing dancing with me?'

'Having an invigorating discussion, I thought.'

'Well, you chose the wrong person. I'm not into invigorating tonight! Try your girlfriend!'

'I hate to say this, Miranda, but I'll put you out of your misery. She's not my girlfriend. In fact, she lives in Chicago and she's over here for four days on business. It's fallen to me to entertain her, something I have no objection whatsoever to doing as I'm very good friends with her husband and godfather to her youngest child. There, you little spitting kitten, feel better now?' He drew back so that he could inspect her face, then slipped his hand through her hair, cupping the back of her neck.

'It doesn't matter to me one way or another.'

'Oh, yes, it does. You're jealous as hell! Just like I am of that computer nerd you brought with you tonight. And don't think that I'm going to let you off the hook. You're gong to stay wrapped up in my arms on this dance floor until you tell me what's going on between the two of you.'

Miranda tried very hard to bristle at the masculine possessiveness in his voice, *possessiveness to which he had no right whatsoever*, but she had a moment of soaring glee.

'Who is he?' Luke demanded. 'Which plank of woodwork did he crawl out from?'

'You know who he is. His name is James, and he hasn't crawled out of a plank of woodwork. He happens to be a computer analyst and very interesting with it.'

'If you happen to like indulging in never-ending conversations about the mysteries of the computer.'

'It's very informative, actually. Did you know that there are some theories circulating that libraries will eventually die out because books will all be accessible on the computer? So...' she smirked with satisfaction, '...you'd better hang on to those decrepit detective novels in the cabin. They might be worth something one day.'

'You can't be interested in a guy like that.' His grip tightened around her so that she was pulled further into him, until the scent of his maleness filled her nostrils like incense and circulated in her head, making her giddy.

'Why not? I happen to like him. A lot.'

'I know you're lying,' Luke whispered into her ear.

'Oh, really?'

'Oh, really.' He repeated her coolly incredulous protest with frankly assured assertion. 'Do you think you need something to distract you from your memories of what we did? Is that it? Why don't we go somewhere a little quieter so that we can discuss what a big mistake you're making if that's the case?'

'You can't leave your date on her own!' Miranda protested, appalled. She glanced around to discover that his 'date' seemed to be perfectly fine and deep in conversation with one of the men from her group.

'I don't think Eleanor will miss me for a short while.'

He had cleverly managed to steer her sideways across the dance floor; and, as soon as the music dulled, he draped his arm over her shoulder and led her out of the dark jazz area into a side room which was comfortably furnished with cosy chairs. It was evidently used as a casual lunch area when there was no live music: a relaxing room with tables strewn with newspapers and a bar area that was currently shut.

'You seem to know this pl—'

'Shh.' Instead of moving towards the chairs, he pushed her against the wall. 'I missed you.'

'You wanted to talk,' Miranda said weakly.

'Yes. Talk about why we're fighting the attraction we

feel for one another. Talk about how much you want me and how much I want you.'

There was that word again.

'I don't want you.' She could feel her breasts pushing against the lacy covering of her bra, straining towards his fingers, aching with the anticipation of being caressed. She felt that if he just touched her body, even through the black tight sheath of her dress, she would explode and be swept away on those treacherous wings of longing that would leave her wanting more. More than it was possible for him to give her.

'Oh, yes, you do.' He snaked his fingers through her hair, capturing her face between his hands, his eyes hot and intent. 'You want me to kiss, to take you right here, right now. I know it. *I can smell it.*'

Miranda's eyes closed and she felt the descent of his face towards hers, then the bitter sweet joy of his mouth on hers, hungrily devouring her and her fragile principles, the thrust of his tongue as it squirmed against hers, compelling her to succumb to desire.

And she did. For a while. For that split instant when all her good intentions were suspended in time under the furious assault to her senses. She kissed him back with a hunger that matched his own, not protesting as his hands groped along her thighs, shifting her dress higher, his fingers hooking over the elastic top of her satin suspender belt.

He had meant it! He would take her here and now, hang the possibility of interruption!

This was the definition of *wanting*. It was something that defied all convention and crashed through all obstacles in a greedy need to be sated. She felt it, too. Felt passion rush through her like molten lava, filling every inch of her body.

Her violent push took him by surprise and she used that window of hesitation to wriggle free of his captive grip.

'No!' she said, shaking. She wrapped her arms around her body in an unconscious gesture of defence.

The glazed look in his eyes began to diminish as his brain rapidly deciphered what she was saying. Miranda moved swiftly to one of the chairs and sat down, not knowing whether he would follow and half hoping that he wouldn't.

'No?' He followed her but, instead of sitting down, remained standing over her, looming with the dark intensity of an avenging angel. 'No?' He shook his head, she didn't know whether from disbelief, bemusement or just plain pique at having his plans to seduce her scuppered at the eleventh hour.

No, she amended silently to herself. *Not his plans to seduce her.* Seduction implied having to work at persuasion, having to lure and entice and enthral, and Luke knew that there was no need for him to do any of those things.

'Why not?' he demanded. 'Isn't it a bit late for maidenly outrage? Isn't it a bit like trying to shut the stable door after the horse has bolted?'

'I don't care what it's like,' Miranda told him shakily, plucking her dress between her fingers, her head flung back so that she could look at him.

'This is ridiculous,' he stormed. He slammed his hands onto the back of the chair facing her and bent forwards, his body thrusting towards her. 'A bizarre charade. We made love, Miranda. Do I need to remind you? We made love in every possible way. Don't tell me you're somehow going to pretend that that never existed!'

'I—I've had a chance to think, Luke,' she replied almost inaudibly, so that he had to crane forward to catch what she was saying. 'I've—changed, and making love is no longer part of my plan.'

'So you've decided to become celibate, have you?' His mouth twisted in cynical disbelief.

'I've decided that wanting someone isn't a good enough reason to sleep with them.'

'And what *is* a good enough reason, Miranda?'

'I want a relationship—I want—I don't know what I want…'

'I'm offering you a relationship.'

'You're offering me a good time.'

'Is there a difference?'

Miranda looked at him hopelessly.

'Is this some protracted brand of revenge?' he asked softly. 'Is that it? A way of paying me back for my so-called betrayal? No, it's not, is it? Then what? Are you hoping that I'll ask you to marry me? Is that it?'

The little pulse in her neck began to jump.

'And what if I did? What if I asked you to marry me? Would you suddenly decide that sleeping with me might be permissible after all?'

'No, I wouldn't!' Her blue eyes flashed angrily as she detected the scorn in his voice. Scorn for a gold-digging woman who had suddenly decided to cling to her principles in the hope that they might reap bigger dividends than a temporary bed companion. Wouldn't it be just like him to bypass the little technicality of love and move straight on to exploitation? Hardly surprising, she thought with sudden savagery, considering how familiar he was with that particular method of handling other people!

'No, you wouldn't *what*? Marry me? Or sleep with me? Would you wait until the gold band was on your finger?'

'I wouldn't dream of marrying you, Luke Decroix! What happened between us, well—it happened, and so what if I'm still—still attracted to you? That doesn't mean that I'm going to jump into the sack with you. I'm beginning to realise that life is about more than just taking advantage of passing pleasures. It's about responsibility and consequences and—and—'

'Self-denial? Why not throw that on the list as well? I was fine to bed just so long as we were in the middle of nowhere, but now that you've become a fully functioning adult with a fully functioning conscience, it's a different story. Is that it?'

'Yes!' Miranda said defiantly. Let him believe the worst. Anything other than believing the truth. Because if he even suspected how far she had fallen in love with him, he would know that his persistence would guarantee the result he wanted. And she would be lost. Even more lost than she already was.

'Fine!' He pushed himself back from the chair and turned his back on her, his hands bunched into fists.

'I'm sorry,' Miranda said impulsively, realising that she *was* sorry. Sorry that she could not give him what he wanted because she wanted it so badly herself.

He turned round very slowly to face her and only a tell-tale dark flush belied the illusion of perfect self-control.

'For what?' He laughed dismissively. 'Believe it or not, I do actually think that it's a woman's prerogative to say no and to be respected for saying no.'

This wasn't what Miranda wanted to hear. She didn't want proof of his inherent fairness.

'I'll understand,' she said awkwardly, 'if you don't want me to finish the project. If you think that things might be a bit uncomfortable between us.'

'What on earth would make you think that?' He frowned and then smiled mirthlessly. 'We have a contract, Miranda, a binding contract and I have no intention of allowing you to wriggle free of it so that you can escape the inconvenience of seeing me and having to deal with your decision whenever I'm around. Business is business, after all.'

'I just thought...'

'That you had scarred me for life?' His mouth twisted into a mimicry of a smile, one that sent shivers racing down her spine. 'I think I'll live,' he said, 'to fight another day. Or maybe *fight* isn't quite the word I'm searching for...'

She knew what word he was searching for and what he was trying to tell her: that walking away from her would not be a problem. He had tried his hand and had lost, but his loss was a temporary irritation. It confirmed everything she had suspected, and her expression hardened into sour understanding.

'So I shall see you, as usual, on Monday...'

'Oh, yes. Monday, as usual.' His fingers curled around the handle of the door. 'And I'll want a deadline. You'll be wanting to move onto other jobs, I'm sure, and I want to see things wrapped up as quickly as possible. Don't you agree?'

'Absolutely,' Miranda said, with an expression as freezingly distant as his own.

It would be hard, but it could be done.

Little did she suspect as she slumped into the chair once he had left, how hard it would be.

CHAPTER NINE

SHE only began to realise when, on Monday morning, she arrived at the house to see his car parked outside. She had anticipated an hour or two, at least, of relative calm before he made his appearance. Normally, he dropped by. She had never actually arrived to find him fully installed.

Miranda slowly edged her way out of her car and walked quickly towards the front door, her books of fabric and wallpapers clutched like a barricade in her arms. He said he wanted speed and, accordingly, she would make sure that as many of the soft furnishings were chosen in the course of the week as possible. That way, she could begin the process of farming out the orders for curtains and spreads; and, with any luck, she might even be able to arrange with the decorator to start painting and wallpapering the rooms that were already finished.

She heard voices before she entered the house. The distinctive sound of Luke's deep, commanding voice intermingling with Tom's slightly higher far more plummy tones. She took a deep breath, pushed open the door and, for a few seconds, was destabilised by the sight of Luke in his faded jeans and thick black jumper shoved up to the sleeves to reveal the sprinkling of black hairs on his powerful forearms. His arms were folded and his head was thrown back as though she had interrupted him in the middle of delivering a tirade. He handled his workforce with fairness, but woe betide any one who thought they could relax on the job when he was around, because he was not averse to using invective when he thought it would do the trick.

They both turned at precisely the same time as she walked in and Luke said in a clipped voice, making a show of checking his watch as though he didn't know what time it was, 'I thought you might have been here a bit earlier.'

'I had to stop by to get some fabric books.'

'If we'd known you were going to be this late, we wouldn't have…arrived so early…'

'We?'

'Oh, of course…' He did a poor imitation of absent-mindedness and then called out in a voice rich with implied intimacy, 'Helen! The interior designer's here!'

Helen walked briskly out of the kitchen and Miranda's mouth opened in staggered surprise. She only had the wit to snap her teeth back together into a smile when the small curvaceous blonde emerged from the kitchen with a broad smile on her face. She had a heart-shaped face and the sort of unruly fair hair that still managed to maintain a hairstyle without slipping into the category of unkempt.

Miranda dizzily noticed that, whoever or whatever the woman was, she was certainly not dressed for the business of scouting around a house that was still full of rubble and bits of wood. Her emerald-green suit was far too short and figure-hugging and her shoes were of the kind that necessitated lots of rests in between walking.

'Helen…' he slipped his arm cosily around her shoulders and they faced Miranda as a united front '…this is the interior designer.'

'Whose name happens to be Miranda,' Miranda said, stretching out one hand and allowing Tom to relieve her of her weighty tomes.

'This is fabulous, isn't it?' Her slanting green eyes were

lazily speculative and Miranda swallowed down the surge of bile that had risen up her throat. Her immediate impression was of a woman in her early twenties but, on closer inspection, she could see the fine lines fanning around the eyes and mouth that pointed to someone older, perhaps in her mid-thirties.

'Fabulous,' she agreed hollowly.

'I mean, when this great lug told me that he was renovating a house in the middle of nowhere, I had no idea that by *house* he meant *mansion*.'

'Oh, really,' Miranda said, for want of anything else better.

'Helen's fascinated by what you've done,' Luke said, idly playing with a tendril of fair hair. Miranda noticed that his arm, loosely resting on Helen's shoulders, hovered provocatively over the breasts, which were extraordinarily large for someone of beguilingly diminutive proportions. She folded her arms and forced a smile on her face, tilting her head to one side so that she could assume an attitude of interest, instead of revealing her sudden machiavellian desire to murder.

'Perhaps she could trail along behind you while you work? Maybe even give you a helping hand at choosing colours? Or whatever? It's always so much better to have a second opinion on things like furnishings, wouldn't you agree?'

'I work better alone,' Miranda said tightly.

'Oh, but I think the input would be useful. Have another female opinion to go by. And I *am* your employer.' His cobalt eyes were repressively insistent, and she gave him a curt nod in acknowledgement of the trump card he had played. So much for giving in with good grace! His ego had taken a beating and he was going to rub her nose in it.

'Sure.'

Helen's feline green eyes narrowed in satisfied victory and Miranda beamed back. A fairly terrifying beam. The five foot nothing slip of a woman with the curves that would make a centrefold queen envious, made her feel like a towering Amazon. The fact that she was devoid of all make-up and was garbed in a pair of old baggy jeans and an even older baggier jumper didn't help. 'If you follow me, Helen, we'll start with the kitchen, shall we?'

'And I think I'll come along for the ride.' The rogue arm had returned to its original position across Helen's shoulders, and she linked her tiny fingers through his as they followed Miranda into the kitchen.

'Now,' Luke said, 'why don't we all sit down and have a look at what you've brought along for us to see?'

At the end of forty minutes, during which Miranda had been subjected to account for her choice of everything, from floor tiles to wallpaper border, she felt as though she was going mad. She was forced to endure little shows of affection, the casual brushing of his hands on Helen's arm, the overplayed attentiveness to whatever piece of super-fluous advice her new replacement happened to voice, the high-pitched, girlish voice that seemed so at odds with the coolly assessing expression on her face.

When Helen asked where the nearest bathroom was, Miranda almost expected Luke to spring to his feet and escort her there, but he didn't. He sent her on her trip upstairs, following every inch of her voluptuous movements across the kitchen and then shaking his head with a little sigh when she was out of the room.

'Don't you think there's something *peach-like* about her?' he asked Miranda, his eyes still lingering at the empty space of the doorway.

'I hadn't noticed.'

'No?' He seemed to be having difficulty in dragging his eyes away from the vacant spot which would soon be filled by the swaying figure of his latest conquest. 'I'm surprised. Helen has never been able to walk into a room without attracting stares from everyone, men and women alike. She's a qualified chartered surveyor, you know. I used to go out with her years ago and, as luck would have it, I happily bumped into her yesterday.'

Miranda snapped shut the book in front of her. And where, she thought acidly, had he managed to bump into her? His little black book perhaps? Let him play his puerile games, she thought venomously.

'She may well be a qualified chartered surveyor, but you can't really intend to paint the kitchen in bright orange. And I don't care what she says about it being good feng shui.' Especially, Miranda thought, when she had made it sound as though not knowing the ins and outs of feng shui indicated some kind of dinosaur attitude towards interior design.

'A charming suggestion, I thought.'

'Charming but hideous. A bright orange kitchen would look vile.'

'According to you.'

'According to anyone with a modicum of good taste.'

'Perhaps. Toss us that colour chart again, would you?' Which he then proceeded to inspect with the thoroughness of a bank manager inspecting an overdue account. 'Maybe it's a little on the vibrant side. Leave it with me for a few days. I'll think it over.'

'I thought you wanted to get this whole thing finished as soon as possible,' Miranda said nastily. 'Mulling things over for days on end isn't going to get the job done quickly.'

'More haste, less speed. Now, shall we have a look at

the bedroom next?' He raised one dark eyebrow expressively and Miranda gave him another of those stiff, practised smiles. She could hear Helen clipping her way back to the kitchen and there was no need to glance around to watch the satisfied gleam on the cheeks. She could very easily imagine it judging from Luke's lingering look at the woman standing behind her out of sight.

'Did I hear the word *bedroom*?' Helen said, and Miranda gritted her teeth together and stood up.

'Oh-h-h, this is gorgeous, Luke!' Helen opened her arms wide in an all-encompassing gesture as soon as they had stepped into the bedroom, from which the two workmen had hurriedly exited, though not before casting appreciative glances at the small blonde.

The wooden flooring was now fully under way and almost laid and it was, Miranda admitted, a gorgeous bedroom. Large and airy, with two massive bay windows that overlooked the sprawling acres of garden. Despite the condition of the house, the garden had been well-maintained and was landscaped with those imaginative touches that spoke of a previous owner whose focus had been primarily on the lawns.

'Where's the bed going to go?' Helen strolled to one of the bay windows and perched on the edge, her eyes flirting with intent on Luke, who was standing and looking around him, his hands stuffed into his pockets, in a lord-of-all-I-survey attitude.

'I thought greens and creams might suit in here,' Miranda interrupted, dumping two of the books on the work table in the middle of the room.

'Hang on. I haven't answered Helen's very pertinent question. Hmm. Now, where should I put that bed of mine...?'

'Just make sure that it isn't with its back to a window,'

Helen said. 'Very bad feng shui. And, personally, I think bedroom feng shui is *very* important.'

'I really had no idea chartered surveyors were so informed when it came to Oriental house design,' Miranda said blandly. 'Is it part of the course these days?'

She flicked to the page she was looking for and pointed to the colour combination she had in mind.

'Hmm. A little dull, darling, don't you think? We want *alive*, we want *dangerous*, we want something a little more *interesting*.' Helen swivelled the book so that it was facing her and flipped through the pages, finally lighting on a colour scheme comprised of reds and blacks at which she proceeded to jab one well-manicured finger. 'Now, Lukey, isn't this more like it? A girl could be persuaded to do all sorts of things in a room with these colours. They're wild, they're passionate, they're...almost demanding abandon, wouldn't you agree? They're literally *red hot.*'

'Lukey?' Miranda couldn't help a little snigger and Luke gave her a quelling look.

'That's my little pet name for him.' She gave him a quick embrace and then slipped her arm around his waist.

'Charming,' Miranda said. 'Though, personally, I've always thought that pet names should be left for pets.' Besides, she could think of quite a few, more appropriate, pet names for Luke Decroix and they all involved dangerous animals with sharp teeth. 'And what does Lukey thing of the *red* option?' She smiled brilliantly in the face of his scowl. 'I certainly agree with Helen that they would lend a certain frisson to any bedroom.'

'I'll take it into consideration,' he muttered.

'Something else being taken into consideration?' Miranda frowned with apparent bewilderment. 'If you tell me what particular reds you want, I can make sure to order the wallpaper today. I believe, Helen, you said you liked…this one?' She pointed to an alarming wallpaper comprised of swirling deep red patterns interlaced with black and gold.

'I *said* I'll think about it.' Luke slammed the book shut and looked at her. 'You might have to carry on without us,' he said abruptly. 'Just choose the colours for the other bedrooms.'

'On my own?' Miranda opened her blue eyes wide. 'But I thought you wanted more female input? I think it's a splendid idea if Helen shared her thoughts on the décor.'

'I've got to get back to London for a meeting this afternoon.'

'Well, then, why doesn't Helen stay and give me a hand? I'm dying to hear what other innovative ideas she has in mind.' Miranda allowed herself the sheer pleasure of seeing him wallow in the consequences of his own ill-considered plot to humiliate her but her enjoyment was short-lived.

'She can't. She's coming down to London with me…' His blue eyes sent a very distinct message which had Helen gurgling with anticipation.

'But what about your meeting?' she asked coyly, snuggling against him.

'Some things can wait.' As he said that, his eyes flicked to where Miranda was standing awkwardly in the centre of the room. 'So you just get along without us and let me have your decisions by tomorrow lunch-time. Think you can manage?'

'Perfectly.'

'Good. Then we'll leave you to it.' At the door, he paused, his arms still around the small blonde. 'Actually,' he said in a thoughtful voice, 'I have an idea… Why wait until tomorrow when, as you say, I want this whole thing wrapped up as soon as possible…? Helen and I are going to be dining at my club this evening… Why don't you join us for a pre-dinner drink and you can bring samples of what you think I might like. That way, I can make my decision and you can begin sorting it all out in the morning, first thing…'

'I'm busy this evening.'

'In that case, you'll just have to cancel, won't you?' He gave her the address of his club, as though her social life was something that barely qualified to be a minor detail, never mind a reason for refusing his order. 'Be there for seven, would you? That way, we should have the whole thing sorted out and wrapped up by eight-thirty and you can do whatever you had planned…'

Instead of going, he resisted Helen's eager tugs and continued staring at Miranda, waiting for her to speak. It crossed her mind that perhaps he was waiting for more than mere agreement with his high-handed redistribution of her free time. Was he waiting for her to tell him what plans she had? Even though he had no right, was he still jealous that she might be seeing someone? The thought made her fizz with resentment.

An evil little spark sizzled inside her and she lowered her eyes. 'That sounds fine,' she said. 'And I'm sure James won't mind if I meet him a little later.' She risked glancing up at him and, for the merest of seconds, their eyes tangled, but his expression remained unrevealing. What was revealing was the kiss he gave the woman nestled against him. A long, lingering kiss that was more like a taste of the red puckered mouth than a friendly brush of lips against lips.

'See you later,' he murmured, as a red flush crept treacherously along her neck and flooded her face. He smiled and she felt a rush of resentment that was so overpowering that she was tempted to heave the wallpaper book at his dark handsome head.

But she didn't. She spent the rest of the day simmering instead. If he had wanted to prove to her just how little she had meant to him, then he had succeeded; because even if the big-breasted Helen was not the love of his life, she certainly was the embodiment of the transience of his lust. It had been perfectly clear from the body language, not to mention that kiss by the bedroom door which had left precious little to the imagination, that they were bed partners.

The thought of that was so abjectly painful that she tried to shove it away, but throughout the day it hovered there, like a malign imp taking delight in torturing her.

In anticipation of what Helen might be wearing, and she was certain that it would involve a sufficient lack of fabric to enhance her prominent breasts, Miranda went down the road of the opposite extreme. Nothing stretchy, nothing that emphasised her body, nothing that revealed the length of her legs. Instead, she chose to wear a plain grey trouser suit twinned with a light blue cashmere jumper and some flat black shoes.

In deference to the unusually sober attire, she combed her hair back into one long French plait, on either side of which she placed a tortoiseshell hair grip.

When she inspected her reflection in the mirror, she decided that this was an outfit in which she could cope. She felt efficient and professional in it. A woman immune to the attractions of the opposite sex, and of one man in particular. A woman who was the archetypal working woman and therefore would not succumb to feelings of raging jealousy.

She could safely ignore Helen in an outfit like this and if Luke really got on her nerves, she thought with a little nervous giggle, she could always hit him with the robust black leather bag she intended on using.

But when she finally arrived at the club at a little after seven and was shown into the cavernous sitting area around which were strewn small tables, comfortable chairs and faded Persian rugs, it was to find that Helen had not yet arrived.

'There's no need for anyone else to get involved at this stage of the proceedings,' Luke drawled, summoning a waiter apparently from thin air and ordering a bottle of white wine.

'Oh? But what about the importance of additional female input?' Miranda sat back in the chair and crossed her legs. With her samples in her thick folders on the ground and in this austere suit, she could almost maintain the illusion of their boss, employee relationship.

'Perhaps I overestimated that,' he muttered under his breath.

'Well,' Miranda leaned over and collected her folders, opening out the top one on the table in front of them '...shall we get on with choosing these colours?'

'I'll have a look at them when I'm ready.' The waiter materialised, again seemingly from thin air, and poured them both a glass of wine. 'And I'm not ready yet.'

'Well, shouldn't we get this done with before Helen arrives? You might find that she's not happy with the selection and doesn't like the idea of being sidelined.'

'She won't be arriving.'

'Oh.' The single monosyllable spoke volumes and Luke's eyebrows met in a frown.

'That's right. *Oh.*'

'What happened?' She felt a satisfying, sweet singing in her ears and had to force herself to remember that one woman's disappearance from his life meant nothing. It certainly didn't suddenly transform him into a man who was ready to take commitment by the horns, least of all commitment to her. He would just move onto Helen Mark two.

'I decided that anyone who seriously considers decorating a bedroom in deep reds wouldn't be the kind of girl I'm interested in.'

'But you two made such a perfect match!' Miranda sipped her wine and glanced around her idly. 'And she seemed so *enraptured* with you. What a let-down for the poor woman!'

'She *was* a bit disappointed,' he admitted, 'but I managed to paint such a black picture of myself that, by the time she left, I could hear her thinking that perhaps it was for the best.'

'What did you tell her?'

'That I was a serial womaniser with a penchant for train-spotting.' He drained his glass and looked at her over the rim, his black-fringed eyes unreadable. Then he poured himself another, tilting the bottle at her and leaning forward to top up her drink, but she shook her head.

'Anyway, there you go. As they say about the sea and fish…' He stretched his long legs out in front of him and watched her. Miranda was not going to let herself respond to the taunting challenge in his voice.

'I haven't got all evening,' she said politely. 'So if you wouldn't mind…?'

His jaw hardened fractionally. 'Sure. As a matter of fact…' he consulted his watch '…nor have I. Shall we get on with it?'

They spent the next half an hour looking at the various samples she had brought with her, but his mind was elsewhere. She could sense it. He agreed with everything she showed him and it slowly dawned on her that his agreement had more to do with his urgency to get the house finished and her out of the way, than with any inherent good taste she might have displayed.

'So I'll go ahead and order all of these, shall I?' she asked a little uncertainly and he shrugged, not bothering to glance in her direction.

He was looking at the door. Involuntarily, Miranda followed his gaze and felt numb when a tall, dark-haired woman appeared, looking around her before recognising him and waving.

'Candice,' he said in a low voice. 'I thought you might have finished a bit sooner, but…'

'Candice?'

He shrugged helplessly and gave her a charming smile. 'Would you like to stay and meet her? I think you two would get along, actually. She's into houses…'

'She's an interior designer?'

'No, no. Buy and sells properties. Useful contact for you to make, in point of fact.' He was getting to his feet and Miranda hurriedly and dazedly followed suit. Before her brain could catch up with reality, she found herself shaking hands and muttering something polite, while Candice exclaimed over her job, gushingly informing her that they were always on the lookout for new designers.

'And you must be good if Luke trusts you to overhaul his house.'

'Miranda hadn't worked for a while. I was merely lending her a helping hand.' He smiled in a self-effacing manner and Miranda choked back her inarticulate furious muttering.

'Oh, and what were you doing before?' Dark eyes narrowed on her. 'You're much too young to have been bringing up a family…'

'Oh, Miranda was just…'

'Travelling. Anyway, I must dash.'

Trust the rotten swine to start exclaiming about the night being young; and why not stay at least to finish the bottle of wine; surely she and Candice would have so much to chat about. Miranda could quite easily have killed him on the spot. But instead, she threw him a killing smile and gathered her folders together.

'No, as I said, I've got another appointment tonight.' She extended her hand politely to the other woman. 'Have fun.'

She didn't glance back once as she walked the five-mile plank, or so it seemed, from table to door, nodding curtly at the porter as he tipped his hat at her.

If only James had been around, she thought viciously, as the evening air clipped her cheeks and made her sprint to hail a taxi back to the house, he might have been in luck. She might not have been so pre-emptive in being a good girl and telling him that she wasn't interested. She might have played the Devil at his own game.

Of course, she thought wearily, she wouldn't have. Why bother to kid herself? Luke was too big a part of her soul for her to try and discard him in a series of pointless affairs. Or even one pointless affair.

She awoke the next morning with the dull, heavy feeling of not having slept very well.

Now that most of the structural work was under way and the various colour schemes and designs had been chosen, her presence at the house would, of necessity, be less intense. She might be able to go along perhaps every other day, just to supervise that her various touches were being adhered to. Likewise, there was no need for Luke to appear with such regularity. She wasn't surprised when she got to the house, to find that he hadn't made an appearance.

Miranda trailed through the rooms, her mind not focused on the job at hand, but rather on the spectre of Luke in the arms of other women. And, for the looks of things, a line of women without much discernible gap between them. If he intended to use distraction as a means of getting over her, then he was certainly entering into the spirit of easy oblivion with boundless energy.

On the spur of the moment, she found herself ringing James and arranging to see him that evening.

'Perhaps we could go out for a meal,' she suggested desperately, 'and then maybe come back to the house for coffee. Dad has gone away for the next few days. And I...' she drew in her breath and vacantly let her gaze wander around the rolling countryside that spread like a thousand-hued blanket around the house, dwarfing her as she stood by her car, mobile in hand '...I need to talk to someone. Someone impartial...'

'Ah. Just friends, I take it?'

'Just friends.'

'Good. Because you're far too short and plain for me. Okay. What say I pick you up about seven and we go somewhere for a quick meal, then back to your house for coffee and confidences? You can tell me all about him.'

'About who?'

'The man who broke your heart.' He laughed down the end of the line. 'I have three sisters, Miranda, and I've eavesdropped enough conversations as a lad to know that when women say they want to talk, it's usually because someone's broken their heart.'

If only, she thought as, later, she sat in a noisy Italian restaurant with James. If only Cupid went around choosing his victims with a little more discernment, because James was a good listener, and if she were just a little different, then maybe she could have fallen for him and thereby spared herself the promise of lifetime's misery.

As it was, she spent the better part of an hour pouring her heart out, with intermittent breaks during which she apologised profusely and promised not to be such a relentlessly boring female the next time they met.

'He's just trying to make you jealous,' James said, as she lingered over yet another detailed description of replacement number two, and Miranda snorted.

'Of course he's trying to make me jealous. He wants to make sure that I realise how much I want him and absolve himself of all blame. He wants to prove that however much he wanted me, it wasn't enough to make him pine when I turned him down.'

It was nearly nine by the time they returned to the house and she felt pleasantly tipsy and marginally better than when she had set out two hours earlier.

As she let them in through the front door, she held his hand, guiding him towards the sitting room and giggling as she groped along the side of the wall for the light.

'My father is obsessed with switching lights off,' she whispered, still feeling the wall for the switch, her body turned towards James and her face tilted as she giggled merrily. 'I've told him a million times that it makes no sense to pretend to save money on electricity, then have a tumble drier, but he's never seen the logic of my argument. You do, though, James, don't you?'

She realised that she was asking more than an answer to that simple question. She was asking him to justify the decision she had taken to walk away from Luke when an insidious voice in her head kept telling her that maybe she should just have taken what was on offer and run. If she was going to suffer, then why not have something to show for it at the end of the day, instead of a halo that felt too heavy for her head and a lot of pious self-pity that made the worst bed companion. Wasn't it better to be hung for a sheep than a lamb? Or something like that? Her brain, after three glasses of very average wine, felt a little fuddled.

She was still leaning into James when her finger found the switch and the sitting room was flooded in a soft mellow light that swam over the centre of the large room, leaving the corners in semi-darkness.

'Honestly, James,' Miranda said huskily, with a sob at the back of her throat, 'it's been so good being with you. I'm really glad we got together. Shall we have a coffee? And carry on if you're not too tired with the whole thing?'

She tugged him by his wayward tie into the room and only became aware that something was wrong by the expression that registered on his face as he looked beyond her. The smile froze on his lips and he said, in a low, singsong voice,

'Uh-oh.'

Miranda turned around very slowly, and Luke's voice reached her ears before her blurry eyes could discern him sitting on a chair towards the back of the room.

'You were saying, Miranda? About carrying on? Please, don't let me stop you in mid-sentence.' There was dangerously reined control to his words that made her nervously turn to James for support. James however did not look like a man who was about to rush into the arms of danger in his continuing role of moral supporter.

'Perhaps I'd better go,' he said slowly.

'No!' Miranda screeched. She hesitantly took two steps into the sitting room, arms folded warrior-style. Then, remembering that it was, after all *her* house, or at least her father's, she boldly took two more steps before stopping well short of her target.

'What are you doing here?' she demanded.

'Hadn't we better dispatch your escort before we launch into conversation?' He lazily clasped his hands behind his head and tore his eyes away from Miranda long enough to say to James, 'Run along, little boy.'

'There's nothing,' Miranda said, with a lot more courage than she felt, 'that you can say to me that you can't say in front of James.'

'I beg to differ. Now, boy, are you going to go of your own accord or do I have to throw you out? Because, make no mistake, I'm more than capable of dispatching you into the street. Head first.' Unconsciously, or perhaps as an unspoken threat, he slowly flexed his fingers.

A successful ploy as it happened because she heard James say nervously from behind her, 'Will you be all right, Miranda?'

'She'll be absolutely fine.'

'Don't believe a word of what he says!' she exclaimed in a frantic outburst. 'I've told you that he's a congenital liar!'

'So you've been talking about me, have you?' Luke stood up and moved with purposeful slowness towards them.

With a little sign of frustrated resignation, she turned to James and said, 'It's all right. You'd better go.'

'Wise advice.' Luke was now only a couple of feet away from her and up close, with the light more directly positioned over him, she could see the smouldering fury stamped on his dark features. 'I'll give you ten seconds; then, my friend, I want to hear that front door slam behind you.'

CHAPTER TEN

'SOUNDS like he's gone.' Luke lazily relaxed into his chair with a triumphant smile. 'So much for your rescuer. He couldn't wait to run away when the going got a bit tough. You're going to have to do a bit better than that, you know. There's nothing worse for a budding relationship than for the man to feel that his woman is the aggressor. Call me old-fashioned but I happen to think that the healthiest relationships are the ones where the man can consider himself the protector. Now, why don't you sit down?'

'Call me old-fashioned, but I happen to think that breaking and entering is an offence. And I am *not going to sit down*!'

'You sounded a little worse for wear when you came in. Haven't been out drinking, have you? Weak men find it very easy to take advantage of a woman when she's drunk.'

'I am not drunk!'

'No? Well your face looks a little flushed considering you're not drunk.'

'I'm flushed with outrage! *What* are you doing here and how did you get in?' Miranda continued to skewer him with furious blue eyes, her hands placed firmly on her hips.

'Sit down.'

'I will *not sit down*! And stop giving me orders in my own house! How dare you? I don't know how you found your way inside here but...'

'How do you think I got in? Broke a window-pane and crept in? De-alarming the house in the process?'

'Well, how did you?'

'I won't be answering any more questions until you sit down. And I won't be leaving either.'

Miranda flung herself into a chair and her short skirt rode up her thighs, exposing a slither of bare skin where her stockings ended and her suspender belt began. She barely noticed Luke's narrowed eyes as he absorbed the pale strip of flesh, nor did she hear the softly indrawn hiss.

'I came in through the front door,' Luke told her shortly. 'And I switched off the alarm using the code your father very kindly gave me.'

'My father...'

'Knows that I'm here. Why are you dressed like that?'

Thrown off course, Miranda could only stammer out a reply. 'Dressed like what?'

'Like a cheap street walker.'

'Like a...*how dare you*?' She unconsciously held her hand to her throat, pulling together the front break in her tight, fitted woollen top. She could feel the little pulse in her neck throbbing against the backs of her fingers.

'Did you go out tonight with the thought of provoking a response? Is that why you're dressed in a skirt that barely covers your underwear?' His voice was controlled but she could detect a dangerous edge to it that spoke of emotions barely reined in.

'This skirt is perfectly all right!' Miranda snapped, distracted once again from the more perplexing mystery of what he was doing in her father's house. Nevertheless, her fingers fluttered guiltily towards the hemline, vaguely aware that because of the way she was sitting, there was more skin exposed that she cared for.

'I hope you weren't stupid enough to let that little boy touch you...'

'Little boy? James is hardly what I would call a little boy!' She was referring to his height, but she could tell from the sudden darkening in his eyes that his mind had taken her innocent sentence and reworked it into something more sinister. She watched as he clenched his powerful fists, and she felt a stirring of satisfaction.

'And what would you do if I *had* let him touch me, Luke?' she taunted. 'There wouldn't be much you could do about it, would there?' She sat back, allowing her hands to drop to either side of her because there was no reason for her to feel guilty or to be propelled into defending herself against someone who had no right to be there anyway.

'I wouldn't bet on it.' His voice was a low growl, like the rumble of thunder and, before she had time to react, he had moved swiftly to the sofa where she was sitting. 'You don't want to find out what I could do,' he said, positioning his bulky body so close to her that she had to cringe back to avoid physical contact. Along the back of the sofa, his extended arm found her silky hair and curled into it so that she was imprisoned. 'Don't mistake me for one of your mild-mannered businessmen who's scared of a little physical—shall we say—retribution...or for one of your craven playboys who wouldn't know a street fight if it hit them in their pretty little face.'

'Oh, very tough,' Miranda mocked. She kept her head rigidly still, but even so she could still feel the weight of his hand in her hair. The low front slit of her jumper had made wearing a bra pointless and she was uncomfortably aware of her breasts pushing against the fine woollen fabric. Thank heavens only the shape of her breasts was contoured by the wool, which was not thin enough to reveal the circles of her nipples.

'And why does it matter anyway?' she asked in a trembling voice. 'We're not involved with one another, Luke. Or is it all right for you to prance about testing all the fish in the sea, while I sit at home chewing my fingernails and…' think about you, she thought '…watching television… I don't need you checking up on my movements! I'm a free agent and I can do exactly as I please. With *whoever* I want!'

'I haven't been testing all the fish in the sea,' he muttered, flushing, and there was a profound silence that lasted the duration of a heartbeat.

'Oh, and what about Helen, the-woman-who-turns-heads wherever-she-goes-she's-a-chartered-surveyor-you-know? And Candice, the great, important property developer who could help me out because she has so many contacts?'

'Distractions.'

The single word was like a match set to dry leaves and Miranda did something she had never done in her life before: she swung at him. As the soft flesh of her palm made contact with his cheek, she watched in horror as his face swivelled under the impact. His hard jaw line reddened immediately with the imprint of her hand and he nursed it while he watched her with dry amusement.

'I—I'm sorry,' she stammered. 'I—does it hurt? I'll get a wet rag…' She half stood up and he pulled her back down with his free hand, which he left loosely circling her wrist as she tried to fix herself into a less revealing position.

'Don't. I deserved that.'

'You *deserved it*?'

'For being a fool.'

Miranda looked at him, her lips parted. He gave her a rueful glance. 'You pack a hefty punch. I don't suppose you've ever considered taking up boxing as a hobby?'

'I've never hit anyone in my life before,' she said in a stunned voice.

'I consider myself lucky to be the first,' he mused. 'You once told me that you weren't a jealous kind of woman. But jealousy is a very telling emotion, don't you think? I personally think that it's one of the most primitive of human feelings. It can rise out of nothing, and when it takes over, it can command our entire body, make us do its bidding. I shouldn't have used that word. *Distractions*. But that's what Helen and Candice were. Distractions and manifestly unsuccessful ones at that.'

'What do you mean?'

'I mean that I haven't slept with either of them, nor did I want to, despite their obvious physical attributes.'

Miranda felt a tide of relief and joy rush through her.

'I thought…' he began, pausing and searching, apparently for the right words. '…I thought that I would be able to forget…forget you…but it appears not. And you can't forget me either, can you?' He gave a dry laugh. 'I saw it on your face when you met Helen at the house and, I tell you what, just witnessing that expression was enough to have made it worthwhile because I wanted you to be jealous. I wanted you to be eaten with jealousy so that you could realise how much you wanted me and how much you didn't want to share me with anyone else. I wanted you to feel the same way about me as I do about you.'

There he went again, Miranda thought with a little sigh of misery, *want, want, want*. But his still, words were like soothing unguents to her troubled mind. She had fought her love and their intense attraction to one another with the only weapon she'd had at hand; her morality. But it had not been enough. It hadn't even been enough to blunt the intensity of her feelings for him.

He took one of her hands between his and traced the lines of her thin fingers, his head lowered in apparent concentration.

'I wasn't prepared for this,' he murmured inaudibly. 'When you descended on me in that cabin, my first thought was to get rid of you as soon as I could. I figured that I'd met enough girls of your ilk in my life to be able to spot an empty-headed pretty face from ten miles away.'

'I know. You said as much.' Miranda followed the line of his fingers with her eyes, sadly wistful because she could feel her capitulation and what it meant.

'I did, didn't I?' He glanced up at her sombre face and smiled, willing her to smile back at him. 'Then I realised that I knew who you were. Had heard your father talk about you. He's very proud of you, you know, even though you haven't exactly used your talents to their advantage, at least not until now.'

'Oh, thanks very much. Nothing like cutting to the quick.'

'It's the truth.' Luke paused. 'In a way, it seemed as though fate had thrown you in my way and the thought of that amused me. You see, your father had even tentatively hinted once that you and I might be…what shall I say…suitable for one another? At the time, I laughed outright at any such suggestion; but when you arrived, well, you know what happened. If you had been anyone else, I wouldn't have dreamt of concocting any plan to bring you in line.

'But I realised almost immediately that my preconceptions of you were wrong, that you were more complex than I had bargained for, and when your father jokingly suggested that I might be a good influence on you I found myself jumping at the idea. I told myself that it was the challenge, but there was something else. Something I couldn't quite put my finger on, and I've never experienced anything like that before with a woman.'

'I had no idea you knew my father that well.'

'Professionally, mostly. But we did have dinner together now and again, just to cement the bond he had with my own father.' He sighed and looked at her. 'Is this making any sense to you? I'm trying not to sound confused, which is how you make me feel.'

'Oh, what's there to be confused about?' Miranda sighed and stood up, pulling her hand out of his reach and hugging herself as she strolled towards the window and parted the thick curtains a crack to stare outside. Then she let the drapes fall back into place although she remained where she was, leaning against the window sill, which made a soft perch with the heavy fall of velvet cloth.

'I landed on you and practically forced you into sleeping with me.' Miranda looked at him steadily. She was aware that the evocative fluency of his words could start a whole network of hope burgeoning inside her and she wouldn't let that happen. She would be realistic, if nothing else, because what he was speaking of had nothing to do with love.

'Oh, is that what you did? And I thought I might have had some say in the matter.' Luke had angled his big body so that he was facing her but, even with the distance she had put between them, she could still feel the potent effect of his personality curling around her like a suffocating vice.

'What man wouldn't say yes to a woman who throws herself at him?' Miranda asked with a tight laugh.

'This one, actually.'

'Maybe.' She shrugged, determined to summarise the so-called course of their so-called relationship. Because putting it into words would leave no room for the romantic notions festering unbidden inside her. 'So now you tell me that I confuse you. Why? Because you hadn't expected that you might want a one-night stand to proceed into an affair?' Her fingers fiddled restlessly with the woollen top.

'I suppose I should be flattered, should I? Or maybe, it would have died a natural death if I hadn't been an interior designer and you hadn't had a house to design. Maybe then you wouldn't have had an excuse to find me work to do to save me from myself; and then you wouldn't have been thrown into my company so that you found yourself remembering a few hours of lovemaking a million years ago, wanting to turn those hours into a few days or weeks, or however long it takes before a man like you gets bored and needs to stretch his wings and move on.'

She couldn't bear to meet his eyes, so she stared behind him to the doorway. 'And you knew you'd win, didn't you? All you had to do was be patient and, in the end, I'd break down because you could read it on my face. You told me so yourself.'

'Oh, for God's sake, Miranda.' He raked his fingers through his hair and stared at her with frustration. 'Why are you making this sound all so damned sordid?'

'It's all about having a fling, Luke. I'm not making anything sound sordid. I'm just being practical.'

'Well, stop being so bloody practical. You have no idea what I've gone through...'

'Oh, I can well imagine. Sleepless nights wondering how to get me back into bed! Tortured hours thinking of ways to change my mind!'

'Stop it!'

'Why?' Miranda knew that she was going wildly off course now, thrashing about in waters that made her want to break down in front of him, but she couldn't seem to help herself. 'I know what you want so why beat about the bush with fancy talk about feeling confused and confessions of what you felt and when you felt it? Why not just call a spade a spade and we can get down to business. Because you're right. The attraction hasn't stopped for me either.' She reached and pulled her small top over her head, flinging it carelessly on one of the chairs.

'Miranda, don't!' His sharp voice was like the crack of a whip, and she paused with her hands already poised to leap on him. She could feel the hot, blinding force of her tears hovering just behind her eyelids, but she would not cry. Wanting him and sleeping with him was a poor man's substitute for the love she desperately craved, but it would have to be enough; because those few weeks of being in his presence had made her realise that fine principles were one thing, but reality was another.

'Don't,' he said in a more gentle voice. He stood up and walked over to where she had dropped her arms to her sides and he rubbed them with the palms of his hands.

'Why not?' she asked in a small, resigned voice. 'It's what you want, isn't it? It's what we both want.'

'But not like this.'

He slipped one finger under her chin and tilted her head so that she was looking at him. 'I would rather die than ever be the one to make you cry,' he whispered, wrapped his arms around her, and drew her into his great bulk. She could feel the thudding of his heart. It was unbearably comforting.

'I'm not crying,' she said stubbornly, and she felt him smile.

'But you want to, my darling, and it's my fault. I was blind.'

'Don't speak,' Miranda said softly. Sometimes words could be knives and she just wanted to stay where she was, in the cocoon of his arms, kidding herself that everything was going to be all right.

'Don't be afraid,' he whispered into her ear. 'I never meant to hurt you. I just didn't realise that you would get to me the way you did and it frightened me. I've always had my life under control and it was a new experience for me to find myself caught up in an undertow without any idea where it was leading. I would have followed you, you know. Whatever. Yes, it was handy that I had an available excuse but, if I hadn't, I would have just thought of one because, the day you left that cabin, I knew that I couldn't live without you in my life.'

Miranda felt her shuddering body go very still at that.

'I spent those days after you left telling myself that I was a fool, that sleeping with you, however magical it had been, was not essentially different than sleeping with any woman, but I was wrong. I came back over here with your designs, like an idiot on a quest to prove the impossible. I desperately wanted you back in bed with me and I was infuriated that you were so adamant that you would design my house but nothing else would be on the agenda. You can't begin to imagine what I felt when I saw you with that little twerp. It was as though my entire universe had come crashing down on my head. I never want to go through that again, my love.'

He rocked her gently, drawing comfort from having her in his arms. 'Even when you told me that you wouldn't entertain the idea of sleeping with me, I still imagined that you hadn't dealt me a mortal blow, that I could deal with that the way I had dealt with everything else in my life. With efficiency. But I was wrong and I was blind. I need you, Miranda and I've never said that to anyone in my life before. I need you and I want you and I love you.'

'You *what*?'

'I love you.' He drew back so that he could look down at her and gave her a crooked, stupified smile. 'And it just took me time to realise how much that one thing could change the whole equation…'

EPILOGUE

MIRANDA stepped into the room and felt Luke step in behind her, enfolding her in his arms, his hand wrapped possessively around her heavy breast.

It was a small room, with two quaintly shaped semi-circular windows overlooking the gardens, adjoining their own bedroom with an interconnecting door. The intention had been for it to be an upstairs study, to be used if Luke occasionally needed to work at night and didn't want to use the massive and well-equipped den on the ground floor.

Right now, the last rays of the summer sun were dipping through the windows, sending a soft, mellow glow through the room.

'I really liked this wallpaper.' Miranda sighed.

'We could always leave it as it is.' He nuzzled her ear and she squirmed pleasurably against him, feeling her soft body relax deeper into his.

'You know we can't. It's too...*blue* and too masculine.'

'And what do you suggest, my little interior designer?' He slipped his big hand under her jumper and felt the heavy weight of her breast and the taut protuberance of her nipple against his palm. He rolled his hand gently around and Miranda gave a little gasp of pleasure. She could feel his arousal pressing against the back of her and she smiled dreamily before refocusing her mind on the task at hand. But she didn't remove his massaging hand. That felt altogether too good.

'How about something orange...?'

'A little vibrant, wouldn't you say?' They shared a laugh of mutual understanding at this private joke.

'But very good feng shui. And also very neutral. Besides, bright colours suit little children...' She gazed at the room and saw oranges and yellows and turquoises and a small wardrobe with a montage of ducks swimming across the doors and, just there, the cot. She saw a little baby lying in it, with fuzzy dark hair, growing into a toddler, and the hurried, frantic patter of tiny feet racing through a house. She placed her hands on her stomach, already swelling and showing the five months of pregnancy, and Luke's hands covered hers.

Together, they looked around the room, their minds as one, forming the same images.

He turned her to him and stroked her long hair away from her face and smiled tenderly.

'Have I ever told you how much I love you?' he asked softly.

'Every day.'

'So you won't mind hearing it again...'

'Nope.'

'I love you, Mrs Decroix.'

MARRIAGE AT HIS CONVENIENCE

by

Jacqueline Baird

Jacqueline Baird began writing as a hobby when her family objected to the smell of her oil painting, and immediately became hooked on the romantic genre. She loves travelling and worked her way around the world from Europe to the Americas and Australia, returning to marry her teenage sweetheart. She lives in Ponteland, Northumbria, the county of her birth, and has two teenage sons. She enjoys playing badminton, and spends most weekends with husband Jim, sailing their Gp.14 around Derwent Reservoir.

Don't miss Jacqueline Baird's brand new novel out in the summer from Mills & Boon's Modern Romance™!

CHAPTER ONE

LUCAS KARADINES stood before the plate-glass window of his New York office, his dark eyes staring out over the Manhattan skyline without really registering the landscape. He ran a long-fingered hand through his night-black hair, a predatory smile curving his sensuous mouth, and a hint of triumph glittered in his eyes. Lunch had been a resounding success; he had done it! Tomorrow afternoon at Karadines London hotel, he and his father Theo, and the head of the Aristides Corporation, Alex Aristides, would sign the deal that would make Karadines one of the largest international hotel chains, and shipping lines in the world.

Like his own father, Alex Aristides was not in the best of health, but unlike his father he had no son to carry on the family business, one of the oldest firms in Greece, hence the sale to Karadines at a discounted price. Tomorrow night a party would be held for the families, the lawyers, and a few friends to celebrate the deal.

Lucas turned back to his desk, his glance falling on the telephone; as for the rest, a brief frown marred the perfect symmetry of his strikingly handsome face. It was time he made the call. He glanced at the gold Rolex on his wrist—at a pinch he could make it back to London tonight. Amber would not mind him arriving in the middle of the night… Amber was a born sensualist—he had never known a sexier woman. Amber with the long golden brown hair, and the long legs; legs that entwined with his as though they were made to match. He felt the familiar stirring in his loins and for a moment felt a flicker of regret.

No, he ruthlessly squashed the wayward thought. There was more to life than wild, white-hot sex. And he hadn't forgotten he'd had to wait a long time for even that the last time he had returned to London a day early. Amber had been at work and when she'd finally returned to the apartment, had only been able to spare half an hour as she'd had a business dinner to attend. They had made up for it later, but Lucas Karadines was not the kind of man to wait around for any woman, or play second fiddle to a woman's career. Several times he had suggested she resign from her job and allow him to keep her, but she had refused.

No, his mind was made up. In fact his decision had been made weeks ago. Lucas had been in the first stages of delicate negotiations to try and buy out the Aristides Corporation when he'd been introduced to the daughter of the owner, and fate had played a hand. Christina, sweet, innocent Christina, was everything he wanted in a wife. She was the opposite of Amber. She had absolutely no desire for a career other than marriage and children. She was Greek with the same cultural background and traditions as himself. And Christina adored him and hung onto his every word. They were totally compatible, and she would make a brilliant wife and mother.

The timing was perfect. After his father's last Angina attack he had confided in Lucas his ambition to see him happily married with a family of his own before he died. Lucas needed no urging to propose to Christina; he was ready to settle down and raise a family. His father was delighted at the deal and the prospect of Lucas marrying was icing on the cake.

Lucas knew he owed everything to his father. He had rescued him at the age of thirteen from the streets of Athens. His mother had left a letter with the Karadineses' lawyers before she died, giving proof that Lucas was the illegitimate son of Theo Karadines. His father had searched for him, found him and taken him into his home, paid for his education, given him his name and moulded him in his own image, for which Lucas was eternally grateful. Lucas's much older half-brother had been killed with his wife in a plane crash when Lucas was twenty-six. Without hesitation his father had made Lucas head of the company and he had repaid him by expanding and increasing their holdings and profits a hundredfold.

He turned, strode to his desk, and picked up the telephone, one long finger jabbing out the number he knew by heart. He straightened his broad shoulders beneath the exquisitely tailored dark blue silk jacket, and shoved his free hand in the pocket of his trousers, and with a look of grim determination on his face he listened to the ringing tone.

Amber Jackson walked back into her office with a dazed look in her lovely eyes and a broad grin on her face. She'd just had lunch with Sir David Janson, the chairman of the merchant bank by the same name, and she was still in a state of shock at what he had revealed to her. The ringing of the telephone brought her back to reality with a jolt. It might be Lucas, and, dashing across to her desk, she picked up the receiver.

'Amber, good I caught you. I'm sorry, but I won't be able to see you tomorrow. It will be Saturday before we can meet, pressure of business, you understand.'

The happy expression that had illuminated Amber's face when she'd picked up the receiver and heard the deep rich tones of her boyfriend's voice turned into a disappointed frown.

'Yes, I understand.' What else could she say? Lucas was

the managing director of his family firm, a large hotel and leisure company, and he spent much of his time travelling between the main offices in Athens and New York, and the various holdings around the world. In the year she had known him, she had accepted the fact he could not be with her all the time. She had a high-powered job herself as a dealer with Brentford's, a large stockbroking firm, and she knew all too well the pressure of work. 'But I'm not very happy,' she added huskily. The sound of his voice alone was enough to make her pulse race, and she was missing him quite madly. 'It is almost two months since I saw you. I was really looking forward to tomorrow—it is the anniversary of our first date and I have some marvellous news for you. You won't believe it.'

'I have some news for you as well,' he drawled, and the trace of sarcasm in his tone wasn't very reassuring. 'But it will keep until Saturday.'

It was not the response she would have liked, but then for the past few weeks Lucas's telephone calls had been few and brief, and her confidence in his love had begun to waver a little. She told herself she was being stupid. He loved her, she knew he did. But she knew the last time he had come back unexpectedly early hoping to surprise her he had been chillingly angry because she had refused to leave her office the moment he'd called and she'd insisted on keeping her work commitments. Later that night he had suggested yet again she give up her job, declaring a man of his wealth did not need a girlfriend who worked. Amber had tried to make a joke out of it, by answering with, 'I will when I am married and pregnant, but not before,' hoping he would take the hint and ask her to marry him. He hadn't. But when Amber had had to go back to work on the Monday he had casually informed her he had to go to New York for a while. The while had stretched into two long months.

Amber was desperate to see him again. She had taken tomorrow, Friday, off work especially to be able to meet him. Now he was saying Saturday, and she could have wept with frustration. But she wanted nothing to upset their reunion, and so she responded with determined good humour.

'Okay, but I miss you. It has been so long and I'm suffering from terrible withdrawal symptoms. I expect you to cure me on sight,' she said throatily.

'Sorry, darling, but it is only one more day—but it might be more if I don't get off this line and back to work.'

The prospect of their reunion being delayed even further was enough for Amber to end the conversation within a minute. She replaced the receiver, her smile somewhat restored at his use of the endearment and his apology for the delay. She had waited so long, she could easily wait another day.

But on leaving the classic old building that housed the prestigious offices of the Brentford brokerage firm, she could not help a pensive sigh escaping. She thought her surprise was special, but would Lucas? Lucas had come into her life like a whirlwind and she'd changed from a serious young woman of twenty-two, who had never worn a designer dress in her life, into the sophisticated, elegant creature she was today. But sometimes when she looked in the mirror she did not recognise herself...

Securing the gaily wrapped parcel she was carrying more firmly under one arm, Amber waved down a passing cab by swinging her briefcase in her other hand. She was completely oblivious to the admiring glances of the dozens of men pouring out of the city office. At five-feet-seven, with a slender but curvaceous body clad in a smart navy suit, the short skirt ending inches above her knees, and the snug-fitting jacket enhancing her tiny waist and the soft swell of her breasts, she was an enchanting picture. She moved with a natural, sensuous grace. Her long light brown hair, gleaming like the colour of polished chestnuts, fell from a centre parting, and was loosely tied at her nape with a pearl clasp, before falling like a silken banner almost to her waist. Her face was a classic oval with high cheekbones, a small straight nose and a wide, full-lipped mouth, but it was her huge eyes, hazel in colour and tinged with gold, shining beneath extravagantly long lashes, that animated her whole face.

'Where to, miss?' The cab stopped at her feet, and with a bright smile she slid into the back seat and gave the driver the address of her friends Tim and Spiro.

She alighted from the taxi outside the door of a small terraced house in Pimlico, and, after paying the fare, she glanced up at the white-painted house. It was hard to believe it was five years ago since she had moved into the house with Tim, a lifelong friend from the small Northumbrian village of Thropton where they'd both been born and brought up. Tim had comforted her when her mother had died when she was seventeen, and he had been in his first year at art college when Amber had been about to start at the London School of Economics. It had been Tim's suggestion she move into the spare room where he stayed. The house actually belonged to Spiro Karadines, a Greek student who was studying English at a language school before going to work at the deluxe London hotel which his family owned to learn the business from the bottom up. He reckoned he needed to let the rooms to students to pay for the upkeep of the house, because his closest relative was an uncle, Lucas Karadines, who controlled his trust fund, and was as mean as sin.

Lucas would not be pleased if he knew Amber was visiting his nephew Spiro, but he had been a good friend to her whatever Lucas thought about him. She rang the bell and waited, a reminiscent smile on her face. It was exactly a year ago tonight, Spiro's twenty-second birthday, when she had first set eyes on Lucas. He had arrived unannounced at the party, and, after a furious argument with Spiro, Lucas had calmed down and accepted a drink.

For Amber it had been love at first sight. She had taken one look at the tall, dark-haired man, incongruously dressed in a house full of motley-clad students in an immaculate grey business suit, and at least a decade older than anyone else, and her heart had turned over. She'd been unable to take her eyes off him; her fascinated gaze had followed him around the room.

Well over six feet tall, broad-shouldered, and long-legged, with thick black hair slightly longer than the present fashion, he'd been *the* most handsome man she had ever seen. Even when it had been obvious he'd been hopelessly out of place in a room where quite a few of the men had been openly gay, he'd exuded a powerful sexuality that had been totally, tauntingly masculine. When his dark eyes had finally rested on her, he'd smiled and she'd blushed scarlet, and when he had casually asked her to have dinner with him the next night she had agreed with alacrity.

Spiro had tried to put her off. He had told her his uncle was a predator of the first order, a shark, who would gobble up a little girl like her for breakfast. He was thirty-five, far too old for her. He liked his women smart and sophisticated—women who knew the score. Amber had replied she was smart, and Spiro had laughed.

'In the brains department, yes, but you dress like—a blue stocking, I believe is your peculiar English term.'

Amber had thumped him, but had ignored Spiro's warning and gone out to dinner with Lucas anyway.

It had been a magical evening. Lucas had asked her all about herself, and she'd responded by telling him her ambition to be a successful investment analyst. How she had just completed her first year at work and was delighted to have earned a huge bonus. She'd even told him she was the only child of an unmarried mother, but he had not been shocked. Finally, when Lucas had seen her to her door he had asked her if she would like to accompany Spiro and Tim to the family villa on the Karadineses' private island of the same name in the Aegean Sea for Easter. Amber had again accepted his invitation. The kiss-on-the-cheek goodnight had been a bit of a let-down. But after questioning Spiro the next day about Lucas, she had blown a few thousand pounds of her first year's bonus in buying a wardrobe full of designer clothes, visiting a beautician, and transforming herself into the sophisticated kind of woman she thought Lucas liked.

By the end of the island holiday, she had met the senior Mr Karadines, and Lucas had no longer been seeing her as a student friend of Spiro, but had been looking at her with blatant male sexual speculation in his dark eyes. On returning to London he had called her and wined and dined her half a dozen times, but the relationship had not developed past a goodnight kiss, admittedly each one more passionate and lingering than the last, but nothing more. Then he had gone to New York on business and she had thought he had forgotten her. Two weeks later he'd been back, and the next dinner date they'd shared she'd ended up in his hotel suite and they'd become lovers.

He was her first and only lover so she had no one to

compare him with, but she did not need to. She knew she had found her soul mate. He only had to look at her and her stomach curled, and when he touched her he ignited a fire, a passion she had never known existed. She had a vivid mental image of his magnificent naked body looming over her, his powerful shoulders and hair-roughened chest, the long, tanned length of him, all straining muscle and sinew as he kissed and caressed her, and taught her the exquisite delight only two people who loved could share. Within a week, at Lucas's insistence, she had moved into the loft apartment he had bought overlooking the Thames, and their relationship had gone from strength to strength. Just thinking about him made her heart pound, and brought a dreamy smile to her face.

'What are you looking so happy about?' Tim's demand brought her out of her reverie.

She looked into the sparkling blue eyes of the blond-haired man holding open the door. 'Happy memories,' she said, and, walking past him, she brushed her lips against his smooth cheek. 'Where is the birthday boy? I have a present for him.'

With the ease of long familiarity Amber strolled into the small living room. 'Happy birthday, Spiro.' She grinned at the slender dark-haired man elegantly reclining on a deep blue satin brocade sofa, and, gently dropping the parcel she was carrying onto his lap, she kicked off her shoes and sat down on the matching sofa opposite.

'My, I am honoured. My esteemed uncle has actually allowed you to visit us. It must be over six months since we saw you,' and, lifting an enquiring eyebrow to his part-ner, he added, 'or is it more, Tim?'

'Cut the sarcasm, Spiro. Amber is our friend, even if we do abhor her taste in men. Open your gift.'

'Yes, Spiro, where Lucas is concerned we've agreed to

differ. So open the present—I'll have you know I went to great trouble to find just the right gift,' Amber declared with a grin.

'So-rry, Amber,' he drawled dramatically. 'You've caught me in a bad mood; I am finally beginning to feel my age.'

'At twenty-three!' she exclaimed. 'Don't make me laugh.'

'You deserve to laugh, Amber. You deserve to be happy,' Spiro suddenly said seriously.

'I am happy.' She grinned back. 'Now open the parcel.'

Two minutes later Spiro was on his feet and pressing a swift kiss on Amber's cheek. 'I love it, Amber,' he said, his gaze straying back to the small sketch of two young men, clad in loincloths, facing up as if to wrestle. 'But it must have cost you a fortune—it is an original from the nineteenth century, isn't it?'

'Of course, I would not dare give you a fake,' she replied, and all three laughed. Amber knew Spiro hated working for the family firm and his burning ambition was to set up his own art gallery.

Unfortunately she also knew Lucas controlled the purse strings, and Spiro could not inherit his late father's share of the firm until he was twenty-five, or married. Spiro had a very generous monthly allowance, but he spent every penny.

The week after she'd moved in with Lucas, she had tried to put Spiro's point of view to Lucas but he had withdrawn behind a cold, impenetrable mask and told her curtly to keep out of their family business, and also suggested she keep away from his nephew.

The ease with which he had turned into a hard, remote stranger as though her thoughts and opinions were nothing had scared her. Amber had wanted to argue, she'd tried, but Lucas had simply blanked her. Unfortunately it had put a strain on Amber's friendship with her former flat-mates. She did keep in touch with Tim on a regular ba-sis—they talked on the phone every week or so—but Spiro was right. It was months since she had seen them both.

'I bet my uncle does not know you spent a fortune on this for me?' Spiro said, propping the framed sketch on the cast-iron mantelpiece, before turning back to look down on Amber.

'It has nothing to do with Lucas. I found out two weeks ago my bonus at the end of this financial year, on the fifth of April, is—wait for it, boys,' and with a wide grin, she said, 'almost a quarter of a million.'

'Well done, Amber, love,' Tim exclaimed. 'I always knew you were a genius.'

'This calls for a double celebration! Break out the bub-bly, Tim, and let the party start,' Spiro added his con-gratulations. 'The three musketeers are back in action.'

Moisture glazed Amber's eyes at Spiro's reminder of what the three of them used to be nicknamed by their friends when they had all lived together. She'd changed and moved on, and the carefree days were long gone, but not forgotten.

The champagne was produced and toasts drank to Spiro, to Amber, to Tim, to life, and anything else they could think of. It was like old times.

Two hours later, her jacket long since removed and the clip taken from her hair, Amber was curled up on the sofa with a glass of champagne in her hand when Spiro dropped a bomb on the proceedings.

'So, Amber, what do you think of this idea of Lucas's to get married? I saw Grandfather yesterday—he is staying at the hotel while having a check-up at his Harley Street doctor, and he is delighted at the news.'

Suddenly the world seemed a wonderful place to Amber, even in her half-inebriated state. 'He told you that? Lucas is thinking of getting married! I can't believe it!' she cried happily. Lucas had actually told his father they were getting married; she couldn't wait for him to get home to ask her. Of course, she would have to pretend she didn't know. 'I spoke to Lucas this afternoon and I was disappointed because he can't make it back from New York until Saturday.' Her golden eyes sparkled like jewels in her flushed face. 'But he did say he had some news for me, and I never guessed.' Her not-so-subtle hint about giving up work when she was married and pregnant had obviously worked after all, she thought ecstatically.

'According to Grandfather, Lucas has news for you, all right, but—' Spiro started to speak but was cut off in mid-flow by Tim.

'Shut up, Spiro. Amber does not need to know second hand.'

'Please, Spiro, tell me what your grandfather said. I have only met him the one time we were all in Greece but I thought he liked me.'

A harsh laugh escaped Spiro. 'Oh, he likes you, all right, but not for what you think.'

'Spiro, no. It is none of your business,' Tim interjected again. 'We are having a good time—leave it.'

'Why? Amber has been our friend for years—she deserves to know the truth. Do you really want her to find out cold?'

Lost in her dream of wedded bliss, she was only half listening but it slowly began to dawn on Amber that the two men were arguing. 'What's the matter?' She glanced from one to the other. They looked serious. Straightening up in the seat, she drained her glass and placed it on the floor at her feet. 'Come on, guys, find *what* out cold?' she demanded cheerfully.

The two men looked at each other, and then Tim nodded. 'You're right, she deserves better.'

'Better than what?' Amber queried.

Spiro jumped to his feet. 'Better than my bastard of an uncle.'

'Oh, please, Spiro, not that again. Why can't you just be happy that Lucas and I love each other? We accept you and Tim are partners, why can't you return the favour and accept Lucas and I are partners just the same, instead of bleating on about him being a bastard?'

When she'd first told Tim and Spiro she was moving out to set up home with Lucas, Spiro had tried all ways to get her to change her mind. Finally, in a rage, he'd told her Lucas was the illegitimate child of his grandfather, and his mother was little better than a prostitute, notorious in Athens for her string of lovers, and Lucas was no better. Amber had refused to listen then and she refused to listen now. 'In case you've forgotten, I never knew my father. So what does that make me?'

Spiro, his anger subsiding, looked at her with glistening brown eyes full of compassion. 'I didn't mean it literally, though that is true. I meant it figuratively, Amber. Lucas does not consider you his partner. He considers you his mistress, nothing more, and easily dispensable.'

'Only married men have mistresses, Spiro,' Amber snapped back. 'You know nothing about my relationship with Lucas.' Her face paled at Spiro's hurtful comments. 'And I think it's time I left.' Rising unsteadily to her feet, she glanced down at her old friends. Tim was watching her with compassion, and that hurt more than anything else did. Tim had known her since infant school, surely she should be able to count on his support? But apparently not.

'Listen to Spiro, Amber. It's for your own good,' Tim said quietly.

'Lucas is good for me and to me, and that is all I need to know.' Picking up her purse, she slipped her shoes back on her feet.

'Wait, Amber.' Spiro stood up and caught her arm as she would have moved towards the door. 'You are a lovely, highly intelligent girl, with a genius for picking winners in the money markets, but you're hopelessly naive where men are concerned. Lucas is the only man you have ever known.'

'He is the only man I want to know. Now, let go of my arm.'

Reluctantly Spiro let her go. 'Just one more thing, Amber. I know who Lucas intends marrying, and it is not—'

Amber cut in angrily. 'I am not listening to any more of this,' an inexplicable fear made her yell. Spiro was half drunk and he was lying, he had to be. 'You're lying, and I know why—you can't bear to see Lucas and I happy together. You want to hurt Lucas by trying to break us up, just because he won't give you your inheritance ahead of time. I can read you like a book, Spiro, you have to dom-inate everyone around you. Tim might be happy to let you get away with it, but Lucas won't and that is what sticks in your craw. Grow up, why don't you?'

Spiro shook his dark head. 'You're blind, Amber, plain blind.' His dark eyes sought Tim's, his exasperation show-ing. 'Now what?'

Tim grimaced. 'Give it up, Spiro, she will never believe you.'

'All right, Amber, think what you like.' Spiro held his hands up in front of him. 'But do me one favour—I am dining with my grandfather at the hotel tomorrow night. He is having a bit of a party to celebrate a business deal and hopefully his return to good health. He has asked me to bring you along, and, as you say Lucas will not be back until Saturday, there is nothing to stop you. Will you come?'

Amber was torn. She didn't want to go anywhere with Spiro, but on the other hand… 'Your grandfather actually asked you to invite me?' she queried.

'Yes, in fact he was insistent.'

'In that case, yes.' How kind of him, Amber thought, the old man must know Lucas was not in London, and so had asked Spiro to bring her to his party.

'Good, I'll pick you up at your place at eight.' She never saw the gleam of determination in Spiro's eyes, that made him look uncannily like his uncle for a fleeting instant, as she said her goodbyes and left.

Later that night as she slipped a satin nightgown over her head she walked restlessly around the large bedroom she shared with Lucas. Spiro's bitchy words had upset her more than she wanted to admit. She slid open one of the wardrobe doors that lined two walls, and let her hand trail across the fine fabric of a couple of Lucas's tailored suits. The faintest lingering trace of his cologne teased her nostrils, and somehow she was reassured. Lucas loved her, she knew he did, and on that thought she climbed into the king-sized bed and sleep claimed her.

Amber glanced at her reflection for the last time in the large mirrored doors of the wardrobes that formed one wall of the bedroom. She looked good, better than good. Great, she told herself. Her hair was washed and brushed until it shone dark gold, and she had clipped the sides up into a coronet on top of her head, while the rest fell down her back like a swathe of silk. She had opted for a classic black DKNY dress—the fine black silk jersey clung to her body like a second skin, the sleeves long and fitted, the skirt ending inches above her knees. The low-cut square neckline exposed the gentle curve of her firm breasts, setting off to perfection the emerald and diamond necklace she had clasped around her throat. The matching drop earrings glinted against the swan-like elegance of her neck. Both had been presents from Lucas. On her feet she wore three-inch-heeled black sandals, adding to her already tall stature.

Picking up her purse and a jade-green pashmina shawl, she walked down the spiral staircase to the vast floor area of the apartment. She loved the polished hardwood floor, and the carefully arranged sofas that picked out the colour in the cashmere rug. In fact she loved her home. But where was Spiro? He was ten minutes late.

She crossed the room to a large desk, her hand reaching out for the telephone. She would try one last time to ring Lucas in New York. Picking up the instrument, she dialled the number. Two minutes later she replaced the receiver, the same reply as she had got earlier echoing in her head. 'I'm sorry but Mr Karadines is not in the office today, if you would like to leave a message…' She had also tried his suite at the Karadines Hotel in New York, and got no reply.

The bell rang and she had no time to worry where Lucas was. Spiro had arrived.

Two minutes later she was seated in the back of a taxi-cab with Spiro looking very elegant in a conservative black dinner suit and white shirt; the only hint at his rebellious personality was a vibrantly striped bow-tie in red, green and blue.

'You look rather nice,' Amber said with a grin. 'Though I don't know about the bow-tie.'

'And you, dear girl, look as stunning as ever.' But there was no smile in his eyes as he reached out and caught both of Amber's hands in his.

'Where to now, Gov?' the taxi driver asked.

'Hold it a minute or two,' Spiro responded, then, glancing back at Amber, he added, 'You must listen to me and believe me. Tim made me promise that I would tell you before we arrive at the hotel so if you want to cancel you can do so. I am sorry, truly sorry, Amber, but Lucas will be at the party.'

Her hands jerked in his hold but he did not set her free. His brown eyes held hers, and there was no doubting the sincerity and sadness in their depths.

'How...?' All the blood drained from her face. 'How do you know?' she asked quietly.

'Because, a rare occurrence for me, I admit, I actually went to work for a few hours this afternoon in my capacity of Assistant Manager at the hotel. I saw Lucas arriving with two guests, Alex Aristides and his young daughter Christina. They went to Grandfather's suite. Ten minutes later I escorted the two family lawyers to the same suite. Karadines have bought out the Aristides Corporation. The deal was signed this afternoon. Needless to say they didn't need my signature, although I own half the company. My trustees did it for me. I was given the task of amusing the teenage daughter for an hour. An hour spent standing around in the boutiques in the hotel lobby. The girl could shop for the world.'

'So it was business—Lucas said he was tied up with business, he would not lie to me,' she declared adamantly. Though he had lied by omission—he had led her to believe he was staying in New York...

'Stop, Amber.' Spiro squeezed her hands in his. 'Please don't do this to yourself. Christina Aristides is eighteen years of age and obviously part of the deal.'

'No, no, Spiro, you're wrong. Lucas would never do that to me,' Amber said firmly, but deep down inside a tiny voice of dissent was telling her he might.

'He is a chip off the old block, as you English say. How do you think Grandfather made his money? As a young man he went to sea on a cruise liner as a waiter. Twelve months later he married the owner's daughter, a woman ten years older than him, but for a waiter that was some step up. To give him his due, under his control the firm went from strength to strength. But my grandmother was no fool—she knew he had several mistresses and Lucas's mother was one of them. So she kept the stock in her name, and on her death half went to Grandfather and half to her son, my father. Do you really think Grandfather would have risked his whole business on taking Lucas in, and giving him his name, if my grandmother had still been alive? My parents did not object because they already had half the business.'

'But that does not mean Lucas would marry for money. He does not need to,' she defended him staunchly.

'Amber, Grandfather wants this deal, and Lucas is exactly like him. They are both very Greek, very traditional. Everything is business to them. Lucas will marry the girl. You have no chance, Amber. Believe me, you never did.'

'You don't know Lucas as I do. He might just be stringing the girl along until the deal was signed…' She stopped, realising how desperate she sounded, as if she would rather think of Lucas as a ruthless, manipulative businessman than face the fact he might leave her.

'Well, I suppose it is a possibility and if that is what

you want to believe...' Spiro shrugged his broad shoulders...'we might as well go.'

'You say Tim told you to tell me this.' She looked at Spiro with icy eyes. 'I don't believe you. Tim would never be so cruel.'

'You're right, of course—Tim has not a cruel bone in his body. I, on the other hand, wanted to walk you straight into the party and let you come face to face with Lucas. In fact I was hoping you would cause a scene in front of my grandfather. Then my precious uncle would be seen for the devil he is, but Tim would not let me.'

'You actually believe all you are telling me,' Amber whispered, the full horror of Spiro's revelation finally sinking into her troubled mind.

'You don't have to take my word. You can go back into your apartment and bury your head in the sand like an ostrich for one more night. Or you can come with me and see for yourself.' A challenging smile curved his full lips. 'If you have the nerve.'

Amber had never refused a challenge in her life and she was not going to start now. Besides which, she did not believe Spiro. Her heart would not let her...

CHAPTER TWO

AMBER, tall and sophisticated in the black silk dress with
jewels gleaming at her throat, handed her shawl in to the
cloakroom attendant, and turned back to Spiro.

'Ready.' She smiled. Spiro had to be mistaken, she told
herself yet again, her golden eyes straying to the wide
open doors of the private function room where the party
was being held.

'Take my arm, Amber.' Spiro picked up her nerveless
hand and slipped it through his arm as they walked into
the elegant room.

Lucas Karadines saw Amber before she had even got
through the door. She looked sensational. Shock held him
rigid for a second, then he looked away hastily but not
before seeing her companion, Spiro! Lucas's black eyes
closed briefly. Oh, hell! He almost groaned out loud. For
the first time in his adult life he felt about two inches tall.
He knew deep down he should have made the effort to
see Amber some time today and finish their relationship,
but he had been reluctant to do so. But what the hell was
she doing here? He did not need to ask. Spiro, of course.
Spiro would find it amusing.

He felt a tug on his sleeve, and looked down into the
round open face of Christina. Thank God his betrothal to
Christina was not to be announced until next week—at
least that would give him time to explain to Amber. He
would not wish to hurt her for the world. His dark eyes
were fixed on Christina, but more worrying was that in his
mind's eye he was seeing the stunningly sensual naked

24

figure of Amber, the night he had given her the necklace as a birthday present, the emeralds blazing around her neck her only adornment. Brutally he squashed the image, much the way he would like to squash Spiro for putting him in this position. Determinedly he smiled down at Christina, and, slipping an arm around her shoulder, continued the conversation with their respective fathers.

Amber's golden gaze urgently scanned the crowded room, hoping against hope she would not find the man she was looking for. Then she spotted Lucas. It was two long months since she had seen him, and she could not help it as her eyes drank in the sight of him. Why he was here instead of New York didn't matter, he was here…now…

He was the tallest, sexiest man in the room. His superbly muscled frame was clad in a black dinner suit, the exquisitely tailored jacket fitted perfectly across his broad shoulders, the pure white of the dress shirt he wore contrasted starkly with his bronzed skin. Her heart squeezed in her chest, her gaze slanting down over the long, elegant length of him with loving, hungry eyes. She knew every inch of his magnificent body as intimately as she knew her own. She would have gambled her last penny that neither one of them could have walked into a room without the other being instantly aware of it. She waited for his head to turn, for those incredible dark eyes to meet hers, for his smile of delighted recognition. But she was wrong… Lucas wasn't aware of her at all…

She blindly allowed Spiro to lead her slowly through the crowd of guests; she had eyes for no one but Lucas. He was standing at the far end of the room with a group of three other people: his father, another elderly gentleman, and a young girl. He was smiling down at the girl with a look of such tenderness in his eyes that an inexplicable fear made Amber's blood run cold. His head was

slightly bowed, his shoulders curved in a protective attitude towards the girl, and Amber's heart froze in her
breast. She was vaguely aware of the long table they were
standing beside; for a second her eyes flickered to the centre point, a magnificent ice sculpture of a sailing ship.
Wildly whimsical, she wished she could get in it and sail
away, but inevitably her gaze was drawn back to the small
group. It was just a business deal, it had to be, she told
herself. She dimly felt Spiro squeeze her hand, and heard
through the roaring in her ears.

'I hate to say it, Amber, but I told you so...'

'Thanks.' She cast a furious sidelong glance at Spiro;
he was enjoying this. 'But it still does not mean you are
right. Lucas might not have had time to call me if, as you
say, he had a business meeting this afternoon.' She had to
hope; she could not face the alternative or it would destroy
her.

'If you believe that, you will believe anything. Where's
your pride, girl?' Spiro queried, raising one elegant brow,
but, sensing her distress, he added, 'Chin up, Amber.
Don't let the devil get you down.'

'He is not a devil,' she defended Lucas, but without her
usual conviction, and, glancing back at the group, she finally looked at the young girl at Lucas's side.

She was short and very Greek with an olive-skinned
complexion and long black hair tied back in a ponytail.
Pretty if a little plump. The dress she was wearing was a
concoction in pink satin with a gathered skirt, probably
ruinously expensive, but it did nothing for the girl's figure.
The girl was gazing up at Lucas, with a dreamy smile on
her face. One of her hands rested on his arm, and the other
was on his chest—there was no mistaking the intimacy of
the gesture.

'Is that child Christina Aristides?' Amber asked. 'The daughter you mentioned.'

'Yes.'

'Then you're wrong, Spiro. Lucas is no cradle-snatcher and that girl is young enough to be *his* daughter.' Her gaze strayed helplessly back to the dark head of her lover, and at that moment his head lifted, and his dark eyes clashed with Amber's.

She stared at the man she loved with all her heart, and she saw the coldness in his hard gaze as their glances locked. He did not even look surprised to see her. But she noticed his pupils dilate slightly, and the flare of desire in his eyes before he lowered his gaze, to sweep down over the shapely length of her and return blandly to her face.

Lucas Karadines shifted uncomfortably and shoved his hand in his trouser pocket. He had thought he had got himself under control enough to look at her again, but his body thought otherwise, much to his disgust. What the hell was she doing here with Spiro, anyway? He had told her to keep away from Spiro and she had deliberately defied him. But then that was Amber—she took a delight in challenging him on every level. A trait he could put up with in a girlfriend but not a trait a man wanted in a wife.

She looked stunning as always, her waist-length chestnut hair gleaming gold in the artificial light, the sleek black dress lovingly clinging to every curve of her magnificent body. Every man in the place was secretly eyeing her, he knew. She was sex personified, and his body had reacted instantly. He cursed under his breath. No man in his right mind would marry a girl like Amber, a girl who would have to be guarded every minute of every day from other predatory males. He smiled down at the young girl by his side. He had made the right decision; Christina would never cause him a moment's worry. Then he eyed Spiro

again, and any guilt he was feeling at his own behaviour
he transferred to Spiro. He might have guessed it was his
damn nephew's entire fault. He had done it deliberately to
embarrass him.

Amber watched Lucas shove his hand in his trouser
pocket and knew he still wanted her. The beginnings of a
smile curved her full lips as she waited for him to acknowledge her. But his desire was quickly replaced by
anger as his dark eyes moved to narrow on her companion.
The smile died from her lips before it was born as Lucas,
with a dismissive arch of one dark brow, turned slightly
and said something to his father, and then, smiling at his
young companion, he took her hand in his and moved
through the crowd, stopping as various people spoke to
them.

Amber took the drink Spiro handed her and immediately
took a long swallow; she needed something, anything. She
was shaken to the core; she had never felt so utterly humiliated in her life. It was like being trapped in a nightmare, unable to move, or breathe. A frantic glance around
the room, and she was amazed no one seemed to be aware
of the enormity of what had just happened. Lucas had
looked at her as if she was of no more interest to him than
the dirt beneath his feet. It had to be a mistake, and for a
wild moment she thought of flying over to him, and
snatching his hand from the young girl.

'Any minute now, Amber, be cool,' Spiro murmured,
his dark head bending towards her, shielding her face from
view. 'Take a deep breath, don't let him see he has hurt
you, don't give him the satisfaction.'

Hurt didn't begin to cover how she felt, and a slow-
burning anger ignited in the pit of her stomach. She took
a few deep, calming breaths, schooling her face into calm
immobility.

'That's it,' Spiro said, and moved to her side just as Lucas and Christina stopped in front of them.

'Glad you could make it, Spiro, and you too, Amber,' Lucas said smoothly, and proceeded to introduce his companion. 'Allow me to introduce Christina Aristides. I have just acquired her father's business, and this evening is to celebrate the deal.'

Amber wanted to smash her fist in his face, scream and yell, demand to know why he had lied to her, but this was neither the time or the place. Instead she straightened her shoulders and pinned a smile on her face as she shook the young girl's hand. It wasn't the poor girl's fault, it was Lucas who was the swine.

Christina smiled demurely, and then, turning to Spiro, she punched him playfully on the arm. 'My, you are a dark horse, Spiro, you never mentioned that you were bringing your girlfriend with you tonight.' And then she added for Amber's benefit, 'I hope you did not mind me stealing your boyfriend for the afternoon, but Lucas was too tied up with business to go shopping with me.' The inference being Lucas was her boyfriend.

The tension between the other three was electric. Amber's eyes flew to Lucas's face—surely he would say something, deny it. She saw the cold anger in the depths of his eyes. He was furious she was here. Her presence had obviously upset his glittering celebration, or maybe for the first time in his life he actually felt embarrassed. But in a second Amber knew she was wrong. He stared back at her, his gaze chillingly remote. Amber had seen that look only once before when she'd tried to argue with him about Spiro—it had scared her then, but now it confirmed what she had probably known for the past twenty-four hours but refused to admit.

Shattered by his duplicity, she let her gaze trail over his

tall, muscular body. He was the sexiest man alive, but also heartless. She finally saw him as the hard, ruthless Greek tycoon that he had always been, but love had blinded her to his real character. She tilted back her head, her golden eyes challenging him, but he avoided her gaze, his whole attention fixed on the young girl.

'Don't worry, Christina. I'm sure Amber didn't mind,' Lucas said softly, and, turning to Spiro, he added, 'Though I did not know you and Amber were still seeing each other.'

'Oh, yes, Amber is not the sort to desert her friends, are you, Amber, darling?' Spiro drawled pointedly, and, clasping an arm around her slender waist, he pulled her into his side and pressed a swift kiss on her brow.

Amber let him—in fact she was glad of his support. Her stomach churned and she wanted to be sick as the full extent of Lucas's betrayal hit her. Her beautiful face lost what little colour she had. How dared he introduce her to Christina as though she were merely an acquaintance, a friend of his nephew, instead of the woman who had shared his bed for the best part of a year?

'So I see,' Lucas drawled mockingly. He knew Spiro was gay.

His mockery was the last straw for Amber. Her wild golden eyes clashed with Lucas's. 'I wonder, can anyone say the same about you, Lucas? But, no, I seem to remember you telling me once you had no real friends. Perhaps because you only use people.' She saw his jaw clench, a dark tide of colour surging up under his skin, and a leap of fury in his eyes. Serves him right, Amber thought.

'My, Lucas, a woman who does not admire you unreservedly, that must be a first,' Christina piped up.

'Amber is an old friend, and she and Spiro delight in

trying to needle me, it's just a joke.' Lucas smiled down at Christina, his voice softening. 'Nothing for you to worry about.'

Fury such as she had never known sent all the blood rushing back to Amber's head. Old friend! He had a nerve. The hand holding her glass of wine began to rise. Spiro, guessing her intentions, grasped her wrist.

'I am starving and I think you need a top up, Amber. Excuse us.' With his arm at her waist, he urged her away from the other couple. 'It would have been a futile gesture, Amber, throwing your drink over him—your glass is virtually empty,' he murmured, turning her back to the crowd to face the buffet table.

Amber was shaking, visibly shaking. She'd never felt such overwhelming rage in her life. 'I wasn't going to throw it over him,' she denied, turning blazing eyes up to Spiro's. 'I was going to screw the glass in his arrogant, lying face,' she confessed fiercely.

She was not a violent person, she had never harmed a living thing in her life, but for a second she had completely lost control. Suddenly she was appalled at her own actions, and her anger subsided. 'Thank you for stopping me, Spiro.' She tried to smile. 'Your better nature got the better of you—you said earlier you wanted me to cause a scene, and I thought you were joking. But the joke is on me and I've never felt less like laughing. I want to cry.'

'No, Amber. Tim was right and I was wrong.' His arm dropped from her waist and he lifted a hand to her chin and tilted her head up to face him. 'I should never have brought you here. I have to speak to my grandfather but then I am taking you straight home. Ten minutes at most, can you do it?'

A film of moisture hazed her glorious eyes, and she blinked furiously. 'I have to, I have no choice.' Imperceptibly she straightened her shoulders, her back ramrod straight as she fought for control, and won.

Spiro's hand fell from her chin, his dark eyes admiring her elegant form. 'You are the most beautiful, elegant lady in this room. You have more class in your little finger than the whole of this lot put together, and don't you forget it.'

Before Amber could respond old Mr Karadines interrupted them. He gave Spiro a hug and spoke to him in Greek, before turning to Amber.

'Amber, isn't it? Good to meet you again, and I'm glad to see you are still keeping this grandson of mine in order.'

'Hello, and I'm trying,' was as much as she could manage to say. A blessed numbness had enveloped her. She felt as if she were viewing the proceedings from outside her body—the pain was waiting for her, she knew, but her heart had not broken, it had simply solidified into a hard black stone in her breast.

'Good, good. I have been hearing great things about you from Clive here. Allow me to introduce you. Clive Thompson, my grandson's friend, Amber Jackson.'

Amber didn't have time to wonder why the old man had referred to her as Spiro's friend as the name of the tall, elegant blond-haired man registered, and she was holding out her hand to him. He was a top manager with Janson's merchant bank. He was only forty but already his reputation was legendary in the City.

She sensed rather than saw Lucas and Christina walk up and join the group, but she did not dare look. If she did she knew she would break down. Her hand was still held by Clive and she was grateful because it enabled her to find the strength not to tremble at Lucas's towering presence beside her.

'I have been longing to meet you as soon as Theo told me your name. Allow me to say you are as beautiful as you are brilliant, if not more so; a truly stunning combination.' His bright blue eyes smiled down into hers, and, lifting her fingers to his lips, he kissed the back of her hand before letting go.

'Oh, how gallant, Mr Thompson!' Christina's accented voice interrupted.

Amber glanced sideways and saw Lucas had moved closer to her with Christina clinging onto his other arm. Quickly she returned her attention to Clive, and saw his slightly raised eyebrows and brief polite smile at the young girl, before he returned his attention to Amber again and continued as if the other girl had not spoken.

'Brentford's are very lucky to have you, is the word in the City. Apparently you got your clients out of...' and he mentioned a high-tech company whose shares were on the way down and out '...even better than I did,' and he gave her an appreciative smile that Amber returned. They discussed the company in question in some detail. They were like-minded people.

'I was lucky,' she finally finished. Anything to do with business and she was not in the least intimidated. It was only in the love stakes she was a total idiot, it seemed.

'People make their own luck, Amber—I may call you Amber?' Clive grinned.

'Of course.' She heard what sounded like a grunt from Lucas, and felt the slight brush of his trouser-clad thigh against her hip.

Lucas did it deliberately. Inexplicably it angered him to hear Amber discussing business with the elegant Englishman, and he wanted to disconcert her, but she simply moved away. In that moment Lucas recognised the truth and his arm tightened around Christina. Amber did not need a man for anything other than sex and even that, as he knew to his cost, could be delayed because of her work. He had never been in love but his idea of it was to protect and care for his wife and family. Christina needed his protection and in return he knew that as she was a well-brought-up young Greek girl, her husband and children would always come first.

Amber felt as if she could feel Lucas breathing down her neck and carefully moved closer to Spiro as Clive slid one hand into the inside pocket of his jacket to withdraw a gold-edged card. 'Here is my card—if you ever feel like changing firms, I promise we will offer you a much better package.'

A wry smile curved her full lips; she could not help it. The ultimate irony. From her surprising lunch on Thursday it had been like a roller-coaster ride of highs and lows, finally to this, the worst night of her life, when it was taking all her strength to simply keep standing, she was being head-hunted by Janson's of all firms...

'And would your chairman, Sir David Janson, agree to your proposition?' she prompted with an enviable touch of cynicism, considering the tall, dark presence of Lucas was within touching distance; the familiar scent of him that filled her nostrils had her nerves at screaming-point.

'It would depend on the proposition, would it not, Clive?' Lucas's deep voice queried sardonically.

'Oh, I'm sure Amber and I could work out a mutually satisfactory arrangement.' Clive's blue eyes, gleaming with very male appreciation, didn't leave Amber's as he tagged on, 'And Sir Janson, of course.'

'I'm sure Amber does not want to talk business all night with you men,' Christina inserted, smiling across at Amber. 'I thought this was supposed to be a party.' Then she added, 'Let's go find the rest room, and we can have a gossip. I love your dress, and your necklace and earrings are gorgeous; you must tell me where you got them.'

The bluntness with which Christina changed the subject stopped the conversation dead. Lucas's black eyes clashed with Amber's over the top of Christina's head, and she saw the warning glint in their depths, but she ignored it. Boldly she held his gaze, contempt blazing from her hazel eyes. For the first time that evening she felt in control.

'They were a birthday and Christmas present.' Amber smiled down at Christina. 'And, yes, I'll come with you,' she said, taking the young girl's arm. Let the swine sweat, let him wonder if she would tell his innocent *girlfriend* exactly who had given Amber the jewellery, she thought bitterly. Her rage was the only thing that kept her going as she walked out of the party and along the quiet hall to the powder room.

'Thank God we've escaped,' Christina groaned as they entered the powder room together, and, walking across to the row of vanity basins and dropping her purse on the marble top, she admired herself in the mirror above. 'An hour of my father and his friends and I feel like climbing the walls.' Turning to Amber, she added, 'You're lucky Spiro is young and doesn't take himself seriously. Lucas can be mind-bendingly boring, you've no idea.'

Shocked into silence, Amber watched the younger girl pull at the pink satin bodice of her dress. 'I ask you, Amber, would you be caught dead in a dress like this?'

'Well...' How to be diplomatic? Amber pondered. 'You must like it.' A high-pitched laugh greeted her comment.

'You're joking. I hate it, but then you are not Greek so you would not understand.'

Slowly Amber crossed to stand beside Christina. Her eyes met the other girl's in the mirror, and suddenly Christina seemed so much older and harder. 'Understand why you wear a dress you hate?' Amber prompted.

'Because my father expects me to look like his innocent

young daughter, and of course Lucas expects his fiancée to look like a shy young virgin, otherwise I would not be caught dead in pink satin.'

'Your fiancé!' Amber exclaimed, unable to disguise her horror.

'Yes, didn't Spiro tell you?' And, not waiting for an answer, Christina continued, 'Next weekend at our home in Athens my father is holding a huge party for my be-trothal to Lucas and three weeks later we are getting mar-ried. He would have announced it tonight except it looks a bit too blatant even for a Greek to sign the business deal and sell your daughter in one afternoon.'

So it was all true. Amber's brain reeled under the shock. Spiro had not been exaggerating. She looked into the face of her rival and asked the question uppermost on her mind. 'Do you love Lucas?'

Christina laughed. 'No, but he loves me, or so he says, and it does not really matter anyway. I want to get married, the quicker the better.' Christina fiddled nervously with the clip of the small satin purse on the marble bench. 'Once I am married, I'm free. I get the money my mother left me, and, to give Lucas his due, he is renowned as a shrewd operator, so I have no doubt he will greatly in-crease the wealth of the family company. Therefore mine,' she said with some glee, and, finally noticing the look of shock and horror Amber could not hide, Christina laughed out loud. 'Don't look so shocked; it is a typical Greek arrangement.'

'But…but…' Amber spluttered '…you are so young.'

'I have just spent a year in a Swiss finishing-school, and those ski instructors are something else again. I'm not that young,' she offered with a very adult smile. 'Though I know what you mean—Lucas is a bit old. But Spiro did me a favour this afternoon. I think he was trying to warn me, but actually I was delighted when he told me Lucas apparently keeps a mistress, so I don't think he is going to be bothering me much in bed even when we are married.'

'You really don't mind?' Amber said slowly, the callousness of Christina's statement ringing in her ears. 'You don't care if your husband is unfaithful to you?'

'Not in the least, why should I with a fortune at my disposal?' And, picking up her purse, she opened it and withdrew some rolling tobacco. 'Do you want a smoke?'

Amber looked at the girl and the tobacco. 'No, I don't smoke.' Amber wondered why with her wealth she rolled her own.

'Pity.' Placing a hand on Amber's arm, Christina said, 'Don't look so surprised, and do me a favour, go out and tell Lucas I will be another five minutes. He does not know of my little vice.' She chuckled as she urged Amber towards the door.

Amber found herself out in the corridor without realising how she had got there.

'Where is Christina?' Lucas's deep voice demanded. Amber lifted her head, her stunned gaze meeting his dark brooding eyes. He was standing in the middle of the hall, his large body tense, waiting… But not for Amber…

'She said give her five minutes,' Amber stated bluntly. 'She also said you are her fiancé. How can that be, Lucas?' she hissed furiously. 'You live with me, it has to be a horrible mistake.'

'It is not a mistake.' The dark-lashed brilliance of his eyes clashed with hers; she was too upset to try and hide the hurt and anger in her own gaze. His expression hardened. 'I regret you had to find out this way. But then I had no knowledge of your continued association with my nephew or that he would bring you here tonight…'

Amber's mouth opened but no sound came out. The colossal arrogance of the man! Lucas was as good as saying it was Spiro's fault, that she had discovered his wicked betrayal.

'Look, Amber—' he laid a large hand on her arm, and furiously she brushed him off '—we have to talk.'

'A bit late for talk,' she snapped.

He straightened, squaring his broad shoulders. 'Keep your voice down,' he commanded, his dark eyes narrowing on her flushed, furious face. 'I will call tomorrow morning as arranged and explain.'

'My surprise,' she whispered, realising the full horrific extent of his betrayal. 'Christina was going to be my surprise!' Her voice rose an octave.

'Someone talking about me?' Christina came sauntering out of the cloakroom, her dark eyes almost feverishly bright, her smile brilliant.

Immediately Lucas curved a protective arm around Christina's shoulder, making it very clear where his loyalty lay. 'We were just discussing the engagement party next weekend. It was supposed to be a secret, you're very naughty.' He chided the young girl with such indulgence Amber felt sick.

Spiro sauntered up and slipped an arm around Amber's waist. 'What's all this? Plotting in corridors now.' He chuckled, and Amber clung to him like a life raft in a storm-tossed sea. Her knees were buckling and she thought she would faint; there was only so much hurt one body could stand and she was at the limit. Spiro, sensing her desperation, tightened his grip on her waist and listened as Christina, seemingly inexhaustible, went on at great length about the following weekend and extended an invitation to the party.

Finally when the young girl paused for breath Spiro

leapt in. 'Well, on behalf of both Amber and I, our heartiest congratulations to you, and we hope you both get the happiness you deserve!' he drawled sarcastically. 'Now, you will have to excuse us, but we have a prior engagement.' And within minutes Amber found herself out in the foyer of the hotel.

'I'm sorry, I am truly, truly sorry, Amber, I should never have brought you here.' But Amber wasn't listening. She'd been functioning on shock and adrenalin for the past hour, and now she was as spent as a burst balloon—she wanted to curl up and die.

'Take me home, Spiro.' And he did.

Sitting in the back seat of the cab, with Spiro's protective arm around her, Amber asked bleakly, 'Why, Spiro? You said your grandfather invited me. Why would he do that knowing Lucas and I…?' She broke off, to swallow the lump rising in her throat, her lashes wet with tears. 'How could he be so cruel?'

'You still don't see it,' Spiro said ruefully. 'I've avoided the subject for too long. I should have told you at the time, Amber, but it seemed a harmless enough deceit.' He glanced apologetically down at her tear-stained face. 'Remember the first time you saw Lucas, when he arrived at my party madder than hell? Well, it was because he had just discovered I was taking Tim to our villa in Greece for the Easter holiday and I was about to confess to Grandfather that I was gay. Lucas tried to talk me out of it, saying it would kill the old man if he thought his only grandson was gay. Which is why he asked you out to dinner, and asked you to accompany Tim and I on holiday. Lucas is not above using anybody to protect the old man. Consequently, he subtly let Grandfather know you and Tim were like brother and sister. But you and I had a much closer relationship; after all, you had been living in my house for four years. Lucas can be very convincing, as you know.'

'You mean all this time your grandfather has thought you and I are a couple? But that's impossible...' But was it? she asked herself. Lucas had made no approach to her until they had returned to England, and she had never met his father again until tonight.

Then she remembered their very first dinner date. When Lucas had invited her to the villa, he had also asked her to do him a favour. He knew she was close to Tim and Spiro, and he had asked her to use her influence on the pair to tone down their behaviour in front of his father when they were all at the villa. The old man was rather old-fashioned that way. Of course, Amber had said yes.

Now it all made a horrible kind of sense. Lucas would do anything for his father, including marrying a suitable rich little Greek girl. Spiro was right...

'Think about it, Amber. Has Lucas ever taken you anywhere in public where Grandfather was likely to hear about it? No. While you thought you were building a relationship, a home, with a thoroughly modern man, Lucas had no such intentions.'

Amber's face was bleak, her mouth bitter and twisted as the full import of Spiro's revelation sank in. She tried to speak and found herself shivering compulsively. She could not believe she had been so blind, so stupid...

CHAPTER THREE

AMBER knew once she let the first tear fall that she would never be able to stop. Kicking off her shoes, she locked the door and padded across the polished wood floor to the spiral staircase. Grasping the rail, she ascended to the galleried sleeping area like an old woman. Spiro had asked her to go back to his place, but she'd refused. He had done enough for her for one night, she thought bitterly.

Stripping off her clothes, she walked into the huge bathroom. She glanced at the circular white marble Jacuzzi sunk into the floor, and quickly away as too many memories flooded back. Skirting the bath, she stepped into the double shower. She turned the tap on full, and stood under the power jets and let the water pound her slender body. She closed her eyes, but she could not block out the image of Lucas naked on his knees in the shower with her. Soaping every inch of her tender flesh from the tips of her toes to her head in what she had thought was complete adoration.

Why? Why had Lucas done this to her? her mind screamed, and the iron control she had exerted over her emotions all evening finally broke. The tears slowly squeezed from her eyes to slide down her cheeks. The trickle became a flood as she wept out her pain and grief, the tears mingling with the powerful spray until Amber fell to her knees, her arms wrapped around her middle, her head bowed, completely broken, defeated...

Her body shivering, Amber slowly opened her eyes. She was huddled on the floor of the shower. When had the hot water run out and turned to icy cold? She had no idea. She was freezing, her limbs numb. Slowly she staggered to her feet, turned off the tap and stepped out of the shower. Pulling a large bath towel from the rail, she wrapped it toga-style around her shaking body. She caught sight of her reflection in the mirror above the vanity basin—her eyes were red-rimmed and puffy, her skin pale and cold as death.

She was still wearing the emerald necklace and earrings. Carefully she removed both, and, walking out of the bathroom, she dropped them on the dressing table, then pulled out the seat and sat down. Picking up the hair-dryer, she switched it on and methodically began drying her long hair.

Lucas had loved to see her naked with her hair smoothed silkily over her breasts. Her eyes filled with moisture at the memory, and, leaping to her feet, she staggered across the room and flung herself down on the bed. She turned her face into the pillow, shaken by another violent storm of weeping.

When it was over she felt curiously calm, and as it was just dawn she got to her feet and began to dress. She did not bother with a bra, she had no need for one, but slipped into skimpy white lace briefs. She withdrew grey- and blue-checked trousers from the wardrobe and a V-neck button-through matching blue cashmere cardigan, and put them on. She slipped her feet into soft leather loafers and descended the spiral staircase. She crossed the vast expanse of the living area to the kitchen, and opened the door just as the first rays of sun shone though the window.

Amber switched on the kettle, made herself a cup of instant coffee, and, taking it back with her into the living room, she sat down on one of the soft-cushioned sofas. She picked up the remote control for the television and switched it on. It was the twenty-four-hour news channel. She watched and waited...

Amber heard the key turn in the lock, and, switching off the television, she stood up and slowly turned to face the door.

To the man entering the room, she looked cool, calm and collected, and beautiful. 'Amber, I am glad you are here. I thought you might have gone back with Spiro after last night,' Lucas said smoothly, closing the door behind him and striding towards her.

Amber watched him approach. He was casually dressed in faded denim jeans, a cream-coloured roll-neck sweater and tan leather jacket. His black hair was windswept; he had never looked more attractive to her, or more out of her reach.

Her heart hardened against his masculine appeal. 'Why would I do that, Lucas? This is my home,' she queried coolly. A bone-numbing anger had replaced her earlier grief.

'Good, I hoped you would be sensible.' His long legs slightly splayed, he stopped about a foot away from her, his dark eyes sweeping over her long hair falling loose to her waist, and back up, lingering for a second too long on the proud thrust of her breasts against the soft cashmere sweater.

Amber saw his pupils darken, and the sudden tension in his broad frame. He was not immune to her, that much was obvious, and it simply fuelled her anger. 'Sensible is not the word I would have chosen,' she declared bitterly. 'I don't feel in the least sensible after last night, I feel madder than hell, and demand an explanation. I thought you were my boyfriend, my partner. We live together, for

God's sake!' she cried, aware of the consuming bile rising in her throat as she studied his hard features.

Abruptly Lucas stepped back a pace, and she had the satisfaction of seeing his face darken with suppressed anger, or was it embarrassment? He didn't appreciate being called to account for his behaviour. 'I agree,' he said curtly. 'And I apologise—last night should never have happened. Christina should not have told you we were getting engaged next weekend. But then you should not have been at the party. You have Spiro to thank for last night's fiasco, not I.'

'Oh, no, you can't blame this on Spiro, you lying swine,' she shot back furiously. 'You told me you could not get back from New York until Saturday—pressure of work, you said. What a joke!' Blazing golden eyes clashed with his and what she saw in their obsidian depths sent an icy shiver down her spine.

'I did not lie. I said I could not *meet* you until Saturday, which was perfectly true. I had a prior engagement for Friday evening,' he drawled cynically.

'An engagement for the rest of your life, if Christina is to be believed. I have never been so embarrassed or humiliated in all my life, and I want to know *why*? You owe me that much,' Amber demanded, her voice rising stridently.

Lucas stepped forward and closed a powerful hand over both of hers. 'Calm down and listen to me,' he snapped back, his black eyes hard on her lovely face. 'I had no desire to embarrass or hurt you in any way. I had every intention of telling you our affair was over before announcing my betrothal. I have never in my life begun a sexual relationship with a woman without first divesting myself of her predecessor. It is a rule of mine.'

'Bully for you!' she snorted inelegantly, but just the

touch of his hand on hers made her pulse race and she despised herself for it. 'You are so moral,' she managed to drawl sarcastically. 'Is that supposed to make me feel better that you are dumping me?'

'Dumping…' a grimace of distaste tightened his hard mouth '…is not how I would have put it. Our affair has reached its conclusion, and I hope we can part friends.'

This is not happening to me, this cannot be happening to me, Amber told herself over and over again. The blind, arrogant conceit of the man was unbelievable. *Friends*— he wanted them to be *friends*… Didn't he know he had broken her heart, destroyed her dreams, her life? She looked up and saw the flicker of impatience in his dark eyes, the aloof expression on his handsome face, and she had her answer. It was obvious he was wondering how to extricate himself as quickly as possible.

'And what about me?' Amber asked quietly, amazed that her voice didn't break.

'Amber, we have had some great times together, but now it is over, it has to be. I have reached the age—' he walked away from her, pacing the length of the room '—when it is time for me to settle down. I want a wife, a family, a home, and Christina is going to give me all that.' Then, spinning on his heel, he walked slowly back towards her.

'You're bright and ambitious, I know you have a brilliant future ahead of you. But, for me, Christina is the answer. You understand.'

The numbness that had protected her for the past few hours vanished. He was ripping her heart to shreds with every word he spoke. 'No, no, I don't.' She raised her eyes to meet his. 'I thought we were a couple, and that this was our home.' Even as she said the words, she saw the gleam of cynical amusement in his dark eyes as he glanced around the room and back at Amber.

'Oh, come on, Amber, don't play the innocent, it does not suit you. This was never meant to be a home, a living area with an open-galleried bedroom and a sybaritic bathroom. Could you see me entertaining my family and friends in this place?' One dark brow arched sardonically. 'I think not...'

Amber exploded; her hand swung in a wide arc and smashed across his face. 'I should have done that last night,' she yelled. 'You arrogant, conceited, two-timing bastard.'

Lucas raised a hand to his cheek, and rubbed where she had hit him. 'Perhaps I deserved that, so I'll let you get away with it, Amber, but only once,' he declared grimly. 'Accept it is over between us and move on. I have.'

She watched the dark stain appear on his cheek where she had hit him, and immediately regretted her action. Involuntarily she raised her hand, intending to stroke the side of his face, but her wrist was caught in an iron grip. 'No.'

She moved forward and lifted her other hand to rest on the soft wool sweater covering his broad chest. 'I'm sorry,' she murmured. But the familiar feel of his hard muscles beneath her fingers sent shivers of delight arcing though her body. She loved this man with all her heart, and helplessly she tilted back her head and looked up into his darkly attractive face. 'Please, Lucas.' She felt him stiffen, and she moved even closer, and slid her hand up over his chest and around the nape of his neck.

'We are so good together, Lucas, you know we are.' It had been two long months since she had felt the warmth of his caress and she ached for him. Suddenly she was fighting for her man, and using every skill at her disposal. She saw his pupils dilate as her breasts brushed against his hard chest, and involuntarily her fingers trailed with tactile delight up through the hair at the back of his neck. 'Kiss me, Lucas, you know you want to.' Gently she urged his head down towards her eager lips.

'No, Amber.' His large hands gripped her shoulders to push her away just as she brushed her lips against his, the tip of her tongue darting out to gain access to his mouth. She heard the intake of his breath as his arms jerked her to him and their bodies met in searing contact, and she was lost in the dark, heady hunger of the kiss for an instant, before his hands caught her shoulders and he forced her back at arm's length.

Lucas Karadines didn't like the way she affected him. His dark eyes glittered dangerously. His own mother had been addicted to sex, one lover after another until she'd died. Her last lover had kicked a young boy of thirteen out on the street. So he fought the temptation and won. 'You are a very sexy lady, Amber, but I am not such a bastard as to take what you're offering. It's over.'

'But if you want a wife, why not me? I love you, Lucas, and I thought you loved me,' Amber pleaded, raising an unsteady hand and tenderly brushing a few black silky strands of his hair from his brow. 'I could give you children, anything you want.' She was laying her heart, her life, on the line, begging him. She had lost all pride, all anger, and she didn't care. She looked deep into his dark eyes, her own beseeching his. She thought she saw a flicker of uncertainty in the depths of his, but she was mistaken.

'No, Amber.' A grim smile twisted the corners of his sensual mouth. 'I never lied to you—I never once mentioned love.'

His words lashed her like a whip flailing her alive; she closed her eyes for an instant, searching her mind. He was right, he had never said he loved her. How had she made such an enormous mistake? His hands fell from her shoulders and she opened her eyes. She could actually see him mentally withdrawing from her as he physically moved back a step.

'You are a lovely girl, but you are not the wife and mother type.' His breathing was heavy but his dark eyes held unmistakable, unyielding will-power. 'You're a career woman—you compete in a male-dominated industry, and you are as good as, if not better than, most of the men, by all accounts. You wouldn't last six months as a stay-at-home wife. You would be bored out of your skull. So don't fool yourself, Amber. You're strictly lover material.'

She listened with growing horror. 'Is that really what you think?' she muttered sickly. 'All this time you saw me as your lover, a sex object, nothing else.'

He shrugged his broad shoulders. 'The term is not important. What we shared was a mutually agreeable relationship.' His dark eyes skimmed over her shapely figure and he made no effort to hide his masculine appreciation. 'And great sex.'

His deliberate sensual scrutiny made her breasts swell in instant awareness, and hot colour flooded her cheeks and he noticed. 'Be honest, Amber, you're no shy young maid, never were. You're a born hedonist, you thrive on sensual pleasure, the pleasure I gave you. But you're a sophisticated lady—admit it, if we have spent six months together since we met it would be a miracle, and that mostly in bed. Ours was a sexual relationship, nothing more.'

For him maybe, but for Amber it had been everything. She only had to look at him to remember the powerful strength of his all-male body when he possessed her, caressed her. 'Nothing more,' she parroted his words with horror.

'Exactly.' He sounded relieved, actually believing she had agreed with him. And blithely carried on adding insult to injury. 'But Christina is different. She is sweet and innocent and has no desire to do anything other than be my wife, and bear my children.'

Her teeth had bitten into her bottom lip as she listened to him praise his Christina, and the salty tang of blood coated her tongue. 'I was innocent until you seduced me,' she reminded him, the hurt almost too much to bear. He knew she'd been a virgin when he'd first made love to her. She had given him the greatest gift a woman could give a man, her heart, body and soul, and he had the gall to label her a hedonist…

'Ah, Amber…' He shook his dark head in a mocking gesture. 'You know as well as I do that it was no great moral conviction that kept you a virgin. It was probably the fact you had spent the last four years living with a couple of gay men and their friends and hadn't much opportunity. You would have jumped into bed with me the first day you arrived at the villa.' Lucas shot her a cynical smile. 'With your minuscule bikinis, and designer clothes, you were no retiring violet. You were desperate for a man, and it was my restraint, my strict rule not to take on a new lover without first leaving the old that meant we waited until I had got back from New York. Seduction did not come into it.'

'I see.' And she did… She closed her eyes for a brief moment, blocking out the picture of his hard, cynical face, her hands clenching into fists at her sides. He thought of her as a sexy woman who had been easy to take, who could respond to any man's caress with equal fervour, not just his. Eagerly she had followed where he'd led, plunging the erotic depths with a hunger that had known no bounds, confident that he'd loved her, and everything had been permissible between two lovers. Her own innate honesty forced her to admit it was not all his fault. She had deliberately set out to appear to be the sort of woman she'd imagined he wanted. 'Hoist by her own petard' was the phrase that sprang to mind... Lucas did not know her at all, never had, and, worse, did not want to.

'Tell me, Lucas, if I had held out for a ring, would you have married me?' Amber demanded, black anger filling her heart at his chauvinistic attitude, never mind his betrayal.

He stared at her, his hard mouth suddenly cruel. 'With you the question would never arise. If you remember, I did ask you to give up work so we could spend more time together, and you could not even do that. So the answer is no. You're a thoroughly modern woman, equal to a man, you work hard and play hard.'

'And your Christina is not?' She arched one delicate brow in a gesture of mocking disbelief. 'A year in Switzerland, all those hunky ski instructors,' she taunted him, the memory of the young girl's conversation last night still clear in her mind.

That appeared to catch him on the raw, and for a moment he looked almost savage. 'Leave Christina out of this,' he ordered curtly. ' You disappoint me, Amber, I did not think you could sink so low as to maliciously malign a young girl's reputation, a girl you hardly know,' he drawled contemptuously.

Amber stared at his hard, cold face, willing herself not to feel hurt by his immediate defence of the girl. Then it hit her. 'You've never slept with Christina, and you think you love her. I'm right, aren't I?' she demanded, not sure whether to laugh or cry. Lucas Karadines, a powerful, dynamic businessman viewed with fear and awe by his competitors, was fooled by a pseudo-innocent eighteen-year-old going on eighty.

'Yes, I love Christina, and I am going to marry her.' He gave the only answer he could. He wasn't sure he believed in love. His mother had fallen in *love* with depressing regularity, when basically it had been sex. He had no intention of making the same mistake. He had chosen carefully and made the commitment to Christina and both of their families in traditional Greek fashion, and he was determined to honour it and make his marriage a success.

Amber stared at him. Oh, heavens, she silently screamed. It was true. She saw the absolute sincerity in his dark eyes, heard it in the tone of his voice, and was convinced. Never mind business, Lucas honestly thought he loved the girl. Her shoulders drooping, she closed her eyes for a second, all the fight draining out of her, and a dull acceptance taking its place. 'I suppose I'd better go and pack.'

'No.' Lucas caught her shoulder and turned her back to face him. 'Sit down, Amber. I am not so unfeeling I would see you deprived of your home.'

It never was a home, he had made that abundantly clear, but her traitorous limbs gave way beneath her and she sank thankfully down onto the soft cushions. 'No.' Amber looked at him towering over her, with all the bitterness of her feelings in her eyes. 'Then what now, Lucas? If you're waiting for my blessing, you're wasting your time.' He was sliding something from the inside pocket of his jacket—a long manila envelope.

'You have no need to leave—I am going. I'll send someone round this afternoon to collect the few things I have here, and you'd better keep these—you will need them.'

The last half-hour had been the hardest of Lucas Karadines's life. It had taken all his monumental control not to take what Amber had been offering. He would not dare come back himself, because deep down he knew he would not be able to resist making love to her one more time. He dropped the envelope and his set of keys to the apartment down onto the sofa beside her. 'Goodbye, Amber.' He hesitated for a second, his night-black eyes lingering on her pale face. 'I'm…'

'Just go.' Her lips twisted; if he said sorry she would kill him. His dark head bent towards her and she felt the brush of his lips against her hair and flinched. She didn't need his pity. And, flinging her head back, she sat rigidly on the edge of the sofa, her golden eyes hating him.

Lucas straightened up. 'Look after yourself.' And, brushing past her, he headed for the door. He opened the door and paused, finally turning to add, 'By the way, if you're thinking of taking up the offer Clive Thompson made you, don't. The man is not to be trusted.'

A harsh laugh escaped her. 'It takes one to know one. Get out.' And, picking up a scatter cushion, she flung it at him. It bounced harmlessly off the closed door and fell to the floor.

Amber looked around her at the apartment that she had mistakenly thought was a home with new eyes, and groaned out loud. Lucas was right. How could she have been so stupid, so gullible? She had tried to add a few touches, the scatter cushions, a couple of framed photographs of her mother, and Tim. A painting she had bought on a trip around a gallery with Spiro. The rug was the only thing in the place that she and Lucas had chosen together. It was exactly as Lucas had said: a bachelor pad, or a love-nest.

She had to get out, she thought brutally. It didn't matter

where as long it was somewhere that did not remind her of Lucas. But first she had to pack up his clothes—hadn't he said he was sending someone over to collect them?

She jumped to her feet and the manila envelope fell from her knee to the floor; she bent down and picked it up. Slitting open the envelope, she withdrew a folded document. She read it, her eyes widening in amazement that quickly turned to fury. Her first thought was to rip it up, but she hesitated... The paper dropped from her hand to flutter back to the floor.

It was the deeds for the apartment in her name, and it was dated two weeks ago. She felt sick and defiled; he had paid her off like some cheap whore. Perhaps not cheap, she amended, but her fury knew no bounds. She marched into the kitchen and took the scissors from the kitchen drawer, and then headed straight upstairs. With grim determination she slid back the wardrobe door. Earlier she had run her hands over Lucas's clothes, in need of reassurance. Now she touched them for a completely different reason.

Working quickly, Amber emptied the wardrobe and drawers of every item that belonged to Lucas, and packed them in one suitcase. That told her something. Her mouth tightened in a rare grimace of cynicism. If she had needed any further convincing that Lucas had considered her nothing more than a convenient bed partner, the fact that he had left so few clothes in the place she had thought was his home said it all.

When a little man called a few hours later and asked for Mr Karadines's luggage she handed over the suitcase without a word, and closed the door in the man's face. She only wished she could close the door to her heart as firmly on the memory of Lucas Karadines.

*   *   *

A few hours later on the other side of London, Lucas Karadines stood in the middle of his hotel bedroom and stared in fury at the pair of trousers his father's valet was holding out to him.

'I'm afraid, sir, I've checked, and all three suits in the luggage I collected from the lady's apartment are the same.' The little wizened man was having the greatest difficulty keeping the smile from his face. 'The fly panel has been rather roughly cut out of all of them.'

A torrent of Greek curses turned the air blue as Lucas stormed across the room and picked up the telephone and began pressing out the number he knew by heart. Then suddenly he stopped halfway through, and replaced the receiver. No, there was no point—Amber was out of his life and he wanted it to stay that way. But a reluctant smile quirked the corners of his firm mouth. He should have expected some such thing. Amber was a passionate character in every way; it was what had drawn him to her in the first place. A shadow darkened his tanned features as he instructed the valet to press another suit. With brutal honesty he recognised Amber had some justification. She should never have discovered by a third party their relationship was over, and certainly not in so public a manner.

CHAPTER FOUR

CARRYING her mug of coffee, Amber made her way to the kitchen. Draining the last dregs, she rinsed the cup in the sink, and dried it with the tea towel.

It was little more than a week since Lucas had told her he was marrying Christina and walked out of her life. She had gone to work as usual, and she had waited. Waited and hoped for a miracle—for Lucas to change his mind. But by Wednesday she had bowed to the inevitable and set the wheels in motion to move out of the apartment. And if in the deepest corner of her heart hope lingered, she ignored it.

When Spiro had called her Sunday afternoon from Athens, confirming that the engagement party of Lucas Karadines and Christina Aristides the previous evening had been a great success, it was simply the final nail in the coffin that held all her dreams.

If she needed any more confirmation, she only had to look at this morning's newspaper lying on the kitchen bench open at the gossip page. A picture of the couple was prominently displayed. She crushed up the paper and wrapped the coffee mug in it. Then she carefully placed it on the top of the rest of the kitchen implements already packed in the large tea chest that sat in the middle of the kitchen floor. Finished...

She had applied on Friday to have today, Monday, off work, because realistically she'd known she would be moving out. Everything was packed, the For Sale sign had been erected an hour earlier by the carpenter employed by the estate agent she had consulted to dispose of the apartment. She could not live in it, and the proceeds would help some charity. She did not care any more.

Since the night at the London hotel, and the sleepless nights since, she had gone beyond feeling pain into a state of complete detachment. It was not completely Lucas's fault. She should have remembered 'To thine own self be true.' She had transformed herself virtually overnight into a sophisticated lady in her determination to win Lucas, and that was how he had seen her. She had never let him see the naive young country girl she had been, who just happened to have a gift for figures. Now it was too late. He had fallen in love with someone else, and she would never be that girl again anyway.

On Saturday she'd made a start on getting her life back. She had rented a small cottage with a garden in the village of Flamstead, within manageable commuting distance of the City. Amber recognised she had loved unwisely and too much, but she had silently vowed no man would ever be able to hurt her like that again.

Amber walked back into the living room, and glanced at the gold watch on her wrist. The removal firm was due to arrive at three. Another two hours to kill.

The telephone was still connected: she could call Tim, but she had no desire to talk to him or Spiro for that matter. She was still mad at Spiro's revelation yesterday that, at the engagement party, for a joke he had hinted to his grandfather and Lucas that his engagement to Amber might be next. Spiro was a wickedly mischievous devil—he could not help himself.

She heard the knock on the front door and sighed with relief. Good, the removal men were early, almost unheard of in London. Walking over to the door, she opened it, the beginnings of a smile curving her generous mouth. At last something was going her way. Her smile vanished, her mouth falling open in shock as she found herself staring into the hard black eyes of Lucas Karadines.

Her first instinct was to slam the door in his face but he anticipated her action by brushing past her and into the centre of the room.

Mechanically, she closed the door behind him. 'What do you want?' she demanded, her mind spinning, fighting to control the tremor in her voice and the swift surge of hope his appearance aroused in her. On a completely feminine note Amber wished she were wearing something better than a battered old cotton shirt and a pair of scruffy black leggings from her student days.

Spinning around to face her, Lucas regarded her silently for what seemed an interminable length of time, but Amber quickly gathered from the harsh expression on his dark, slightly saturnine features that he had certainly not sought her out for reconciliation.

'I said, what do you want?' she repeated coolly. He looked dynamic and infinitely masculine, his casual jeans and heavy wool sweater barely detracting from the raw vitality of the man. His eyes didn't leave hers for a second, and she began to feel a rising tide of bitter resentment as the blood raced through her veins in the old familiar way.

'I want to study what a woman scorned really looks like,' Lucas stated with studied indolence, his eyes raking over her from the top of her head, over her face, her hair hanging loose about her shoulders, down over the firm thrust of her breasts clearly outlined against the fine cotton, then lower to her slim hips and long legs perfectly moulded by the black leggings. His narrowed gaze rested on her bare feet, then back to her face.

'I ignored the destruction of a few suits,' he drawled silkily, taking a step towards her.

She swallowed painfully, colour flooding her cheeks. She'd forgotten about her futile attempt at revenge: the mangled suits, and all the gifts he had ever given her flung on top. But it was as nothing to what he had done to her. Her head lifted fractionally. Pride uppermost. 'You can afford it,' she snapped.

One eyebrow lifted slightly. 'A bagatelle, I grant you, compared to the price of this apartment. I see you have wasted no time in trying to sell it,' he opined silkily and moved closer. 'I ignored the insult intended by the return of the presents I gave you.' And, catching hold of her hand, he drew her towards him, despite the struggle she made to break free. His glance spearing her ruthlessly, he added, 'But I will never allow you to marry Spiro simply so he can get his hands on his inheritance before he is of age. I'll see you in hell first.'

The statement was quiet and deadly, and Amber suddenly realised his temper was held in check by a tenuous thread. 'Let go of me,' she demanded, her own anger rising. as she tried to escape his steel-like grasp.

'I will when I have your promise you will stay away from Spiro.'

She almost laughed out loud. Lucas actually thought Spiro had been serious when he had voiced the prospect of marrying her to his grandfather. But she saw no reason to make it easy for Lucas. How dared he come here and threaten her?

'I can live with who I like and I can marry who I like, and it has damn all to do with you. In case you have forgotten, you are engaged to be married. In fact, I am amazed you could tear yourself away from the arms of your fiancée so quickly after your betrothal. Not as passionate as you hoped, hmm?' she prompted. 'Now, let go of my arm and get lost.' And with a fierce tug she freed her wrist from his grasp and swiftly stepped around him, heading for the stairs.

With an angry oath he spun around and caught the back of her shirt, bringing her to an abrupt halt. She strained forwards and he tugged harder so she fell back against him, the buttons popping off her shirt at the rough treatment. She tried to elbow him in the stomach. But he quickly turned her around and held her hard against the long length of his impressive frame. She began to struggle in earnest, striking out at him with her fists, making little impression on the broad, muscular wall of his chest.

'Let go of me, you great brute.' Her temper finally exploded. 'I know your game. Not content with marrying a poor kid half your age for her father's business, you're so bloody greedy that you're terrified Spiro will manage to get his hands on his half of the business. God, you make me sick!' she told him furiously.

Her wrists were caught and held together with effortless ease behind her in one large hand, his dark eyes leaping with rage as they burned into hers. 'You foul-mouthed little bitch! You would marry a man you know is gay simply to get back at me.'

'Don't flatter yourself,' she jeered. 'I don't give a toss about you.'

'But you enjoyed what I could give you,' he said harshly as though he wasn't really making a statement but remembering. 'Something Spiro is not capable of.'

If Amber had not known better, she might have thought he was jealous on a personal level, but she knew he was only worried about retaining complete control of the company. Once Spiro came of age, heaven knew what he would do with his share. He was a loose cannon in the business sense, her own intelligence told her that. But it was still no reason for Lucas to try and bully her.

'How would you know what Spiro is capable of?' she taunted him. 'He could be bisexual. But it does not really matter because Spiro is a friend, and with you for an uncle he needs all the friends he can get,' she opined scathingly.

'And of course you have no ulterior motive in befriending Spiro,' Lucas drawled cynically. 'What did my nephew promise you for marrying him—a percentage of his inheritance, or is it pure, old-fashioned revenge you're after?'

He towered over her, dwarfing her not inconsiderable height. Suddenly she became aware of the hard heat of his body. His aroused body! Her eyes clashed with his, and his darkened as the chemistry between them renewed itself with frightening force.

'Certainly not his body, we both know that is not his scene,' Lucas drawled huskily, his dark gaze moving down to the luscious outline of her lips.

Amber could not help it. She regarded him hungrily, his harshly etched features as familiar to her as her own. She lowered her eyes in case he might see the need, the hunger flooding through her, and suddenly she became aware that in the struggle her shirt had come open almost to her waist. One firm breast was completely exposed, the other only partially covered. But she was not alone in her discovery; Lucas's sharply indrawn breath and something in his eyes that had always warned her in the past of his stirring hunger for sex made her tremble. His free hand slid cool fingers down her flushed cheeks, circling the outline of her full mouth.

Amber realised she should be fighting him, but could only gaze at him mesmerised as his hand captured the gentle curve of her nape, and electric tension filled the air.

'*Christos!* But you probably could turn Spiro!' He laughed harshly. 'You are sinfully sexy.' His gaze swept

down to her bare breasts, and her nipples peaked in telling
arousal; she was incapable of hiding her response to him.
In that second Lucas knew he should never have come
back here—she was utterly irresistible.

Speechless, Amber remained pinned against him, her
pulse racing wildly out of control, and suddenly she realised with blinding clarity she did not want to hide her
response. The musky scent of masculine arousal teased her
nostrils, and, as she felt the muscles of his powerful thighs
pressing against her, she tilted back her head and saw his
eyes were all black pupil, his desire a primitive need as
great as her own. Involuntarily her back arched ever so
slightly, lifting her breasts to greater prominence.

She heard his guttural curse a moment before his mouth
found hers, kissing her with a bruising, demanding hunger,
grinding her lips back against her teeth. A wild, basic recklessness filled her, and she responded with a fiery fervour,
her mouth opening to his. She forgot he was engaged to
another. She forgot he had betrayed her. There was only
the moment...

He kissed her with a searing passion, and she shuddered,
responding to his passion, matching it with her own. The
kiss they exchanged was primitive and out of control.
Every bit of Amber burned with a need, a hunger that was
almost pain, and when he trailed sharp, biting kisses down
her throat and finally closed his teeth over one pouting
nipple she whimpered, but not with pain.

Her hands were set free, and instead of pushing him
away she gloried in her freedom to touch him. Her hands
worked frenziedly beneath his sweater. Lucas helped her
by lifting his head and tearing his sweater off, before hauling her back against him. Her fingers traced over the
breadth of his chest, finding the hard male nipples in the
silky mat of hair and doing some tantalising of her own.

It had been months and she hadn't realised how needy she had been.

Lucas lifted her high in his arms and laid her down on the hardwood floor in one smooth motion. 'Damn you, Amber,' he growled, following her down, his chiselled features dark with passion.

His words hurt and angered her, but nothing could stop the storm of desire sweeping through her. He removed her leggings and briefs with enviable ease, while Amber fumbled with the belt of his trousers; quickly he guided her hands and in a second he was almost naked.

She heard the sharp intake of his breath as her fingers slid along his thigh and his mouth ground down on hers with furious greed. Their bodies met with a searing impact that made her shudder with pleasure.

Lucas lifted his head, his black eyes sweeping almost violently over her naked body. His head bent and he suckled the hard, aching peak of her breast as swiftly he parted her legs. Every other time he had enjoyed making love to her long and slow, teasing and tantalizing, drawing out the experience for ages. But this time it was like a dam bursting, sweeping everything before it, as without hesitating he positioned himself between her slender thighs and joined them fiercely together.

Amber gasped and writhed, half mad with wanting him, the hardness of the floor, the anger not love that fuelled the joining—none of it mattered. It was enough he was here with her—in her—and if it was to be the last time, she didn't care. He wanted her.

Hot and breathless bodies wet with sweat, they moved together in a mind-blowing, consuming passion. The climax when it came was a shuddering ecstatic release that lifted Amber to another universe, where her mind closed down, and the body was everything. The ecstatic shivers went on and on long after Lucas lay heavily on top of her, the rasping sound of his breathing the most wonderful music to Amber's ears.

She refused to believe he could behave like this with her and yet love someone else, and when he moved to roll off her she followed him around. Sprawled across his wide chest, still joined, she looked into his darkly flushed handsome face, but his eyes were closed.

'Lucas,' she tenderly murmured his name, and, reaching up, she brushed the sweat-slicked hair from his brow. Slowly his eyes opened and he looked at her with such contempt she almost cried out.

'Amber,' he grated, mockingly brushing her off him as if he were swatting a fly and jumping to his feet, as though he could not get away from her quickly enough.

She lay where he had left her and watched him. He had not removed his shoes, and he should have looked stupid with his trousers around his ankles, but he didn't. She let her eyes stray over every perfect inch of his bronzed body, committing every curve and muscle, pore and hair to memory, because she instinctively knew this was the very last time she would ever see him this way.

His dark eyes wandered insolently over her as he pulled up his trousers. The taut line of his mouth gave way to a thin, cruel smile. '*Christos.*' He laughed harshly, and slipped his sweater over his head. Adjusting the sleeves, he added, 'I was right about you—as sexy as sin and far too seductive to wed.'

Lucas knew he was being cruel, but it was a pure defence mechanism. He could not believe what he had just done! He had lost control completely, and he hated himself for it. He was strongly puritanical when it came to women, totally monogamous for as long as the relationship lasted, and he had every intention of being totally faithful to his wife. Hell! He almost groaned out loud. Betrothed three days to Christina, and already…

'You're no saint,' Amber's voice cut into his tortured thoughts.

His black eyes roamed over her lovely face, her cheeks burning with angry colour. She was exquisite, and briefly he closed his eyes, a deep black pit opening up before him, his supreme self-confidence shaken to its core as for a moment he doubted his decision to marry Christina. He opened his eyes. It was too late now. He was Greek, first and foremost, he was engaged to a Greek girl, his father was delighted, Christina's father was ecstatic. He had made the right decision. It was simply he had been celibate for too long, he told himself, and *almost* believed it…

'So much for your moral code, off with the old before the new,' Amber declared fiercely, breaking the tension-filled silence, and, sitting up, she pulled the shirt that was hanging off her back around her chest.

He smiled down at her mockingly, forcing himself not to weaken. 'Oh, for heaven's sake, get dressed.' If she didn't he was in grave danger of falling down on top of her again, eyeing her flustered attempt to pull her shirt around the luscious curve of her breasts. Shame and guilt made him add, 'You disgust me. I disgust myself.'

Amber bowed her head for a moment, the long curtain of her hair hiding her face from his glittering gaze. She squeezed her eyes tightly shut to hold back the tears. She disgusted him, he had said, and yet she was only what he had made her, and in that instant the new Amber was born.

Swiping back the mass of hair from her face, she rose to her feet. Ignoring Lucas's looming presence, she picked up her briefs and leggings and, turning her back on him, took her time about putting them on. Then, straightening her shoulders, she turned to face him.

She lifted hard golden eyes to his. 'What are you waiting for?' she demanded bluntly. She was furiously angry at the undisguised contempt in his expression. But she refused to show it. 'I thought a man of your high moral values would be long gone,' she mocked him. She had learnt her lesson well. Never again in this life, she vowed, would she show any man how she really felt.

'The floor show is over,' she said facetiously. 'If you're hoping for a repeat performance, forget it—go back to Christina and I wish you both joy. Though I have a suspicion you will not find her quite the pure, malleable little bed partner and wife you imagine. After all, she already knows you have a mistress—' she wanted to hurt him, dent his arrogant pride '—and she doesn't care, which must tell you something.'

She had gone too far. He stepped towards her, his hand lifted as if to hit her. Involuntarily she flinched and stepped back.

'No.' His hand fell to his side, his fingers curling into a fist, his knuckles white with strain. 'You are a lying little bitch.' Amber knew he would never believe her or forgive her for her comments. 'And you will never speak to my fiancée or mention her name again.'

Amber stared at him, her anger dying fast as his glance roamed contemptuously over her. There was sheer hatred in his eyes, and a clear message he would not touch her again if his life depended on it. But then she already knew that, she thought sadly. The last half-hour had been nothing more than animal attraction fuelled by rage on his part. He didn't want her love, never had… The realisation was the end of everything for Amber. 'Just go,' she said wearily, brushing past him towards the door. Good manners decreed she see him out, she thought, and had to choke back hysterical laughter.

She opened the door and held it. Lucas reached out to grasp her arm, but she pulled away. 'Goodbye, Lucas.' The finality in her tone was unmistakable.

He went rigid. 'Not so fast, you still have not given me the promise I asked for. I...I want your word you will not marry Spiro.'

She was sick at heart and halfway to being physically sick. 'Okay.'

'I mean it, Amber,' Lucas said with deadly emphasis. 'If you marry him your life will not be worth living, and you will find no solace in your work, that I promise.' The taut line of his mouth gave way to a thin cruel smile as he paused. 'I will personally make sure no one in the financial world will ever employ you again.' He had to convince her for his own sanity to break all ties with Spiro. If the last hour had taught him anything it was that there was no way on God's earth Lucas trusted himself to be in the company of Amber ever again. Not even a simple social occasion, or he was in danger of succumbing to the same sickening addiction to sex his mother had suffered from. The realisation of his own weakness shocked and horrified him, and he reacted with the same icy determination that made him a ruthlessly successful businessman. 'I will totally destroy the career you love, and, believe me, I can and will do it.'

It was no idle threat, and the really scary part was that Amber had no doubt he could destroy her career with a few chosen words to her most influential clients. 'Your threat is unnecessary. I have no intention of marrying Spiro.'

Amber's golden gaze roamed over Lucas as though she were seeing him for the first time. He stood in the entrance door, tall and broad and as still as a statue carved in stone. She registered the soft wool sweater moulding the muscles of his broad chest, the hip-hugging jeans. Raising her gaze, she noted the thick black hair, the broad forehead, the perfectly chiselled features—he was incredibly handsome, but his face was hard, cold, the inner man hidden. One thumb casually hooked his leather jacket over a shoulder, but there was nothing casual about the man. Spiro had called him a shark and Amber finally realised it was true.

It was a revelation to Amber's bruised heart. Lucas thought he loved Christina, but it was not what Amber considered love to be. It was no great consuming passion on Lucas's part, he was incapable of the emotion. He had simply planned to fall in love with Christina with the same ruthless efficiency he planned a takeover bid. Christina simply met his criteria for a wife. Amber's golden eyes met his, black and not a glimmer of human warmth in their depths, just a ruthless determination to succeed be it business or private, family or friend. He was incapable of differentiating between them. How had she ever thought she loved this cold, frighteningly austere man?

'If you knew your nephew a little better, or at all,' Amber said softly, one perfectly arched brow lifting eloquently, 'you would have realised he was only winding you up when he said it. Now please go.'

With the door closed behind him, Amber silently added, If Lucas allowed anyone to know him, he might possibly develop into a halfway decent human being. But she had a suspicion he never had, and he was too old to change now.

Three weeks later in the same Monday morning paper Amber viewed the wedding photo of Lucas and Christina with a cynical smile. She read the gossip that went with it, the gist of it being that there were great celebrations at the high society wedding in Athens and the joining together of two great Greek families, not to mention the amalgamation of two international corporations to make one of the top leisure companies in the world.

Amber settled into her small house, bought a neat Ford car to drive into work, and as the days and weeks went past tried to put her disastrous love affair out of her mind. During the day she could block Lucas out of her thoughts with work. But at night she was haunted by memories of the sheer magic of his lovemaking—only it hadn't been love, she had to keep reminding herself, and then the tears would fall. The only thing that kept Amber from a nervous breakdown over the next year was her growing relationship with her father. The news she had wanted to tell Lucas so eagerly, after lunching with Sir David Janson.

Two weeks after Lucas Karadines had left her, Amber had met Sir David again for lunch at a restaurant in Covent Garden. Much to Amber's surprise his wife Mildred had accompanied him. It could have been embarrassing, but Mildred quickly explained she did not blame her husband or Amber's mother. At the time Mildred had left her husband and two children and had lived with another man for over a year. Sir David had found solace with his secretary and Amber was the result.

Sir David quite happily acknowledged Amber as his daughter, saying a certain notorious Member of Parliament had recognised an illegitimate daughter without any ill effect, so why shouldn't he? It was a one-day wonder in the papers, and his family—a married daughter and a much older son—were equally welcoming.

But Amber refused to take a job with her father's company. Her feminine intuition told her she shouldn't. Sir David's son, Mark Janson, accepted her in the family, but as heir apparent to the business he was nowhere near so happy about having her in his father's firm. Especially as Sir David told all and sundry Amber had obviously inherited her skill in the money markets from him.

CHAPTER FIVE

FIVE years later…

As Monday mornings went, this had to be one of the worst, Amber thought sadly. She'd just returned from two weeks' holiday in Tuscany at her father's villa feeling relaxed, and revitalised. June in Italy was beautiful; unfortunately June in London was rain, the stock market had dropped three per cent, and now this…

Her long fingers tapped restlessly on the document lying on the desk. She'd read the letter countless times, but she still could not quite believe it. The letter was from a firm of lawyers in New York, the lawyers dealing with the estate of the late Spiro Karadines. It was dated eleven days ago. Spiro had died the day before, apparently, and it was informing her of the time and place of his funeral in Greece, and a legal document in the usual lawyer speak that 'Amber Jackson may learn something to her advantage'. Amber didn't think so… Spiro was trouble…

A sad, reminiscent smile curved her wide mouth. It was four years since she'd last seen him, and they had not parted on the best of terms.

She had gone to New York for the grand opening of his art gallery. Spiro had been so excited as he had shown Amber around the exhibition. It had been incredible, or perhaps unbelievable was a better word, Amber had thought privately. Spiro had told her the artists whose work was on display were all up and coming in the modern art world. To Amber's untrained eyes it looked more as if they had been and gone… Gone crazy…

'Are you sure about this stuff?' she had asked Spiro, recoiling from a massive red and green painting that appeared to be bits of body parts.

'Yes, don't worry, in half an hour people will be fighting over these paintings. Trust me!'

Her smooth brow pleated in a frown as she fiddled with the letter on her desk. She'd trusted Spiro when he had assured her that if she gave him the money from the sale of the loft apartment to start his art gallery, he would never tell Lucas, and return it with interest when he came into his inheritance a year later. He had persuaded her that charity could wait, and, being honest, Amber admitted she had thought it was poetic justice, letting Spiro have the money as it was Karadines money after all. He had also told her Lucas would not be at the opening. Spiro had lied on both counts...

Although it had been over a year since she'd last seen Lucas, the gut-wrenching pain she had felt when she'd turned around from viewing the 'Body Parts' painting to find him, and Christina his wife, his *pregnant* wife, standing behind her had been almost unbearable.

She'd glanced at Spiro, and seen the devilment in his eyes, and known he had done it deliberately. Shifting her gaze to the couple, she'd made the obligatory greeting portraying a sophistication she had not felt. She'd even managed to congratulate the pair on their forthcoming happy event. But she'd been shaken so badly she'd had to clasp her hands behind her back to hide their trembling.

But Lucas had had no such problem. His eyes had slid over her with cool insolence, stripping away the stylish green silk sheath dress she'd worn to the flesh beneath, but Amber had forced herself to withstand his scrutiny, and done some scrutinising of her own. Thick dark hair had curled down over the collar of his impeccably tailored light linen suit, he'd been leaner than he had been the last time she had seen him, his features slightly more fine drawn, but as devastatingly attractive as ever, until he'd spoken.

'It seems congratulations are in order for you too, Amber. Spiro tells me you are his partner and put up most of the money for this little venture,' Lucas said smoothly. 'A remarkable achievement for a young woman. Your passion...' his hesitation was deliberate '...for finance must be truly exceptional,' he opined with mocking cynicism.

Amber felt the colour burn up under her skin. Lucas wasn't referring only to her passion for business. He obviously knew where the money had come from and for a moment she felt like strangling Spiro. But instead she forced herself to look at Lucas. 'Luckily I seem to have a gift for it.' Amber stared at him, deliberately holding his eyes. 'But I'll never be in your league. Men have a certain ruthlessness...' and it was her turn to pause '...in business, women find hard to emulate.'

'Not all women,' Lucas said flatly, and Amber surprised what looked very much like a flicker of regret in his dark eyes before he turned his attention to his wife, and began a conversation in Greek, ignoring Amber completely.

Instead of being insulted Amber was glad to escape the attention of Lucas; breathing an inward sigh of relief, she turned away. It hurt her more than she wanted to admit to see the two of them so close, and she was going to have a very serious talk to her so-called partner. Spiro was talking animatedly to a guest in the now crowded gallery. He could wait!

Spying Tim, she'd begun to walk towards him when suddenly someone grabbed her bare arm. The tingling sensation of the long fingers on her bare flesh was electric. Lucas...

'What?' Amber snapped.

'Will you follow Christina to the rest room, make sure she is all right?' he asked, his expression one of deep concern, the worry in his dark eyes there for all to see as they tracked his wife heading for the powder room.

Amber did see. His request reinforced what she had tried to deny. Amazing for such a predatory male, Lucas, a man who was ruthless in the business world, a man whom she'd thought incapable of love, was actually madly in love with his wife.

'She is pregnant, not sick.' Amber shrugged off his hand and stalked away without looking back. Listening to Christina rhapsodising about Lucas and the soon-to-be family was the last thing she needed. Lucas was a fantastic lover, and, once Christina had discovered the wonder to be found in her husband's arms, she had to have fallen in love with him, even if she had not been at the beginning.

After a furious row with Spiro, Amber left New York the next day, and she had not seen or spoken to Spiro since. As for the money she had given him, she had written that off long ago.

With the benefit of hindsight Amber had come to realise that Lucas had been right about Spiro. She should never have given him the money, because within a week of the gallery opening Tim and Spiro had split up. Spiro had been having an affair with the artist of 'Body Parts'.

Tim had returned to England, and back to his home in Northumbria. Six months later he had received a brief note, not from Spiro, but from a New York clinic telling him to get himself tested. Spiro had been HIV positive, as had been the artist lover who had somehow forgotten to mention the fact!

Restlessly Amber swivelled around in her chair, and stared out of the plate-glass window of her office, not really seeing what was beyond. She felt guilty and half blamed herself for Spiro's illness. If she hadn't given him the money, he would not have gone to New York, and it might never have happened.

Tim was a successful wildlife artist living and working from his home in the north and perfectly healthy. He had told her over and over again, it was not her fault Spiro had done what he had. Tim firmly believed Amber and himself had both fallen victims to the charm of the Karadines men; it was that simple, and they had both had a lucky escape.

Swivelling back to face her desk, Amber picked up the telephone and dialled Tim's number in Thropton. He had a right to know Spiro was dead.

The conversation was not as difficult as she had expected. Tim was quite philosophical about it: the past was past—so they had lost a good friend, but in reality they had lost him years ago.

'You're right, Tim...' Suddenly her office door swung open and someone walked in unannounced. Amber lifted her head. Recognition was instant, her golden eyes widening in shock. 'I'll see you soon, love,' she finished her conversation, and replaced the receiver.

She was thankful she was sitting down because she doubted her legs would support her. Lucas Karadines... She didn't dare meet his cold black eyes, and, carefully taking deep breaths, she sought to calm her suddenly erratic pulse. She should have expected this as soon as she had read the line 'something to her advantage' she realised too late.

He was standing in the middle of her office as though he owned the place. Amber's first thought was that Lucas at forty-one looked little different than he had done when they had first met. His body beneath the conservatively

tailored charcoal-grey suit was still lithe and firm, his face
was still handsome, but the harsh symmetry of bones and
flesh mirrored a cold bitterness that she had never noticed
before. He looked lean and as predatory as ever, but he
looked older, harder than she would have expected for a
happily married man, was her second thought. The lines
bracketing his mouth were deeper, the hair at his temples
liberally streaked with silver. But nothing could detract
from the aura of dynamic, vibrant male he wore like a
powerful cloak, masking his ruthlessly chauvinistic nature.
He would be a handsome devil to his dying day, Amber
acknowledged wryly.

Amber felt colour creeping under her skin as he made
no immediate attempt to either move or speak. His hands
were slanted casually into his trouser pockets, accentuating
the musculature of his long legs. His eyes were hooded so
she could not tell what he was thinking as they slid slowly
over her head and shoulders to where the collar of her
blue silk blouse revealed a glimpse of cleavage. She
fought the impulse to slip her suit jacket off the back of
the chair and put it on. This was her office, and Lucas was
the intruder, and as he made no attempt to break the tense
silence between them she finally found her voice.

'What do you want?' she asked abruptly.

Lucas Karadines for the first time in his life was struck
dumb. The instant tightening in his groin shocked him into
silence. His body had not reacted this way in years. His
memory of Amber had not done her justice. She'd matured
into the most exquisitely beautiful woman he had ever
seen. His dark eyes drank in the sight of her. The hair
scraped back from her face only accentuated the perfection
of her features, the elegant line of her throat, the shadowed
cleft between her luscious breasts her conservative blouse
could not quite hide.

'Not a great welcome for an old friend,' Lucas finally murmured, his dark eyes gleaming with mockery, before scanning the elegant office. 'So this is your domain.'

A corner suite with windows on two sides, it was light and airy, and in keeping with her present position in the firm as the youngest partner, and Amber was justifiably proud of her achievements. 'Obviously,' she said dryly.

'You have done well for yourself, but then I always said you would.' Lucas's glance skimmed lightly over her desk as he moved towards it, noting her hand still on the phone. 'Sorry if I interrupted your conversation with your lover, but you and I have some pressing business to discuss.'

Her hand gripping the telephone was white-knuckled, and, realising she was betraying her shock, she smoothly slipped her hands to her lap and managed to smile coolly back at him. She was fiercely glad that the sophisticate she had pretended to be when they had first met was now a reality. She refused to be intimidated by Lucas—or any man, for that matter.

'I can't imagine we have anything to discuss, Mr Karadines. As far as I am aware you are a client of Janson's and I am not in the habit of poaching my father's clients.' It gave her great satisfaction to say it. Whether Lucas was aware Sir David was her father, she did not know. But she was making it abundantly clear he was not about to treat her like some inferior being to be discarded like yesterday's newspaper as he had before.

'Yes, I heard. I'm surprised you didn't choose to join Sir David's firm,' he opined smoothly. 'I seem to remember Clive Thompson was rather keen on the idea.'

'He still is,' Amber shot back, angry that Lucas had the nerve to remind her of that horrible party. 'But I like it at Brentford's and I don't believe in nepotism,' she said with a shrug. 'Nor mixing business with pleasure.' Let him make of that what he liked. She'd been dating Clive for the past year and part of the reason she had spent the last couple of weeks on holiday was to decide if she should accept Clive's proposal of marriage.

'Very wise of you. I dispensed with their services myself some months ago.'

That did surprise her. Neither Clive nor Mark, her half-brother, who had been the head of the firm since their father had retired two years ago, had mentioned the fact.

'I didn't know,' she said blandly, implying that she didn't really care.

'Now, if there is nothing further, I am rather busy.' Tilting back her head, she stared up at him, deliberately holding his eyes. 'And it is usual to make an appointment.' The sarcasm in her tone was very evident. 'I am a busy lady.'

Lucas was not the slightest bit fazed. 'I'm sure you are, Amber—a little too busy, it would seem.'

Amber raised her eyebrows. 'Too busy, says a man who was the most driven, competitive workaholic!' she mocked lightly. 'Marriage has changed you. How is the family? Well, I hope.' She was proud of her ability to ask the conventional question, and was surprised to realise it actually did not hurt at all.

Lucas stilled, his handsome face as expressionless as stone. 'I have no family. Spiro was the last—that is why I am here.'

Amber's face went white. Oh, God! In her shock at seeing Lucas again, she had forgotten all about Spiro's death. How could she have been so callous? 'I'm sorry, Lucas, truly sorry,' she hastened into an explanation. 'I only found out this morning. I've been on holiday, and the news hasn't really sunk in yet. I'm sorry I missed the funeral. Please sit down.' She indicated a chair at the op-

posite side of the desk with the wave of her hand. 'I'll
order some coffee.' She was babbling, she knew, and,
pressing for her secretary, she quickly asked Sandy to
bring in two coffees.

He lowered his long length into the chair she had indicated. 'Cut out the phoney sympathy, Amber,' he commanded bluntly. 'We both know Spiro hated my guts, and
the fact he left everything he possessed to you simply un-
derlined the fact.'

'He what?' she exclaimed, her golden eyes widening in
astonishment on Lucas's hard face, and what she saw in
his night-black eyes sent a shiver of something very like
fear quivering down her spine. 'No, I don't believe you,'
she amended quickly. 'Spiro wouldn't.' Then she remembered the 'something to her advantage'.

'Yes, Spiro would, and did, and your innocent act does
not impress me,' he said harshly. 'You knew damn fine
you stood to inherit Spiro's share of the business.'

'Now wait just a minute—' Amber began, but at that
moment Sandy walked in with the coffee.

Amber sat bristling with frustration as she watched her
secretary, the girl's eyes awestruck as she asked Lucas
breathlessly how he took his coffee.

'Black, please.' He favoured her with a broad smile and
just sat looking dark and strikingly attractive until the flustered girl handed him a cup of coffee. 'Thank you.'

Amber thought Sandy was going to swoon. No wonder
she had let Lucas in without an appointment. Even her
secretary, who had only been married a few months, was
not immune to Lucas's lethal male charm.

When Amber had first seen Lucas walk into her office
she had been in shock, but now the shock had worn off,
and another much more dangerous emotion was threatening her hard-won equilibrium. Lucas was a handsome

devil and he still had the power to stir her feminine hormones.

Amber hastily picked up her cup of coffee and took a long drink of the reviving brew. The days were long gone when she was a slave to the sexual excitement Lucas could arouse with a mere look or touch. He had killed them dead when he had accused her of being an oversexed female, excellent lover material, but never a wife, and then had gone off and married Christina.

For months after his desertion her self-esteem had hit rock-bottom. She'd questioned her own worth; perhaps Lucas had been right about her. She was sex mad, the hedonist he had called her. She certainly had been when she'd been with him. In consequence she had, without really being aware of doing it, adjusted her style of dress to elegant but conservative—no short skirts, or revealing necklines. She wore little make-up and kept her long hair ruthlessly scraped back in a tight chignon, and she had no idea she looked even more desirable.

The door closing as Sandy left brought Amber back to the present with a start, and, straightening her shoulders, she was once again in command. She looked at Lucas with narrowed hostile eyes. 'I don't need you to tell me what I do or don't know,' she said curtly, and, picking up the letter from the desk, she held it out to him.

'Read that. I saw it for the first time this morning, and as yet I have not had time to respond, basically because I have an unscheduled guest. You.' His fingers brushed hers as he took the document from her outstretched hand, igniting a tingling sensation on her soft skin. Her golden eyes narrowed warily to his face, sure he had done it deliberately, but he was unfolding the document.

She waited as he read the letter, and then with slow deliberation folded the document back up again. 'This proves nothing,' Lucas said bluntly, dropping the letter back on her desk.

'I don't have to prove anything to you, Mr Karadines.' She shrugged dismissively. 'Now finish your coffee and leave. I have work to do.' Yes, Amber congratulated herself, she was back on track; the cool businesswoman. 'And when I get around to contacting the lawyers, and discover the true state of affairs, then if I need to get in touch with you, I will.' When hell freezes over, she thought silently. Standing up, she drained her coffee-cup and replaced it on the desk, before walking around heading for the door, her intention to show Lucas out as swiftly as possible.

'Well, well. The hard-bitten businesswoman act,' Lucas drawled sardonically, rising to his feet, and when she moved to pass him he reached out for her.

Amber felt every hair on her skin leaping to attention as his long fingers encircled her forearm. 'It is no act. Believe me!' she retaliated sharply. If he thought he was going to walk all over her again, he was in for a rude awakening.

'You don't fool me, Amber.' His voice dropped throatily, his fingers tightening ever so slightly on her arm. His eyes wandered over her in blatant masculine appraisal, taking in the prim neckline of her blue blouse, the tailored navy blue trousers that skimmed her slender hips and concealed her long legs to the classic low-heeled navy shoes, and then ever so slowly back to her face until she thought she would scream with the effort to remain cool and in control. 'You may dress like a conservative businesswoman, but it doesn't change what you are. I always knew you had a passion for sex, but it was only after we parted that I realised you had an equal passion for money,' he drawled cynically.

She wrenched her arm free from his hold, her whole

body rigid with anger. Just who the hell did he think he was? So now she was a gold-digger, as well as a sex maniac in his eyes… With the greatest effort of will, Amber managed to control her fury and say calmly, 'What exactly do you want, Lucas, barging into my office un-announced? I have neither the time nor the inclination for playing games. You obviously know something about Spiro's will, which concerns me. So just spit it out and then go.'

His eyes darkened, and for a moment Amber saw a flash of violent anger in their glittering depths, and she knew she had been right to feel threatened. Then he was smiling mockingly down at her. 'You used to like playing games,' he reminded her, his eyes cruel. 'Sexual games.' His finger lifted and stroked down the curve of her cheek.

'Cut that out,' she snapped, taking a deep, shuddering breath. 'You're a married man, remember.' Her golden eyes clashed with his, and as she watched it was like a shutter falling down over his face.

Lucas's hand fell from her face, his black eyes cold and blank. 'No, I am not. I told you before, I have no family.'

Confusion flickered in Amber's eyes. Had he? Then she remembered, but she had thought he'd meant Spiro. 'But what about Christina and your child?'

'The child was stillborn. My father died three years ago, and Christina was gone the next,' he informed her in clipped tones.

Her soft heart flooded with compassion, and unthink-ingly she laid a hand on his arm in a tender gesture… Such tragedy must be heartbreaking even for a man as hard as Lucas. 'I am so sorry, Lucas, I had no idea.'

'These things happen…' he brushed her hand away '…and, as you never cared much for any of them, I can do without your hypocritical sympathy. I would ask you not to mention the subject again. Except for *Spiro*, of course,' he demanded with chilling emphasis.

Why was she wasting her sympathy on this man? Lucas meant nothing to her. He was simply another irritant in an already bad day, she told herself. So why did her cheek still burn where he had touched her, her pulse still race? It wasn't fair that one man could have such a terrible effect on her senses. She glanced up at him, and briefly his towering presence was a threat to her hard-won sophistication, then she casually took a step back.

'You want to talk about Spiro, fire away,' she said flatly, retreating behind her usual hard shell of astute business-woman, and deliberately she lifted her wrist and scanned the elegant gold watch she wore. 'But make it quick, I have a lunch appointment.'

'You have changed, Amber.' His lips quirked in the semblance of a smile that did not quite reach his eyes. 'I can remember a time when you begged for my company, you couldn't get enough of me and pleaded with me to stay with you,' he said silkily.

The unexpected personal attack made her go white, a terrible coldness invading her very being that he could be so utterly callous as to mention the last time they had been alone together. 'I can't,' she denied flatly. He might even now make her heart race, but no way was she foolish enough to get personal with Lucas Karadines ever again.

'Liar.' He smiled sardonically. 'But I'll let it go for now, as you say you are busy, and we have a much more pressing item to discuss, *partner*.'

'Partner.' She bristled. What on earth was the man talking about? She'd rather partner a rattlesnake.

'All right, pretend you're innocent, I don't really care. But, put simply, the will Spiro made when you invested in his art gallery made you his heir if anything happened to him.'

'Oh, no!' Amber exclaimed, a horrible suspicion making her face pale. It couldn't be. But one look at Lucas's dark countenance confirmed her worst fear. When she had given Spiro the money he had insisted on making a will naming her his heir as collateral for the loan, until he could pay her back.

'Oh, ye-es,' Lucas drawled derisively. 'Spiro never changed his will. You are now, or very soon will be, the proud owner of a substantial part of Karadines.'

He was watching her with eyes that glittered with undisguised contempt and something else she could not put a name to.

Amber simply stared at him like a paralysed porpoise, her mouth hanging open in shocked horror. How typical of Spiro. He would get a bee in his bonnet about something, do it and then forget all about it. His business sense had always been negligible, but Amber hadn't seen it until it was too late.

Lucas laughed, but there was no humour in it. 'Struck dumb; how very typical of you. The silent treatment might have worked for you in the past with Spiro,' Lucas drawled, a smile creasing his firm mouth, 'but not this time. I am a totally different male animal to my late nephew.'

He'd got that right! Amber had a hysterical desire to laugh—a more ruggedly aggressive macho male than Lucas would be impossible to find. Her lips quirked, while she damned Spiro for landing her in this mess.

'You find something amusing in this situation?' he challenged icily.

The ring of the telephone saved her from answering. 'Yes, Sandy, what is it?' she asked briskly. 'Clive.' She glanced sideways at Lucas and caught a thunderous frown on his dark face.

'Tell him two minutes, my client is just leaving,' she informed Sandy before turning towards Lucas. 'My lunch date has arrived, I'm afraid I must ask you to leave.'

'Clive Thompson, I might have guessed—he was lusting after you the first time he met you,' Lucas opined bluntly. His dark eyes swept over her cynically. Her wide, oddly coloured gold eyes, and the full sensual lips that begged to be kissed. Her startling beauty combined with a slender yet curvaceous body was enough to make a grown man ache. Lucas was aching and he bitterly resented it. 'Obviously he has succeeded, but by your ringless fingers I see you have had no success getting him to the altar yet,' he taunted.

The arrogant bastard, Amber thought angrily. He was still of the opinion she was good enough to bed, but not to wed. Well, he was in for a big surprise.

'Ah, Lucas, that is where you are wrong.' Amber smiled a deliberately slow, sexy curve of her full lips. 'Clive appreciates my talents.' Let the swine make of that whatever his lecherous mind concluded. 'He has asked me to marry him, but I have yet to give him my answer—perhaps over lunch,' she said. 'So, if you will excuse me.'

He moved so fast Amber didn't have time to avoid him. One minute there were six feet of space between them, and the next she was hauled against the hard-muscled wall of his chest. Before she could struggle, one large hand slipped down over her buttocks, pressing hard against his thighs, and she felt the heat of him searing into her even through her clothes. 'No, I won't excuse you,' he rasped.

Amber's throat closed in panic. The years since they had last met might never have been. It was as if Lucas had rolled back time, his sexuality so potent that it fired her blood, making her once again the young girl who had been a slave to her senses. Then his dark head descended and he kissed her.

'Lucas, no,' she managed to croak as his mouth plundered hers, as he ground the tender flesh of her lips back against her teeth in a brutal travesty of a loving kiss. But even as she hated him, her body flooded with a feverish excitement and she fought the compulsion to surrender with every ounce of will-power she possessed, but it was not enough. The sexual chemistry between them had always been explosive. The years had not dulled the effect, and with a hoarse moan she responded. Lucas's hold relaxed as he sensed her surrender, and, realising how completely she had betrayed herself, she swiftly twisted out of his arms.

'Get out,' she ordered in a voice that shook, her arms folded protectively across her breasts as she put as much space between them as her office allowed.

'*Christo!* It was only a kiss—since when have you ever objected to a kiss?' he derided savagely. 'I was wrong, you haven't changed. You can't help responding. It is to be hoped Clive knows what he is taking on.'

The cruelty of his attack drove every last vestige of colour from her face.

His narrowed eyes studied her pale face for a long moment before a self-satisfied smile tilted the corners of his mouth. 'Well, well, you haven't told Clive about you and I.' He was far too astute; he had seen the answer in her lowered gaze.

Lifting her head, she looked straight at him. 'There is no you and I,' she declared angrily. 'There never was, as you were at great pains to point out when you married Christina.' Her eyes sparkled with cold defiance.

His temper rose as swiftly as her own. 'Leave Christina

out of this,' he commanded. 'And if you want Clive to stay in ignorance…' he paused, his narrowed gaze cold on her lovely face '…you will have dinner with me tonight. I will pick you up here at six and we will continue our talk. We have a lot to discuss.'

Panicked by his kiss, her lips tingling with the taste of him, Amber had forgotten Lucas's real reason for seeking her out. There was still the will to discuss…

'All right,' she said curtly. 'I'll check with New York this afternoon. The sooner this matter is settled, the better.' The thought of Lucas back in her life filled her with horror and fear.

'Amber, darling.' Clive strolled into the office, saw Lucas and stopped. 'Lucas Karadines.' And he held out his hand for Lucas to shake. 'Thinking of changing bankers yet again?' Clive asked conversationally.

'No, nothing like that. A private matter concerning my late nephew Spiro. Now, if you will excuse me…' Lucas glanced at Amber, his dark eyes holding a definite threat '…until later.' And he left.

Clive quickly crossed to Amber's side, and put a comforting arm around her shoulder. 'I forgot to tell you when I spoke to you yesterday. I heard about Spiro a week ago. I know he used to be a good friend of yours; it must have been a shock.'

A tragedy. A calamity that Amber had a sinking feeling was only going to get worse.

Lunch was a disaster. Amber toyed with the food on her plate, her mind in turmoil. One kiss from Lucas Karadines, and her carefully considered decision taken after two weeks in Italy to accept Clive's proposal of marriage was shot to hell…

Clive was very understanding when she told him she needed more time. But she saw the hurt in his blue eyes when they said goodbye outside her office building, and she hated herself for it. He was a true friend.

CHAPTER SIX

RETURNING from lunch, Amber stopped at her secretary's desk. 'Sandy...' she looked hard at the pretty brunette '...what possessed you to let Mr Karadines walk straight into my office? You know the rules. No one gets in unless they have an appointment, especially not Mr Karadines, you must inform me first. Do I make myself clear?'

'Sorry.' Sandy apologised and then grinned. 'But he said he was an old friend and he wanted to surprise you, and I couldn't resist. I thought you would be pleased. I know *I* would. Smart, charming and sexy as hell; what more could a girl want?'

'He is also a domineering, chauvinistic pig, with the mind-set of a medieval monarch,' Amber declared with a wry grin. Sandy was an excellent secretary but a hopeless romantic. 'Now get back to work,' Amber commanded and walked into her office, closing the door behind her. She couldn't blame Sandy. Lucas had a lethal charm that few women, if any, could resist...

A fax to New York was her first priority and then Amber spent all afternoon trying to work, but without accomplishing much. It was five in the afternoon when she finally received a reply to her fax. She read it, and groaned; her worst fear was confirmed. Lucas, damn him, was right! She was Spiro's sole heir, and clarification of what that entailed would follow by mail.

Amber did not need to know. She'd made up her mind that whatever Spiro had left her she would give to Lucas. She wanted nothing to do with Karadines ever again...

She'd been badly burnt once and only a fool put their hand in the flame a second time. Ruthlessly she squashed the wayward thought that Lucas was a single man once more. He probably wasn't, she thought dryly. Lucas had a powerful sex drive, he was not the sort to do without a woman for very long, and there were millions of women out there only too ready to fall into bed with the man.

She was walking out of her personal washroom when the telephone rang. Crossing to her desk, she pressed the button on the intercom to hear Sandy at her most formal announcing the arrival of Mr Karadines.

'Send him in,' Amber responded briskly.

A moment later with an exaggerated flourish Sandy flung the door wide open. 'Lucas Karadines.' Strolling past Sandy, Lucas gave the girl a smile and a thank-you.

Even though Amber was ready for him, her heart still missed a beat, and anger with herself made her tone sharp. 'Thanks, Sandy, you can leave now. I will see Mr Karadines out myself.'

'As I have no intention of leaving without you, your last statement was rather superfluous, wouldn't you say?' Lucas queried sardonically.

Amber forced herself to meet the mockery she knew would be in his eyes. 'Not at all. I think when you hear what I have to say, this meeting will be over in a few minutes.' She was slightly reassured when she realised he was still wearing the same charcoal suit as before. Like her, he had not bothered to change; with a bit of luck, she could avoid having dinner with him.

'Really?' he drawled silkily. 'You intrigue me.'

'Yes, well. I have checked with New York, you were right about Spiro's will. I don't have the details yet, but it does not matter, because I have decided to sign everything over to you.'

'Such generosity, Amber.' He was laughing at her, she could see it in the sparkle in his black eyes. 'But then you were always very generous, at least in one department,' Lucas drawled softly, a flick of his lashes sending his gaze skimming over her with deliberate sensual provocation.

She shivered, with what must be cold, she told herself as she stared at him in silence for a second, then lowered her gaze to the desk and picked up her briefcase. She was over Lucas. She had been for years. He had humiliated her, and caused her more pain than any woman should have to bear. So why? Why did the sight of him, the sound of him, still have the power to disturb her? With no answer, she continued as though he had never spoken.

'That being the case, I don't think there is anything for us to discuss at this time. When I am in possession of the full facts of Spiro's legacy, I'll have my lawyer contact yours as soon as possible.' Clutching her briefcase, she stepped forward, about to stalk past him, but his hand reached out and his fingers bit into her shoulder. Instinctively she froze.

'It is not that simple, Amber, and you promised to join me for dinner,' he reminded her pointedly. 'I'm holding you to that.'

She wanted to deny him, but his closeness, his hand on her shoulder were a brittle reminder of her own susceptibility to the man. She was not indifferent to Lucas, no matter how much she tried to deny it. Whenever he came near her she was rigid with tension. Her heart pounded and her mouth went dry, a throwback to the time they'd spent together, and something she'd thought she'd got over long ago.

'If you insist,' Amber managed to say coolly, and, shrugging her shoulder, she slipped from under his restraining hand. 'But it is totally unnecessary. I've told you, you can have the lot.'

'If only it were that easy. You're a businesswoman, Amber, you should know better,' Lucas opined sarcastically. 'But now is not the time to discuss it. Unlike you, I missed lunch and I'm starving. Let's go.'

She didn't really want to go anywhere with Lucas, but one glance at his granite-like profile and she knew it would be futile to argue. Much better to go along with him now, than put off the discussion to another day. 'Okay,' she agreed, and preceded him out of the office. Entering the lift, she tried to ignore Lucas's brooding presence lounging against one wall, apparently content to remain silent now he had got his own way.

Her mother had always told her it was better to take bad medicine in one go, and Lucas was certainly that where she was concerned. How bad could it be? A couple of hours in his company and then she never need see him again. Amber consoled herself with the thought as the lift hummed silently to the ground floor, and she stepped out into the foyer, her chin up, her expression one of cool control.

'There is quite a nice little Italian restaurant just around the corner from here,' she offered with a brief glance at Lucas, tall and indomitable at her side.

'No, I have already made arrangements.'

Amber shot him a sharp glance. She didn't like the sound of that, but as they were exiting the building the early rain had given way to brilliant sun and dazzled her eyes for a moment. When she did focus, Lucas was opening the door of a black BMW parked illegally at the kerb.

She stopped. 'I have my own car, tell me where we are going and I'll follow you.'

'Not necessary. Get in, I can see a traffic warden coming.' His large hand grasped hers, urging her forward. 'Don't worry, I'll bring you back.'

Amber didn't want to get in his car, but a brief glance along the road told her he was telling the truth, at least about the traffic warden, so she did as she was told. It was only as he deftly manoeuvred the car through the rush-hour traffic that she realised to a man of his wealth a traffic ticket was nothing. When he stopped the car outside the impressive entrance to the Karadines Hotel, Amber's face paled. Lucas had to be the most insensitive man alive, or else he had brought her here deliberately and was just plain cruel.

'Why here?' Amber queried as Lucas helped her out of the car. She didn't want to put her hand in his, but she did, refusing to let him see how much he still affected her. 'Not very discreet of you.'

'It is too late for discretion, you own part of the place.' Lucas's hard, intent gaze held hers. 'So follow my lead and behave.'

She stared at him, their eyes warring for a second, and she was the first to look away. 'All right.'

The foyer was relatively empty, but even so the hotel manager appeared and greeted Lucas effusively. Amber, to her consternation, was urged forward and Lucas insisted on introducing her to the man as a partner in the business.

'What did you do that for?' she snapped as soon as the man took his leave of them. 'I have not the least intention of—'

'Keep it till we get to the suite.'

'Wait a minute. I am not going to any suite with you.' She stopped dead and looked up into his cold dark eyes. 'The restaurant will do perfectly well.'

'And run the risk of some employee tuning into our

business discussion?' he drawled sardonically. 'I think not, Amber.'

'Then you should not have brought me here in the first place,' she snapped.

Lucas's dark head bent towards her. 'I thought you would appreciate somewhere you knew,' he suggested softly, his breath feathering across her cheek as his hand settled in the middle of her back and he urged her across to the bank of lifts and into a conveniently empty one.

'You thought wrong,' she declared angrily, twisting away from his hand, her body taut with tension. She stared at his broad back as he pressed the required button and the doors closed, entombing them in the small space.

Slowly Lucas turned and lounged back against the carpeted wall, his dark eyes narrowing speculatively on her furious face. 'It can't be the place, because you are familiar with the hotel. So why the anger, Amber? I could almost believe you are afraid of me.'

He hadn't moved, but all at once the atmosphere had become charged with sexual tension. Amber's mouth was dry, the blood moving rapidly through her veins. 'I'm not afraid of any man.' She raised her eyebrows, her air of sophistication firmly back in place. 'And I am not familiar with the hotel,' she said sweetly. 'I have only been here twice, and *both* times were a disaster. The first you dragged me into bed, and the second you drove me out.' She managed to say it all with a light, even tone of voice, and she watched with interest as a red tide of colour ran up under his skin. 'Or had you forgotten in the old days you had a preference for discreet little restaurants, as I suggested earlier?'

The lift came to a halt, and Amber had the distinct impression Lucas was relieved he did not have to respond. Stroke one up for her, she thought irreverently as she followed him down a short corridor, and brushed past the door he held open for her without a glance.

The elegant sitting room was exactly the same with its luxury fitted carpet and period furniture. The large patio doors leading out onto the terrace were wide open and she had a glimpse of a table set for two. Some of her hard-won sophistication evaporated as she recalled the only other time she had been in this suite. The first time they had made love.

She stared at the floor with unseeing eyes. She had been a virgin, and totally ignorant of the power of love. She had been shy at first but so desperately eager. She felt the colour rise in her cheeks at the memory. A few passionate kisses and he had carried her into the bedroom and she had let him strip her naked—helped him, in fact. Then he had told her to undress him, and she had fumblingly complied. With breathtaking expertise he had taken her to the heights of ecstasy over and over again, and from that night on she had been completely addicted to the man. She had been madly in love, and willingly she had followed where he'd led. With hindsight she realised she should have guessed then for Lucas it had only been sex. She felt a deep ache in the region of her heart, and gritted her teeth. She hadn't expected the memory to hurt so much…

Lucas walked past her, discarding his jacket and tie on a low velvet-covered sofa, and headed straight for the drinks trolley. 'What will you have?' he asked, and only then did she lift her head and glance at him.

'Nothing,' she croaked. With his shirt half open and a tantalising glimpse of silky black chest hair exposed and his pleated trousers resting snugly on his slim hips, he looked exactly as he had all those years ago.

One ebony brow rose enquiringly. 'You must, I insist.'

'No, I'm driving later.' She swallowed hard and looked away. 'A fruit juice, maybe,' she amended.

A moment later Lucas was handing her a glass of orange juice. She took it with a steady hand but made sure her fingers did not come into contact with his.

'You look hot,' he opined, his dark eyes searching on her flushed face. 'Let me take your jacket.'

'No, no.' With a glass of juice in one hand and her briefcase in the other, there was no way she could remove it, and he certainly wasn't going to. She had no faith in the fine silk of her blouse hiding her body's reaction to his intimidating male presence.

'Please yourself, but at least let me take this.' And before she could react, his large hand prised her fingers from the death-like grip she had on her briefcase. 'We are eating on the terrace. Are you sure I can't persuade you out of your jacket? It is a warm night.'

Warm did not begin to describe how Amber was suddenly feeling and she almost fell over her feet to rush out onto the terrace, and take a great gulp of air.

A moment later Lucas followed her out with a glass of whisky in one hand, and, casting a sardonic glance at her stiff body standing by the balustrade, he pulled out a chair at the perfectly set table.

'For heaven's sake! Sit down and relax, Amber. I'm not about to jump you.'

'I never thought you were,' she responded with admirable poise and took the seat he offered.

Surprisingly Amber enjoyed the meal, probably because she had hardly eaten any lunch, but also because Lucas was at his charming best. Not a hint of innuendo, or mention of the past. The conversation was topical; some politics, the latest show to open in the West End, which Amber had seen, Lucas had not.

'I didn't know you liked the theatre,' Lucas remarked. 'I never thought to take you when we were together.'

Sitting back in her chair, sipping at a cup of black coffee, Amber almost choked. He was back to personal and she did not like it. 'You never took me anywhere,' she said flatly, draining her cup.

'You're right. Except to bed, of course, as I recall we had the greatest difficulty leaving the bedroom.'

Hot colour flooded her face but Amber wasn't touching that one with a bargepole. 'Shall we stick to business? I meant what I said earlier—whatever Spiro has left me, you can have. I know the will must have been an oversight on his part, or laziness. Either way you are the rightful heir. I don't see any problem.'

'Even if I believed your offer, there are several huge obstacles,' Lucas intoned cynically. 'Never mind the death duty, which will be quite substantial, his medical bills are enormous.'

'Did he die of Aids?' Amber asked, but she'd already guessed the answer.

'Of course, after a protracted illness,' Lucas stated flatly. 'I gather you have not had much contact with Spiro.'

'I hadn't spoken to him in four years,' she said, nervously fingering the waist button on her jacket and slipping it open. She felt terribly guilty, though she knew deep down it wasn't rational. Spiro had been a law unto himself.

'Okay. In that case I'd better fill you in.'

For a brief second she imagined his long body, naked, literally doing just that, and to her horror her own body betrayed her, a wave of heat washing over the surface of her skin, her breasts swelling against the constraint of her bra. Thankfully Lucas did not seem to be aware of the effect his simple statement had aroused.

'Well, you know Spiro,' Lucas prompted, exasperation lacing his tone. 'From taking control of his inheritance, he spent money like a madman. He bought most of the pictures in his art gallery from the artists himself. ''Friends'', he called them. For the last few years he has hired a house on Fire Island every summer, apparently a very popular place with the gay community, and he always took a crowd of pals along to share it with him. He sold off twenty per cent of his share of Karadines without my knowledge. I don't think he did it deliberately to harm the company, but it didn't help. He needed money fast and a friend fixed it for him.'

'How so Spiro,' Amber groaned with feeling. 'Even in death he caused chaos.'

'You knew him well,' Lucas commented dryly. 'But settling up after my father and Christina has left me with a bit of a cash-flow problem. I haven't got the capital to buy Spiro's shares at the moment—but if I don't own them, the company will be very vulnerable to predators.'

And he should know, Amber silently concluded. Lucas was the biggest predator she knew. She glanced across at him, her golden eyes narrowing shrewdly on his darkly attractive face. That was it! Amber saw the flaw in his argument. Lucas *should* know the solution. He had a brilliant brain and was a sharp operator of worldwide renown. He was also wickedly sexy with his shirt unbuttoned, came the unbidden thought. Stop it, Amber. Concentrate, she told herself firmly. Lucas was up to something, but what?

'But why can't I just give you Spiro's share?' she asked, feeling her way.

'I have never taken money off a woman in my life and I am not going to start now. I will buy your shares, eventually.'

'When you're over your cash-flow problems.'

He nodded. His eyes were hooded, masking his expression. Hers were hopefully blandly business-like. The treacherous thought did flicker through her mind that she was in the perfect position to exact a devastating revenge on the man who had thought of her as little better than a slut, a sex object to be used and discarded when he felt like it. For a fleeting moment she let her mind dwell on the idea of selling to another party. It was no more than Lucas Karadines deserved; her lips curved in a wry smile. But she knew she couldn't do it…

Rising abruptly from the table, Lucas said, 'It is getting distinctly chilly out here, we can carry on our discussion inside.'

Amber's mouth opened to deny him, but, catching the cynical expression on his handsome face, she thought better of it. She had the distinct impression he had read her mind and was not talking about the weather at all.

Rising, she followed him back into the sitting room, and, carefully positioning herself on the edge of an armchair, she refused his offer of a brandy. She simply watched and waited.

'My solution…' having poured himself a generous helping of brandy into a crystal goblet, Lucas turned and walked towards her…'is as I said earlier today… You and I, Amber, are now the major partners in Karadines. As you have probably worked out, you can make life very difficult for me, and I could hardly blame you, after the way I treated you.'

His answer floored her. He actually sounded contrite. Her golden eyes widened to their fullest extent on his, and he smiled down at her, a small smile, but a smile nevertheless.

'Don't look so surprised.' His gaze narrowed and swept over her tensely held body perched on the end of the chair, lingering at where her breasts were outlined beneath the fine silk of her blouse. She had forgotten she had undone her jacket. 'The past four years have taught me that love is an illusion and what we shared was a lot more honest emotion.'

Amber gulped, and jumped to her feet. No way was she going there! And, fastening the button of her jacket, 'This is all very interesting but I really must be going. And if you want my advice…' she said briskly, spying her brief-case leaning against the end of the sofa and she headed towards it. Picking it up, she turned and finally glanced up at Lucas. 'I'm a stockbroker—if you need to raise money, float the company on the stock market.'

'Come now, Amber,' he drawled mockingly. 'Do you really think that I, Lucas Karadines, would ever give up control of Karadines?'

His impregnable confidence made her suddenly angry; her golden eyes flashed. 'You might have to.'

'Not if you agree to my plan, Amber,' he murmured, his glance intent on her lovely face as he towered over her. 'If you are as honest as you say, you know Spiro would never have intended the family firm to fall into other hands or even collapse.'

Lucas was right. Spiro used to rant and rave about his family, but deep down he had cared for them. Amber's golden gaze studied Lucas, and her pulses raced. She'd been struggling to keep her eyes off him all evening, the tempting view of his near-naked chest, and with only inches separating them she knew she had to get away.

'What exactly is your plan?' she asked abruptly. She would listen to him, agree and get out fast.

'It's quite simple,' he murmured. His black eyes lingered on her high cheekbones, the thick, curling lashes framing her wide-set golden eyes, and then lower to the full curve of her lips, and lower still to the soft swell of her breast.

'Get on with it,' Amber prompted, terrified by the latent sensual gleam in his dark eyes.

He was too close. Far, far too close. 'Just—just *tell* me,' she stammered, somewhat breathlessly. *Turn, run,* her mind screamed. But she had waited too long.

Lucas hauled her hard against him, his dark head swooped down and his mouth closed over hers. Amber gasped, and his tongue gained instant access to the moist, dark interior of her mouth. Her briefcase fell from her hand and clattered to the floor. But Amber was unconscious of the fact. She was only aware of the hard heat of Lucas, the rock-like strength of his arousal pressed against her lower body, the greedy hunger of his mouth as he ravished hers, and her own instant fierce response.

His hands slid down from her shoulders, and she lifted her own to clasp them around his neck. She clung to him, as one large hand delved down the front of her blouse to cup the soft curve of her breast, long fingers slipping under the strip of lace that was her bra. Amber shuddered as he flicked a nail over a nipple, bringing it to a rigid, pulsing peak. With his other hand closed over her bottom, she instinctively rotated her hips sensually against his hard thighs, wanting more.

Lucas lifted his head, his breath hot against her cheek, and watched her with night-black eyes. 'You haven't changed,' he said huskily with an edge of triumph in his tone. 'Still the sexiest girl alive.' His lips caressed hers softly.

Amber stiffened, her hands fell from his neck, and she turned her head away from his searching mouth. He was right, damn him… Nothing had changed in the intervening years, she realized. She was still helplessly enslaved to the potent sexuality of this one man... But she was older and wiser...and, fighting for every bit of will-power, she flattened both hands on his chest and pushed.

'Let me go,' she demanded bitterly. She could feel the heavy pounding of his heart beneath her hand, the angry tension in his body. She lifted her eyes to his, and caught a flash of something violent that quickly vanished.

'As you wish, Amber.' He threw his arms wide and stepped back. 'I have discovered all I needed to know.' His dark eyes had a glitter in them, and more than a hint of triumph.

Amber gazed at him, her eyes clouded with puzzlement and the lingering traces of passion. To hide her confusion, she bent down and retrieved her briefcase, and, straightening up, she smoothed her jacket down over the curve of her hips with a trembling hand. 'If you want my co-operation over Spiro's legacy, you can cut that out for a start,' she said icily. 'Otherwise you can sort Karadines' problems out yourself. I'm sure you're more than capable.' She headed for the door.

'I am.' Lucas smiled, catching her wrist and spinning her back to face him. 'The solution is simple: I marry you,' he declared, a hint of satisfaction in his voice. 'You did ask me once before, remember?' He taunted softly.

Amber would have given everything she owned not to. Her face went ashen, the passion and the pain inextricably linked in her mind. She had swallowed her pride and begged him to love her. Until finally he had told her the truth—that she disgusted him.

'Over my dead body.' Wrenching her wrist from his grasp, she looked at him with loathing in her eyes. 'My God! Your arrogance is only exceeded by your colossal conceit in daring to ask the question.'

'I did not ask a question.' His black eyes glinted mockingly. 'I made a statement of intent.'

CHAPTER SEVEN

As AMBER tried to find her voice through the anger that consumed her she told herself, He has to be joking! But Lucas did not look particularly amused. In fact, the cold determination in his black eyes sent an icy shiver of fear slithering down her spine. 'I don't have to listen to this,' she declared forcibly. 'I'm leaving.'

'No, you are not,' Lucas countered coolly, and slipped an arm around her waist, drawing her ruthlessly closer. She felt the heat of him searing her even through her clothes. Amber's lips went dry, her throat closing in panic. Lucas was holding her tightly. She tried to struggle free, but he simply increased the pressure, crushing her to the hardness of his body. 'I have no intention of letting you go,' he muttered, 'ever again.' He grasped her chin with one large hand and tilted her head back. 'Look at me!' he commanded.

She wanted to escape, and planted her hands firmly on his chest intending to push him away, but the old familiar sexual chemistry held her in thrall, and had he actually said 'ever again'? The notion was beguiling and the best she could do was stare up at him with puzzled, angry eyes.

Her anger seemed to amuse him, and as his dark gaze bored into her she felt the surge of blood in her cheeks, and began to tremble, her legs suddenly weak as with a faint, mocking smile he told her exactly what he wanted.

'You and I will marry a week on Saturday in Greece.' His fingers traced up over her lips in intentional provocation. 'I can take you to bed now, and remind you how it was with us, or we can wait for the wedding. But that is the only choice I'm giving you.'

Amber knew she should be fighting him, but could only gaze at him in shock, with increasing need and desire scorching through her. 'No,' she denied. But his mouth found hers, deriding her negative with a demanding hunger that had her weakening helplessly against him. With sensual expertise he deepened the kiss until a drugging passion had emptied her mind of everything but a growing physical need, an ache she had to have assuaged.

He was using the potent force of his sexuality to get his own way, and even as she recognised the fact Amber suddenly did not care! A wild recklessness filled her, sweeping away the years since Lucas had held her like this, kissed her like this, and, slipping her hands over his chest, she clasped them behind his neck, pressing her slender body to his mighty frame. It was only when he broke the kiss and held her slightly away from him, his breathing ragged, she realised the full extent of her capitulation.

'Come to bed with me, you know you want to.' His dark eyes blazed with triumph; he had sensed her complete surrender and taken it as a yes, now he was simply discussing the terms. 'Now or next week, what does it matter?'

Amber would have denied him, even as her body was on fire for him. His assumption he only had to kiss her and she would give in was an insult to her pride, her self-esteem. But then he groaned.

'*Christo!* I certainly need you.' The hand at her chin was suddenly gentle, and he stared deep into her golden eyes. 'Say yes.' She gulped at the unguarded hunger, the desire she saw in expressive eyes. 'I'll wait for the wedding night if you insist,' he said, his smile almost tender.

It was the tenderness that did it. She wanted him. Oh!

How she wanted him, and why not? her sex-starved body demanded. She was not going to marry him, she was no longer a lovesick girl, or a fool, but with every nerve in her body screaming with frustration she murmured, 'All right.' At least she could have this one night.

Lucas smiled, a slow, sensual twist, then raised his hands to her head and deftly unpinned the severe chignon, and trailed his fingers through the long length of her hair, spreading it over her shoulders. Eyes closed, Amber trembled as his arm slid down around her waist and he rested his head in the curve of her neck, breathing in the fragrant scent of the tumbling mass of hair.

'I have been longing to do this,' he murmured. 'From the second I walked into your office today and saw your magnificent hair scraped back, my fingers ached to set it free. It should always be free.' His lips moving over her burning cheek finally found her mouth.

The years since they had last met might never have been. Her pulse leapt as Lucas kissed her with a wild, yet tender, passion she was helpless to deny. She didn't want to. She felt the sudden rush of damp heat flooding her lower body, and feverishly she clung to him, silently abandoning herself to the sheer ecstasy of his kiss, his touch.

Swiftly Lucas swept her up in his arms. She put her arms around his neck and she kissed him very slowly and long. Amber wasn't really conscious of him lowering her to her feet and removing their clothing as desire mounted fiercely inside her. She touched a slender finger to his lips, remembering, tracing the firm outline—he had such a sensual mouth. Lucas drew a ragged breath, and urged her down onto the bed. She felt the mattress at her back, and stared up at him with passion-glazed eyes. He was magnificent in his nudity; his shoulders were broad, his hips were narrow and his belly flat and hard, and the awesome sight of his aroused manhood made her shudder in almost fearful anticipation.

For a long, tense moment Lucas looked down at her, drinking in her naked beauty with black hungry eyes, then, leaning over, he kissed her, his mouth possessive and urgent on her own.

Then, rearing back, he touched her and she quivered like a leaf in the breeze. His hands swept slowly down her body in a long, sinuous, almost worshipful motion, then up again, his palms flat on her stomach until they reached her breasts. He teased her gently, the fingers of one hand grazing slowly over the tips of her breasts, first one and then the other, bringing them to rigid, aching peaks, while his other hand smoothed back down between her legs that parted involuntarily at his caress. She was moist, ready, aching for him, and with a delicate, erotic touch he caressed her until desire mounted crazily inside her and everything else was blotted from her mind.

He caught her to him, and their mouths met and fused, and she arched herself blindly against him. With tactile delight she slipped her hands down across his shoulders, and along under his arms, across his taut abdomen, and then they swept around the outside of his thighs and finally to his inner thigh, her slender fingers curving around the hard, pulsing strength of him. She wanted him now…

She heard the sharp intake of his breath as his head tilted back. 'No, Amber.' And he closed his hand over hers, pulling it from his body. For a horrible second she thought he meant to deny her. 'Not yet. I was a brute the last time,' he rasped. 'I vowed…'

She could see the muscles of his thighs bunch with tension in the effort of control. But after five years of celibacy Amber didn't want to talk. So she wrapped her arms around his neck, and pulled him back down over her.

He kissed her with a wild hunger, his tongue exploring deep in her mouth, his hands caressing every inch of her burning flesh with sensual delight, and she responded with equal passion and helpless moans of pleasure.

She sank back under his hard, hot body, whimpering with need. But Lucas was not to be hurried. He kissed her mouth, her breasts, her thighs, until she jerked helplessly beneath him, her senses swimming with desire. 'Please, Lucas, don't make me wait,' she begged.

And as though he'd been waiting for her plea Lucas moved between her parted thighs. Amber tensed for a second. It had been a long time for her. The hard length of him moved slowly, easing himself deeper and deeper inside her, sometimes to his full length and sometimes with shallow strokes that teased and enhanced the pleasure almost to pain. Amber had never felt such need, such fiery tension, until her inner muscles convulsed around him in a shattering completion. But still he moved, their bodies locked together.

Lucas rolled onto his back and brought her up above him. His hands clasping her hips, he held her against him, but now he could kiss her breasts. Amber cried out at the feel of his mouth on her taut nipples, and shockingly felt the excitement building all over again.

'Yes, yes,' Lucas cried, and as he held her fiercely down on him his great body bucked violently beneath her as he reached his climax. At the same time Amber cried his name, and tumbled over into her own headlong fulfilment yet again.

She collapsed on top of him, breathless and mindless, feeling the sweat of passion cooling on her skin. She buried her head on his shoulder. She did not want him to see her, not yet. Not until she had recovered some of her shattered control. She felt his large, warm hand stroke her back gently, and she could almost fool herself it was love… But not quite…

Rolling off him, she lay flat on her back, and swallowed a despairing sigh—from the heights of ecstasy to the depths of despair in a few moments. Amber knew herself well—no way would she allow any man the intimate liberties she had gloried in with Lucas unless she loved him. The enormity of the realisation made her heartsick.

She loved him, she always had and probably always would. But she had been too badly hurt before to believe he wanted to marry her for any other reason than Spiro's legacy. Tonight would have to be enough. It was ironic in a way, she thought as a wry smile curved her love-swollen lips. Lucas had called her a gold-digger, but in fact it was Lucas who was now in that position.

'What are you thinking?' Lucas propped himself on one elbow, his dark, slumberous eyes boring into hers, his breathing still unsteady. 'That smile looks decidedly smug.'

It was a question she did not want to answer, not truthfully. The night was young and she intended to make full use of it. She lifted her hands and trailed her fingers through the silky mat of chest hair, caressing his body. As her finger grazed a hard male nipple she felt his magnificent body tremble, and she smiled again. 'I was wondering how long it takes you to recover these days,' she murmured throatily, her eyes gleaming with invitation.

Surreptitiously Amber glanced at her wrist-watch—it was the only thing she was wearing. It was close to one o'clock in the morning. She looked down into the face of Lucas Karadines. Somehow he seemed much younger in sleep. His eyes were closed, his long dark lashes brushing his cheeks. He was deeply asleep, not surprising after their second encounter, Amber thought, remembering his seemingly insatiable desire. But she could not sleep—she had to leave. Even now, with her passion for him momentarily quenched, she felt no lessening of desire, but she knew on Lucas's part it was only lust... He had told her so quite truthfully years ago. Dear heaven! What was it going to take for her to get over him? Death?

On that morbid thought she stifled a sigh and slid out of bed, and by moonlight she managed to find her clothes and get dressed. Slipping her shoes on, she crept quietly towards the door. She turned for one last look at his bronzed body spread out on the bed, and almost went back to join him. Instead she closed the door on the temptation he provided.

She didn't get far! Finding her jacket on the arm of the sofa, she slipped it on, and, picking up her briefcase, she stepped towards the exit and escape, just when the bedroom door was flung open.

'Amber.' Lucas walked into the sitting room, totally unconscious of his nudity. 'What are you doing?'

'I am leaving.'

Lucas glared at her for a startled second. 'What the hell is wrong with you? Are you out of your mind? We have just shared mind-blowing sex and now you are sneaking out of my bed in the middle of the night!'

Pushing the tangled mass of her hair behind her ears in a futile attempt to tame it, she glanced up at Lucas. He had the angry, puzzled look of a child who had had his favourite toy snatched from his grasp, and his crude comment on sex simply angered her further. 'Why, was I supposed to wait until you left first?' she asked cynically.

If tonight had taught her anything at all, it was that she had to stay away from Lucas. Because, loving him as she did, she had no resistance against him; she was his for the

taking. Even now the temptation to close the distance between them and run her hands over his hard, tanned body,
to feel once more the wonder of his possession, was almost
irresistible. But one thought stopped her. The memory of
his leaving her naked on the floor in the apartment they
had once shared was something she would not let herself
forget. She moved to walk past him, but his hand shot out
and he captured her arm in a steely grip.

'I have no intention of leaving you—' he glared down
at her pale face and bruised, swollen mouth '—or of letting
you go. You belong to me!'

'Spiro's money belongs to you is what you really
mean.'

He frowned at her acid comment. 'If that is what you
want to think, so be it. But it does not alter the fact you
are marrying me. I had hoped willingly.' His black eyes
raked appreciatively over her. 'You're a very beautiful,
intelligent woman; any man would be proud to make you
his wife.'

A harsh laugh escaped her. 'Oh, please, Lucas,' she
drawled scathingly, tugging her arm free and stepping
back. 'It's a bit late for compliments.' Five years too late,
she thought bitterly.

His dark eyes blazed angrily for a second before adopt-
ing his more usual expression, coldly remote. 'If you say
so.' He shrugged his broad shoulders. 'But if not willingly,
I am quite prepared to use coercion. The end result will
be the same.'

He sounded so uncompromising that Amber flinched.
'But why?' she demanded in exasperation, trying not to
look at his naked body. 'I have told you to contact my
lawyer. I will put it in writing here and now, if you like.
You can have the lot.' Her temper was frayed, she was
tired and beginning to be afraid. There was something

about his insistence on marriage that was finally getting through to her. He was deadly serious.

'Because of the time-scale, Amber, even if I believe your assurance that you don't want Spiro's legacy, I don't want you to give it to me,' he insisted for the second time, much to Amber's puzzlement. 'I will pay you the going rate for your holding. But first there is the small question of probate. It usually takes months for a will to get through, and in the meantime the company will become vulnerable to rumour as to how you intend to disperse Spiro's shares,' Lucas answered grimly. 'You will be in-undated with offers, and, much as I want to believe in your altruistic nature, I prefer to make sure. As my wife it will be apparent to any predator the company is being kept firmly in the family.'

Amber had enough business sense to realise there was a flaw in his argument. 'In that case the answer is simple. I will give you first option to buy the shares at a knock-down price when I finally inherit. Problem solved,' she said jauntily.

'I prefer my solution. We both know there is the pos-sibility of you marrying Clive Thompson—' he almost spat the name out '—and there is no way he is getting anywhere near my business.' Lucas's glittering glance was full of macho rage. He knew Amber would not be easy to fool, she was too damn smart. But after the great sex they had shared there was no way on God's earth he was letting her get away again. He had spent far too many long, lonely nights frustrated as hell. He looked grimly down at her. 'And if you have any fondness for your new-found father and family, you will do as I say.'

To Amber's ears that sounded suspiciously like a threat. A terrible coldness invaded her and, cautiously lifting her head, she looked into his jet-black eyes. 'What exactly do you mean by that?' she demanded quietly.

'Wait here while I dress,' Lucas commanded and strode back into the bedroom, leaving Amber standing in an agony of suspense. She considered walking out, but didn't dare. Lucas had been so chillingly confident, she had to know what he meant.

When he returned, Amber's wary gaze swept over him. He looked casually elegant. Light-coloured linen trousers hung easily on his lean hips, a fine knit roll-neck sweater covered his muscular chest and his black hair was brushed firmly from his broad brow. 'Good, you waited. I rather thought you might,' he stated silkily. 'Now, where were we?' he asked, smiling.

She felt like knocking the grin off his face, but instead gathered all the will-power she possessed and took a couple of steadying breaths. 'You were about to tell me why I should not marry Clive but marry you instead. Personally I thought it was my own choice. How silly of me,' she managed to say facetiously.

Lucas's smile vanished. 'You have no choice.' His dark eyes narrowed to angry slits. 'Not if you value your father's good name.' Amber felt a sick feeling in the pit of her stomach as Lucas continued. 'Since Sir David retired, his bank has not, how shall I put it…?' He hesitated; his black eyes, glittering with triumph, clashed with hers. 'His son Mark is not a patch on him. Last year, although it saddened me to do it given the long association between Karadines and Janson's, I had to cut all ties with the bank. It was only out of deference for Sir David that charges were not brought against them.'

'I don't believe you,' Amber said sharply. 'My father is an honest man.'

'Yes, I agree. Unfortunately the same cannot be said for his son,' Lucas opined cynically.

Amber went white, and in a voice that shook she asked, 'You're telling me that Mark has done something illegal?' The horrible part was, Amber realized that she was not completely surprised by Lucas's statement.

Lucas shot her a caustic smile. 'What else would you call using money from a client's account to fund a yacht in the Med and keeping a very expensive mistress?'

Amber turned her head aside, unable to meet his eyes. Mark had bought a yacht, that much was true, and the mistress didn't surprise her much either. His poor wife Mary was the mother of three delightful daughters, and spent her whole time apologising for not producing the son her husband wanted.

Lucas walked over to her, his long fingers clasping her chin. 'If you don't believe me, ask him, Amber,' he challenged.

She had a terrible feeling Lucas might be right, and she hid her confusion with an angry accusation. 'You would use the feeling I have for my father to blackmail me into marrying you?' she derided. 'In your dreams, buster.'

His jaw tensed and something violent flashed in his eyes before he drew a deep breath. 'Not in a dream, but in reality, yes. If that's what it takes to get what I want. Yes,' he reiterated bluntly.

She searched his lean, strong face, sure he must be kidding. Surely no man in the twenty-first century could force a woman into marriage? He didn't mean it. But she could not help noticing the implacable determination in his gaze. How had she forgotten what a ruthless bastard he could be? She'd fooled herself into thinking she could have him for a night and walk away. Amber felt her stomach curl sickeningly with fear as her eyes skimmed over his magnificent physique, the vibrant raw energy of the man that fascinated her even as it repelled her. She had underestimated Lucas. But she'd also overestimated her own ability to control her chaotic emotions. Her eyes widened in horror. 'You're crazy,' she bit out as realisation dawned. He was serious, and, worse, much worse, she was tempted...

One ebony brow lifted while a ruthless smile curved his sensuous mouth. 'Perhaps, but how would you live with yourself knowing you could have saved the reputation of your father's firm? A father who went to great lengths to find you and acknowledge you.'

She was trembling. 'You're a bastard, Lucas,' she said, her strained features reflecting her inner turmoil. 'But I'm not afraid of you. I will ask Mark, and—'

He cut across her. 'You *do* that. I made my decision a while ago, I'll give you until the day after tomorrow to make yours.'

Amber heard the car drive up, the engine stop and the car door slam. Her full lips tightened in an angry grimace as she glanced out of the window of her living room. Lucas was pushing open the wrought-iron gate that led up the garden path to the front door of her cottage.

Since the night when she'd fallen like a ripe plum into his arms, in his hotel suite, her life had become chaotic. The following evening she'd met Mark, her half-brother, for a drink, and as soon as she'd mentioned Lucas Karadines he had gone white, and within minutes she'd had the whole story: it was true. It would have been risible if the consequences had not been so tragic for Amber.

Wednesday morning Lucas had called at her office. Loyalty to her father's family and her guilty feelings over Spiro's legacy had forced her to accept Lucas's proposal. Because she knew she did not deserve to gain by Spiro's death. He had been a good friend for many years, as a student and after. Yet she had not contacted him in over four years because he had invited his uncle to the opening of his art gallery without telling her, and told Lucas that she'd put up the capital for Spiro's venture. Worse, she could not shake the notion that if she had not given Spiro the money to go to New York when he had, he might not have contracted the disease that had killed him. But the fact that Lucas the devil had won did nothing to soothe her anger.

That weekend, at Lucas's insistence, she had taken him to her father's house in Surrey, and dropped the bombshell of her forthcoming marriage the following Saturday. Lucas had charmed Sir David and his wife Mildred so much so that Mildred had insisted on throwing an engagement party. Amber had been glad to get back to work on the Monday and away from Lucas, who had business in New York for a few days. But then she'd had the unenviable task of lunching with Clive and telling him she was marrying Lucas Karadines. She had felt an absolute worm by the time they had parted, because she hadn't been able to tell Clive the real reason for her hasty marriage, and he'd taken her rejection with a brave smile and an honest desire that they remain friends.

Then mid-week she'd discovered Lucas had spoken to the chairman of Brentford's. The firm had given her three months' holiday. When she had discovered from one of the other partners why, she had been furious and deeply hurt in equal proportions.

She heard the doorbell ring. They were flying out to Greece today and tomorrow was their wedding day. 'Unfortunately,' Amber muttered darkly, smoothing the fine buttercup silk summer dress she had chosen to wear over her slender hips, and, taking a deep, calming breath, she walked out of the living room, along the hall and opened the front door.

Lucas stood on the path, tall and dark, and the expression on his strong face was one of amusement. 'I don't believe it—you live in a country cottage with roses around the door. It is not you at all, Amber,' he drawled mockingly.

Put out by his opening comment, Amber snapped, 'How the hell would you know?' Her heart had leapt at the sight of him—she had not seen him since last Sunday.

A green polo shirt fit snugly over his wide shoulders, and outlined the musculature of his broad chest in loving detail. Khaki cotton trousers clung to his hips and long legs. A pair of sunglasses was shoved carelessly back across the thick black hair of his head, revealing his perfect features in stark beauty. It wasn't fair; no man should look so good. Even the summer sun glinting on the silver wings of his hair only enhanced his vibrant masculine charm.

Lucas straightened. 'As I recall I know you very well.' His dark eyes roamed over her face and down over her shapely figure in a blatant sensual caress.

'Only in the biblical sense,' Amber returned, and, turning back into the hall, she grabbed the case she had packed and walked to the door. 'I'm ready. Let's go.' She did not want to invite him into her home, because she knew her marriage to Lucas would only last as long as it took Spiro's will to pass probate. She loved her cottage; she had bought it from her landlord three years ago, and had had great fun renovating it. She wanted no memories of Lucas to haunt it when she returned.

'Is that all your luggage?' Lucas demanded, one dark brow arching incredulously on the single suitcase. 'We are getting married in the morning, we will be in Greece for at least the rest of the summer. Where are all your clothes? Surely not in that thing.' He flung an elegant tanned hand at her admittedly rather battered suitcase.

'Let's get one thing straight here, Lucas. I don't need anything special for a civil marriage that is strictly business and will be terminated as soon as possible; the dress I am wearing will do. Easy-care wash and dry as are the other clothes I have packed. I don't need much to bum around on a Greek beach for three months, which is *all* I will be doing since you took it upon yourself to get my employer to give me a holiday. Understood?' Amber told him belligerently, squaring up to him, her golden eyes flashing. If he thought for one second she was going to socialise with him, or play the part of the loving wife, or climb into his bed like a good little girl, he was in for a rude awakening.

Black eyes clashed with hers, and she saw the glint of fury before he successfully masked it with self-restraint.

'Amber, you can walk around naked, if that is what you want,' he drawled mockingly. 'In fact, I would prefer you to.' His eyes, flaring with sensual heat, roamed over her body. She looked breathtakingly beautiful, the buttercup silk dress outlining her luscious curves in loving detail. Her eyes were wide and lustrous, with just a trace of vulnerability in their golden depths that her anger could not hide. She was nowhere near as confident as she wanted to appear.

'Oh, that is not what I mean and you know it,' she snapped.

Lucas knew now was not the time to argue. 'It was a joke, Amber, I hear what you are saying. A business arrangement.'

Expecting an argument, Amber was surprised at his easy agreement, and for a moment felt ridiculously disappointed. But then what had she expected? She remonstrated with her foolish heart. Lucas had not wanted her five years ago, he was hardly going to be desperate to marry her now. On that sobering thought she brushed past him, dropped the suitcase on the path, and turned to lock the door of her little cottage.

'What exactly do you intend doing with this place?' Lucas asked, picking up her suitcase in one hand, his other hand settling at the base of her rigid spine as he urged her away from the house.

'Why, nothing,' she informed him dulcetly. 'I expect to be back at work in three months.' Lucas wasn't getting it all his own way. He had ridden roughshod over all her objections, charmed her father, and bribed her boss to give her a three-month sabbatical, by the simple expedient of becoming a client of Brentford's. He might have blackmailed her into marriage, but he was definitely not blackmailing her into his bed again.

'Well, it is a bit small, but I suppose I could get used to it,' Lucas murmured.

Amber tensed. 'What do you mean by that?'

His sensuous mouth tilted at the corners. 'Why, Amber, darling, once we are married, what is mine is yours, and what is yours is mine.'

Amber's eyes widened in astonishment at his words. 'You're joking.'

'If you want us to live in a cottage rather than a mansion,' he said, shrugging his broad shoulders. His dark eyes watched the myriad expressions flicker across her exquisite face, and then flicked appreciatively over the soft curve of her breasts, the narrow waist and on down over the slender hips and long legs. 'I don't mind,' Lucas said huskily, his dark eyes dancing wickedly.

He was laughing at her; she should have been furious.

'But—but, I—I mean you have just agreed the marriage is strictly business,' Amber stammered to a halt. He was handsome, a rampantly virile male, and she stared at him, her breath catching in her throat.

'I know *exactly* what you mean, Amber,' Lucas emphasised dryly. 'You are angling for a fight and I flatly refuse to give you one. Business marriage or whatever! If my competitors are to be convinced, we have to live together for as long as it takes. Now relax, the sun is shining, it is a beautiful day, and tomorrow will be even better. Get in the car and let's go.' With a broad grin he urged her out onto the road and into the passenger seat of a black BMW.

She watched him through lowered lashes as he slid into the driving seat after depositing her suitcase in the back. Why had she even imagined for a moment that she would be able to resist Lucas, deny him her body? If he wanted her he only had to smile at her, and she was lost. Why had she even tried to pretend she hated him? She loved him, and the realisation of exactly how vulnerable she was hurt like hell. But it made her all the more determined to defy him.

Starting the car, Lucas turned his dark head and smiled at her again. 'I have a surprise for you when we get to the airport.'

Her own vulnerability to his blatant masculine charm made her respond with biting sarcasm. 'Let's hope it is the same surprise as the last time you said that to me. You are marrying someone else...'

Lucas stiffened, his smile vanishing, his dark eyes staring straight ahead, watching the road. Amber noticed the dull stain of red on his cheekbones and for a second thought he was embarrassed until he spoke. 'No, this time it has to be you. I have no choice.'

Amber opened her mouth to argue and stopped. Shrinking back in the seat, she let her thoughts loose, and winced at her own conceit. She had been so incensed at being conned into marrying Lucas, convinced she was making a great sacrifice for her family; she had never thought for a moment how Lucas had to feel. He had loved his first wife, Christina, and now because of Spiro's will he was stuck with either trusting Amber, or marrying her. His only other alternative was facing a takeover battle for his business.

A very chastened Amber said, 'It is not too late. We don't have to marry. You can trust me to give you Spiro's legacy, Lucas. I won't betray you.'

A large tanned hand dropped from the wheel to curve over her thigh. Involuntarily her leg flexed, electric sensation tingling down to her toes. Lucas shot her a deep and unfathomable look.

'Sorry, Amber,' he said softly, 'but I do have to marry you.' With a brief squeeze of her leg, he returned his hand to the steering wheel.

With her thigh still burning from his touch, she couldn't think of a thing to say. She closed her eyes to be alone with her thoughts. He had said sorry. Did he mean he was sorry for her? Or sorry for himself because he had to marry her?

Trying to fathom out how Lucas's mind worked was doing her head in, and, opening her eyes, she looked out of the passenger window and realised they were approaching the airport.

CHAPTER EIGHT

'SO WHAT is the mysterious surprise?' Amber finally demanded. The long silence, the heightened tension in the close confines of the car, had her nerves stretched to breaking-point.

'You will soon find out,' Lucas said curtly, bringing the car to a halt at the entrance to the airport terminal and, without so much as looking in her direction, he proceeded to unfasten his seat belt. Whatever the surprise was, Lucas obviously had no intention of enlightening her.

'Get out.' The terse command did nothing for Amber's growing resentment at his high-handed manner. She cast him a fulminating glance but it was wasted as he was already sliding out of the driver's seat, his back towards her.

Amber scrambled out of the car with more haste than elegance, and, straightening up, she flicked her mane of chestnut hair back from her shoulders and looked around.

Lucas stood a couple of feet away. She watched as he lifted an elegant tanned hand and, magically, a small, rather wizened man appeared and caught the car key Lucas threw in his direction. The older man looked vaguely familiar to Amber and, walking forward, she stopped at Lucas's side as the strange man withdrew her suitcase from the car, handed it to Lucas and said something in Greek.

Watching Lucas respond in the same language and smile down at the other man, Amber was diverted from her simmering anger by trying to figure out where she had seen him before. Then the old man lifted his head, grinned at her and she remembered.

'Why, it's you,' the asinine comment slipped out, but the man had turned and was already getting into the car. 'That's the man that called at the apartment,' Amber said impulsively, tilting her head to look up at Lucas. 'I remember him.' She beamed, pleased at having placed the stranger.

One dark brow arched sardonically as their eyes met. 'Ah, yes! The symbolic castration! I don't think a trip down that particular memory lane is appropriate, given we are to be married tomorrow,' Lucas drawled cynically.

Instinctively her eyes dropped to a certain part of his anatomy; realising what she was doing, she quickly glanced back up at his face. 'No. No...' she stammered. She had forgotten her vengeful reaction when she'd destroyed the crotch in his trousers, and felt colour burn up through her skin. Through anger, she decided staunchly, not embarrassment.

The look he cast her held a tinge of amusement that was apparent in his voice. 'It was probably no more than I deserved, given the circumstances. Forget it—I have—and give me your passport, we have to get a move on.'

Whether it was embarrassment, anger, or sheer shock that Lucas had actually admitted he might have been at fault, which was surely a first for the great Lucas Karadines, it did not matter. Amber was flustered enough to delve into her bag, withdraw her passport and hand it to him without a murmur.

'Good girl.' And, cupping a large hand around her elbow, he led her through the airport.

Following his broad back up the steps to the aircraft, Amber fumed at the sheer arrogant confidence of Lucas. He had swept them both through customs, with an ease that lesser mortals could never aspire to. She watched him smile at the stewardess waiting at the entrance door to the plane, and saw the stupid girl simpering all over him. By the time Amber reached the door, the same girl simply bared her teeth at Amber.

Walking into the cabin, Amber stopped dead.

'Surprise, surprise,' a cacophony of voices shouted.

Amber's mouth fell open in shock, her golden eyes widening to their fullest extent. Everyone and their granny were on the aircraft, she registered in stunned amazement.

Lucas stepped forward to curve a confident arm around her rigid body. 'This is your surprise...I thought you would appreciate your family attending our wedding.'

She forced a smile to her lips, while her eyes scanned the interior of the cabin. Her father, his wife Mildred, her half-sister Julie, Julie's husband Tom and their son plus Mark's wife Mary and her three girls were all on board.

But the biggest surprise to Amber was Tim's presence. In a flurry of greetings and with the aircraft door closing and the captain announcing take-off, it was some time before Amber caught her breath long enough to look up at Lucas, who had somehow manoeuvred her into a seat and fastened her seat belt.

'Why didn't you tell me? I thought this was supposed to be a quick civil wedding and an even quicker divorce,' she hissed as the roar of the engines signalled lift-off. 'Why on earth involve my family?'

Lucas's dark head bent towards her, one arm resting lightly over her slender shoulders. 'I am Greek, we are very family orientated,' his deep voice murmured against her ear. 'And, though I have lost my family, it would be unthinkable to exclude yours,' he declared, the warmth of his breath against her face sending her pulse-rate rocketing.

Amber stared at him, and Lucas stared levelly back at her, his hooded black eyes giving nothing away.

'But Tim as well, I thought...' She didn't know what she thought.

'He is your lifelong friend,' he explained with a casual shrug of his broad shoulders. Against her will, Amber's eyes were drawn to those same shoulders, straining under the cotton knit polo shirt, and gulped. The popping of a champagne cork was a welcome diversion.

Seat belts were unfastened, and the luxurious comfort of the private jet was enjoyed by everyone. Amber found herself seated on a soft hide sofa, with Lucas apparently glued to her side. She could feel the heat of his thigh through the thin silk of her dress, and almost snapped the stewardess's hand off when she offered her a glass of champagne. Amber needed to cool down quick...

The flight took on a party mood, champagne flowed freely, and toasts were drunk to the engaged couple. Lucas responded by taking the opportunity to sweep Amber into his arms and kiss her thoroughly, much to the delight of everyone except Amber. Who, as soon as she could without it looking obvious, got to her feet and put some distance between them. She engaged Mary in conversation only to have the woman gush all over her, because her three girls were to be bridesmaids.

It was the first Amber had heard of it, and she downed another glass of champagne as more toasts were drunk to just about everyone.

When Sir David raised his glass and offered a toast to his son Mark who unfortunately could not be with them, Amber glanced warily across the cabin to where Lucas was in conversation with Tim. Her fiancé lifted his head, his black eyes clashing with hers as he raised his glass to her, and smiled a chilling smile that was more of a warning.

But, fortified with another couple of glasses of champagne and a delightful cold lunch to settle her nervous stomach, Amber had forgotten the moment by the time the aircraft landed.

'Are you all right?' Lucas asked softly, his hand on her elbow as he guided her towards one of the waiting cars.

'Yes, never better.' Amber flashed him a smile—somewhere over Europe she had given up worrying, or some time after the fourth glass of champagne. 'Where are we going or is that another surprise?' she asked blithely.

Handing her into the back seat of a luxurious chauffeur-driven, air-conditioned car, Lucas lowered his long length in beside her, and, casually throwing his arm over her shoulders, he hauled her into his side. 'We are going to the latest Karadines luxury hotel complex, about an hour's drive up the coast from Athens.' He looked down into her flushed, beautiful face and his eyes gleamed with triumph, and something else Amber was too inebriated to recognise.

'Does that suit you?' he asked with an indulgent smile.

Lucas Karadines could afford to be indulgent. He congratulated himself as he settled her pliant body more comfortably against him; his long fingers lightly squeezed her upper arm. He had her. Amber was here in his car, in his country, and tomorrow she would be his in every way known to man. 'Amber?' he queried, but her eyes had closed and she was fast asleep.

Amber's eyelids flickered half open and closed again. She nuzzled her head into the warm human pillow, blissfully aware of Lucas's arms enfolding her in a warm embrace.

She opened her eyes again, and let her lips brush against the strong brown column of his throat. Her tongue flicked out, and tasted the warm, smooth skin. Amber breathed in the familiar masculine scent of him and sighed with pleasure. She felt the tightening of his fingers at her waist and stirred, tilting her head back to look up into his much-loved face. 'Lucas,' she murmured his name, still in that no man's land between sleep and wakefulness.

Through half-closed eyes, she saw his dark head descending, the mobile mouth with just the hint of a smile, and her tongue stroked out over her softly parted lips in sensual anticipation.

His mouth covered hers, and she sighed her acceptance as his tongue gently explored the soft dark interior, and she reciprocated. His lips were firm yet sensuous, his touch so light, she mused languidly. His strong hand closed over her breast, and she groaned, the nipple peaking in instant reaction to his touch. She snuggled closer and let her own hand drop to his thigh and gently stroke upwards. She heard his hiss of breath and felt his instant reaction. His long, hard body was savagely tense; her slender fingers traced the outline of his rampant arousal through the fabric of his trousers. His dark head bent and he muttered something violent in Greek and captured her mouth again with a raw passion, a ferocious urgency that took her by surprise. Her head swam and she could hardly breathe. Fire scorched through her veins. She heard him moan, and the blast of heat was overpowering. With a violent curse Lucas lifted his head. Amber surfaced abruptly from a whirlpool of passion.

A blast of hot air *had* invaded the air-conditioned interior of the car. The door was open...

'Come on, you two, we are waiting.' A deep masculine voice laced with laughter echoed in Amber's head, and suddenly she was wide awake. Appalled at what she was doing, she jerked back and clasped her hands tightly together across her chest, staring into Lucas's dark face with horrified golden eyes.

'*Christo!* Don't move,' Lucas growled, his arms tightening around her, shielding his body with hers. 'Give me a moment,' he husked with one strong hand stroking slowly up and down her back, his breathing ragged. 'You have the most damnable timing, Amber,' he informed her, slowly withdrawing his arms from around her trembling body.

A rueful smile twisted his firm lips, but the heat in his hungry gaze as he stared into her upturned face was sent wild colour surging over her cheeks. Lucas still wanted her every bit as much as she wanted him. The realisation sent her into renewed shock.

'I must have been drunk,' she muttered, sliding back along the seat to her own side of the car, mortified that she had betrayed herself so publicly. For a moment she had travelled back in time to the younger Amber when she'd fallen madly in love for the first time and had believed her feelings were reciprocated. Hastily she lifted her hands and swept back the wild tumble of her hair behind her ears.

'Then I will have to make sure I feed you champagne for the rest of our lives.' Lucas drove raking fingers through his thick black hair, much the same as she had just done, and stared at her. Dark eyes met her bemused gold, his lips curved back over brilliant white teeth in a dazzling genuine smile, the like of which Amber had not seen in years, and her own eyes widened in wonder. 'But if you keep looking at me like that I think the champagne may be superfluous,' Lucas prompted softly. 'Come on.'

It was a very subdued Amber that stepped out of the car. How had she imagined for a second that she could marry Lucas and not go to bed with him, when a simple smile had her panting? Her knees felt weak and she was actually grateful when Lucas slid a strong arm around her waist as he introduced her to the man who had so casually interrupted them.

'This is Joe, my right-hand man, and tomorrow my best man.'

Amber looked up into the laughing grey eyes of the tall, brown-haired man. 'How do you do?' she said formally.

'Great for having finally met you,' he responded with a trace of an American accent.

'You're American,' Amber said stiltedly. If she had not been feeling so embarrassed she would have immediately liked the man.

'Greek-American and you are very English, and very beautiful, exactly as Lucas described you.' He smiled broadly. 'Pity he saw you first.'

'Cut that out, Joe; the lady is mine,' Lucas said possessively. Amber watched as the two men exchanged an expressive look, and then they were all entering the vast foyer of the hotel.

Immediately Amber's family surrounded them, while Joe, with a few swift commands, had their luggage taken care of. Lucas confidently listed the features of the complex at Sir David's request. Set in two hundred acres with its own golf course, shooting range, and private beach with every kind of water sport available, it was a holiday paradise. Private chalets were scattered all around the complex. But he had arranged for everyone to stay in a number of suites in the main hotel building, as it was more convenient.

Without a word Lucas took hold of Amber's arm and led her towards a lift. The doors swung open as if waiting for his arrival and he urged her inside.

For the sake of something to say, Amber offered, 'Joe seems a really nice man.'

The look Lucas cast her held a hint of wry acceptance and something more she did not recognise. 'Implying I am not?' he taunted gently.

'I never said that.' She tensed, suddenly feeling claustrophobic in the small enclosed lift.

'Relax, Amber—I was joking. All the ladies like Joe. The trouble is, he likes all the ladies. *All* being the operative word.' Lucas, his eyes glinting, flicked Amber a teasing glance, asking her to share his humour.

Lucas in a light-hearted mood was impossible to resist, and a reluctant smile parted her full lips. She could imagine Joe as a ladies' man with no trouble. He had the good looks and easygoing charm, and the banter girls the world over fell for.

'And of course you don't,' she mocked.

His hand reached out and caught hold of Amber's, spreading her fingers as he threaded his own through hers. 'No, I only want one.' And the look he cast down was serious, his black eyes penetrating on her lovely face. 'And I've got you,' he murmured, leading her out of the lift. Amber was powerless to control the sudden acceleration in her pulse, or to deny his hand holding hers was oddly reassuring.

Twenty minutes later she stood in the centre of the elegantly furnished sitting room, and looked around in wide-eyed awe. 'It's magnificent, Lucas.' She turned her beautiful face towards him and grinned. 'It's bigger than my cottage. I could live in here.' He had just given her a tour of the suite. From the long balcony with magnificent views over the bay, through the stylish bedroom with a king-sized bed, from which she had hastily dashed out into the bathroom, with double shower and whirlpool bath all in the finest marble.

'I'm glad you like it. My only regret is I cannot stop and share it with you now. But have patience, tomorrow will be a different story,' he declared with all the arrogance of a supremely confident man. 'And the experience will be all the more erotic for the anticipation, I promise.'

Amber flinched. After her performance in the car it was hardly surprising; he thought she was a pushover. But then Lucas was a typical alpha male, strikingly handsome, lethally sexy, wealthy, sophisticated, and great in bed, and the combination was irresistible. She doubted he'd ever met a woman in his life that would not be happy to fall into his arms at the first opportunity. But it galled her to think he thought she was one, and that he had to apologise for leaving!

She straightened her shoulders, her proud gaze narrowing on his face. 'Providing I am still here. After all, there is nothing to stop me changing my mind, a woman's prerogative and all that,' Amber pointed out. That should give the arrogant devil something to worry about.

Tall and powerful even in casual clothes, Lucas watched her, not a flicker of any emotion showing on his handsome, hard-boned face. 'I'm sure you can leave,' he said softly, moving swiftly across to where she stood. 'But you won't.' Tilting her chin with one long finger, he added, 'That is the second reason for your family's attendance at the ceremony. You might want to walk out on me, but no way will you walk out on them…' He shook his dark head. 'Leaving them dependent on my hospitality. I know you too well, Amber.'

Amber squirmed at her own stupidity. She had actually bought his fairy story on the plane about her family. His second reason was much more believable. The devious devil—in that second she hated him. 'You really are a swine,' she hissed. The fact that his assumption was also correct did nothing for her temper.

His perfectly chiselled features froze into impassivity, but not before she saw the flare of anger in the depths of the hard black eyes that held hers.

'It won't work.' Lucas's fingers tightened slightly on her chin. 'I told you earlier, I am not going to argue with you, so stop trying.' His thumb traced along her full lower lip, and she could not repress the shiver that rippled through her.

'You want me and I want you, so stop fighting it. With our history it is inevitable.'

'No,' she denied, but her body inexplicably swayed forward like a moth to a flame, her golden gaze captured by the simmering sensuality in his night-black eyes.

'Yes.' Lucas smiled a wry sexy twist to his firm lips. His hand dropped from her face. He ached for her with a hunger, a pain she had no knowledge of. But he dared not touch her again. Not yet! He'd made one mistake, and he was not about to risk making another until he had his ring safely on her finger. 'But not now—I have some business to attend to in Athens, but I will be back to take you to dinner at nine. If you need anything, speak to Joe or Reception.' Lucas bent and dropped a swift kiss on her full lips and left.

Tense and frustrated at her own inability to resist him, Amber paced the length of the room and back, her mind a seething mass of conflicting emotions. Was she a woman or a wimp? A few hours ago she'd been determined her marriage to Lucas would be in name only. But one touch and she melted like ice in a desert. And he, damn him, knew it!

By eight in the evening Amber was almost at boiling-point. The first shock had been Reception delivering a wedding dress to her room and a handful of bridesmaid dresses, closely followed by Julie and Mary and her daughters. Amber had stood in the middle of the room like a statue as the other two women had shoved the girls into masses of white froth while Julie had explained it had all been Lucas's idea. He was such a considerate man, she had rhapsodised.

Apparently, he had explained, because it was a second marriage for him Amber was being stubborn and insisting on keeping it low-key—a simple suit had been mentioned. But he did not want to deprive Amber of a white wedding. So he'd asked Julie to choose the gowns for the occasion.

Any thought of depriving the young girls of being bridesmaids or of doing a bunk on Amber's part had been quickly dispelled by the constant visitors to her room: her father, Mildred, everyone, and all in favour of the wedding.

Amber lay in the decadent marble bath, and steamed her temper as hot as the water. Finally she stepped out and, picking up a large fluffy towel, wrapped it around her naked body, and then, using the hair-dryer provided, she spent the next ten minutes drying her long hair. Walking back into the bedroom, she picked white lace briefs from the drawer and stepped into them. She didn't have much time and she wanted to be ready before Lucas arrived. Amber did not want him in her room again; once was enough for one day.

Quickly she withdrew from the wardrobe a blue silk jersey halter-necked dress, and slipped it over her head. Turning, she glanced at her reflection in the wall mirror, smoothing the clinging fabric down over her slender hips. The skirt ended a few inches above her knee, and she adjusted the bodice over her firm breasts, eyeing the cleavage with a wry look. Either she was getting fatter or the dress had shrunk in the wash. With a toss of her head, she dismissed her worries and slipped her feet into matching blue open-toed sandals.

It took only minutes to apply moisturiser to her smooth skin, a touch of mascara to her long lashes, and a plain pink lipgloss completed her make-up. With the ease of long habit, she brushed her long hair back behind her ears and let it fall loose down her back. She fastened the gold Rolex watch, a present from her father, around her wrist. Five to nine, she made it, and, walking into the sitting room, she picked up her purse and left.

Luck was with her, a lift was waiting. Amber walked in and pressed the down button and seconds later she stepped out into the foyer. Julie and her husband and the whole crowd immediately surrounded her. Joe appeared and, heading straight for Amber, he took her arm. 'You look sensational. Where's Lucas?'

'I don't know,' she told the truth. Then she did know, when a strong arm curved around her waist.

'I'm here, Joe, you can unhand the lady now. I've got her.'

Amber tensed, her heart missing a beat. Slowly she turned her head. 'Lucas,' she greeted him.

'Amber, darling, you couldn't wait, you had to come down to meet me—how sweet.' The devilish light in his dark eyes should have warned her. He curved her close into his hard body, crushing her up against him as his dark head swooped and his lips claimed hers.

Amber's pulse went from normal to the speed of light, and then he lifted his head; though he still held her hard against him and she could not help but be aware of his instant, shameless arousal. 'You're sex mad,' she muttered angrily. 'And you had no right to get Julie to buy a wedding dress.'

He silenced her by claiming her mouth again in a long passionate kiss, and when he finally let her up for air she was boneless. It didn't matter how often he touched her, it was always the same. There had always been a devastating chemical reaction between them, and that had not changed in the intervening years. 'What do you think you are doing?' she croaked.

'Not what I want to be doing, that's for sure,' Lucas said bluntly in her ear, and then very slowly eased her away from him.

Her face scarlet, Amber wanted the ground to open and swallow her up. How dared he embarrass her like that in front of her family? Eyes flashing angrily, she looked at Lucas and caught her breath. In a superbly tailored white dinner jacket and narrow black trousers that clung to his thighs and accentuated the long length of his legs, he looked magnificent. A perfect example of a man—the slight dilation of his pupils still evident, although he had controlled his body, only added to his aura of predatory masculine power.

'You look ravishing, Amber.' His dark eyes raked her from head to toe. 'I am a very lucky man.' Lucas smiled— for the audience, Amber thought, but said nothing as he caught her hand and tucked it under his arm.

Dinner was probably superb, Amber decided almost two hours later. It was a pity she had no idea what she'd eaten. The *maître d'* had arranged for a long rectangular table to be set at one end of the elegant dining room so the whole party could eat together. Seated at Lucas's side at the top of the table, she had smiled and chatted and prayed for the evening to end.

'You must try this, *agape mou*.' Lucas's husky drawl

had all the women at the table swooning, while Amber felt like a cat on a hot tin roof. If he put his finger in her mouth one more time she swore she would bite it off.

Finally, when the meal was over and he called her his love for the umpteenth time, and let his long fingers stray over her breast supposedly to smooth back a strand of her hair, Amber turned in her seat and raised her golden eyes to his. 'You are so good to me, Lucas,' she said, and delivered a hard kick to his shin under the table.

Lucas threw back his head and laughed out loud. 'Really, Amber, you are priceless!'

She wasn't priceless, she was furious and frustrated and tingling all over in a semi-permanent state of arousal, because of his tricks.

'Hey, cut us in—what's the joke?' Joe asked with a grin.

'Private, strictly private,' Lucas responded, and settled gleaming dark eyes on Amber. 'It is only between my fiancée and I. Isn't that right, Amber?'

To everyone else it was a casual comment, but to Amber, with his intent gaze lingering on her face, it was very definitely a warning. Their war was private and nothing must upset the success of the evening. She picked up her wineglass and drained it, avoiding his eyes.

'By the way, Lucas, you will have to leave before midnight,' Sir David remarked as they were all being served with coffee after the meal. 'Traditionally it is unlucky to see the bride before the ceremony on the day of the wedding.'

'Well, I am all for tradition, so at midnight I'll make my way back to my lonely bed,' Lucas drawled with mock sorrow, and everyone laughed, except Amber who could only manage a stiff smile.

The urge to smash through the smooth façade he

showed to their guests raged through her. How could they not see the deception behind the clever, striking face? The feeling of being trapped was almost overpowering and she sighed with relief when a trio of musicians arrived and took up positions on the small stage set at the back of the small square dance-floor at one end of the elegant dining room and started to play. Chairs were pushed back, and to Amber's delight Tim appeared at her side.

'Dance with me, Amber. We have hardly had a chance to talk,' Tim asked. With a brief glance at Lucas, he added, 'If you don't mind.'

'Of course he doesn't mind,' Amber answered for Lucas, leaping to her feet. To escape Lucas's overpowering presence for a few moments was just what she needed. Grasping Tim's hand, she almost dragged him onto the dance-floor.

The lights had been dimmed and quite a few people were dancing. Amber slipped into Tim's arms, and felt as if she were home. 'Thank God!' she sighed, and, looking up into his familiar face and sparkling blue eyes, she smiled her first genuine smile of the evening. 'It's great to see you; I had no idea you were coming.'

'Lucas called me last week and told me your good news. My favourite girl getting married! How could I refuse? Then again, your fiancé is a very persuasive man, I doubt anyone dares refuse him.'

'You've got that right,' Amber said with feeling, her smile vanishing.

'Hardly the response I would have expected from a woman in love,' Tim stated quietly, and, tightening his arms around her waist as they moved slowly to the music, he asked, 'What's wrong, Amber?'

'Nothing,' she murmured. It wasn't fair to involve Tim in her problems.

'Come on, it's me, your best pal. I know you better than you know yourself. I've watched you all night—your laughter was forced and your smile strained. That is not like you at all. You're the most genuine person I know.'

Moisture glazed her eyes. 'Thanks for that, Tim.' And suddenly she had the overwhelming need to confess everything. 'You're right, Tim.' And as they moved around the dance-floor she told him about Spiro's will and the consequences of it.

'That's Spiro for you,' Tim remarked dryly. 'Even in death he causes mayhem. But that is not your problem, Amber. All you need to ask yourself is, do you love Lucas? Everything else is superfluous; believe me, I know.'

'Yes, I never stopped loving him,' Amber admitted huskily, the sadness in her voice unmistakable. 'But Lucas had never loved me. I thought he did, and you know what happened. He fell in love with someone else.'

'I'm not so sure about that,' Tim contradicted. 'Lucas Karadines is a very traditional Greek male, and at the time he would have done anything to humour his father—the man was dying. He went to great lengths to hide Spiro's sexuality from the old man. Marrying the girl his father approved of would seem a likely thing for Lucas to do. As for loving her, he might have thought he did, but we men are just as likely as women to mistake our true feelings.'

'Since when did you become such an expert on the sexes?' Amber asked dryly.

'Since I made a huge mistake with Spiro that could have cost me my life.'

'But you did truly love him,' Amber responded. 'I was there, remember.'

'No, it was friendship and infatuation, and the only reason I stayed so long was because Spiro, as the dominant partner, kept telling me we were in love. But once in New York and watching how he behaved, I discovered I didn't actually care enough to even be jealous, and I realised it wasn't real love I felt for him. I know the difference now. I have a new partner, David.' His blue eyes lit up with happiness as he continued. 'He has a picture-framing business in Newcastle and what we share is true love. So you see, Amber, we can all make quite horrendous mistakes.'

Amber looked up into his lovable face, believing him. 'I am glad for you, but it doesn't really help me. Lucas loved his wife—he can't even bring himself to talk about her death.'

'But she is dead, Amber, and she can't come between you any more. Lucas wants a flesh-and-blood woman.' He held her slightly away from him, his blue eyes roaming the luscious length of her, camping it up with mocking male appreciation. 'And you are certainly that!'

Amber grinned at his teasing; she could not help it.

'Look at him—he is watching me like a hawk.' Tim gestured with his head, and, glancing across the room, Amber saw Lucas rising up from the table, his whole attention fixed on her. 'Believe me, Amber, he wants you and badly. He and I had a long talk last week. I'm sure he loves you even if he does not want to admit it. Take a chance.'

'Take a chance on what?' Lucas's deep, melodious voice broke into the conversation. 'You are already taking a big chance, Tim, dancing with my fiancée for so long. If you don't mind.'

'My pleasure.' Tim grinned and, leaning forward, he dropped a swift kiss on Amber's nose. 'Go for it,' he whispered before placing her hand in Lucas's.

'Are you sure that guy is gay? I saw the way he looked

at you,' Lucas queried, slipping a long arm around her waist, and clasping her other hand in his, holding her close to his strong body.

Tilting her head back, she looked up into his oddly serious face. 'Jealous of Tim?' she prompted with a chuckle.

'I'm no fool; if your closest male friend had been straight I would never have invited him in a million years,' he declared bluntly.

Amber couldn't help it, she burst out laughing.

'I'm glad I amuse you,' Lucas said simply. 'I have been trying to all night.'

The hint of a smile quirked the corners of his mobile mouth as his hand laced with hers and raised it to his lips. He brushed a kiss along her knuckles, before moving her effortlessly to the soft strains of the music.

'Is that what you were doing?' Seducing her more likely, Amber thought, and slid a slender arm up around his neck, tangling her fingers in the silky black hair at his nape. 'I would have called it *teasing*.' She pouted and did some teasing of her own, relaxing against him, and moving her hips in an exaggerated sway to the rhythm of the music. Her golden eyes gleamed mischievously up at Lucas.

His black eyes glittered over her lovely face. 'Amber.' One hand caressed her back down her spine, curving her in closer to the hard strength of his body, and heat pooled in her belly. 'Watch it! You're playing a dangerous game,' his husky voice drawled as he curled their joined fists against her breast.

Her sensitive flesh swelled and her nipples peaked into tight buds against the smooth fabric of her gown as desire, sharp and physical, scorched between them. Amber could not drag her eyes away from his. She wanted him so much, she trembled. 'I don't play games,' she whispered, and then, with courage she had not known she possessed, she asked, 'but what about you?' He'd played with her emotions once before; she had no reason to suppose it would be any different this time.

CHAPTER NINE

LUCAS had hurt Amber so much before, it terrified her as she waited for his answer. But Tim had told her to take a chance; after all, Christina was dead and Lucas was very much alive.

Something she was made vividly aware of the next second as, dropping her hand, he placed his through the silken fall of her hair to curve around the nape of her neck and tip her head back. 'No, I never play games,' he contradicted fiercely while his other hand, low on the base of her spine, urged her hard against him. 'Does this feel like a game?' His lean hips moved urgently against her, making her aware of his arousal. 'Do you think I willingly walk around in this state aching for you? The chemistry between us is as strong as it always was, always will be.'

'Not always.' The memory of him walking out on her was ever present.

Lucas stilled, giving up any pretence of dancing. 'Yes, even then,' he confessed harshly. He knew exactly what she meant, and he was ashamed of his behaviour, but at the time he had been too blindly arrogant to see the truth. He had decided it was time he fell in love and married, and had set about doing it exactly the same way as he pursued a business deal. He had been so confident he'd been doing the right thing. Pleasing his father, and expecting it to please himself.

'No,' Amber denied. 'Don't bother lying.' It was all a game to Lucas, anything to get his own way. 'I was *there*, remember,' she prompted scathingly. 'You said I was dis-

139

gusting, a hedonist. You as good as called me a whore,'
she fumed, all the old anger and resentment bubbling to
the surface.

Lucas's arm around her waist jerked tighter. His superb
bone structure tautened and something that looked almost
like pain glinted in his night-black eyes. 'I was disgusted
with *myself*, Amber, never you. Spiro's statement after my
engagement party that he was going to marry you had
enraged me, but deep down I suspected it was a lie.
Though it did not stop me using it as an excuse to see you
again. I had to make sure, I told myself, and, seeing you
so strong and defiant and desirable, I was lost to all reason,
consumed by such an irresistible passion that nothing else
mattered. I betrayed my fiancée, and I hated myself, so I
took it out on you. You have to believe me, and if I hurt
you with my brutally callous remarks I am truly sorry.'

If... He'd almost destroyed her, and he had not even
realised he'd been doing it...and yet, looking up into his
taut, sombre face, she believed him. Plus he had actually
done it, actually managed to say *I'm sorry*. For once the
arrogant, all-powerful Lucas Karadines was admitting he
was as susceptible to making a mistake as any ordinary
mortal was.

'Amber, I swear it was never my intention to hurt you,
then or now. We are getting married tomorrow.' His sensual mouth twisted wryly. 'Can we at least try to forget
the past and make it work? Make it real.'

His strong hand moved restlessly up and down her spine
and with the heat, the strength of him enveloping her, she
was tempted to agree.

'Please,' Lucas pleaded for the first time in his life. He
had behaved like the worst kind of hide-bound, chauvinistic fool when he had let this woman go. Equating great
sex with a girlfriend, but talking himself into loving what

he had considered an acceptable wife. Now he knew better: love was an illusion; lust was reality. He might not like the way Amber affected him so instantly. But he was not fool enough to believe he could live with her without making love to her. He was no masochist.

Amber saw his eyes darken. She knew what he wanted, what he was asking, and was dizzied by the sensations snaking through her. She placed a hand on his shirt-front to steady herself. Involuntarily her hand stroked up over the front of his chest, feeling the uneven pounding of his heart beneath the fine silk of his shirt. He wanted her, and in all honesty Amber knew she ached for him. She was older now and she no longer saw Lucas as the perfect, infallible, godlike male she had years ago, yet she still loved him.

She was under no illusion as to why he was marrying her. He was not prepared to trust Amber's word she would sell Spiro's shares to him. It was ingrained in his character to trust no one; an asset in the top echelons of the business world, but on a personal level more of a liability, though Lucas would never see it as such. But the real question was, was she mature enough to forget all her old bitterness and anger, and take what was on offer? A few months of sexual pleasure at least, and maybe, just maybe Lucas might come to love her. Dared she take the chance?

'Amber...' his long fingers tangled in the silky gold locks of her hair, he urged her face to his '...what do you say?'

She could say no! And deprive herself of six months of pleasure and probably the only sex she would get in her life. She looked into his eyes, and was fascinated by the tinge of vulnerability that even the sensual hunger blazing in their depths could not hide. Or she could say yes! And pray she was mature enough to walk away with her pride intact when the time came.

Her golden gaze meshed with his. 'Yes, I suppose…'

Whatever else she might have said was lost as Lucas covered her mouth with his own, his tongue prising her lips apart, thrusting and tasting with a simmering sensuality, again and again.

'This is becoming a habit,' a laughing Joe exclaimed. 'Break it up, you two, it is late.'

Lucas groaned, and lifted his head. He eased his hand from Amber's nape but still kept his arm around her waist. 'We appear to be the floor show, sweetheart,' he husked, brushing the long fall of her chestnut hair carefully back off her face.

'Oh, heavens!' Blushing bright red, Amber tried to ease away, horribly aware the music was no longer playing, and everyone was watching them with varying degrees of amusement.

Lucas grinned and, clasping her around the waist with both hands, he stepped back, his dark eyes, blazing with masculine triumph, flicking over her. 'It's all right, you look decent,' he murmured huskily. 'But Joe is right. It is late, and I have to leave you before the witching hour, according to your father. If I want to be lucky, and I *am* going to be lucky tomorrow night…' He arched one ebony brow wickedly.

Amber's blush could have lit the room. She walked back to the table with Lucas on legs that shook. Any thought of trying to pretend she was immune to him was banished for ever from her brain.

'Well, any lingering doubts I had about the haste of this wedding are well and truly put to rest, old man.' Sir David slapped Lucas on the back. 'But in future I would try to be a little more circumspect, if I were you.' He chuckled.

'I will, Sir,' Lucas agreed and the two men exchanged a very masculine smug grin. 'And look after Amber for me until tomorrow.' Bending his dark head, he pressed a swift kiss on her brow. 'Go to bed. It's late.'

She did not need looking after, nor did she need to be told to go to bed. But, then again, after the exhibition she had just made of herself, maybe she did.

Noon the next day Amber stood in front of the dressing mirror, and barely recognised herself. The sides of her long hair had been swept up into an intricate crown of curls threaded through with perfect white rosebuds and tiny satin ribbons, and the rest left to fall in gentle curls down her back. Her make-up was light but perfect. The wedding dress was a dream, the soft fabric draped narrowly across her shoulders, exposing just a hint of the creamy mounds of her breasts. Cut on the bias, it shimmied across the shapely length of her body to end at her ankles in a scalloped border embroidered in a rose pattern. She glanced around the havoc of the room, and smiled at the three young bridesmaids. They were standing in a stiff line, terrified of spoiling their finery; their dresses flounced like crinolines from fitted waists and copied the embroidery of the bridal gown.

Someone handed Amber a posy of ivory roses mixed with baby's breath and her father appeared at her side, resplendent in a pale grey suit.

'You look beautiful, Amber. I am so proud to be your father and I want you to know—I deeply regret all the wasted years when I was not there for you. Especially now when I am losing you again.' Tears glazed her golden eyes, and she sniffed as he took her hand and tugged it under her arm, adding, 'Time to go, Amber.'

Suddenly the enormity of what she was about to do hit her and for a second she panicked. 'But I don't even know where I am going,' Amber wailed.

Hoots of laughter greeted her comment and someone shouted, 'Joe has it all arranged,' as everyone moved towards the door.

Amber gasped—it was like something out of a Hollywood movie. Joe had done a superb job. A secluded corner of the vast gardens of the hotel was set out with chairs for the guests, the centre aisle leading to a raised dais covered with a delicate arched pergola beautifully decorated with hundreds of tiny white roses and vines.

The three little girls were solemnly walking down the aisle sprinkling rose petals from decorated baskets, and then it was Amber's turn.

Straightening her shoulders, Amber took a tighter grasp of her father's arm and stepped forward, her gaze fixed on the tall black-haired man standing with his back to her in front of the celebrant. Then he turned to watch her approach.

The clear blue sky and the blinding sun added to Amber's feeling of unreality and only hazily was she aware of the guests seated either side of the aisle, her glance captured by Lucas's intent, unwavering gaze. He was magnificent in an immaculate pale grey silk suit, and white shirt, and a grey silk tie shot through with blue. His thick black hair had been neatly trimmed and he looked exactly what he was: a mature, sophisticated Greek businessman, while Amber, on the other hand, was shaking like a jelly with nerves.

It was stupid, she knew. She'd lived with the man for a year, for heaven's sake! She should not be intimidated by what was really a simple civil ceremony—it was not as if she were marrying him for life.

But as her father left her at Lucas's side, Amber knew that for her it would be a life sentence. She would never love any man the way she loved Lucas. Looking up into his darkly handsome face, she had to blink hard to stop emotional tears blinding her eyes. 'You've had your hair cut.' She said the first thing that came into her head to cover her emotions.

His black eyes widened in surprise and then his lips parted over brilliant white teeth in a beaming smile. 'I'm so glad you noticed,' he murmured for her ears only. 'I was afraid you might have changed your mind, and not deign to look at me.'

Lucas afraid was a novel notion, but she did not have time to dwell on it as she listened to the celebrant and surprisingly a priest appeared. Amber was too nervous to take much in but she must have made the right response. Lucas took hold of her hand and slipped a gold band on her ring finger, and indicated she should return the favour by placing a ring on his finger. Surprised he would want to wear a ring, she glanced up and was captivated by the blaze of emotion in his dark eyes. She hesitated for a moment and Lucas covered her hand with his free one and helped her slip the ring on his finger.

'My wife at last,' he murmured. Then gathered her into his arms and kissed her. It was a kiss like no other, firm but tender, sensual and seeking. Amber's head swam, her pulse raced, her full lips parting to welcome him.

'Break it up, you two. You still have plenty of time for that later. We have to party.'

To Amber's chagrin, once again it was Joe who'd brought them back to their senses. Flushing scarlet, she glanced wildly around at all the grinning faces, then tilted her head to look up at Lucas.

'You really are a blushing bride now,' Lucas said wryly. 'My fault—I got carried away.' Her heart gave a curious lurch at seeing the glittering intensity of his gaze, igniting sparks of sensual awareness through her whole body. 'But you are the most beautiful bride. I don't have the words to tell you how much it means to me you are mine.' His voice was thickened with emotion and he lifted her hand to his mouth and kissed the wedding band.

Amber wanted to believe his sentiment was genuine but, tearing her eyes from his, she mumbled, 'Yes, well, thank you.' She loved him but trusting him again was something else…

The speeches were over, and the wedding reception had taken on the air of a joyous feast. Lucas led Amber from one table to another to say their goodbyes. Amber was stunned at the number of people. Lucas appeared to have a remarkable number of friends, all Greek, and as she could not speak the language she simply nodded and smiled.

It was a relief when Lucas curved his large hands possessively around her shoulders and murmured, 'It's time you changed, we have to leave in a few minutes.'

'Leave. What for?' Amber queried. She glanced up and saw the amusement gleaming in his black eyes, and she simply stared rather helplessly back at him.

Lucas chuckled. 'Because the honeymoon is the best part of the wedding, my sweet.'

Julie burst out laughing. 'Come on, Amber, I'll help you change.' Before Amber knew it she was back in the bedroom of the suite.

Amber removed her bridal gown, and with Julie's help managed to remove the rosebuds from her hair. Five minutes later her hair was brushed, but a little on the wild side because of the curls. Julie was holding an elegant cream trouser suit up for her inspection.

'A present from your husband. Put it on.'

A silk and linen mix—the designer label told Amber it was incredibly expensive. The tiny silk camisole that left her midriff bare prevented her from wearing a bra, but with the jacked fastened it looked great. Chic casual and Amber wondered again where they were going. Two hours later she knew…

'So. What do you think? ' Lucas demanded, his black eyes alight with pleasure. 'Isn't she beautiful? I only bought her a few months ago, and I have not really had the time to try her out.' The pride and admiration in his voice were unmistakable.

Amber stood on the wooden deck and looked around. They had driven to a marina along the coast, and Lucas had just finished showing her around his latest toy—a thirty-foot motor cruiser.

'The joy of this is…' Lucas continued, his handsome face animated '…it does not need a crew, I can handle it myself, and the two of us will have no problem. Everyone sails around the islands, but I thought we could explore the mainland coastline, stopping off to see the places of interest, of course. It will be fun.'

He was wearing cream cotton trousers and a short-sleeved blue checked shirt. His legs were planted slightly apart on the deck. He looked so sexy, the sheer size and virile strength of him hit her like a punch in the stomach. Amber hadn't the heart to tell him she'd never been to sea before, other than on a ferry. For all she knew, she might get seasick.

'It sounds very nice, but I don't know much about boats,' she managed to say, suddenly realising just what kind of intimacy she was inviting if she agreed. She had seen the galley was small and compact, the saloon was beautifully furnished, and comfortable, but not huge. There was one large cabin with a very big bed, a shower and toilet. One small cabin with a couple of bunks and a lot of computer equipment.

'You don't need to.' Lucas caught both of her hands and cradled them in his own. 'I will teach you everything; you will love it, I promise.'

Standing barefoot on the deck, Lucas had insisted she remove her shoes, declaring they were unsuitable for the wood deck, and, with the warmth of his hands enfolding hers, she felt totally out of her depth in more ways than one. 'Yes, well...'

Lucas drew her into his arms, pulling her close so the top of her head tucked under his chin. 'Great. I had intended taking you to a very exclusive holiday island in the Bahamas, but yesterday when I saw your suitcase and you said you only needed a few clothes because you intended to bum around and do nothing, I thought of this.'

'I missed out on the Bahamas!' Amber exclaimed, flashing a mock protesting glance up at him, only to chuckle when she saw his teasing expression.

'I will take you another time,' Lucas countered, his dark eyes suddenly serious. 'I am going to do everything in my power to make sure you never miss out on anything life has to offer ever again.' He gathered her in even closer, and Amber was utterly transfixed by the burning desire in his eyes. A desire Lucas was doing nothing to hide.

She gasped, a soft sound, her lips parting as awareness shivered though her. Lucas lowered his mouth down to hers, and stole the breath from her body.

The kiss didn't last long, but when he drew away and said gruffly, 'Let's go below,' with a nod of her head Amber mutely agreed.

Lucas wanted her, and, dear God, she wanted him. She wanted to feel that sensuous mouth on her own again, those elegant hands on her naked flesh, feel once more the exquisite pleasure only Lucas could provide. There was no point in denying it.

He didn't give her time to change her mind. Clasping her hand, he led her quickly down into the living quarters. His steps were urgent as he hurried her through the salon and into the bedroom.

Kicking the door shut behind him, he let go of her hand and reached for her, quickly opening the buttons of her jacket, and he slid it down her shoulders to drop unnoticed on the floor.

Amber gasped, her breathing was fractured, her pulse was racing, her breasts swelling against the silk camisole. His smouldering eyes burned a path down her body, taking in the bare midriff; at the same time his fingers deftly dealt with the fastening of her trousers. His dark head bent towards her and her lips parted in anticipation of his kiss, but instead he moved lower, his mouth closing over the tip of her silk-encased breast, sucking on it, then biting and nibbling, and her spine arched on a fierce shock of sensual pleasure.

He dropped to his knees, taking her trousers and briefs with him while his mouth slid from her breast to lick down over her bare midriff, and circle her navel, and lower.

'No, Lucas,' she tried to protest at the ultimate intimacy, even as a low erotic moan escaped her. His head jerked up, his black eyes smouldered. Standing up, he whipped the camisole over her head, and tumbled her naked body backwards onto the bed.

Lucas looked down at her, his passionate gaze roaming over every inch of her body as he swiftly stripped naked. 'You're perfect,' he growled, falling down to join her on the bed.

'So are you,' Amber murmured throatily, the sight of his big tanned body, hugely aroused, sending shivers of pleasurable anticipation arching though her.

He leant over her, his mouth capturing hers in a savagely hungry kiss that she welcomed like a sex-starved slave, her tongue tangling with his, relishing the devouring need that had always been between them. His hand slid down over her breast and stomach, along her slender thigh, parting her long legs. He touched her, and she shuddered, her body responding with a wanton life all of its own. She grasped his broad shoulders, her slender hands tracing down his long back, feeling the satin-smooth skin burning beneath her fingertips. She wanted him, wanted him now with a fierce, primitive need.

He broke the kiss. They fought for breath, his dark eyes holding hers asking the question and he saw the answer in her luminous golden gaze. With a low growl he lowered his head and sucked one rigid nipple into his mouth. Her back arched off the bed, and she was lost in the fiery sensations flooding through her. She never heard her own little whimpering cries of pleasure, as with hands and mouth Lucas ravished every inch of her body.

'You want me.' Lucas shifted his weight between her thighs, his arms straining either side of her pulsing body.

She was lost to all reason, her eyes burning like molten gold clung to his. 'Yes, yes, yes,' she pleaded, and involuntarily she lifted her long legs and wrapped them around his lean waist. Lucas thrust into her in one strong stroke, and she cried out at the power of his possession. He was there, where she ached for him.

He filled her, and moved in her in a wild pagan rhythm. Her legs wrapped tighter around his thrusting body as she soared ever higher and higher. Her arms reached for him, pulling his head down close enough for her mouth to meet his. Her tongue sought to repeat the rhythm of their bodies.

Lucas threw back his head, his battle for restraint evident in the damp sheen on the taut bronzed features. He watched her eagerly, as he drove feverishly harder, his hands grasping her buttocks, holding her in a grip of steel as she reached the peak. Her keening cry rending the air as the incredible tension snapped, her tight, pulsing muscles convulsed inside her taking Lucas with her in a fierce dynamic surge of powerful release that shook his great body, totally out of control.

It was a frantic coupling and together they clung in the shuddering aftermath, until finally, their sweat-slicked bodies entwined, they both fought to breathe air into laboured lungs, the pounding of two hearts together.

Amber let her arms fall weakly to the bed as reality intruded. But it wasn't love and she had to remember that, and she tried to move.

Lucas rolled off her, and, lying down beside her, he gathered her tenderly into the curve of his body. She tried to ease away, but he hauled her closer. 'Lie still and let me hold you for a while,' he rasped in a throaty voice. 'My Amber, my sexy wife,' and the satisfaction in his tone was unmistakable.

'Wife,' Amber murmured, her golden eyes widening in surprise as she glanced up at him. The *sexy* she did not like at all—it reminded her too much of their past affair. But the *wife* she did like. Amber Karadines had a nice ring to it.

'Why the surprise?' Lucas grinned and, leaning over her, he kissed her very gently. 'We have just consummated our marriage, and that does make you my wife,' he drawled huskily. 'And if you give me a moment I will prove it to you all over again.' His eyes held hers, glinting with amusement, and Amber could not look away.

His suggestion of a repeat performance was enough to make her stomach curl and her breasts tingle, in shameful awareness of his promise of more sensual delights to come. 'I thought we were supposed to be going out to sea,' she reminded him, to take her mind off more erotic thoughts.

'I know,' he declared with a rueful grin. 'I'm beginning to wonder if a cruising holiday was such a great idea with only me to steer the boat.'

'Serves you right.' Amber laughed. 'You will be stuck at the wheel all day and night.'

'No way.' His head bent and he captured her mouth with his own.

Her lips parted, and her senses stirred again, a slow, deep, salacious curl of excitement that unfurled from her belly to ignite every nerve-end in her body. Lucas thought she was sex mad, always had. Why try to deny it? she wondered with stark reality—after all, this was what she wanted. She let her hands slide up over the bulging biceps to the wide shoulders and up to tangle in the thick black hair, and she held his head to hers and returned the kiss with equal fervour.

It was dark when Amber opened her eyes. She rolled over onto her stomach and discovered she was alone in the big bed. Then she realised the low noise she could hear was the sound of the engines, and the gentle motion of the boat told her he had put out to sea. Struggling to a sitting position, she surveyed the tangled mass of sheets, and her own slightly bruised naked body. She was just reaching for a sheet to cover her with when a light flicked on. Blinded by the light, she blinked for a moment.

'Good, you're awake. Come on.' Lucas smiled, walking over to the bed and lifting her bodily out of it.

'Wait a minute, what do you think you are doing?'

He lowered her down the length of his long body, and, with her feet on the not-so-firm floor, she glanced up at him. 'What time is it?'

'Time you started work, sailor. Hurry and get dressed

and meet me on the deck. If I stay here much longer—' his sparkling black eyes slid lasciviously over her naked body '—the boat will probably run aground.'

Ten days later, Amber leant on the rail of the boat with a cup of coffee in one hand, idly surveying the approaching shoreline. She had just showered and put on a fine lawn sarong skirt in blue and white with a blue bandeau around her breasts. Her long hair hung down her back in wet strands, because Lucas's precious boat with all mod cons did not possess a hair-dryer.

Stifling a big yawn, she lifted the cup to her mouth and took a sip. She grimaced as she swallowed. She needed the caffeine—an unrestricted diet of sex, sex and more sex could be pretty exhausting. For the first four days of their honeymoon, Lucas had anchored the boat in a secluded cove and they had lived on sex and the provisions on board. Lucas was almost insatiable, more so than she re-membered, and, being brutally honest, she was no better herself.

He only had to look at her a certain way and they were straight into bed, or not necessarily the bed—the salon, the galley, the deck, a beach, even the sea, which she was surprised was possible. Maybe Lucas had been right about her all along—maybe she was a sex fiend, but then what did that make him?

She drained her coffee-cup and sighed. He certainly did not love her, the word hadn't been mentioned. Sometimes when she felt him deep inside her, possessing her, de-vouring her completely, she had to bite her tongue to stop crying out her love for him.

The tour of the Greek coastline had been a joke. The only sites Amber had seen were the sea and a naked Lucas. Her lips curled in a secretive smile—not that she was complaining. Lucas was fun to be with, and an experienced and inventive lover, and no woman could have dreamed of a more passionate honeymoon. And they had actually managed to travel through the Corinthian canal a couple of days ago.

They had stopped in the town of Corinth, and dined out for a change, and now they were heading for Karadines Island, and home.

Home was such an emotive word, and Amber felt longingly of her own little house in England. Amber was beginning to have severe doubts about lazing around all summer. It was all right for Lucas—he was going back to work after the weekend. He had told her last night. He had everything arranged: they would live on the island, and Lucas would travel into Athens most days by helicopter, but when he had to travel further afield Amber would go with him—at least until the children arrived, he'd laughed.

Amber had been stunned to think Lucas was actually considering her as the mother of his children. Or had he been joking…? She wasn't sure and so she'd mumbled something and changed the subject.

Before she'd left England she'd visited her doctor and started taking the pill, because, though loath to admit it, she'd known a platonic marriage was never going to work between them. And she wasn't fool enough to risk getting pregnant, much as she would love to have his child, until she was sure their relationship was going to last beyond the probate of Spiro's will. Lucas had let her down before, and she still didn't trust him…

Two large hands slid around her slender waist. 'Time to take up position.'

'What position would that be?' Amber queried teasingly as she turned in his arms to face him. He looked good enough to eat, showered and shaved and dressed in white tailored shorts, and pale blue short-sleeved shirt, and his sensuous mouth curved in a wicked smile.

'How about over the rail?' Lucas prompted, elevating one dark brow enquiringly. 'I think that's one we have missed.' His head dipped and he kissed her, and in an exaggerated gesture bent her back over the rail.

'No, no,' she squealed with laughter as he nuzzled the side of her neck. 'I was only joking.'

'I wasn't,' Lucas drawled mockingly, allowing her to stand up.

'You're incorrigible.' Amber shook her head, but grinned.

'I know. We will save the rail for later. In the meantime would you go to the stern of the ship and be ready to throw the line? We are going to dock in a few minutes.'

Only then did she notice they were a lot nearer the shore. She could see the tiny harbour, and she was vividly reminded of her other visit here with Tim and Spiro. It seemed a lifetime ago now…

Twenty-two and in love for the first time, the only time. Full of confidence and dressed up to the nines, she'd set out to make Lucas Karadines notice her. Hoping and praying he would fall in love with her, and they would live happily ever after. Then believing he had, she'd been bitterly disillusioned when their relationship had ended.

Who would have thought years later she would be coming back as Lucas's wife? Was she making the same mistake again? Amber wondered. No, because it wasn't the same. She was no longer a young, trusting fool; she no longer wore her heart on her sleeve. She and Lucas had a mature adult relationship based mostly on sexual attraction and a growing mutual respect. She kept her love and her innermost thoughts to herself. Perhaps she had finally grown up emotionally…

How times change, Amber mused sadly, her hazel eyes hazing with moisture. She was no longer the carefree girl who had first arrived on this island, but at least she was here. Poor Spiro was dead, and the woman Lucas had really loved, Christina, was also dead, both long before their time. Amber was the lucky one. She had a chance at a good marriage. It was up to her to take it. Life was too short for regrets.

CHAPTER TEN

'THROW it, Amber. Amber!' Lost in her thoughts, Amber had forgotten what she was supposed to be doing until an irate Lucas appeared at her side, grabbed the rope from her hand and threw it, muttering a string of curses in Greek.

She looked at him, and felt her breath catch in her throat. His hair was rumpled, his big muscled chest was bare and he looked supremely male and infinitely desirable.

'What were you thinking of?' Lucas whirled to face her. 'We almost hit the pier.'

'Sorry.' Amber smiled up at him, and, stepping forward, she looped her arms around his neck and, stretching up, placed a swift kiss on his firm lips. 'Guess,' she murmured teasingly.

His arms clasped her loosely around the waist, his dark eyes lit with laughter. 'I'd take you up on that, but the welcoming party awaits.'

Before she could respond, a heavy-set middle-aged man hurried along the deck to meet them carrying two garlands of wild flowers in his hands.

As he approached Lucas greeted him, and, taking Amber's hand, said, 'This is Tomso, he runs the bar-cum-store, and is in charge in my absence—a sort of mayor.'

Amber smiled as Tomso insisted on placing the garlands of flowers over their heads and leading them ashore. 'What did he say?' she asked Lucas as they stepped onto the old stone pier. The row of about a dozen or more whitewashed houses lined one side of the earth road overlooking the bay were the same. But the twenty or so smiling faces of the locals waiting to greet them were a surprise.

'Every new Karadines bride arriving on the island has to be met with a garland of flowers; it's tradition.' Sliding an arm around her shoulders, and briefly kissing her smiling mouth, he added, 'We also have to walk to the villa.'

A great cheer went up as Lucas led her along the road, and suddenly Amber wondered if Christina had enjoyed the same welcome and her smile dimmed a little.

Sensing her withdrawal, Lucas looked directly into her eyes. 'What's wrong? Tired?'

'No, I just wondered how many other Karadines brides got to do this walk,' she replied flippantly.

'You're the first,' he conceded wryly. 'I should have added if we don't have a tradition we invent one.'

Amber's head jerked around and she looked at him with open-mouthed incredulity. 'You invent...' And staring into his sparkling eyes, she shook her head and grinned.

Hand in hand they walked up the winding path that led to the big rambling Greek-style house. Scarlet bougainvillaea made a brilliant splash of colour against one of the white walls. As they drew closer Amber could see the huge iron gates were open onto the forecourt with an ornate fountain in the centre.

'Come on, let me show you the house.' Lucas urged her inside out of the sun.

'I have been here before,' she reminded him easily.

He looked down at her, his dark glance moving intently over her lovely face. 'As a visitor years ago. Now I welcome you to your home, Amber.'

'And was it Christina's home as well?' She wanted to bite her tongue the minute she'd said it. But to her astonishment Lucas grinned and swept her up high in his arms.'

'Never,' he said adamantly. 'Christina was a city girl through and through. Nothing would persuade her to visit the island. But it's good to know you are jealous.'

Whatever she might have said was lost, as Lucas turned to introduce her to a plump lady waiting in the cool of the interior.

'This is Anna, she keeps the place running. If you want anything you just ask. She does speak a little English.'

Anna shook hands with Amber enthusiastically. 'Welcome, welcome. It is hot for you. You like a cool drink? Lemon?'

'Yes, thank you.' Amber looked around her. The impressive reception hall with its central marble staircase looked different, but she could not immediately think why. She turned enquiring eyes up at Lucas. 'It is different,' she said. 'But why?'

'Let me show you.' Grasping her hand in his again, he gestured with his free hand to ornate double doors set in one wall. 'Remember the sitting room? It has been extended into what was the study. The dining room, the terrace and everything else is the same. But I've had the opposite side extended by about thirty feet.' Then she realised the one wall of the hall that had been blank now had two doors set into it. He led her through one of them.

Amber stared around her in amazement. Pride of place went to a custom-made oak desk fitted with all the latest computer equipment. A long low cream hide sofa overlooked a large window that opened onto a vast expanse of lawn, and in the distance there was what looked like a stone patio area. She turned to look up at Lucas. 'This is your new study,' she surmised.

'No.' He folded his arms around her waist, his black eyes holding hers. 'This is *your* study. I know how much your work means to you and this study has everything you need to keep in touch with the world markets, and your office in London. Mine is next door. I did think of having one big study, but I realised if we shared one neither of us would get much work done. Do you like it?'

Like it! She loved it. Lowering her eyes from his, she swallowed the lump of emotion lodged in her throat. More importantly, she loved what it represented. Years ago he had objected to her work, and now he had done this for her. He was not quite the male chauvinist pig she had thought him to be. He understood her need to work, to be her own woman. Hope grew in her heart for their marriage. Building a study for her was not the act of a man who expected to be rid of her a few months later.

'Well?' he prompted when she took too long to answer.

'I love it,' she said simply. She could feel the threatening prickle of moisture in her eyes, and to hide her emotions she eased out of his embrace and walked back to the window and stared out.

'I knew you would.' Lucas followed, slipping a casual arm around her waist.

Amber leant into him, revelling in the hard heat of his body. 'And of course you are always right,' she teased.

'Not always.' He moved to her side, his eyes catching hers again. 'But I am trying, I want you to be happy here…' he lifted one hand, so he could gently comb his fingers through her long loose hair '…with me,' he husked and she trembled, her breasts swelling against her top.

'I think I will be,' she murmured, wallowing in the wonderful heady sense of elation she was experiencing as she stroked a hand up over his broad chest and felt his muscles ripple with pleasure.

'Good.' His black eyes moved lazily over her small face, the expression in the darkening depths anything but good; wickedly sexual, more like.

'Anna will be here any second,' Amber said, reading his mind.

'You're right.' Lucas grinned, stepping back. 'But I shall continue the guided tour until we reach the bedroom.' Looking out of the window, he added, 'There is no sea view, which is a plus for a study, as it would only be a distraction.' He indicated with his hand the patio area. 'But you do have a view of the heliport so you will know the moment I arrive home.'

Amber couldn't help but burst out laughing. Trust Lucas! He had given her a high-tech study so she could continue to work, but made absolutely sure she would know the second he was home. He hadn't changed that much after all...

'What's so funny?' One dark brow arched in genuine puzzlement.

'Nothing—nothing at all,' Amber said, shaking her head, her long golden hair shimmering over her shoulders.

Anna entered the room carrying a tray with the jug of lemonade and two glasses and, thanking the housekeeper, Amber filled the glasses and handed one to Lucas. 'Drink your lemonade and show me the bedrooms.'

His black eyes flared and he drank down the lemonade in one go. Reaching out to flick her hair back over her shoulder, he implored her to hurry up. Five minutes later he was lowering her down onto an enormous bed, and joining her.

'Nice bedroom,' Amber commented, running her fingers up into his hair, and then his mouth covered hers.

Clothes were ripped off, and with eager hands and hot and urgent mouths they explored and gloried in each other, until finally once more they reached the ultimate pinnacle of passion and then slid languidly into the heated comfort of the aftermath.

'All right, Amber?' Lucas's husky demand vibrated against her smooth cheek, as she lay sprawled on top of him.

'Better than all right,' she breathed against his chest, and, pushing herself up, she looked around. She spied her skirt, her *torn* skirt, and, glancing back down at Lucas, she added, 'But we have to stop doing this or I will very soon have no clothes left!'

'I have to go to Milan next week. Come with me and you can shop till you drop.'

She went to Milan with him, and Lucas bought her a complete new wardrobe, and on returning to the island she modelled the whole lot for him, including the lingerie, with countless interruptions.

It was lucky she had because over the ensuing weeks Lucas spent only three days a week in Athens, but numerous business colleagues arrived on the island. Though she had told herself she would not socialise, she did, and she was too much of a professional to greet smart-suited businessmen in cut-off jeans. She contacted her own office and discovered quite a few of her clients had insisted on dealing only with her. With the compliance of her boss, and the state-of-the-art equipment Lucas had provided, she quickly slipped back into work mode and when Lucas was in Athens she spent the time as hard at work.

As the weeks stretched into two months they developed an enviable lifestyle. They went swimming, sailed, ate together and slept together. They also talked, listened to music or sometimes simply sat companionably in the same room reading. The one thing they did not do was talk about their relationship and underpinning all their activities was the simmering desire for each other. Their lovemaking was great. They could not keep their hands off each other.

Amber wandered out onto the terrace and sat down on a conveniently placed lounger overlooking the gardens and the pool, and stared out at the sun-drenched blue of the sea beyond. Her marriage was working better than she had ever dreamed possible. She remembered their early-morning romp and a sensual smile curved her wide mouth. But was sex enough? she asked herself, chewing her bottom lip with her teeth. It was Monday and three weeks today she was supposed to return to England. She would have to go back anyway, because, although she could keep on top of her job as well from the island as England, her clients expected some personal contact, as did the other partners in the firm. She would miss this place, lazing around in only briefs and a cotton shirt, with the greatest lover in the world for company. What more could a woman want?

'Hi, beautiful, waiting for me?' Lucas leant over and brushed his lips lightly over her brow before sitting down on the lounger beside her, flicking open the buttons of his jacket and shrugging it off.

'Yes. But I didn't hear the helicopter.' Amber glanced across at him, and watched as he unfastened the buttons of his shirt and lay back with a sigh. He had been in Athens today and he looked tired—sexy but tired.

With his eyes closed, his long lashes curled on high cheekbones, his firm lips curved in a smile. 'That's because I came back by boat. The helicopter is out of service until Saturday.'

'But what about the rest of the week?'

Lucas dealt her a simmering look from half-closed eyes. 'The rest of the week, I am going to stay here with you.'

Amber rose to her feet and, leaning over him, she murmured, 'Promises, promises.' She pressed her lips to his, probing his mouth with her tongue. Lucas responded by slipping his strong hands up under the soft shirt she was wearing to cup her full, firm breasts with his palms, and groaning. 'This is what I came back for,' he confided hoarsely, and moments later they were in the shuttered coolness of their bedroom.

Amber threw off her shirt, and watched utterly enslaved as Lucas stripped off his, and then with a husky growl tumbled her naked onto the bed.

A long powerful thigh nudged hers apart and she wrapped her arms around his neck and kissed his mouth, his eyes, his shoulder, anywhere she could reach.

His long fingers teased her nipples, traced over her stomach and parted the soft folds of velvety flesh between her thighs. Amber groaned out loud, heat flooding through her, and he took her hard and fast, and she was with him all the way until their mingled cries of release left them absolutely sated in each other's arms.

'Do you think the hot climate in Greece has anything to do with making people feel sexy?' Amber asked lazily.

A great guffaw of laughter greeted her remark, and Lucas, propping himself up on one elbow, stared down at her. 'You know what I l...' And he stopped, an arrested expression in his black eyes. He focused on her flushed face, her swollen mouth, thick black lashes screening his gaze. 'What I adore about you, Amber, for all your brains and beauty, you can be so naive.'

Amber forced a grin to her lips, but for a moment there she had been sure he was going to say he loved her. 'Better naive than world-weary, like some I could mention.'

He didn't rise to her teasing but looked at her for a long while with disturbing intensity. 'You're right.' And, rolling off the bed, Lucas strolled over to the bathroom. 'I need a shower.'

Ah, well! Amber sighed happily. They had the whole week together. But she was wrong…

After dinner Lucas retired to his study to make a few calls and Amber headed for bed. Fifteen minutes later, showered and wearing a peach-coloured satin negligée, Amber walked back into the bedroom, the material floating around her as she moved. Tiny shoestring straps supported the bodice—a delicately embroidered web of fine lace revealing tantalising glimpses of her full breasts and dusky nipples. Outrageously sexy, it had been chosen for her by Lucas and Amber felt great wearing it. She crossed to the dressing table, and, opening a drawer, withdrew the small box that held her contraceptive pills, a dreamy smile on her face. Lucas would be joining her soon. Flipping open the top of a delicately lacquered box, she picked up a pill and lifted her hand to her mouth.

'What the hell are you doing?' Lucas's deep voice roared, and the box went flying through the air, pills cascading on the floor, and suddenly her wrist was caught in an iron grip. 'Drop it. Drop it now,' he said in a rough threatening voice, with menace in his dark eyes.

The single pill fell from her fingers, and Amber felt a frisson of fear run down her spine. She had never seen Lucas in such a violent temper.

He pulled her towards him, the strong dark planes of his face contorted with rage. 'What are they?' he demanded, fury in every line of his body. 'Tell me, damn you.'

She opened her mouth to speak but no sound came out. The tension in him was so strong that she shivered at the impact of it. She stared at him, and the violence leaping in his eyes scared her witless. Amber told herself she had no reason to fear him, she had every right to take birth control pills.

'Answer me, woman,' he raged, his hand falling from her hair to curve around her throat, tipping her head back. 'Tell me or so help me I'll—'

'You're hurting me.' She choked, the breath squeezed from her lungs.

Suddenly he released her, but he still held her wrist. She tried to jerk away, shaking from head to foot, but he forcibly pulled her closer.

'Birth control pills,' she muttered in a low, frightened voice.

'Not amphetamines,' Lucas grated between his teeth, some of the anger easing from his body. 'You're sure?' His simmering black eyes fixed on her face.

Some opinion he had of her that he dared suggest she would take drugs. Anger tightened her mouth, and she returned his look with a hard, level stare. 'They are my birth control pills,' she reiterated.

'My wife, and you—'

'Thought I was a junkie,' Amber cut in hardly.

She saw him stiffen 'One cannot be too sure nowadays.' His dark eyes were hooded and curiously blank when he added, 'You'd better pick them up, as you seem to think you need them.' Letting go of her wrist, he spun around and stalked off into the bathroom without another word.

Amber crawled around the floor trying to find her remaining pills, and then, placing the box back in the drawer, she climbed into bed. Lucas's reaction puzzled her—it had been out of all proportion, and totally out of character.

The bathroom door opened and Lucas approached the bed, a small white towel flung precariously around his hips, and with another towel he was rubbing his damp hair. Helplessly Amber's eyes trailed over his magnificent tanned torso, and she forgot their brief argument, her body warming at the sight of him.

Lucas slid into bed and, leaning over her, brushed a few strands of hair from her forehead, his fingertips stroking down the curve of her cheek. 'Do you like children, Amber?'

'Yes,' she murmured, but warning bells rang in her brain.

'So why the pill? You're a married woman,' he asked silkily, his dark eyes intent and a little speculative on her lovely face.

Amber didn't want this conversation, not now, not yet… Easing away from his side, she looked up at him, and, choosing her words carefully, she said, 'You told me to take it the first time we were together, so naturally I do now.'

'And if I told you to stop? If I told you I wanted you to be the mother of my child,' he suggested, 'how would you respond?'

Her heart missed a beat, but her own sense of self-preservation made her cautious. 'That it was not a very sensible suggestion if we are to part in a few months.' She waited with bated breath, hoping and praying for him to ask her to stay for ever, tell her he cared. She was disappointed…

For a space of ten seconds he didn't speak. She saw the muscles bunch at the edge of his jaw, and if she had not known better she would have thought he was shocked. 'That could be ignored,' he finally offered.

'Why?' She had to know. She had swallowed her pride once where Lucas was concerned and she wasn't doing it a second time. It was his turn…

'I'm forty-one, it is time I had a family, and you are twenty-nine next week. It makes sense.'

There was nothing in the world she wanted more than to have his baby, but the cold calculation in his words and his unsubtle reminder of her age were not what she had wanted to hear and her disappointment was intense. 'I'll take it under consideration,' she mocked, evading a direct answer. 'But right now, I'm tired, can we have this conversation some other time?'

'There is nothing more to say.' Amber flinched at the finality in his tone, the cold derision in the eyes that met hers, and when he turned his back on her and went to sleep she had a sinking feeling the honeymoon was over.

Wednesday afternoon she answered the telephone in her study, and smiled at the sound of her father's voice. She needed something to cheer her up, as her marriage was going down the pan fast. Yesterday Lucas had buried himself away in his study, only surfacing for meals. Last night they had lain in the same bed, but as far apart as it was possible to be. Amber could sense him both physically and mentally withdrawing from her and she could do nothing about it. But realistically she knew a relationship built only on sex was bound to fail. The only question was *when*?

Five minutes of listening to all the city and family gossip cheered her up.

'We had visitors at the weekend—your friend Clive.' Her father chuckled.

'Clive?' Amber responded in surprise.

'Yes, he wanted to know if you will be back for your birthday next week.'

'Not next week, but I will be back soon.' Amber didn't see Lucas standing at the open door of her study or the murderous expression on his face as he turned and left. A few minutes later she concluded the conversation.

Turning back to the computer, she tried to work. The

mood Lucas was in there was no point in joining him, she thought acidly.

'Are you busy?' The man occupying her thoughts walked into the room.

Amber swung around on her chair. 'Not if you can think of something better to do,' she teased with determined cheerfulness. He was wearing a beige linen suit, and the desperate thought occurred to her that, if she got him almost naked in the pool, perhaps they could get back to the way they had been. 'It's so hot I thought I might go for a swim.' Rising to her feet, she walked towards him.

'Don't let me stop you,' he said bitingly. Her golden gaze winged to his and she froze at the contempt she saw in his black eyes.

'I thought you might join me,' she said quietly.

His mouth twisted into a mockery of a smile. 'Sorry, but I have to go to Athens after all, something has come up.'

'I thought the helicopter—'

'It is repaired,' he said, cutting her off. Anger gleamed cold as ice in the darkness of his eyes, but there was reluctant desire too, and it was the desire she responded to when he pulled her into his arms and kissed her with a fierce, possessive passion. Then just as fiercely he put her away from him.

'I won't be back until Saturday. If you need anything, call me—Tomso has the number.' He strode out of the room.

What she needed he could not give her, she realised with a despairing sigh, the sound lost in the whirring sound of the helicopter arriving. He had not even said goodbye.

Amber watched from the window as the helicopter rose

in the air and vanished. It was happening all over again—Lucas running out on her. The truly sad part was, Amber realised stoically, she wasn't even surprised she had no faith in him. She'd been expecting it.

CHAPTER ELEVEN

AFTER spending the night alone, Amber was nowhere near as stoic. She missed Lucas desperately. She had not slept. She couldn't work, and finally mid-morning she decided to walk down to the pier. Tomso waved her into the bar and over a cup of coffee he rhapsodised in fractured English over Lucas and their marriage, informing her they had never seen Lucas so happy, and if anyone deserved to be happy he did after the terrible loneliness of the past few years.

Amber presumed Tomso meant the deaths of all Lucas's family members and it made her think. She had acquired a whole new family that had taken her into their home and hearts while Lucas had lost his. His grief must have been horrendous. Strolling back along the beach, she sat down on the hot sand and took a long, hard look at herself, and was not impressed at what she saw.

She claimed she loved Lucas, but she was too proud and too frightened of being hurt to tell him. But she was hurting now anyway. If she truly loved him, and she did, she should be declaring it from the rooftops, not hiding it as though it were something shameful. Was she really so lacking in courage?

As for Lucas, he had an inherent need to be in control at all times. He was a dynamic, arrogant man, but not a man to talk about his feelings or show them. He was a loner; he withdrew behind a cool, aloof mask at the least sign of challenge to his real emotions. Yet when they made love Amber was almost sure he was as overwhelmed as she was, but far too proud to admit it. But then so was she...

Lucas had hinted she stay with him and have his child. Perhaps that was as near as he could get to admitting he wanted her every way a man wanted a woman, and not just as the sex object he had once labelled her. Christina was dead, and Amber was pretty certain there was no other woman in his life. Dared she take a chance and tell him how she felt? Was she strong enough to cope if he rejected her love? The answer to both questions was yes.

The bible said, 'hope deferred maketh the heart sick,' and it was happening to her. Surely it was better to know the truth one way or the other and get on with her life? And, with that thought in mind, she had made her decision.

The following morning Amber dressed with care in one of her Milan purchases. A sleek white linen dress, with a slightly scooped neckline, buttoned from top to bottom and skimming her slender body from shoulder to mid-thigh, with a matching fabric high-heeled sandals and shoulder-bag to complete the outfit. Her long hair was swept up in a twist on top of her head, and even in the late summer heat she looked coolly sophisticated. She had talked Tomso into bringing her to the mainland by boat and he had also arranged the taxi to carry her to the tower block that housed the offices of Karadines International.

Getting out of the taxi, she hitched her bag on her shoulder and took a step towards the entrance and froze. She blinked and blinked again. It couldn't be—she was seeing things. The woman was dead...

'Amber, it's good to see you again. I was sorry to hear about Spiro, but I hear congratulations are in order, and, hey, Lucas isn't a bad old stick. Even after our divorce he still looks after me, though he does not have to. We have just been to see him.'

It was Christina, a slim, beautiful, positively glowing with life Christina, and obviously pregnant, accompanied by a very handsome young man whom she proudly introduced as her husband with love shining in her dark eyes.

The blood drained from Amber's face. She was poleaxed. She said something and it must have been okay, because a few minutes later she was standing on her own, her dazed eyes watching Christina and her husband walk down the street.

'Hi, Amber.' She vaguely heard her name and turned her head; it was Joe. 'Are you okay? You look like you've seen a ghost.'

'Maybe I have,' she said without thinking in her shocked state, her stomach twisted with nausea and sweat dampening her smooth brow.

'Funny! I'm glad to see you haven't lost your sense of humour. Lucas has been acting like a bear with a sore head for the last two days. For the sake of his poor beleaguered workforce, try and cheer him up, will you? You are going up to see him?

'Oh, yes.' See him! She was going to kill him... Lucas had lied...

'Come. I'll show you to his private lift.' With Joe leading the way, Amber stalked into the Karadines building. Joe ushered her into the small lift.

'It opens into his private office suite. I'll probably catch you later,' Joe said with a grin as the doors swished shut.

Amber sank back against the wall, her mind a mass of teeming emotional pain, humiliation, sheer disbelief. It was a horrible thought, but until now she had not realised how much she had counted on Christina being finally out of his life to win Lucas's love. Tim had told her to take a chance, but she had never had one... Lucas had told her his wife was dead. It was a lie of such magnitude no one with any sense of morality could forgive it. Not only was Christina alive and well, but she had divorced Lucas and married a gorgeous young man and was pregnant. But Lucas was still looking after her.

With blinding clarity Amber saw it all. It must have been a hell of a jolt to Lucas's colossal ego to be rejected by the woman he loved, the woman who had lost his child, and then to see Christina happily married and pregnant again.

Amber had felt sympathy for him and had hoped that once the grieving was past he would fall in love with her. Only last night she'd decided to tell him how much she loved him, and all the time the swine had lied to her. His request she have his baby took a much more sinister turn in the light of Christina's pregnancy. Lucas hated to lose at anything. If his ex-wife could have another child, then so could he. Lucas didn't care about her, Amber realised. She was obviously a convenient pawn to be used in the competition with his ex-wife, and Spiro's legacy was an added bonus.

Amber had been second best once in Lucas's life and she was damned if she would be again. She didn't need the lying, conniving pig, and she was about to tell him so. By the time the lift stopped Amber's overriding emotion was murderous rage.

Her golden eyes leaping with fury, she strode out of the lift, and on past a stunned-looking secretary who cried, 'You can't go in there,' as Amber thrust wide the door of Lucas's office, and slammed it shut behind her.

The object of her fury was sitting behind a large desk. His head shot up as the door slammed, his black brows arching enquiringly, and not a flicker of emotion disturbed his hard-cut handsome features. 'Amber, to what do I owe this honour?'

'Honour, honour!' she screeched, striding across to the desk and planting her hands flat on it. 'You don't know the meaning of the word, you devious, lying bastard.'

'Be careful what you say, Amber.' Lucas shoved back his seat and stood up, moving around the desk. 'A Greek will not allow anyone to cast a slur on his honour. Even you, my beautiful virago,' he drawled mockingly, but with a hint of steel in his tone.

'How could you?' she demanded wildly. 'How could you tell me Christina was dead? What kind of sick joke was that? You want to get down on your knees and pray for your immortal soul or you will surely go to hell.' She was in full flood now. Her golden gaze clashed with his. 'The night before our wedding Tim convinced me to take a chance on you growing to love me. After all, you were a man with a man's need and your first wife was dead. So I did.' Amber didn't see the brilliant flare of triumph in Lucas's eyes—she was on a roll. 'The other night when you flung my pills from my hand...' she accompanied the word with the gesture, knocking a desk lamp flying to the floor with a resounding crash, but even that did not stop her '...then you suggested I have your baby, I, idiot that I am, actually felt guilty for denying you. I spent all yesterday thinking how really you were a caring guy, but too shy to show your emotions!' A hysterical laugh escaped her. 'Shy! You don't have any genuine emotions, only devious plans!'

'Amber,' Lucas slotted in, 'you've got it all wrong.' Reaching out, he grasped her upper arms.

'No. I have finally got it right! After five long, miserable years I am over you. I actually came here today to tell you the opposite. What a joke! I got out of the taxi and, low and behold, risen from the dead on your doorstep I meet Christina, the woman you really love. God! How it must have dented your pride to have your young wife discard you. But I am through being a substitute for any woman.'

'Shut up and listen to me.' His hands tightened on her arms. 'You're screaming like a fish wife, and there is no need.'

His eyes were black but there was fire in them that mirrored the violent emotion in her own. 'Need. What would you know about need? Everything is sex and money to you,' she retorted, trying to pull free, but his grip tightened.

Suddenly aware of how close they were, she felt a trembling start deep in the pit of her stomach, and she stared at him in blazing, humiliating anger. 'I am through listening to you,' she said, feeling her hands clenching into fists at her sides. 'I am leaving you. I never want to see you again. As for Spiro's legacy, see my lawyer.'

His mouth curled in a chilling smile. 'Very convincing but don't pretend you're leaving on my account. I heard you yesterday on the telephone talking to Clive, telling him *not next week but soon*. Three nights without sex too long for you, Amber?' he asked with biting sarcasm.

Her hand flew out and slapped his face in blazing anger. His head jerked back and his eyes leaping with rage clashed with hers for a second, before he hauled her hard against him, his mouth crashing down on hers, kissing her with a raw, savage fury that left her with the taste of blood in her mouth.

She tried to struggle, but he was too strong, and when he finally lifted his head she stared at him with bitter, pain-filled eyes, tears burning at the back of her throat because his last crack had told her his opinion of her had never changed. She froze in his arms and pride alone made her tell him the truth.

'I spoke to my father yesterday. He mentioned Clive

had visited him, and as a friend asked if I was coming back for my birthday. A *friend* that is all Clive has ever been. But you,' she said, her lips trembling, 'you never saw me as anything but an easy lay. You have the mind of a sewer rat.' The tears she had restrained for so long filled her eyes; she blinked furiously, but one escaped down the soft curve of her cheek. 'And I am leaving you.' She tried to push him away, the tears falling faster now as the trauma of the last few days, few months, finally caught up with her and Lucas's callous comment had been the last straw.

'Oh, hell, Amber.' Lucas groaned, hauling her tight against him. 'Don't cry. I can't bear to hear you cry.' With one strong hand he stroked her back, while his other hand lifted to her face and his fingers smoothed the wetness from her cheeks.

She choked back a sob. 'I am not crying,' she murmured, but long shudders racked her slender frame.

Suddenly the door opened, and Lucas turned his head and said something violently to his poor secretary, but the interruption gave Amber the strength to break free from him, and, rubbing the moisture from her face, she fought to regain her self-control. She was not shedding another tear over the fiend, and on shaky legs she stepped towards the door.

'No, Amber. Please.' Lucas swept her up in his arms. 'You have had your say, now it is my turn.'

'What do you think you're doing? Put me down,' she demanded hoarsely.

'What I should have done years ago, but never had the guts,' Lucas admitted and, sitting down on the sofa, he held her fast in the cradle of his arms. His face was only inches away from hers, and the black eyes caught hers with brilliant intensity.

Even in her abject misery, to her horror, the scent, the heat of him invaded her senses, reawakening the familiar awareness she always felt in his presence. 'Let me go, Lucas. Your secretary.' She was grasping at any excuse; she had to get away.

'No, I am going to keep you here until you hear me out,' Lucas informed her bluntly. 'Even a condemned man is allowed to speak.' His features were harsh, brooding as he studied her tear-streaked face.

She nodded—she did not trust herself to speak. Better to hear him out and get out, before she broke down completely in front of him.

'Forgive me for what I said about three days without sex. I didn't mean it. But to hear the mention of Clive's name is enough to drive me insane with jealousy.'

He was jealous, and it gave her hope.

'But I believe you, I know you have to go back to London. You love your work, and I had every intention of taking you. I even got your father to purchase the old rectory for us in the village near his home. I thought we could split the year between Greece and England.' And tilting her chin with one finger, he looked deep into her tear-washed eyes. 'But I wanted it to be a surprise for your birthday.'

Surprised! She was amazed. 'You bought a house?' she murmured. He had been planning for their future together, including her career.

He nodded and continued. 'But I don't believe you meant what you said about Christina. Would you really wish her dead? Because that is what you implied.'

'No, never.' She found her voice. Horrified to think how callous she must have sounded. Then she remembered why she had behaved as she had. 'But you lied.'

'I never lied, Amber. That day in your office I told you

my father had died, and Christina had gone the next year. Perhaps my grasp of English is at fault, but since when had *gone* meant the same as *dead*?'

'Then why did you not tell me you were divorced?' she demanded huskily.

'What man wants to discuss the biggest mistake of his life,' he said slowly, and she felt his muscular body lock with tension, 'with the woman he loves?'

She was held in his protective arms, with the warmth of him surrounding her, and for him to suggest he loved her was the cruellest cut of all to her bruised heart. 'Please, Lucas, no more lies: you loved Christina, you told me so. You probably still do,' she said sadly.

His dark eyes locked on hers as if they would see into her very soul. 'No, I lied to you and myself, and I paid for it with the worst few years of my life.' His dark eyes clouded with remembered pain. 'It was my own fault, but the worst part is knowing in my arrogance I hurt you.'

He brushed her lips with his in a bittersweet tenderness that squeezed her heart. This was Lucas as she had never seen him before. 'I got over it,' she muttered.

'You should not have had to.' He eased her off his lap onto the sofa beside him as if she were the most fragile Dresden doll, and placed an arm around her shoulders, holding her turned towards him. 'I need to explain why I behaved the way I did.' His dark eyes clouded with painful memories. 'My mother was a stunningly beautiful woman.' Amber could believe that. Just look at her son!

'Men adored her. She had numerous affairs—her last one ended at her death of a drug overdose when I was thirteen.' Amber gasped—she had not known that.

'Yes, not very pleasant.' Lucas's lips twisted cynically. 'Though the man we were living with at the time was quite good about it. He gave me a thousand drachmas, and told me I was big enough to look after myself and not to think of my mother as a drug addict because she wasn't. She did not need to get high to be the sexiest lady around.'

'It must have been hard for you.' Amber was shocked, the image of Lucas as a young boy living such a life filled her soft heart with compassion.

'I don't want your pity, Amber,' he said hardly. 'I don't deserve it because I let my mother colour my relationship with you. I didn't see it at the time, but I realised it when it was too late.'

Amber sat up a little straighter—this insight into Lucas's character was so unexpected she could not help but be moved and she wanted to hear more.

'When you came to the villa the first time, you were not as I remembered. You had metamorphosised into an elegant, gorgeous girl who made no secret of what she wanted. I, to my shame, had asked you simply so I could fool Father into thinking you were Spiro's girl, and—'

'You don't need to explain—I know all about that.' Amber felt the colour rise in her cheeks; she had been blatant in her pursuit of Lucas.

'Of course, Spiro told you. Anyway, when we became lovers, although you were a virgin, you were so eager, so uninhibited, you were everything I had ever fantasised about. I wanted you morning, noon and night, and it angered me. I vowed never to be like my mother—addicted to sex—and yet around you I was. I had no control where you were concerned. The year we were together I deliberately forced myself to stay away from you for longer than I needed to, just to prove a point. Then, when I did come back early, you had no time for me, so I began to blame you. Stupid, I know, but though I enjoyed everything you had to give I convinced myself you were too sexy, too career-minded, too free-spirited to be anything other than a girlfriend. Too like my mother.'

His mother had a lot to answer for, Amber thought bitterly. She had coloured his view on relationships from a very early age. But she made no comment as Lucas continued.

'The odd occasion marrying you crossed my mind, I quickly dismissed the notion, and not least because I would also have had to tell my father you had never been Spiro's girl. And I had implied it to hide the fact he was gay. I was an arrogant, conceited bastard, I admit it. When the chance came to make a deal with Alex Aristides, I leapt at it. My father was delighted, and when I met Christina, I was at the right age to marry.' He shrugged his broad shoulders beneath his tailored white silk shirt. 'I am Greek; we are strong on tradition and family. I had just had an argument with you about work, and Christina appeared as a sweet, malleable female. Someone I could love and look after.'

'This is all very interesting, Lucas,' Amber cut in, 'but I really don't need to hear any more.' She was not sitting listening to him telling her how much he loved Christina yet again, and, rising to her feet, she was abruptly pulled back down onto Lucas's lap.

'Damn it, Amber. I am putting my pride on the line here.' He held her firm on his lap and his mouth swooped down on hers and he kissed her with a driven urgency that awakened the same response in her, so that in seconds she was flat on her back on the sofa with Lucas lying over her.

'I am trying to tell you I love you. I always have, being brutally honest.' He clasped her head between his large hands, forcing her to look at him, his black eyes dark and glittering with emotion. 'I knew the last time we were together in the loft but I wouldn't admit it, not even to myself.' He kissed her again. 'I knew when I walked into your office three months ago. But still I told myself it was just sex. I had behaved abominably towards you, and I didn't think you would give me the time of day, so I forced you into marrying me.'

'You wanted Spiro's shares,' she reminded him.

'You think so?' His mouth quirked in self-derision as he continued, 'I already have most of them, as you will discover when you hear from the lawyers. You knew Spiro—did you honestly think he would be able to hang onto his inheritance for one year, never mind five? He invested in every crackpot scheme his friends suggested, and then some. At least a dozen times he sold me blocks of his stock.'

'What, you tricked me?' Wide-eyed, she stared at him, her thoughts in chaos.

'Another lie.' His jaw clenched. 'Haven't you realised yet? I would lie, I would cheat, I would do anything to have you.' Lucas groaned, burying his head in the glorious gold hair. 'But, God help me, Amber, I do love you.'

If he did not marry her for Spiro's legacy, then… Amber reached up to him, her slender fingers lacing around the back of his neck, the blood pounding through her veins. 'I think I am beginning to believe you,' she whispered, incredulous hope growing in her heart.

'Spiro's will gave me the excuse to see you again. I took one look at you sitting behind the desk in your office, and I was determined to have you back in my life. When you told me you might marry Clive I was frantic. I freely admit I lied to get you back. I wasn't taking any chances.'

'But you told me you loved Christina.' Amber could not get over that fact. 'I saw you with her in New York—

when she was pregnant you were so crazy about her you asked me to go and look after her.'

A harsh laugh escaped him. 'I had to look after her, but I never loved her. The marriage was over before the honeymoon finished. You can guess what I discovered on my wedding night, you had already hinted as much. But that did not matter. I tried to make the marriage work, though we were rarely together because she refused to travel. Until I discovered the final irony when she was pregnant, and then the gods really laughed at me. Christina was a drug addict, and had been since the tender age of fourteen, which is why she would not go to the island. Too far away from her supplier and, as for sex, she would do anything with anyone for a fix. I never touched her again.'

'Oh, my God, no.' Amber tightened her arms around him, feeling his anguish as if it were her own. 'The night of the party she was rolling her own cigarettes and I wondered why,' she murmured out loud. 'Her little vice, she said.'

'Cannabis was the least of her addictions. Our baby was stillborn two months before the due date because Christina had been taking heroine all along.' Lucas ran a hand over his eyes as if they hurt him.

'And Christina now?' Amber asked.

'I look after her business interests—a promise I made to her father, but I divorced her as soon as my father died. I persuaded her to go into rehab. She met her new husband there. He is a doctor and much more competent to look after her than I. She has been clean for over a year.'

'I see.' Amber looked deep into his night-black eyes and she knew he was telling the truth.

'Do you? Do you really?' His sensuous lips tightened in a grim line. 'Have you any idea what it did to me the other night seeing you with a pill in your hand? Just a few hours earlier I had almost told you that I loved you, and I had to walk away because I suddenly realised the enormity of my mistake. I did not deserve you. You gave me your love once with all the joyous abandonment of a true innocent and I in my arrogance took it as my due and walked out on you for the sake of what I thought would be an easy marriage. I stood in the shower and I could not believe how blind I had been. Then later when I saw the pill in your hand I nearly died. I thought you were on drugs, and after the last few months together I could not live if anything happened to you. When I realised it was a birth control pill I was relieved but I was angry—I wanted you to have my child, but I had not the courage to tell you I loved you. The next day, hearing you talk to Clive, I was gutted.' The expression in his eyes nearly stopped her heart, so full of anguished love that it was almost painful.

'You do love me,' she whispered, hardly daring to believe it was true.

'Believe it.' And he lowered his head, his mouth finding hers in a kiss of aching tenderness. 'You are in my blood, my bones.' His throatily murmured words made Amber tremble inside. She looked up into his darkly handsome face and was stunned by the slight vulnerability in night-black eyes. 'Forgive me, Amber, stay with me, and I swear I will spend the rest of my life trying to win your love.'

'I forgive you, and you won't have to.' Amber smiled. She had a better understanding of why he had behaved the way he had in the past, and if their marriage was to work she had to believe in him, trust him. She moved sinuously against him, her hands reaching up to clutch at his broad shoulders. 'I do love you, Lucas. I always have and always will—there has never, ever been anyone else for me,' she confessed, and pulled his head back down to hers. Her tongue touched his and she felt the shuddering intensity of his response.

They kissed and clung to each other, and with shaking fingers Lucas unfastened the buttons down the front of her dress, and parted the fabric exposing the near naked length of her to his view. 'You are so beautiful, so exquisite inside and out,' he grated, shrugging off his clothes and dispensing with her briefs in seconds. His great body arched over her, his eyes glittered down into hers. 'And you really are all mine at last.' Then his head swooped down, and his mouth covered hers in a kiss of pure possession before burning a red-hot trail of fire down her slender throat to her swollen breasts.

He filled up her senses as never before, she was drunk on the wonder of their declared love. Amber moaned as he found the rosy peaks and licked them with his tongue. Her seeking hands stroked up over his back, traced his spine, and her nails dug into his flesh as he suckled the rigid tips each in turn, until Amber cried out and her back arched involuntarily seeking more.

Lifting his head, he looked down at her. 'I love you, Amber,' Lucas groaned, his voice thick with hunger. 'I want you.' His fingers spread over her flat stomach, caressing all the erotic places he knew so well.

'And I want you always and for ever.'

With a low growl deep in his throat, he slid between her thighs and made her his. With huskily muttered words of love and need, Lucas told her everything she had always wanted to hear fall from his passionate mouth. Their coming together was better than anything that had gone before, because this time their bodies and minds as one added a new dimension. Love.

Surfacing from the exhausted aftermath of their lovemaking, Amber stirred in Lucas's arms and looked around.

'Get up, Lucas, get off.' She shoved at him and he sat up, allowing her to do the same.

'No regrets, Amber, you are not going to change your mind,' and she was stunned to see a trace of doubt in his slumberous black eyes.

'No.' He loved her, she could feel it in her soul, and she did not like to see her dynamic, powerful husband uncertain. 'But look where we are, is the door locked?' She grabbed the front of her dress and began frantically fastening buttons.

'No.' His dark eyes, brimming with love, held hers. 'But my secretary would not dare disturb us,' he said with all the arrogant confidence Amber recognised.

She smiled. 'I'm taking no more chances,' and, standing up, she continued dressing, glad to see Lucas was doing the same. 'I can't believe we made love in your office.'

Lucas, looking utterly gorgeous with his hair disheveled, his trousers on and his shirt hanging off his shoulders, pulled her into his arms. 'I can, but if it perturbs you so much…' he grinned down at her '…what about trying the rail we missed on the boat? Another honeymoon?'

And they did…

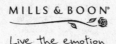

Modern
romance™

THE DESERT VIRGIN by Sandra Marton

Cameron Knight is a ruthless troubleshooter on a dangerous mission in the desert kingdom of Baslaam. He finds himself rescuing Leanna DeMarco, a ballerina who's been abducted by the Sultan of Baslaam. But escaping with Leanna across the sands is more temptation than Cameron can handle…

AT THE CATTLEMAN'S COMMAND
by Lindsay Armstrong

Rugged Australian Tom Hocking's reputation is legendary throughout the Outback – he's a breaker of horses and women, and a maker of deals. Chas has made up her mind to keep out of his way. But during her first night at the Hocking homestead Chas gets into Tom's bed by mistake…

THE MILLIONAIRE'S RUNAWAY BRIDE
by Catherine George

Coming home to the country, Kate wanted a settled life. But there was a complication: her ex-fiancé, millionaire Jack Logan. The attraction between them was still electric, and it would have been easy for Kate to let Jack seduce her. But not so simple to explain the secret she'd kept hidden for years…

HIS SECRETARY MISTRESS by Chantelle Shaw

Jenna Deane is thrilled with her fabulous new job. Life hasn't been easy since her husband deserted her and their little daughter. But her handsome new boss, Alex Morrell, expects Jenna to be available whenever he needs her. How can she tell him that she's actually a single mother…?

On sale 3rd March 2006

0206/03a

MILLS & BOON®

Live the emotion

_Medical romance™

HIS SECRET LOVE-CHILD by Marion Lennox

Surgeon Cal Jamieson never gets involved. He never wants a family – that's why Gina Lopez had to leave him. But Gina returns, with the son he didn't know he had. Can Cal face up to fatherhood? Can he risk losing Gina again? Can he persuade her to stay – this time for good?

CROCODILE CREEK: 24-HOUR RESCUE
A cutting-edge medical centre.
Fully equipped for saving lives and loves!

HER HONOURABLE PLAYBOY by Kate Hardy

Registrar Alyssa Ward is not pleased when she wins a date with A&E consultant the Honourable Sebastian Radley – he's a renowned womaniser! Seb has never been one for monogamy – so why does he find that one date with Alyssa just isn't enough…?

POSH DOCS Honourable, eligible, and in demand!

HIGH-ALTITUDE DOCTOR by Sarah Morgan

High-altitude medicine expert Dr Juliet Adams is about to take on the most gruelling challenge of all – Mount Everest! Brooding Dr Finn McEwan is also on the expedition and his instinct is to protect his beautiful colleague. He knows she has secrets – on Everest there's nowhere to hide…

24:7 Feel the heat –
every hour...every minute...every heartbeat

On sale 3rd March 2006

Available at WHSmith, Tesco, ASDA, Borders, Eason,
Sainsbury's and most bookshops
www.millsandboon.co.uk

MILLS & BOON®

0206/03b

Live the emotion

_MedicaL
romance™

THE SURGEON'S PREGNANCY SURPRISE
by Laura MacDonald

At a friend's wedding, Chrissie Paige falls for the best man – fellow surgeon Sean O'Reagan. After one passionate weekend together they go their separate ways. Chrissie can't stop thinking about him. Then she finds that not only is Sean her new boss, but she's pregnant with his child!

A FRENCH DOCTOR AT ABBEYFIELDS
by Abigail Gordon

When Dr Giselle Howard arrives at Abbeyfields she has no intention of leaving her Parisian lifestyle behind. But the welcome she gets from the villagers, not to mention the affection she has for local GP Marc Bannerman and his two young children, creates a bond she can't ignore…

Abigail Gordon charms us with her enchanting depiction of the warmth and community of English village life

IN HIS LOVING CARE *by Jennifer Taylor*

Lewis Cole's life has changed in an instant – he has a daughter! No longer single city surgeon, he's single father and country GP. He's determined to give little Kristy all the love she needs, but there's also room in his heart for beautiful Dr Helen Daniels. Helen, however, needs more – a child of her own…

Bachelor Dads – Single Doctor… Single Father!

On sale 3rd March 2006

Available at WHSmith, Tesco, ASDA, Borders, Eason, Sainsbury's and most bookshops

www.millsandboon.co.uk

Queens of Romance

An outstanding collection by international bestselling authors.

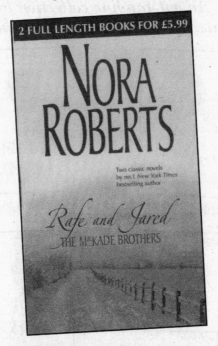

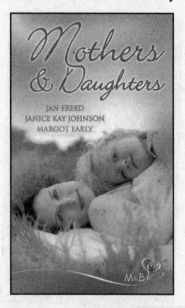

Suzie is a glamorous newspaper columnist –
attractive and flirtatious, she's out on a date every
night. Then, on the Eurostar, she meets a successful
younger man she thinks may be The One.

Alice is a life coach and reluctant TV personality
– after her husband left her for another man, she's
understandably wary of romantic relationships.
But a handsome new client is chipping away at
her defences.

Problem Number One:
Suzie and Alice have fallen for the same guy.

Problem Number Two:
Suzie is Alice's MOTHER!

17th February 2006

This season's must have!

Vig Morgan is lost in a sea of associate editors at *Fashionista*—an aggressively hip magazine that oozes glamour and is ultimately about absolutely nothing.

Instead of putting her journalism degree to good use, Vig writes about *which* star wore *which* designer to *which* party. Yes, she'd rather be writing something of substance but the egomaniacal editor-in-chief isn't interested. So when a cabal of *Fashionista* employees approach Vig with a plot to overthrow their leader, Vig's interest is piqued…

17th February 2006